DISCARDED
STARK COUNTY DISTRICT LIBRARY

The Darkness Within Him

Untwisted Book One

The Darkness Within Him

Untwisted Book One

Alice Raine

Published by Accent Press Ltd 2015

ISBN 9781783753956

Copyright © **Alice Raine** 2015

The right of **Alice Raine** to be identified as the author of this work has been asserted by the author in accordance with the Copyright, Designs and Patents Act 1988.

The story contained within this book is a work of fiction. Names and characters are the product of the author's imagination and any resemblance to actual persons, living or dead, is entirely coincidental.

All rights reserved. No part of this book may be reproduced, stored in a retrieval system, or transmitted in any form or by any means, electronic, electrostatic, magnetic tape, mechanical, photocopying, recording or otherwise, without the written permission of the publishers: Accent Press Ltd, Ty Cynon House, Navigation Park, Abercynon, CF45 4SN

People are like stained glass windows. They sparkle and shine when the sun is out, but when the darkness sets in, their true beauty is revealed only if there is a light from within.

Elisabeth Kubler-Ross

ACKNOWLEDGEMENTS

I'd like to express my greatest appreciation and thanks to my editors Elizabeth Coldwell and Alexandra Davies not only for dedicating countless hours to editing my work and answering my multitude of questions, but for taking a chance on me in the first place.

I must also thank everyone at Accent Press, in particular Beth Jones, Stephanie Williams and Ieuan Matthews. Whilst too many to name individually I must also extend my thanks to all the other people and departments at Accent who have made my dream to become published a reality.

A special thank you must go out to my long-term friend Helen L. for all your support throughout this process. For staying up late reading drafts, suggesting improvements, and being amazingly supportive. Without your friendship and encouragement, this book would never have left my computer!

My thanks also to Ruth W. and Charlotte B. for reading and advising. Charlotte, you have become my ideas guru ;) – thank you for loving my characters enough to spend time with me discussing possible plot lines and pushing me to expand Nathan's character.

Also my test readers, Karen W, Debbie, Rosie M, and

Olivia M for reading through my book during the writing process. Your support, feedback and advice was invaluable. Also thanks to newer friends made via social networking – Laura Mc and Katie N. We're all going through the new author experience together and you two have made the difficult times so much more bearable!

Thank you to my husband for indulging me when I told him, 'I want to be an author,' and for never once complaining when I sat at my laptop night after night tapping away and generally ignoring him, I love you.

Finally, thanks to my family for their support of my writing – not that they will ever be allowed to read this book!

Alice x

PROLOGUE

What the fuck had he been thinking?

Clearly, he hadn't been thinking at all. In fact, in all his twisted years alive this was probably the closest he'd ever come to losing it, *really* losing it.

Apart from the time long ago when he had very nearly lost everything, Nicholas thought with a grimace, finally picking himself up from the floor and pushing his dark hair from his clammy face in agitation.

Looking back to the empty bed in disgust, he attempted to pull on his discarded shirt, but paused as he felt a strange sensation growing in his chest like a steel band being tightened around his ribs. Tighter and tighter it went, until it was practically crushing the air from his lungs and Nicholas was gasping for breath and staring hopelessly at the bed before him.

The silk scarves that, up until ten minutes ago, had held the wrists of Rebecca as he'd knelt over her provocatively now hung limply from the bedposts, and as his eyes strayed across the crumpled white sheets, Nicholas saw small red dots expanding on the cotton in several places.

Blood.

Fuck, he'd never drawn blood before. But as horror spread across his face, Nicholas counted at least ten red dots of blood from the cane he had used on Rebecca's beautiful arse. Lovely, unsuspecting Rebecca whose only wrongdoing had been to make him think he might be falling in love with her.

But he didn't do love, *couldn't*. His past had taught him that, and now Rebecca was gone. Gone for good if she had any sense.

He'd completely lost control, which was so unlike him – and a cane? Why the fuck had that seemed like a good idea? Engrained, dark memories of his childhood had ensured

Nicholas never used canes in his twisted sex life, so why had he done so today? With a grunt, he shook his head in disgust; deep down, he knew exactly why he'd picked the cane, but he refused to listen to the voice in his head telling him he'd chosen it on purpose to show her *why* she should leave him.

In a sickening realisation that had him bent double and clutching at the mattress, choking for air, Nicholas knew he hadn't wanted Rebecca to go at all. He'd only doubted his feelings because of his damn brother. God, he felt like he was going to throw up.

Swallowing down the hot bile that had risen in his throat Nicholas rolled his head back and stared at the ceiling. All he'd really wanted was for her to help take the pain of his past away, hold him and reassure him that how he lived was OK.

But it wasn't, she hadn't, and now she had walked out.

Shaking his head, Nicholas ran his hands roughly through his sweat-slicked hair as he remembered the look upon Rebecca's face when she had left. Tear-stained and utterly furious, apparently at both him for his actions and herself for believing that she could ever change him.

He closed his eyes. Nicholas' nostrils flared as he thought of her beautiful face again. If only Rebecca knew just *how* much she had changed him over these last months, he thought as he dragged the sheet from the bed, unable to bear the sight of it any more. But it was too late now. He would never get the chance to tell her because Rebecca had gone and there was no way she was coming back – not after what he had just subjected her to.

ONE

One week turned into two, and two merged miserably into three as I struggled through each post-break-up day in a trance-like bubble. As much as I hated to admit it, I was finding life without Nicholas a lot tougher than I had first imagined it would be. We'd been together for nearly four months; not that long a time, really, but they had been four incredibly intense, passionate months, and it had felt like so much longer.

Knowing what Nicholas had done to me with the cane should have made it easy to leave him, walk away and never look back, but the haunted, almost terrified expression on his face as I'd left for the final time was still plaguing me daily and haunting my dreams at night, until I woke soaked in sweat and unable to get back to sleep.

Following the same pattern, last night's pathetic attempt at sleep had been yet another fitful one – as was now the norm. With more time spent on taunting nightmares than actual rest, I probably got three hours, maximum, which was nowhere near enough for a sleepaholic like me – especially as my nights had *all* been like this since the break up – and believe me, three weeks of sleepless nights equalled some seriously big bags under my eyes. As such, it really wasn't surprising that I found myself exhausted and leaving my little flat earlier than usual to head to work. Anything was better than sitting still and allowing my mind to saturate itself thinking about my failed relationship with Nicholas Jackson. Again.

Taking a breath as I prepared to leave, I forced thoughts of Nicholas momentarily from my head and tried instead to focus on the positive things in my life. I'm blessed with good health, a loving family, and a secure job, so I really should stop with the whining. Who needs a saucy love life anyway, I thought with a roll of my eyes as I exited my flat and slammed the door with far more force than necessary.

As the bang of the door reverberated around the small landing, I grimaced at the thought that I had probably just woken the three neighbours who shared my floor. So as I ducked out of the landing I made a conscious effort to close the second door more quietly, while wondering if maybe subconsciously I'd been using the slam to try once and for all to shut out memories of Nicholas too. Sighing wistfully, I shook my fuzzy head. It would be so good if it were that easy – to shut out my feelings like closing a lid on a box. If only.

To be honest, my thoughts and behaviour had been so erratic since my spilt from *him* that I'd given up trying to self-analyse my actions. I doubted that even a week-long session with a team of top psychologists could unravel the myriad of messed-up issues currently lurking in my head.

Tramping across the landing, I made my way down the stairs dragging my feet out into a bright, cool morning, tucking my hands into the pockets of my worn leather jacket as I went. It was a beautiful day and I *almost* smiled to myself as I glanced around at the light, fluffy clouds and bright blue sky. As pathetic as it might seem, there hadn't been too many smiles on my lips recently – another thing to blame on Nicholas, I thought with a scowl. Seeing the already busy street, I tried to straighten my shoulders and appreciate my situation in life because I'm lucky enough to live in Camden Town, a very popular and sought-after part of London.

If I turned right from my front door I could be at Chalk Farm tube station in under two minutes, hop on for one stop to Camden Town station, and then be at my bookshop in less than five minutes. But with last night's tumultuous dreams of Nicholas still lingering in my mind, I wanted to distract my brain the best way I could, and for me that was to walk for a while.

No matter what the time of day or night, Camden seemed to be pulsing with energy; there was always something, or someone, new to look at and being ever so slightly nosey it was perfect for me because I simply loved people-watching. So it was a walk I did whenever I had enough time. Or needed a good distraction, like I did today.

By taking just a small diversion off the main road on to some of the side streets and courtyards, I knew I could immerse myself into the fizzing bustle of the Camden markets and their multitude of colourful stalls, which is exactly where I headed this morning. Even in my current mood, there was just something so all-consuming about the bohemian atmosphere of the place. It seemed to seep into my veins and recharge me, and would be a perfect distraction for me today.

After just a few minutes' walk, I crossed the busy main road and headed under a railway bridge and up a familiar side street into The Stables, the first of the famous markets that draw thousands of tourists every year. Dragging my fingertips gently across the soft moss on the stone wall to my left, I allowed my mind to be swamped with the images and delicious smells wafting around me; bacon and fresh coffee teased my nostrils and stalls lined with jewellery, T-shirts, and paintings drew my inquisitive gaze. After a few moments, I even felt the muscles in my face protest as I smiled genuinely for the first time in what seemed like weeks. Even with the big-city-loneliness that I inevitably felt on occasion as a resident of the sprawling metropolis of London, Camden somehow had a way of making me feel like I belonged.

Cutting under a brick archway, I made my way up a short flight of stairs to a bridge that curved over the railway, but just as I was about to descend on the other side, a sound caught my ears and I came to an abrupt halt. The man behind me ran straight into my back, nudging me rather painfully with what I hoped was the point of an umbrella, but to be honest I was so distracted I almost didn't care. He muttered a curse as he shoved me unceremoniously to the side before he and a stream of other uptight suits made their way down the steps toward their highly important destinations.

For several seconds I was unable to move, frozen to the spot as my ears searched for the sound that had stopped me so suddenly in the first place. I strained my hearing so hard that blood started to pound in my eardrums, but just as I thought I'd imagined it, the taunting noise washed over me again, stealing every molecule of air from my lungs.

Piano music.

Someone nearby was playing a piano. It seemed a crazy thought, as I was standing on a bridge in the middle of an outdoor marketplace, but as I listened to the notes flowing over me, there could be no mistaking it. It felt like every single hair on my body had risen to attention as I stood there stock still, and uselessly rubbing at my arms to try and ease the tingling sensation running across my skin. The bustling stalls around me instantly vanished and instead I saw Nicholas in my mind's eye, sitting with graceful elegance at his impressive grand piano, a focused expression on his devastatingly handsome face as his fingers moved skilfully over the keys to produce the most beautiful music I had ever heard in my life.

The sound was so incredibly poignant to me because it had been Nicholas' exquisite piano playing that had brought us together in the first place. I'm not a skilled pianist myself by any means, but I do love listening to music, and three years ago, I'd attended a concert by a jazz group comprised of Nicholas Jackson, Anthony Gurage, and Isla Burren.

The concert was fabulous, I mean out-of-this-frigging-world good. As musicians go, the trio were some of the most skilled I'd ever had the pleasure to listen to. As was my habit, I wrote an online review of the concert afterwards, expressing my appreciation for their skill and stating my completely unqualified belief that they had the potential to become some of the best jazz musicians our country had seen for decades.

Somehow, somewhere, a hotshot musical producer called Greggor Marks happened upon my review and, going purely on gut instinct, tracked the three of them down. At the time, they had been relatively unknown, playing gigs at small concert halls and churches, but in a bizarre twist of fate, Marks signed them on the spot strictly on the basis of my review – and no doubt a quick personal performance.

Things had spiralled rapidly out of control and Anthony,

Isla, and Nicholas pretty much became stars overnight, playing with jazz bands and orchestras all over the world, and even working with several big Broadway productions as musical advisors. And that as they say, is that.

All because of *moi*.

Well, more specifically, my compulsive habit of writing online blogs. As an avid lover of books and a wannabe fiction writer, my obsessive blogging about everything I did was as close as I had ever got to being "published", and spoke volumes about the amount of free time I had. Social life? Ha! Hardly. And now I didn't even have a boyfriend, I thought bitterly.

Even after accidentally making the trio famous with my blog, I'd never had the opportunity to meet Anthony, Isla, or Nicholas. I'd seen them from afar at the concert all those years ago, of course, and spoken to Isla on the phone once, but they had been so swept up in their newfound fame that saying thanks to the girl who wrote a nice review probably hadn't been high on their list of priorities.

Stumbling numbly to the side of the steps, I took hold of the handrail to support my suddenly wobbly legs and clear the stairs for other morning walkers. Blinking wildly at how deeply the mere sound of a piano had shaken me, I shook my head in an attempt to clear the fog that had descended on my already tired brain. I couldn't believe it had come to this. More precisely, I couldn't believe *I'd* come to this; a quivering, pathetic shell of my former self, embarrassing herself by having some sort of breakdown on a bridge in the centre of a busy marketplace. God, it was positively shameful.

I sighed heavily and pushed some of my wayward blonde hair from my face, wishing now that I'd never been to that stupid concert or written the damn review. In short, I was wishing I'd never met Nicholas Jackson. You know the saying "It's better to have loved and lost than to never have loved at all?" Well, it's a load of rubbish as far as I'm concerned, and it certainly didn't carry much weight with me at that moment. Not that I was actually in love with Nicholas, I thought, frowning. *Was I?* I didn't think I was, but I supposed the explosiveness of our final time together might have tarnished the view I had of him.

As hard as I strained my ears, the piano melody had vanished. Scowling, I shook my head; perhaps my twisted mind had conjured it up in the first place to taunt me further about Nicholas. Even without the music, I somehow felt reluctant to leave the bridge, so I retreated up the three steps to a small coffee shop at the top and bought myself a cappuccino to go. Maybe a dose of caffeine would kick-start my brain back to usefulness.

Returning to the railings, I resumed my position overlooking the marketplace so I could watch the tradesmen set up their stalls and banter easily with each other.

As I took the first sip of my coffee, it practically scalded the taste buds from my tongue and I grimaced, my entire face scrunching up in discomfort. I only just managed not to spray it out down my front and over the stalls below. *Marvellous*, an incinerated tongue. Just another thing to be joyous about today.

Peeling off the protective lid to allow the coffee to cool, I indulged in a little people-watching while I considered how my world had changed so drastically over the last year. My social life was still basically non-existent, and apart from the kinky fling with Nicholas, my love life also remained pitifully empty. However, thanks to some significant inheritance money from my granddad, I now owned the bookshop I'd worked in for the past seven years.

Mr Garland, the previous owner, had been only too happy to sell up when I'd made an offer and was now enjoying his well-earned retirement somewhere on the sunny coast of southern Spain, no doubt with a margarita in one hand and a señorita in the other.

The business was doing well, keeping me busy, but this meant my blogs had to take a bit of a back seat. It was quite ironic, really, that the thing that had led me to Nicholas in the first place was now leaving my life, just as he had. Although, technically, it was me who'd left him, I remembered with a dry swallow as I turned my now misty eyes over the first busload of early-morning tourists rushing about below me.

Stupidly, as I forced my tense body to relax against the cold metal railing, I let my mind wander back to better times, memories that would only cause me pain but that I couldn't stop flooding into my brain. Memories of Nicholas before I knew about his darker side, before I had begun to fall headfirst for a man so completely wrong for me that he had left my heart, body, and soul crushed into pieces.

A shuddering sigh escaped me as I played back the events that had led to my first meeting with Nicholas Jackson, my now ex-boyfriend, a dominant and passionate man and the only person I'd ever thought I might actually be able to fall in love with.

Several months ago, I had got a call out of the blue from Greggor Marks, the music producer who had signed Nicholas, Isla, and Anthony all those years ago. He had informed me that the trio's schedules were easing then went on to say that they were in London for some concerts at the Palladium so would I like to meet them? I had been quite touched that he remembered me, and at the time had thought, would I like to meet them? Hell yes. If I'd been ill that day and missed his call, or turned down his offer, I wouldn't now be making a complete fool of myself in the middle of Camden Market, nursing a broken heart. But I hadn't. I'd been thrilled and of course accepted his offer immediately.

After getting the Tube down to Euston, I changed onto the Victoria line for the short journey to Oxford Circus. Holding on to the rail inside the carriage I fidgeted nervously on the spot as the train trundled through the tunnels towards its destination. Tugging self-consciously at my jacket I glanced around the other commuters and was glad that my dressed-up attire – high heels, black trousers, and a silk camisole – didn't stand out among the assortment of outfits being worn around me. This was London in all its impersonal glory; you could wear whatever you wanted and people would simply look the other way and ignore you as if you weren't even there. There was even one guy sat opposite me wearing hot pants and purple ankle warmers and no one was paying a blind bit of notice. Ah, the joy of big-city living.

Emerging from the station, I traversed through the bustle of commuters and early-evening shoppers on the rain-slicked pavement of Oxford Street, before turning off and heading down a side street toward the impressive frontage of the London Palladium. The stretch of pavement outside had become a waiting area and was full of similarly dressed people loitering around and talking excitedly about the performance they were about to watch, so I sidled up to them and fiddled with my phone to kill some time.

Two hours later, after what had possibly been the best night of live jazz music I had ever heard, I found myself waiting to be escorted to the backstage area. Still flushed from the heat in the theatre itself, I knew my face was also red from excitement because in about two minutes I would get to meet the trio I had inadvertently made famous by blogging about them on the internet – Anthony Gurage, Isla Burren, and Nicholas Jackson.

Tonight's performance was the opening night of a new musical called *Keys,* set around the development of jazz piano playing over the years. Nicholas had agreed to perform at the première, with all proceeds to charity, before another skilled pianist would set off with the orchestra and tour the country with the show. Apparently, he was too in demand to do full tours these days. If I were big-headed, I'd take the credit for that too, but luckily, my ego was well in check so I merely let the thought flit through my mind with a small, indulgent smile.

As planned, Greggor Marks met me at my seat immediately after the performance. He was exactly what I had expected of a super-successful producer; sharp suit, immaculate hair, and a rushed, impatient air about everything he did. Even the way he walked was somehow in fast forward and I immediately struggled to keep up with him in my high heels. He was like the living personification of a tornado and put my already frayed nerves even further on edge.

He led me speedily down a maze of corridors backstage, but I was so intent on maintaining his pace without tripping that I barely got a chance to look around me. As I followed close on his heels, a shrill and rather unpleasant ring erupted from his suit and had him reaching into his jacket pocket with an inpatient grunt. Arriving at a dressing room door, he excused himself with an apologetic gesture to his ringing phone before ushering me towards the door with a flustered wave of his hand.

Great, I had to go in alone. Swallowing loudly I licked my lips, tucked some stray hairs behind my ear, and tried to compose myself. Confidence was usually a strong point of mine, but this was different – these were real live famous people I was about to meet. Huffing a huge breath to calm my nerves, I pushed open the door.

And there they were.

Well, not all of them, but Anthony Gurage and Isla Burren stood about ten feet in front of me, involved in what looked like a deep and slightly heated conversation. I couldn't see Nicholas Jackson anywhere, although the dressing room was surprisingly large and appeared to go round a corner at the back.

Standing nervously in the doorway, I pushed my long, blonde hair behind my ear again and watched as Isla frowned at Anthony before suddenly turning her attention on me with a broad smile. God, I wished I felt half as confident as she looked. I knew that Isla was a decade older than me at thirty-five, and was one of the most skilled female saxophone players around. She was also far prettier up close than her publicity shots showed; in fact, with her short, glowing auburn hair, high cheek bones, and bright green eyes she looked a lot like a pixie, and was really quite stunning.

'Rebecca, how lovely to meet you at last, we really should have got together to thank you years ago.' Isla blushed in embarrassment. Anthony, a trumpet player and six years her senior, came to shake my hand too. He was tall and broad with a mop of unruly blond hair and warm, dark brown eyes. It was odd, knowing so much about these people who I'd never met before, but my review had been quite thorough and it's amazing what you can dredge up on the internet these days.

'Yes, it really was rather amiss of us to leave it so long. Unfortunately, Isla has just had a call requiring her attention, I'm afraid we are going to have to leave.'

Already? My eyebrows popped up in surprise and I felt a sharp tug of disappointment in my stomach; I'd only just arrived! That must have been what the deep discussion was about. I also happened to know that Isla and Anthony were dating, so I assumed whatever required her probably needed him too.

'Oh, no problem, I hope it's nothing too serious,' I mumbled limply. Well, at least I had got to watch the performance free of charge, I supposed. Although I'd stuffed a wad of cash into the charity bucket at the end, probably more than the ticket was worth. But you can't attend a concert with all proceeds to charity and not donate, can you?

Isla and Anthony were already headed for the door, as I stood there, rather unsure what to do next. Nicholas didn't seem to be around anywhere, and I'd definitely get lost in the maze of backstage corridors if I tried to navigate them on my own, so perhaps I should follow Isla and Anthony.

'Nicholas, we have to leave,' Isla called into the seemingly empty dressing room, making me frown. 'Well done tonight. Miss Langley is out here to meet you,' she finished, before turning to me. 'Sorry again for rushing off, but we'll leave you in the capable hands of Nicholas.' Her smile was almost apologetic as she dashed out with Anthony, leaving me feeling distinctly uncomfortable in the large, unfamiliar space.

Presumably from her comments, Nicholas was around here somewhere then. Isla's talk of capable hands had me thinking back to Nicholas Jackson's performance on the grand piano tonight and my breath hitched a little as I felt a warm flush cover my cheeks. Wow, it had been just stunning. I hadn't been close enough to see properly, but his hands had seemed to flow over the keyboard so knowingly, as if it were just an extension of his body. He had been truly magnificent to watch and listen to, and had kept me entranced for the entire performance. In fact, I'd been so enthralled by Nicholas that I don't think I'd even graced the other musicians with more than a brief glance.

'Hello?' I called nervously, and then, after several moments of complete silence, I nervously edged forward and peered around the corner into a small, lit area adorned with chairs and make-up mirrors. And Nicholas Jackson.

He faced away from me, bent over the counter doing something with a small red tub. Obviously, he wasn't rushing to return my greeting, which he surely must have heard. He was just ignoring it. Ignoring me. How charming.

In truth, Nicholas was the one I had been most nervous about meeting. I knew that Isla and Anthony had reputations for being warm and sociable and I'd been counting on them to keep the conversation going, because by all accounts, even at the relatively young age of twenty-nine, Nicholas Jackson was brusque, intimidating, and not particularly sociable at the best of times.

Taking the opportunity to glance over at him while he was otherwise engaged, I saw he was tall. Taller than I had expected, actually, with surprisingly broad shoulders. Then, catching a glimpse of his glorious reflection in the mirror, I briefly stopped breathing. I mean the air literally caught in my lungs, and wouldn't move. From just this brief flash of his profile, I saw it was clear that his publicity shots hadn't done him justice either. Nowhere near.

He was still wearing his smart black trousers, white shirt, and waistcoat, but I noticed his tailcoat and bow tie were laid over the back of the chair next to him. Hmm, the figure I could see under the shirt was actually rather nice, certainly better than I'd expected from a sedentary piano player. He appeared lithe and athletic looking, his waistcoat pulled tight over apparently taut muscles below, but as I allowed my eyes to trace back up his body I caught sight of his reflection in the mirror again and saw that he was looking at me.

Oh God, he was watching me as I watched him. How embarrassing. There simply weren't enough swear words to encompass how mortified I felt at that exact moment. My heart rate soared as my skin heated with a blush at being caught in my assessment of him, and all I could do was hope my blatant appreciation of his body hadn't been visible in my expression. Which of course it probably had been. Great.

'Hi,' I squeaked, forcing a limp smile onto my burning face and nervously stroking my hair to flatten it.

'Miss Langley, we meet at last,' he observed dryly with a tweak of one dark eyebrow. 'Just give me a second to finish off here.' Glancing at his hands, I saw he was actually applying hand cream to his long fingers and it briefly distracted me from my nerves.

'You use hand cream?' I blurted without thinking, surprised that a man as apparently tough as Nicholas Jackson would bother with something so, so … well, girly.

Finally, he turned to face me, still rubbing cream into his hands slowly and smoothly and, if I'm honest, rather distractingly. Why the sight of Nicholas rubbing his hands together like that was making me feel so giddy I had no idea, but it was; my temperature must be at fever point by now, my pulse was racing in my veins and I was fairly sure my hands were shaking. Reaching sideways, I rested a hand on the wall to steady myself, hoping my action looked nonchalant and casual and didn't give away just how unsteady my legs had suddenly become.

As I continued to stare at his hands, a small shiver ran through me at the thought of his fingers doing that to me. How would it feel if they were rubbing across my skin, in teasing circles and long massaging strokes? Probably unbelievably good … As my mind wandered, an incredibly loud swallow forced its way down my throat, bringing me back to reality with a bump. I had to get a grip – I was twenty-five, not some hormonal teenager

Abruptly breaking my fantasy, he spoke again. 'Actually, no.' What looked like a sardonic smile tugged at his lips. 'It's a special mixture containing tiger balm. After playing for an extended time like I have tonight, my fingers get stiff, and this helps relax them. It's warming and makes them tingle, reducing the ache,' he explained softly, finally hanging his hands back at his sides and giving me his full attention.

Unlike Isla and Anthony, who had seemed to exude a naturally relaxed vibe, Nicholas positively radiated tension. His entire body seemed wound like a spring, and his posture screamed authority like I'd never experienced before. For some crazy reason my body seemed to want to move towards him, making me grip the wall even tighter in my attempt at nonchalance.

Now I didn't have the almost hypnotic sight of his rubbing

hands to look at, I finally raised my eyes to his face. Thankfully, I already knew what Nicholas looked like and had prepared myself for this moment, because as well as being an incredible piano player, he was also a very handsome man.

And I mean breath-taking, heart-stopping, toe-curling good looks.

It was almost as if I was hypnotised by him, as intense as his stare was, I just couldn't seem to look away, and as I held his gaze, my heart sped up in my chest I found myself blinking rapidly, almost in time with its beats. Even though I knew I was staring at him, I just couldn't help it. Dark hair, short at the back but slightly longer on top, fell messily as if he'd recently run his hands through it, and his features were classic; strong jaw, defined cheekbones, and devastatingly dark blue eyes which I were still boring into mine. At least I wasn't the only one openly staring, I suppose

I swallowed again out of nerves, and with the tight ball of apprehension in my throat I realised it had probably been loud enough for him to hear it. Damn, even with all my preparation and intentions of being calm and professional, I still found Nicholas Jackson just as intimidating as all the papers said he was.

'Your playing tonight was superb, Mr Jackson, so beautiful,' I remarked, trying to break the awkward silence that was hanging between us. Despite my intentions of being aloof, my voice was a tad higher than usual, no doubt betraying my nerves.

'Thank you,' he acknowledged with a short nod.

'It gave me goose pimples,' I said with a wistful smile, before wincing as I realised what a stupid thing that was to say. Engage brain before speaking, I reminded myself irritably. Nicholas didn't respond to my comment apart from a slight narrowing of his eyes as he tilted his head to observe me like some newly discovered curiosity.

'Do you play an instrument, Rebecca?' he asked softly in a low, smooth tone that made my stomach tighten, but instead of lingering on his voice and the peculiar reaction it was causing inside of me, I instead focused on the fact that he had remembered my first name, which I found surprising.

'I play the piano, *very badly*,' I added with a roll of my eyes. What I did clumsily with my keyboard at home could in no way be compared to the skilful things Nicholas did with his grand piano. 'And feel free to call me Becky, everyone else does.'

'Would you like to see the piano here, Becky? It's a Steinway, one of the best in the world,' he murmured in that alluringly low tone again, and I nodded keenly, wanting nothing more than to escape this isolated room and the strange tension that seemed to be emanating from Nicholas and somehow clinging to my skin.

'Come, follow me,' he instructed, not waiting to see if I followed, which was lucky because my first few steps were embarrassingly wobbly.

Nicholas walked incredibly fast, almost gliding in his easy elegance, and was clearly familiar with the maze of small corridors backstage at the Palladium. A couple of minutes later, just as I was getting breathless trying to keep up with him, I found myself following him past a set of huge thick red velvet curtains and out onto the stage. Wow. I stopped dead, drawing in a shocked breath as I took in the scene before me; the theatre looked huge from up here and quite scary with the house lights lowered and the auditorium bathed in shadows. How did people ever perform without freezing from nerves?

'Quite something, isn't it?' he murmured from just next to me, but when I looked at him I saw his dark eyes were on me again, and not the view. The silent intensity of Nicholas' gaze made my stomach lurch unexpectedly and as my teeth clenched with nerves I accidentally bit on the inside of my cheek and flinched. He seemed pleasant enough on the exterior, but something about this man was making me feel distinctly uneasy while simultaneously attracting me, a very confusing feeling which wasn't helped one bit by the waves of heat I could feel radiating from his body.

I nodded jerkily, ripping my gaze away from his probing eyes and looking out at the seats again, trying to calm myself. Even with the lighting low, I could see the grandeur of the place and I noticed a team of cleaners moving between the rows of seats, collecting the rubbish and stubs from tonight's performance.

Nicholas led me toward the piano that just for tonight had been raised up from within the orchestra pit onto the side of the stage. I suspected this more visible position was all in his honour, because he had developed a bit of a celebrity status in the last few years. His supreme skill, immense dislike of publicity, and stunning good looks had made him a popular focus for the press. Seeing him first hand, in all his shuttered-off masculine beauty, I could now understand why.

'It's beautiful,' I murmured, my eyes sweeping over the black glazed mahogany of the huge grand piano. Up close, I was actually surprised by just how large it was. I'd only ever seen ordinary pianos or keyboards before, never one as huge as this.

Nicholas slid one hand into his trouser pocked and ran the other almost lovingly over the closed lid of the piano, and for a ridiculous second I returned to my earlier fantasy, desperately wanting to be that piece of wood and have his fingers running over my body.

I quickly shook myself to ease the magnetic effect this man seemed to have on my body. What the hell was wrong with me?

'Can I touch it?' I whispered, returning my gaze to the piano to distract me from the view of Nicholas and the bizarre sensations currently running through my mind and body.

'Of course,' he replied, possibly with a trace of humour in his voice, although I deliberately avoided looking at him to see if he was smiling. I was already struggling to control myself around him, but God only knows how I'd react if I actually saw his handsome face smiling.

I could feel Nicholas' eyes burning into me as I tentatively reached out and stroked the cool wood of the beautiful instrument; it was smooth like silk beneath my fingertips and I couldn't help but let out a soft gasp. Suddenly awed by both the instrument and the man in front of me, I felt my legs going rather weak again.

'Can I sit?' I croaked, indicating to the piano stool, desperately hoping he would say yes, otherwise there was a high possibility that I was about to collapse into a pile on the floor.

He observed me with that same tilt to his head for several seconds before ignoring my question and asking one of his own instead. 'You are very ... *well trained*. Do you always ask permission before doing something?' he asked, with a peculiar tone to his voice.

I frowned at his words. What a strange thing to say – well trained. He made it sound like I was a dog, I thought, almost laughing out loud from my nerves.

'No ... it's just that you ... Uh, I ...' I hesitated, a flush spreading on my cheeks at my ridiculous lack of control around this man. Honesty was probably best, I decided. 'Well, you're rather intimidating, Mr Jackson,' I admitted finally.

'I am,' he agreed with a curt nod, offering no apology for my obvious discomfort and not asking me to call him Nicholas either. 'Sit. You may play it if you wish.'

Gratefully lowering myself onto the soft leather of the piano stool, I allowed my tense muscles to relax marginally before contemplating his offer, and then shaking my head regretfully. 'I wouldn't be able to do it justice. Would you play something for me?'

A flash of annoyance seemed to knit his dark brows and I realised how rude I was being because not only had he already been playing for hours, but I'd also completely forgotten my manners too. '*Please*?' I added quickly, and once again, I saw the faint flicker of amusement on his lips before he finally nodded and joined me on the piano stool.

The sudden close proximity between us made my breath catch in my throat. He didn't actually touch me, but there could only have been a centimetre or so between our thighs and I was suddenly incredibly aware of every tiny millimetre of that space. Warmth seeped into my skin from Nicholas' body and if that wasn't bad enough it suddenly registered in my nose that he smelled absolutely divine too; some spicy cologne or soap that I recognised vaguely, and that suited him perfectly.

Just drawing in a normal breath suddenly felt like the most complex task on earth. I was filled with such a strong urge to reach across and touch him that I had to stare fixedly at the piano keys before me, and ball my hands into fists in my lap to avoid the temptation. The heady combination of this evening's nerves, the excitement of the show and now his closeness were making my brain feel fluffy and obviously affecting my sensibilities. My body was swept with a wave of warmth as I experienced an adrenaline rush like I'd never had before. Bungee jumping, which I'd done once a long time ago (and screamed like a baby for the entire five minutes), was nothing compared to the thrill I was experiencing sitting at the piano next to Nicholas Jackson.

Thankfully oblivious to my floundering state, Nicholas settled himself, shrugged his shoulders to get comfortable, and then extended his hand to place them on the keys. Shaking the shirt cuffs back from his wrists he then proceeded to play the most beautiful piece of music I think I have ever heard.

Holding my breath, partly in awe of his skill, and partly to avoid his scent and the disastrous things it was doing to my composure, I watched in fascination as Nicholas' fingers flowed over the keys so rapidly I could barely keep up. His lithe body swayed to and fro with the music as he used the pedals below the instrument, his shoulder missing me by mere millimetres each time. In shirt, his masterful control of the piano completely blew me away.

At one point while he played, I caught sight of an ugly scar on his left wrist and frowned – it stood out to me because it was the only part of him that didn't seem immaculate. Whatever had done that would have caused him serious pain, but I was so absorbed in his beautiful music it didn't even cross my mind to ask. Not that I would have been brave enough to ask him such a personal question anyway.

There really was something so attractive about a man who could play the piano well. To be honest, I hadn't watched any other men play it, but the sight of Nicholas' fingers striking the keys continued to do disastrous things to my stability and I was certainly grateful to be sitting down.

What was going on? I'd never felt this sort of instant attraction with a man before. All my previous relationships had always bloomed from friendships and gone from there. They'd been satisfying enough but never magnetic like this. My body seemed to be physically drawn to Nicholas Jackson, and it was still a minute by minute struggle not to reach out and touch him.

From absolutely nowhere my mind was suddenly filled with the image of Nicholas gripping my waist with his long, skilful fingers, bending me across the piano, and making love to me over the keys. Gasping out loud, I blinked in shock at this erotically errant thought and as well as my blush deepening significantly, I had to clench my thighs together to ease the sudden ache that had bloomed between my legs.

From this insight you'd think I'm a complete sex maniac, but believe me, nothing could be further from the truth. This was *totally* unlike me, and as I fought to control the alien thoughts that had taken over my body, I realised if I stood any chance of leaving here tonight with my dignity intact I needed to get a grip of myself, and fast.

Finishing his piece, Nicholas turned and looked at me quizzically with a narrowing of his heavy-lidded eyes, a look that even from our short acquaintance I noted he seemed to use regularly. If he was wondering why I was so red he thankfully didn't ask, but I did see a hint of a smirk tweak at the corner of his mouth, as if he knew exactly what I had been imagining, and I felt my tongue dry up like cotton wool.

This was awful. I felt so uncomfortable with these peculiar feelings that I was just thinking perhaps I should make excuses to leave when he spoke. 'Play me something you know,' Nicholas instructed quietly, and I found myself happy to move on from my crazy fantasy and his silent scrutiny of me, but not happy to embarrass myself by playing in front of someone as talented as him.

'No, I'm really not very good,' I muttered, staring at the keys and trying unsuccessfully to force my heartbeat to decrease. What polite reason could I give that would allow me to leave right now? Because it was definitely time I got the hell away from this man

'I'd like you to play something for me, Rebecca,' Nicholas repeated. This time his tone was low and silky, but also authoritative, and for some reason his words didn't seem like a request, they sounded like an order.

Braving a glance across at him, I saw Nicholas' face was passive, but his dark blue eyes were hooded, as if challenging me to say no to him. The effect of his steely gaze was nerve-racking to say the least, and I actually struggled to take in a breath for several seconds as my eyes remained glued to his. From nowhere, a shiver of fear ran through me that made my entire body shudder. He really was a very intimidating man, and clearly used to getting whatever he asked for, so with some reluctance I raised my hands and saw his eyebrow tweak when he noticed my trembling fingers.

'Are you nervous here alone in the dark with me, Becky?' he asked in a tone that made the hairs on the back of my neck stand up and my senses heighten.

What a strange comment, I thought. Surely only a dangerous person would ask that. Glancing around, I saw to my surprise that the theatre was now deserted and eerily dark beyond the stage. The cleaners had finished and left and the lights were all off apart from the ones above the piano. If it were possible, my heart accelerated even further until my chest actually began to ache.

Looking back to Nicholas, I straightened my back and swallowed the lump in my throat. Yes, I was nervous, for whatever reason I found the man slightly scary, but he was also sexy as hell, which could go a long way to explaining my nerves. Not that I was going to admit either point to him.

At last, finding some shred of my usual confidence, I answered. 'Should I be?' I asked with a raise of my eyebrow, my voice thankfully far bolder than I felt.

Surprising me completely, Nicholas rolled his head back and laughed, a sound so lovely that it amplified the heat between my legs, but also made me smile, before he played a few random chords on the piano and then turning back to me.

'Diversion by answering my question with one of your own. Very clever, Becky.' As I bravely maintained my composed silence, he looked intently at me for a few seconds before almost smiling again. 'And to answer your question, no, you don't need to be scared of me. Not in here. Now play,' he instructed, indicating the keys in front of me.

My shoulders were about to relax when my brain grabbed at three of his words. *Not in here* ... what the hell did that mean? That I was safe with him here, but not elsewhere? Why would he say that? Trying to clear his odd comments from my mind, I shook my head and began to play a very simple version of John Lennon's 'Imagine', a song I had learnt when I first got my keyboard two years ago.

'Interesting song choice,' Nicholas said, looking as if he knew exactly what I had been imagining just minutes ago. I blushed crimson as the fantasy flashed in my mind again, but the more sensible side of me thankfully pushed it away so I could concentrate on playing. Finishing my piece – which had been stuttered and clunky – I stared at the keys, too mortified to meet his gaze. This was so awkward; I felt like a teenager again, and it wasn't a pleasant sensation at all.

Never in my twenty-five years had I had such explicit fantasies, not even in my dreams or the privacy of my own bedroom, so why the hell was my mind suddenly giving me them now, as I sat next to Nicholas Jackson? It might have something to do with my recent period of celibacy I suppose, or perhaps his sexiness and intimidating persona, which I had to admit was rather attractive, but the timing was certainly inconvenient, I thought, rolling my eyes at my own stupidity.

'What are you thinking, Becky?' Nicholas asked suddenly, a smile once again evident in his tone but barely showing on his lips. Biting my lip I drew in a fortifying breath. That 'nearly there' smile was so teasing that it was very likely going to be the death of me.

'Nothing,' I mumbled, shoving my hair behind my ear. Smug bastard, it was almost as if he'd read my frigging mind again. Was I really that transparent or were his comments just coincidental?

Thankfully, he didn't push it and instead turned his attention back to the music. 'Your F-chord is slightly wrong; your first finger is slipping onto the G key and affecting the chord quality,' he explained patiently.

'Show me your hand position,' he instructed, so I did. 'Raise your forearm slightly,' he ordered. God, he was so bossy. There was no pleasantness in his manner; it was just barked orders. But something in his tone told me I shouldn't disobey a man like Nicholas Jackson, so I did exactly as I was told and actually found the chord easier to play.

After I had played my horribly clumsy tune a few more times, he gently closed the lid over the keys, which I took as a hint that our impromptu lesson was over. Thank goodness for that. He was probably sick of my dreadfully slow chord changes by now, and to be honest I wasn't sure I could take our close positioning for much longer without saying or doing something completely stupid anyway.

'You follow instructions well; you would be a good student,' Nicholas mused, his eyes still focused intently on mine and now blazing with something that I couldn't determine. 'I could give you some lessons if you like?' he offered, to my complete surprise, causing my eyes to widen significantly. 'For free, of course, as a thank you for getting us spotted and signed.'

Crikey, I thought, piano lessons from Nicholas Jackson would be amazing; literally learning from the very best. But I hesitated; considering the bizarre reaction in my body since I'd met him, I wasn't sure it was such a good idea to spend any more time in close proximity to him … After all, he was scary intimidating, *and* sexy, not forgetting that I'd fantasised about him three times already.

Quite explicitly, and with all the sweaty details still vibrant in my mind.

Licking my dry lips I considered his offer. I definitely found him hugely attractive, and there seemed to be some sort of buzz between us that I'd never felt before that would be quite interesting to explore if I was brave enough. I tried to weigh it up in my mind. In the short time I'd known him, Nicholas had already fascinated and unnerved me more than any man I'd ever met, plus he'd no doubt be an amazing teacher. My inner conflict was disturbed by his voice breaking into my tumbling thoughts. 'Is that your tell?' he asked, amusement again tinting his tone but not showing on his features. How did he do that? It was like trying to laugh without engaging your cheeks – almost impossible.

'Excuse me?' I asked, blushing and raising my eyes to his in confusion.

'It appears to me that when you are nervous you tuck your hair behind your ear, Becky,' he observed lightly, rubbing his hand absently across the piano lid.

Oh. Did I? I hadn't even been aware I was doing it. Not wanting him to think I was weak or lacking in confidence, which usually I wasn't, I sat straighter and forced my hand to stay in my lap and not touch my hair any more, which I suddenly realised it was itching to do. Damn, he was right.

'I have no idea, but I'm not nervous,' I lied boldly. 'I'll accept your lessons, Mr Jackson, thank you.' Ha, who was nervous? Not me. Well, not much anyway.

'Call me Nicholas,' he requested, a smile breaking on his lips – the first time he'd smiled properly all night, and it was just as incredible as I'd thought it would be, instantly sending a delicious shiver down my spine.

'Do you ever use Nick?' I said casually, feeling sure that a shorter, less formal name might help me see him as a less daunting character. Something unpleasant flickered across his face, tightening his features, and making his lips thin as his brows drew lower in a grimace so dark it almost managed to taint his handsomeness, and caused my stomach to clench uncomfortably.

'No, call me Nicholas,' he stated flatly. In the blink of an eye, his earlier smile had been erased, leaving behind no trace of his better mood and instead projecting the shuttered exterior I was now looking at.

God, what was I getting myself into?

TWO

Being quite a sensible person and thinking myself a good judge of character, I should have seen the warning signs from Nicholas flashing like great big neon bulbs and run away as fast as I could. If I'm really honest with myself, I *had* seen the signs during our first encounter – in short, he'd been controlling, intense, and formidable – but I'd stupidly ignored them, preferring instead to take a risk and allow myself the chance to experience the thrill of being near such a domineeringly sexy man. And believe me, Nicholas Jackson was *sexy,* his looks, posture, clothing, demeanour … Goodness, even the tone of his voice had got me excited.

Huffing out an impatient breath, I pushed off the railings and ran a hand through my hair, tucking it behind my ear. Immediately, I scowled at the stupid nervous habit that I was now fully aware of thanks to Nicholas bloody Jackson. Of course he had spotted it straight away, *my little tell,* as he'd called it. And he'd been right, I did fiddle with my hair and push it self-consciously behind my ears when anxious, which since we'd spilt up seemed to be every frigging five minutes.

Managing to bring my focus back to the present, I realised I must have been standing on the bridge for at least ten minutes now, staring out across the marketplace like a complete loon. Once again I was immensely glad I lived in Camden, where you could look like an idiot and no one cared one little bit, much less commented on it.

Just as I was downing the final dregs of my lukewarm coffee, the sound of a piano hit me again and my whole body tensed in reaction, including my hand, which crumpled the empty paper cup. Closing my eyes, I forced my hearing to come to the forefront of my senses and traced the music to somewhere very nearby, softly mocking me with its notes.

Tilting my head, I listened more carefully. The tune kept faltering and repeating as if someone was learning it, or perhaps tuning the instrument as they played. Gripping at the railing with increasingly white knuckles, I opened my eyes and tried once again to trace the source of the piano music.

Looking down the stairs to my left, I craned my neck and could just see the wooden façade of a shop I'd never noticed before. *Camden Piano Restorers*, its aged sign stated. Sitting at an upright piano by the open door was a man, playing the battered old instrument and tuning it as he went. My throat tightened against my will, letting my emotions beginning to get the better of me. He wasn't Nicholas, as my desperate imagination had hoped, and the piano was a far cry from the elegant beauties Nicholas played, but still the coincidence had left my mind reeling.

Finally regaining the feeling in my legs, I pushed off the railing, dumped my crushed coffee cup in a bin, and made my way down the steps past the piano shop toward the canal, making a mental note not to come this way through the markets again. A canal boat was working its way through one of the brightly painted gates and part of me wished I could jump on board and leave my nagging and annoying memories behind and sail away with the occupants.

Remembering the better times wasn't going to help me get over Nicholas, but it was all I seemed to do lately. While my body was physically functioning and going through the motions of living and running my bookshop, I couldn't have been more unproductive if I'd tried. My fluctuating moods made interactions with other people difficult to say the least, so it was just as well I didn't have a packed social life to rearrange, and thankfully, at work I had my employee Louise to rely on. Since my split with Nicholas, she'd been an absolute legend, keeping the shop running while I tried to get my head back on straight.

My mind was like a cinema these days, replaying each step of our failed relationship in high-definition detail, and I was starting to think my subconscious was trying to torture me slowly to death. Pausing by the canal, I placed my hands on the damp stone wall and watched the boatmen tug and push at the locks on the gates. One shouted commands and the other followed them without hesitation – just as I had with Nicholas, I thought with a scoffed, humourless laugh. Even though it had been three weeks now, I could still remember the precise timbre of Nicholas' voice, his divine fragrance, and even the exact conversations we'd had at my first piano lesson …

My lessons with him had started almost immediately, three days after our first meeting at the Palladium, in fact, when I set out on foot to work my way to his Primrose Hill address. Of course Nicholas would live in Primrose Hill, wouldn't he? It's one of the most sought-after addresses in London and perfectly suited his "only the best is good enough for me" style.

Primrose Hill is exactly what its name describes; a hill – more precisely, a large, grassy park containing said hill. Seeing as I was born and bred in the Lake District, hiking my way to the top of the hill is just like coming home for me, and I've lost count of the number of times I've packed a blanket and book and headed up there to watch the sunset. An hour on Primrose Hill resets my outlook on life like the "refresh" button on a computer. Regardless of what type of day I've had, it never fails to remind me of just how much I love living in the chaos that is London.

Luckily for me, it is also extremely close to where I live, and after searching out Nicholas' address on the map, I worked out that it would probably only take me fifteen minutes to walk there. Seeing as I didn't want to arrive for my first piano lesson sweaty and red, I gave myself half an hour and walked at half my usual speedy pace, allowing myself the indulgence of window shopping in several upmarket boutiques along the way.

When I arrived at Nicholas' house, I had to check the address three times before I finally believed I had it correct. It was enormous. Practically palatial. Just looking at the stunning frontage of the Victorian townhouse made me nervous. Nervous and hugely envious because the house in front of me, with its gleaming white paintwork and shiny front door, was complete with gorgeous, plant-lined bay windows. Three stories in height, it had a small, neat front garden and perfectly trimmed ivy growing up one side. It was the embodiment of what most people would describe as their dream home, and even without entering, I knew the inside would be just as stunning.

Funnily enough, as nervous as I was feeling when I rang the bell, my tension was distracted by the total look of surprise on Nicholas' face when he opened the door. He was dressed in a pale blue shirt and navy suit trousers, and staring at me with apparent shock in those dark blue eyes of his. I attempted a smile as I took in his appearance, but was so nervous I probably just ended up looking constipated. His hair was tousled like last time, and as I saw that peculiar half-smile tweaking the corner of his mouth again like a trademark, I already knew deep down that I was a lost cause.

'Becky, you came. I thought you might cancel,' he mused, stroking his chin thoughtfully before opening the door wider and gesturing for me to enter.

My heartbeat had rocketed from just the sight of him, but I forced myself to stay calm on the outside. 'Why?' I asked with a frown. Always inquisitive, that was me.

'You said you found me intimidating, I thought you might reconsider having lessons with me here.' He shrugged, taking my coat and handing it to a man standing behind him who I hadn't noticed at first.

'This is Mr Burrett; he works for me, keeps my life on track,' Nicholas explained with another of his almost smiles.

Mr Burrett smiled at me fully before hanging my coat in a cupboard and then tactfully disappearing. Was he Nicholas' personal assistant? Or perhaps a butler of sorts? From his smart-suited appearance, it was the only conclusion I could come to. I'd never known anyone with house staff before. How very opulent, not to mention terribly British, I thought, hiding a smirk.

'I do find you intimidating,' I continued brightly, following him through a minimalistic but beautiful hallway and up a wide flight of thickly carpeted stairs, feeling braver now I knew there was someone else in the house with us. 'But I'm more than capable of standing up for myself, Nicholas,' I added coolly, secretly rather pleased by the slightly shocked look on his face as he glanced back at me. I had decided before arriving that I would be ultra-calm and confident today, unlike our last encounter, and no matter how much he disturbed my equilibrium I was going to stick to it. Or at least try my best to, I amended, as I followed him up the stairs and my pulse quickened when my gaze focused on his long legs and firm behind. Mmm, what a sight. My palms were tingling with the urge to reach out, but I flattened them to my sides instead.

Nicholas ushered me into a room on the first floor that was so spacious I could have easily fitted my entire flat into it. Glancing around, it was immediately evident that this was his music room; the space was dominated by a large grand piano and stool that sat toward the back of the room next to floor-to-ceiling picture windows overlooking a tree-lined garden. The only other furniture in the room was a soft white armchair, a solid-looking bookcase, and a desk that was covered in sheet music, most of which appeared to be handwritten.

Annoyingly, even though Nicholas still made me anxious with his height, looks, and penetrating gaze, my traitorous body was also still drawn to him. I had foolishly thought that maybe just the excitement of meeting him backstage at the theatre had caused me to feel that way last time, but once we were seated at the piano, I definitely still felt the same strange tug of attraction.

Even more distractingly, now I was in Nicholas' house, sitting at his piano, I found my mind kept wandering back to my fantasy about the rude things he might do to me over it. Puffing out a flustered breath, I felt my skin heat at the saucy images that had taken root in my dreams since meeting him three days ago.

Maybe lessons with Nicholas weren't such a good idea after all, I thought, shifting awkwardly in my seat and letting out an irritable breath.

Luckily, I was proved wrong and the lesson went well. Nicholas was brisk with his instructions as I had expected, but clear and precise with his advice and, surprisingly, I could hear the improvement in my playing within the hour. Sitting back, I stretched out my arms and smiled at my much-improved version of 'Imagine', but upon seeing his gaze on me, I looked away in embarrassment.

'Don't drop your eyes,' he instructed quietly, and for some reason, even though I felt totally mortified by my body's ridiculous response to him, I found myself looking back. Nicholas' eyes were bright and burning into me, and I just knew my cheeks were going to flush again. Seconds later, they did; in fact, my face felt like it was on fire and I dropped my gaze again and pushed my hair behind my ear in frustration at my lack of control.

'Eyes up,' he growled softly. 'I won't tell you again, Rebecca.' Wow! I sucked in a quick breath at his tone, which had sounded quite a lot like a threat, but for some reason I just couldn't defy him and I found myself raising my wide eyes to his once again; my heart feeling like it might explode from my ribcage at any moment.

'That's better. You have such beautiful eyes,' he murmured soothingly, looking like he wanted to touch me, but refraining.

I blushed again at his compliment; wondering exactly how red a person could go without their blood vessels actually exploding. He was still staring at me intently and although it seemed crazy, I wondered if it were somehow possible that this godlike creature felt the same attraction I did.

'There's that tell again, Rebecca; playing with your hair.' He tutted softly, as his glance flicked to my ear and back again. 'It looks better down,' he informed me, somehow managing to un-tuck my hair from behind my ear without actually touching my skin at all. Still, just knowing that his fingers had been in my hair made my scalp tingle, and I had to fight the urge to finger the strands that he had moved.

My head was spinning. Nicholas' proximity, smell, and peculiar comments were confusing me – *did* he like me too? It was possible, I supposed. My friends always told me I was pretty, but I knew I wasn't in his league. Even if it were the case, why had he gone to such lengths to avoid touching me? He'd actually sat on a chair to escape sharing the piano stool with me, for goodness' sake.

In fact, as I cast my mind back to our meeting after the concert, I couldn't recall him having touched me then either.

Not a handshake, not a brush of his fingers over my arm; no contact at all. How peculiar.

Then, as if nothing had occurred between us at all, Nicholas resumed his lesson on the basic chord changes, leaving me reeling once again, God, he was so confusing. Halfway through instructing me on how to play a G-chord correctly, however, he once again shocked me with his changeable ways by turning to me and closing the music book so I couldn't continue with my piece.

I turned to him in confusion, thinking that perhaps I had done something wrong.

'Are you single?' he asked me bluntly.

Completely thrown by Nicholas' random question and odd tone, I frowned and answered hesitantly, 'Um ... yes.'

After almost having recovered from his earlier "beautiful eyes" comment, my heart was once again pounding in my chest to the point of pain. I thought that after my affirmative response Nicholas might act, ask me out, perhaps, but he didn't. Exasperatingly, he merely nodded, reopened the music, and continued my lesson.

What the heck had that been about? This man was infuriatingly difficult to read! Mind you, compared to the other men I'd dated, Nicholas made them look like inexperienced boys. He somehow came across as a real, manly man, completely self-assured and confident; something I had recently discovered was a rather appealing combination.

From the corner of my eye, I could see Nicholas' continued assessment of me, but saw that he wore an expression that seemed to be a mix of arrogance and derisive passiveness. Apparently, he was unmoved by my single status.

It was ridiculous, but his obvious rejection of me stung like a burn across my skin. As I left that night, I made a conscious effort not to look at Nicholas or show my disappointment. I also decided I'd call him in the week and cancel all future lessons. The piano was fun but I didn't need an unrequited crush on a ridiculously handsome man to complicate my life.

THREE

The rasping noise of a harmonica broke me from my reverie, and as I blinked back to the present I realised I'd walked the entire length of Camden High Street in a daze. Trying to push away my daydreams of Nicholas and focus on the more important reality of living my life, I looked down at the familiar figure of Max, a local busker and harmonica genius, whose favourite spot is just on the end of the road where my shop is located. After chucking him a quid and a KitKat from my bag – they're his favourites – I headed for the junction that leads up the smaller road to my bookshop.

Turning off the High Street, I was almost instantly surrounded by a refreshing calmness as the number of people surrounding me died down to barely a handful. It always amazed me that by just walking ten or so paces away from the main road you could somehow escape the noise and bustle so quickly. Even though I knew that Camden was still happening back there in all its colourful, crowded, noisy glory, I now felt a million miles away.

The side street that my book shop is on also has a few markets of its own, but these predominantly sell fruit and vegetables and, while still busy, it's nothing compared to the crowds on the main drag.

I smiled at Johno on stall five as I passed. He's my fruit guy and always has the freshest, most tasty figs I've ever been lucky enough to ingest.

Once I walk past the fruit stalls, the road starts to look more residential, lined with pretty, brick-built townhouses laden with overflowing hanging baskets, most of which have shops on the lower floor like mine. There's a vintage vinyl shop selling records from the 50s, 60s, and 70s, a fancy dress boutique, a hairdresser, and me, the Camden Book Emporium. The name came with the shop when I bought it, might I add, and although my shop is in Camden, its tiny interior is about as far from an "emporium" as you could get. As much as I might dislike the name, however, the business has an established reputation so I've bravely stuck with it.

If only I'd been as brave in sticking to my decision of cancelling my lessons with Nicholas, I thought as I pulled a bunch of keys from my bag and selected the correct one to open the shop. If I had, I might not be standing on the street, still able to remember the slight ache on my rear from the episode with the cane.

But I hadn't called him to cancel, of course I hadn't. I'd fancied him like crazy; why would I cancel? To give myself a little credit, I had tried several times. I'd even dialled his number fully on two occasions but I'd chickened out both times and hung up as soon as I heard ringing. The fact of the matter was that as well as being incredibly attracted to Nicholas Jackson he also made me a little nervous , and because of this I'd been too worried about what he might say if I tried to cancel, so in the end I'd just buckled up my confidence and gone along the following Friday.

To make matters even more confusing, Nicholas had acted in a completely professional fashion at the next lesson. There had been no inquisitive glances or strange questions about my relationship status and I began to wonder if my lust-filled brain had dreamed up his actions that first week.

After several weeks, my piano playing had made a marked improvement and I gradually began to relax my guard around Nicholas. He hadn't tried anything or made any more suggestive comments so I decided to be an adult about it and try to see him solely as my tutor and nothing else.

Unfortunately, this was when all my troubles really began.

After he'd asked me if I was single and then done nothing when he knew I was, I had convinced myself that Nicholas wasn't interested in me. Even though I had promised to view him as

34

my tutor and nothing more, I couldn't help the thrill of attraction that ran through me every time he was near, or the way my pulse spiked if I caught his eye for a moment or two. He was so good-looking that I think even a celibate nun would have had some sort of response to him.

I decided that it might be a one-sided crush, but if I was careful he'd never know, and besides, I'd get over it in time. That was what I told myself anyway, but in the weeks that followed, I noticed that Nicholas developed a certain way of looking at me that made me feel completely transparent to him.

It had continued like this, Nicholas distant and daunting and me uncharacteristically on edge and nervy, until, one evening after I'd forced myself to try and start relaxing around him, he finally touched me.

It occurred just as I was finishing a new piece he had taught me. Unbeknown to me, Nicholas had moved to stand behind me, and as I completed the song, he placed a hand lightly on the centre of my back.

As ridiculous as it sounds, I couldn't help but gasp as the heat from his palm seemed to sear my skin and froze me to the spot. I didn't say anything, I couldn't, so I simply sat there, stunned and mute and soaking up the delicious sensation of his touch. Very slowly, he used one finger to trail a path up my spine before resting his hand on the nape of my neck and seeming to rip the breath from my body as he did so. Every single one of my nerve endings seemed to be tingling now, and I involuntarily shuddered from the intense pleasure of his touch, still slightly shocked that he was touching me at all. Shooting sparks danced across my skin, causing me to jab the piano keys clumsily and make an awful racket as my limbs jerked. It ruined the otherwise successful piece and made me look incredibly foolish to boot.

'Am I mistaken, Rebecca, or do you feel it too?' Nicholas asked in a silken tone as he straddled the piano stool and sat beside me, his hand still on my neck and heat positively radiating from his body. Or perhaps the heat was coming from me – things felt so surreal that I couldn't quite tell.

Part of me wanted to play dumb and say, 'Feel what too?'

but even though I'd tried to tell myself he didn't like me, I wasn't entirely naïve. The tension between us these past few weeks had grown to the point where it was almost palpable; besides, I was dreadful at seduction so I simply nodded shyly.

'Say it,' he instructed, his thumb doing disastrous things to my equilibrium by rubbing a small circle on the nape of my neck, making me groan and lean into his touch.

'I feel it too, Nicholas.' I had dropped my eyes out of embarrassment, but immediately felt his hand stop circling and slip to my shoulder where his grip tightened till it was almost painful.

'Look at me,' he ordered, and I immediately did. I really should be remembering his obsession with eye contact by now; he'd reminded me of it enough times over the weeks.

'Wayward and fiery one minute, yet so obedient the next,' Nicholas mused out loud, seemingly talking to himself. I scoffed at his comment internally.

I was confident yes, headstrong even on occasions, but wayward and fiery? Hardly – especially not when I was in his domineering presence.

'I have tried to avoid the urge, but I would very much like to fuck you over this piano, Rebecca,' he murmured suddenly, causing my eyes to fly open as his grip once again tightened on my neck, causing me to gasp at his crudeness.

Wow, I had not expected that comment in a million years.

But his grip on my shoulder and obvious strength triggered my mind to fill with images of my sister, Joanne, and the horrific ordeal she had been through just over seven years ago, images so awful that I usually worked hard to subdue them, but I couldn't escape them now, and I felt panic start to rise from my belly and flood my chest.

My apprehension must have been all too apparent on my face because I saw Nicholas' eyebrows rise as his lips narrowed into a thin line. 'You look almost horrified by my suggestion, Rebecca, but I'm asking your opinion. This would be completely consensual; if you say no then we simply go back to our lesson,' he finished with a shrug, although his tone wasn't quite as casual as his actions suggested.

Consensual ... which made it completely different to Joanne's encounter, then, I thought, pushing aside the unpleasant memories. I had to admit that even though I'd never done anything as reckless as this before I found Nicholas' proposition an incredible turn-on. His words exactly mirrored the fantasy I'd had several times now and catapulted something inside me to life as I felt my groin moisten and my stomach muscles quiver in anticipation.

'Would you like that, or have I shocked you?' he enquired softly, his thumb rubbing me in gentle motions again, prompting the hairs on my neck to rise and meet his caress.

Now I'd managed to lock away the thoughts of my poor sister I found my voice. 'Your word choice was a bit shocking ... but ... I think I'd like it,' I said, my response causing him to suck in a sharp breath through his nose.

'My word choice? Because I said *fuck*, you mean?' he asked, looking rather amused for some reason, but I nodded jerkily in response. 'I don't do relationships, Rebecca, I enjoy the company of women but usually only for an hour or two. We barely know each other, so I would be lying if I said I wanted to make love to you, so I didn't. I said it as it is; I would very much like to fuck you. And if that's something that doesn't interest you, you can leave now and we will simply continue your lessons next week.'

Oh. He certainly had a way with words, didn't he? So he wanted to *fuck* me tonight and maybe another time or two but then it would be over, probably along with my piano lessons too, because that would just be too weird to continue with afterwards. For some inexplicable reason, though, I found myself shaking my head.

'I don't want to leave.' God, what was I getting myself into? I'd never even used the word "fuck" as a curse, let alone to describe something I wanted to do with a man.

Nicholas released another long, slow breath as if absorbing the moment, then a smug smile tugged at the corners of his tempting mouth. 'Good. Stand up and lean on this,' he instructed, closing the lid over the piano keys so I could rest my behind on it.

Moving himself so he was sitting at the centre of the stool facing forward, Nicholas placed his hands on my waist and, without any warning, jerked me sideways along the piano so I stood between his legs. Swallowing loudly I licked my dry lips as my anticipation built. He hadn't kissed me, had barely even touched me properly, and yet I think I was more turned on than I had ever been in my entire life.

Trailing his hands so they rested on my bare knees, Nicholas ran them teasingly up under the hem of my cotton skirt to my outer thighs and then repeated the journey back down again. My skin was on fire from pleasure, and my head lolled back, my eyes closing with desire, but suddenly I found Nicholas standing up and pressing his hips painfully against mine. One of his hands twisted into my hair, forcing my head back up, and I opened my eyes in surprise, blinking at his forceful movements.

'Eyes open, Becky. You know how much I like to see you.' His sentence was ground out as if I had annoyed him by looking away. Blinking in confusion, I looked him directly in the eyes as a flicker of concern mixed with my arousal.

'Better,' he stated, giving me a sharp nod and looking pleased, before his lips descended on mine with such devastating heat that I gasped for breath, instantly forgetting my concern. Taking the opportunity my gasp presented, Nicholas' tongue lunged into my mouth, searching and teasing and heating my blood until he too had to stop for air.

I was literally panting as his hands began to roam across my body, which I found embarrassing, but no matter what I did I couldn't seem to breathe normally any more. To be honest, simply remaining upright was enough of a struggle right now.

'Rest your arms back on the top of the piano,' he instructed briskly, and I was so captivated by him that I did it at once. Now I was stood leaning against the piano on my elbows as if resting there casually, a position completely at odds with the emotions that tumbled through my body under his skilled touch.

With a low rumble from his chest, Nicholas rubbed the heels of his hands roughly across my breasts, and I felt my nipples tighten and strain against my T-shirt to the point where the lace of my bra almost seemed painful, but in a way that only added to my overall arousal. His touch was far harder than I was used to, but it felt amazing, and I wished the barrier of material wasn't there so I could feel him skin on skin.

'So responsive,' he murmured under his breath, looking me straight in the eye. Without dropping his gaze, he located one of my nipples under the T-shirt and took it between his thumb and forefinger. With a smith he began to tug it gently, making me moan softly and arch myself toward him where I felt his solid erection digging into me.

The feel of his hard length jutting against my thigh brought things into focus for me. This was really happening, Nicholas was this aroused because of *me*. The thought was potent, powerful somehow, and emboldened me enough to push my hand between us and cup the bulge in his trousers, causing a hiss to escape from his lips as I began to squeeze and rub him.

His favourite half-smile seemed to play on his lips as he repeated the treatment on my other breast, this time twisting the nipple more sharply and sending a delicious shudder directly to my groin and making me moan out loud. His movements threatened to undo me, and as he pressed his thigh against the apex of my legs and began rubbing it against my groin through the material of my skirt I thought I might melt.

'*Ahhh …*' I gasped aloud, but somehow managed to maintain eye contact with him, rather than allowing my eyes to close like they wanted as desire shimmied through me and heated my body.

As both his hands continued teasing, rubbing and tugging my nipples, my legs became so rubbery that I began to fear I might actually fall over. It had been a while since I'd been intimate with a man like this, a *long* while, and the sensations washing through my body were almost too much for me to handle.

I don't know if it was Nicholas' deft touches, the feel of his cock twitching in my hand, the added sensitivity from the material of my T-shirt, or just the way he seemed to be adding in painfully hard tweaks that sent desire coursing through me, but with the addition of his teasing leg at my groin I was quickly getting to the point of no return.

As I felt a familiar coiling of the muscles deep in my belly I realised I'd better warn him before it was too late. 'Nicholas ... I think I'm going to come ...' My voice sounded strained and pathetic as I clutched at the piano with trembling fingers.

Pausing, he tilted his head. 'So soon?' he asked curiously, his hands continuing their torture but at a slightly slower pace and his leg relenting from its rubbing. Yes, so soon! I wanted to scream out; it had been bloody ages since I'd been with a man and even then, they'd never aroused me as startlingly quickly as Nicholas had managed to, but thankfully that's not what came out of my mouth.

'Yes ... sorry, but ... what you're doing is ... *oh God* ...' I knew I was rambling, but I could feel myself building closer and closer. What I desperately wanted was for him to be buried inside of me but Nicholas had other ideas. After dropping a short, hard kiss on my lips, he returned his attention to my nipples, increasing the tempo and rubbing his thigh faster and harder against my groin until I exploded in a shockingly hard climax, groaning out his name and gripping the piano with all my might.

'You are so sensitive, so responsive ...' he said, again seeming pleased by my almost violent response to his touch.

My body was humming with desire and floating on a cloud of post-orgasmic bliss, but I was brought back to earth when Nicholas suddenly left my breasts bereft of his touch and pulled me to him for another deep kiss. Apparently, he wasn't finished with me yet because his right hand skilfully pulled up my skirt and gently massaged the quivering skin of my inner thigh. Somehow, he managed to tug my knickers down one-handed, working them down my leg until I felt them fall around my ankles.

If I had thought his leg on my groin felt good it was nothing compared to the sensations that spiralled through me as Nicholas' hand dipped under my skirt again and began to explore between my legs. In fact, I was so turned on that I very nearly climaxed a second time at the first touch of his fingers brushing through the hair at the apex of my thighs. When he found my expectant nub and circled it slickly with his thumb, I whimpered pathetically and parted my legs further for him.

How was he doing this? I didn't think I'd ever been this wanton in my whole life.

'Jesus, Rebecca, you're so wet ...' Nicholas hissed against my neck as two of his fingers slipped along my damp lips and began to explore inside of me. Even though I knew moistness was a good thing, I blushed with embarrassment from his words, but luckily my face was hidden in his shoulder. 'Turn around,' he ordered firmly. Thankfully, my wobbly legs just about managed the job. 'Lie forward across the piano,' he instructed in a husky tone and I did, glad of the support the cool wood offered to my trembling body.

There was the noise of a zip, then the rip of a condom packet as I felt his leg gently nudge at my knees, pushing them wider. Thank God, Nicholas was on the ball enough to think of contraception, because I had been so caught up in the moment that it had totally slipped my mind. Then, before I really knew what was happening, he gripped my hips and thrust into me in one long, swift movement that stretched me deliciously and made me feel fuller than I had in a very long time.

'*Aggh*!' I cried out in relief. Oh, that felt so good, just what I needed to release the frustration that had built up within me. I'd wanted this for weeks.

My own blatantly sexual realisation startled me slightly; I had wanted Nicholas inside me for weeks.

After pausing for a second to control himself, he began to move, pulling his length slowly out before thrusting back into me hard and fast and striking my G-spot with near perfection. Tantalizingly, he repeated this several times, and before I could do anything about it, I came again, very loudly, my body clenching around him as lights seemed to blind me and waves of intense pleasure swept through my trembling body. God, that had been even better than the first one.

It occurred to me that I had barely lasted a minute with him inside me – how embarrassing. 'Sorry ...' I mumbled weakly, then felt him pull out of me. Oh no! He wasn't going to continue because I'd come so quickly! But, contrary to what I thought, he turned me round to face him and once again settled me on the lid covering the piano keys, his eyes blazing with desire.

'You're incredible. I want to see you,' Nicholas said simply, as if explaining the change of position. 'Never apologise for an orgasm, Rebecca – there will be more to follow,' he promised darkly.

More to follow? Could I cope with more? He'd called me incredible, which I rather liked. But before I could speak, he settled himself between my legs once again and slid inside me with a low breath. This time, he controlled the movements by gripping my hips and using the shine of the wood below my bunched-up skirt to assist him in a smooth rocking motion. To break up his thrusts, he occasionally ground himself in a circular motion against me, and it was all I could do to cling to the piano and try to keep up with him. I soon realised what he had meant by *more to follow*, when I felt a third orgasm building deep inside me.

This was sex like I'd never experienced it before; intense, passionate, and sweaty. Part of me wanted it to go on for ever, but another part knew I hadn't had sex for a long time and wondered if my body could handle another orgasm like the last two.

Sensing my imminent release, or perhaps his own, Nicholas suddenly increased the tempo, slamming into me repeatedly until, finally, my body gave up the battle and smashed into another body-shaking orgasm around him. I cried out his name, coming over and over again with each of his thrusts, clenching around him until I thought I could take no more. Finally, he buried himself even deeper inside me and climaxed with a low groan against my neck.

Thank goodness the grand piano weighed a lot and wouldn't roll, because Nicholas was collapsed against me, panting, and I was slumped back against the lid feeling both breathless and boneless.

Several moments later, he peeled himself back and eased out of me, causing me to wince slightly, before he disposed of the condom in a bin to his left, tucked his softening manhood back inside his trousers, and gently rearranged my skirt for me.

We hadn't even removed any clothes! Talk about fast and furious.

'Did you enjoy that, Rebecca?' Nicholas asked softly, running a hand through my hair as I clung to him, trying not to sag to the floor as my body wanted to. God, I was exhausted, and a tiny bit sore, too – not that I minded.

'Yes ... more than enjoyed,' I murmured, still dazed from the intensity of it. I had never had sex like that before in my life. Who knew it could be so good?

'You're very ... assertive, Nicholas. Why is that?' I observed, still gripping his shoulder.

'You noticed,' he said, trying and failing to hide the ironic smile that rose to his lips. 'That's why this won't happen again. I'll be upfront with you and trust you to keep this to yourself ...' But then he paused, narrowing his eyes as though considering if I were worthy of his trust, before giving a short laugh. 'You wouldn't tell anyone, it would implicate you,' he said, confusing me. 'I like control when I fuck. You may not have heard the term but I'm what you call a dominant, Rebecca, and the women I have sex with understand this. I do ... different things with them, it's what they like, but it wouldn't be suitable for you.' His eyes held mine but I couldn't help but frown at his words.

So this was definitely a one-off, then. I actually felt quite disappointed, but who wouldn't after sex like that? And what did he mean he was a dominant? He was right, I hadn't heard the term before, but it sounded kind of kinky, as if he took what he wanted when he wanted it. But if it was anything like what we'd just done on the piano, why wouldn't I be suitable?

'Oh.' I straightened my back, slightly affronted by his assumption. 'Why wouldn't I be suitable?'

He smiled a dark and slightly scary smile. 'Curious thing, aren't you?' he murmured, his gaze wandering over me probingly. 'Let's just say that the women I fuck do what I want and don't ask lots of questions like you do.'

'*Oh*,' I mumbled, blushing. That had been the best sex I'd ever had and now I knew it wasn't going to be repeated. Damn. Deep down, part of me began to put together a plan, wondering if I could change his mind somehow.

I was pretty sure I was dreadful at flirting and never in my life had I attempted the art of seduction, but, somehow feeling brasher and braver after our intimate liaison on the piano, I raised an eyebrow and rubbed my hips provocatively against Nicholas' pelvis as I moved away from him to leave.

'That's a shame, Nicholas; I had hoped you might be up for an encore. Never mind, if I'm too much for you to handle I should probably just go,' I said teasingly, my heart pounding in my chest. Rather proud of my witty little reference to his musical lifestyle, I smiled to myself as I turned for the door.

Before I'd even taken two steps, I felt a sharp tug on the back of my T-shirt and suddenly I was pinned against Nicholas' hard body, my back to his front. One of his strong arms wrapped around my waist, gripping me tightly to him, pinning my arms to my side and pretty much stopping me from moving at all. I couldn't escape if I wanted to, so it was lucky that I didn't want to, I thought with a triumphant smile. With his other hand, he tilted my neck roughly to the side and lowered his head so his lips were brushing against my earlobe sending tingles along my spine.

'Too much for me to handle?' He laughed, deep and low. 'Oh, but you've not met my alter ego yet, have you? Dominant Nicholas could definitely handle you,' he whispered soothingly against my neck, but somehow his words were also full of a dark, sensual promise that made me quiver. 'And I never turn down a challenge, Miss Langley; I think an encore can be arranged, if you're sure you're up to it?'

A shiver of desire ran through me, laced with a touch of fear at the unknown implication behind his words. Was I up to it? Bedding a – what did he call himself? A dominant? What did that even involve?

Without any warning, Nicholas let me go and took a step away from me, immediately leaving me missing the warmth of his body. Confused, I turned to look at him and gasped. His eyes were blazing and desire was clearly evident in the front of his trousers, but a calm arrogance seemed to be lurking in his oddly blank expression. 'I didn't think so,' he said, elegantly pushing his hands into his pockets and leaning sideways on the piano, almost seeming to mock me.

Seeing my obvious confusion, he smiled tightly. 'Your hesitation told me what I needed to know, Rebecca. You feel unsure of me, as you should, my –' He removed a hand from his pocket and waved it in front of him as he picked the best word, '– *lifestyle* would not be suited to you. I'll see you at next week's lesson. See yourself out.'

I winced at the steely tone in Nicholas' voice and watched as an odd expression crossed his face, but it was gone too quickly for me to read. Then he turned, folded away the piano books, and stalked from the room, leaving me feeling breathless and confused but too unsure to call him back.

He was certainly changeable, that was for sure; passionate and intense one second and then cold and condescending the next. I waited until I heard his footsteps fade away and a door close before I quickly made my way out. As I wandered down the stairs, I was glad Mr Burrett wasn't around to see my blushing face and wayward hair. Maybe he only worked for Nicholas during the day because I hadn't seen him at all for the past few weeks. Relief washed over me as I sneaked to the door and let myself out into the cool evening air.

As I made my way back through the open parkland of Primrose Hill, I decided that being near Nicholas Jackson was like standing on a seesaw; unpredictable, dangerous, and likely to get me tipped off and seriously hurt.

FOUR

Thankfully, the key to the shop door didn't stick today, as it seems to do on a regular basis. I should probably get a locksmith out to fix it but I always forget until I'm stuck outside, cursing it in the cold or rain while I wrestle with its unrelenting form.

As soon as I entered the shop I skipped my usual routine of standing just inside the threshold and sniffing the air – that makes me sound really weird but I love the smell of books; the inky, papery scent is just so relaxing that every day as I step into my shop I pause, inhale, and then smile to myself. Not today though – today I left the door unlocked for Louise who would no doubt arrive any minute, and then headed for my office, almost on the verge of tears again from my wandering thoughts about Nicholas.

My bum had only just hit my chair when there was a knock at the door. Why was it that when you wanted company there was never anyone around, but when you desperately wanted to be left alone to sulk in peace there was instantly a frigging knock on the door? At least it interrupted me from continuing my wallowing, which was just as well, really, because I could feel my throat tightening up as fresh tears gathered.

'Come in,' I muttered, rather unenthusiastically.

Looking over at the door, I saw Louise stick her head in with a limp smile on her face that definitely bordered on pitying. Oh God, here we go again, I almost groaned out loud. Louise was lovely, my friend as well as my colleague, but she was yet to realise quite how fragile I was at the moment. Sure enough, after one more benevolent glance from her I had to purse my lips to stop them quivering as I felt tears prick at the backs of my eyes again. Not that it was a hard feat to accomplish; tears never seemed more than a sneeze away right now.

Seeing my crumpling expression she winced and held her hands up. 'Sorry!' she squeaked, her arms flapping as she got more flustered by the second. 'I just wanted to say good morning and give you a cup of tea.' She plonked down a steaming brew on the desk and hastily made for the door again.

'Thanks, Louise,' I murmured thickly. 'And stop being so nice to me!' I yelled after her with an ironic twist of my lips, hoping to finally get through to her.

Wiping my pointless tears away, I remembered how I had really tried to put a lid on the sex side of things with Nicholas after the piano incident. As hard as it had been not to think of the mind-blowing interlude, I'd focused on work, which hadn't been an entirely successful distraction, but I had been busy enough at the bookshop to just about convince myself that I didn't need a sex life. Yeah, right.

Three nights after my piano-tastic sex session, I had been sat waiting for my computer to load so I could check my emails. As I gazed around my flat I had looked at all my usual stuff; comfy sofa, CDs, DVD collection, and photographs, all *normal* for me, and it had got me thinking about what things were *normal* for someone like Nicholas.

Deep down, I'd known at the time I was venturing down a dangerous path, but instead of clicking on my email programme as planned, I clicked on the internet instead, immediately wondering what I should type to find out about his type of lifestyle.

I'd opened up a search engine and after pondering for several minutes had started by typing in what he had called himself. "Dominant".

The first result was a dictionary definition of the word – *"Dominant, adjective: the most important, powerful, or influential"* – and unsurprisingly it made no mention of anything remotely kinky or sexual. To be honest, I can't imagine Collins get too many requests for a definition of a "sexual dominant" in mainstream society.

As well as being too geeky to live somewhere as trendy and cool as Camden, I'm also too reserved to be searching for naughty things on the internet, or at least I thought I was. But as I nervously trawled through the other results, I found an article from an encyclopaedia that looked a bit more promising, so, biting my lip, I opened up the page and began to read.

After just five minutes of reading, I sat wide-eyed and shocked. It was actually quite stunning just how much gory detail they put into these websites for any Tom, Dick, or Harry to read. It had certainly been a learning curve. I had now learnt a little about what Nicholas was. A dominant, apparently, was a term linked to sexual preferences or relationships that involved one partner with a predilection for overriding control instilling discipline within a relationship over another, referred to as a "submissive". The submissive liked to be subservient to their partner, sometimes just sexually, but sometimes in all aspects of their life. So if I wanted to have sex with Nicholas again I'd have to be submissive, would I?

Practically holding my breath, I had continued reading to see what that might entail. Relationships with dominant partners were often termed as BDSM relationships because they used bondage, discipline, submission, sadism, and masochism. *Wow*. This really should have been where I turned the computer off, but I hadn't. After briefly leaping away from the screen thinking something along the lines of "holy cow", but with slightly more explicit word choices, I stupidly sat back down, ignoring the lump of fear building in my throat.

Hindsight is a wonderful thing, isn't it? I can sit here now in the aftermath of my crazy relationship with Nicholas and clearly see this research mission was a huge turning point for my sanity. I should have walked away from the computer, and Nicholas, at this point, but like a complete fool I'd read on regardless. Always one to weigh up both sides of an argument, I remember thinking at the time that it seemed like these relationships could be balanced and pleasurable for both parties, but dominants could also use punishments if and when they saw fit, which sounded a bit scary to me, so I'd skimmed over that paragraph.

Why, oh why had I not bothered to stop and read it? At the time, my subconscious had been diverting me away from the scary side of Nicholas' life and trying to push the positives on me. Maybe if I had been more sensible and read the frigging paragraph on punishments I'd never have been stupid enough to enter into a sexual relationship with Nicholas Jackson and wouldn't be sitting here now reliving it.

I recall now that I had been almost at the point of throwing up from fear as I blindly continued my research that day, but I had at least read one sentence that vaguely reassured me. *"The fundamental motto used by many practitioners is SSC – safe, sane, and consensual, meaning the activities are safe and both parties are in agreement about what will be done."*

That sounded relatively sensible and I remember thinking that if I could just persuade Nicholas that the "activities" we did were just normal sex, perhaps including his piano again, then we'd be fine. Huh. Naive or what?

Perhaps there is a part of me, deep, deep, down somewhere that is a little bit twisted like Nicholas, or maybe it's just the curiosity of human nature, because once I had started reading that day I hadn't been able to stop myself. I'd actually found it quite fascinating. Up until the point where I read a line that had caused me to pale significantly. *"Because of the use of toys and punishments there is a fine line between safe and unsafe activities. For this reason both parties are advised to discuss preferences to avoid accidental harm ..."*

Accidental harm? My sanity had returned at this point and I hadn't bothered finishing this sentence; instead, I had hastily cleared my browser history, turned off my computer, and then taken a long shower to clean off the feel of smut that was lingering on my skin.

After that enlightening half an hour, I had wrapped myself in my nice, fluffy, and non-bondage-like robe, then chewed on my nails for a long time, wondering why I had even bothered to read that stuff and not really finding an answer.

I'd summarised that, yes, Nicholas might have been the best sex I'd ever had, and yes he fascinated me, but even after just that short amount of research it had become clear to me that if he really was a dominant he was obviously in a completely different league to me, living a lifestyle I didn't see myself fitting into in a million years.

Unfortunately, my determination in this decision faltered as soon as I had laid eyes on him at my next piano lesson the following Friday. There was just something about him that drew me to him, it went beyond his deep blue eyes, supreme confidence, and good looks though, not that I could quite put my finger on it, but it was something deeper, some kind of connection I felt whenever I was near him.

For whatever sick reason, my little research mission had made me even more curious about him. I clearly needed to get a hobby or something to occupy my mind and help me avoid my perusal of unsuitable men – perhaps stamp collecting or something equally as drab that would fit nicely with my boring bookshop persona.

As we sat side by side at the piano, the tension between Nicholas and I was awful; so much static filled the room that I actually felt sick but I couldn't tell if it was sexual tension or anger on his part. He'd barely spoken a word to me apart from instructions and I started to feel distinctly like he didn't want me here at all.

That was what I *had* been thinking until halfway through playing a new piece when I glanced over and caught him staring intently at me, his eyes blazing in a way that even I couldn't misunderstand. *He wanted me.*

My breath shuddered to a halt and I gulped like a fish out of water as I repeatedly tried and failed to speak. The realisation that Nicholas still wanted me made me hornier than I could believe, so finally sucking air into my lungs again I ignored my racing pulse, stopped playing, and plucked up the courage to say something.

'I did a bit of research last week, Nicholas,' I mumbled shyly, turning myself marginally so I was almost facing him. *Almost*, but not quite; his dark eyes were too intense to deal with at the moment.

'Research?' he murmured blandly. He had hidden his previous wanton expression but the flash of something else in his eyes definitely indicated that he was more interested than he was letting on.

'Yeah, I looked on the internet about your … um, type of lifestyle,' I said, throwing his own choice of words back at him.

Expecting some sort of response from him I watched his expression carefully, only to be met with a bland, disinterested look. 'Really? I'm sure it made very dull reading,' he said flatly, closing the piano lid but again giving nothing away. God this man was infuriating!

'It was quite an eye-opener, actually.' I blushed and tucked my hair behind my ear before recalling how Nicholas had said he liked it down and quickly flicking it out again. Really, I did this just as much for me as for Nicholas because it was true: my hair did look nicer down. After his comment the other week, I'd experimented with it in the mirror at home. When my hair was tucked behind my ear, my cheekbones looked a bit too pointy somehow.

Seeing my self-adjusted hair flick, Nicholas arched an eyebrow at me but remained silent, so I continued, feeling a renewed surge of confidence.

'So, basically, you like to take charge in the bedroom and dominate a submissive woman for both her pleasure and yours?' I asked in a tiny voice. Hell, I'd started now, I may as well continue. What was the worst that could happen? No more piano lessons? To be honest, I was never going to be the next Chopin, or Nicholas Jackson, so it wouldn't exactly be a huge loss to the musical world, would it?

Folding his arms across his broad chest, he observed me with narrowed eyes for what seemed like an eternity. 'Yes,' he said darkly, 'I like complete control. They do as I say or they get punished.'

'Punished?' I questioned weakly, my brief period of confidence ebbing away as I began to feel rather nervous at his use of the P-word, the one I'd avoided reading about in my research. Stupid girl, I chastised myself.

'Yes. It's common in Dom/sub relationships. The dominant partner, be that the male or the female, will use punishment to ensure their will is done correctly. Didn't that come up on your little research mission, Rebecca?' Nicholas asked sarcastically, his face still confusingly impassive.

'Well, it did, I just didn't think that you ...' But my voice trailed off when I saw the dark look that sprang to his eye. oh how very naive I'd been.

'You didn't think I'd do that?' Nicholas snapped. 'Well, that's hardly surprising, is it? We barely know each other.' His tone was almost bored now. 'You know nothing about me, Rebecca,' he added sourly, turning away and sorting through a pile of piano books as if dismissing me.

My heart was thundering under my skin. He might be acting blasé but something in the tension of his shoulders made me persevere. For whatever reason, since last week's liaison with Nicholas, I felt changed. Gone was the prude who used to carefully select her boyfriends and make them wait weeks before they could so much as touch her; in her place was an independent woman who knew what she wanted – Nicholas. More accurately, Nicholas and his superb sexing skills.

I chewed on my lip as I accepted this realisation. I wanted this man, desperately, and instead of shying away from the embarrassing fact, I was determined to pursue it with everything I had.

'Can't we just have sex?' *Holy fuck!* Was that seriously my voice that had just spoken? Blimey, how had shy, cautious Rebecca suddenly transformed into this wanton hussy I now appeared to be? Apparently, I now swore in my head too, another new development for me. I certainly was changing a lot recently.

Nicholas seemed to half choke, half laugh at my request, creating a noise in his throat that was almost a bark. 'You've researched dominant relationships in all their dirty glory, I've just told you I like to punish the girls I fuck, and yet you still want to have sex with me?'

OK, when he put it like that I did feel slightly stupid. He was mocking me and my naïvety, that much was abundantly obvious, but even I wasn't stupid enough to miss the hint of astonishment and temptation in his voice.

Shit. I was in way out of my depth here, but what exactly

had I expected – for him to fall at my feet and beg me to sleep with him? Hardly, Nicholas was way too controlled for that. He'd been honest and upfront from the start and I was being stupid enough to hope that last week's little sex session on the piano might have left him feeling the same as me – wanting more.

'Do you regularly proposition men like this?' he asked suddenly, his voice darker than before and causing me to glare at him in indignation.

'Of course not!' I retorted, before faltering as I realised just how sluttish my behaviour must have appeared. 'But then I haven't had mind-blowing sex on a piano before either,' I admitted in a low mutter. I hadn't had mind-blowing sex full stop, just normal, run-of-the-mill sex, which paled into insignificance when compared to what I'd experienced with Nicholas last week. Not that he needed to know that. He was arrogant enough already without me further inflating his ego.

My face was seared with a flush of mortification at the way this conversation had digressed, but I decided I might as well say my piece before I left. 'I … I enjoyed last week, Nicholas, more than enjoyed it … and I just thought, you know, if the whole dominant thing was negotiable, or didn't involve pain, then maybe we could have sex again sometime.'

With my eyes averted out of pure embarrassment at the shocking words coming out of my mouth, it was hard to judge his reaction, but it seemed like Nicholas was completely still and silent next to me for an eternity, to the point where I sighed before standing to leave.

A gentle hand on my wrist stopped me. 'Raise your eyes, Rebecca,' Nicholas instructed softly, now standing up next to me, his body so close I could feel the warmth from his chest and wanted desperately to lean into it. Once again, as if under his spell, I immediately did as he asked and met his gaze with my own.

See? I could follow instructions … sometimes.

'I like to see your eyes, so green, so beautiful.' Raising a hand, Nicholas stroked my cheek gently. He sighed as he did so, and I watched as a mix of emotions flooded across his face.

'The dominant thing isn't negotiable, Rebecca. It's who I am, it's all I've ever known … but you have no idea how much I want to have sex with you again … and for some reason you now tell me you want that too …' Nicholas paused, running his free hand over his chin as he considered the situation. 'What a conundrum …' he murmured. Then, with no warning whatsoever, the hand on my cheek moved to the back of my head, knotted through my hair, and dragged my head toward his lips.

Off we went, then!

'Don't punish me,' I implored in what I hoped was a stern tone before our lips met, his tongue instantly seeking mine and exploring my mouth in a kiss that nearly had my head rolling off my shoulders from its level of passion.

Gosh, he really was such a good kisser.

'Do as I ask, Rebecca, and I won't need to punish you,' he muttered hotly against my mouth, making me shudder with exhilaration.

Holy shit, this was really happening! My body was awash with emotions, this was so scary and somehow so freaking hot at the same time that I was hugely turned on already and all he had done was kiss me. It was like Nicholas was able to flick a switch inside me that no other man had ever discovered, and regardless of how illicit it might have been, I absolutely loved the feelings he was stirring within me.

Abruptly tearing his lips from mine, Nicholas now seemed to loom over me, his breath coming heavily, fanning warmth across my face as he ran his eyes over me, apparently absorbing my appearance into his mind. 'Come with me. I need to get you naked, Rebecca.'

OK, there was certainly no misunderstanding that statement. Breathing deeply while I had the chance, I took his hand with my trembling fingers and let Nicholas lead me from the music room. He was moving purposefully now, like a man set on his goal, and headed across the landing toward a corridor I hadn't been to before and then through a door into a darkened room. By this point my heart was pounding in my ears so loudly that I could barely think straight and I was clutching his hand tight enough that it surely must be hurting him. Coming to a stop he flicked a switch next to the door and the room was lit with the soft glow of several wall lights.

I looked around the master bedroom with interest, as I continued to suck air into my struggling lungs, and could detect the familiar smell of Nicholas' aftershave in the air – spicy and musky, possibly with an undertone of pine in it. I loved the way he smelt, so it was a complete turn-on for me. It merely added to my heightened state of arousal.

My eyes continued to sweep around the room. Like the other parts of the house I had seen, the furniture and decor seemed to be expensive and tastefully done. A gigantic four-poster bed sat in the centre of the room; it was made up with pure white sheets but the black wrought iron frame somehow seemed to scream of the illicit things Nicholas could do in here. It was just a normal bed but there were so many bars and finials in the frame's design to tie me to that the possibilities seemed endless ...

Choking on my thoughts, I distracted myself by looking away from the bed and noticed all the walls were neutral colours, but the rest of the furniture was a deep wood, so dark it almost looked black. The effect of the white sheets and walls together with the black furniture made the room feel rather oriental somehow, but neutral enough to fit what I had expected of Nicholas' bedroom.

As I turned, I found him stood in the centre of the room with his arms folded across his chest as he watched me intently; the look in his hooded eyes was one of pure, unadulterated hunger. Hunger for me, I realised, and immediately I flushed again. Why the hell couldn't I control my cheeks!

'Come here,' he commanded in a low tone, and if on autopilot I immediately began to wobble my way toward him on jellified legs. Being a confident, independent woman, I really shouldn't have liked being told what to do like this, but Nicholas' salacious orders seemed to appeal to some primal part of me and I just couldn't help but comply.

I pondered this as I crossed the room because it was an odd sensation for me. I'd always been quite aloof in my previous relationships, happy to be the one setting the boundaries and never particularly bothered when they ended, but with Nicholas I *wanted* to please him and I wasn't sure why. Almost laughing out loud, I realised it was probably because I hoped that if he was happy then in return he might use his supreme sexing skills to make me happy too. I'm sure you get my drift.

Apparently, Nicholas Jackson had managed to bring out my hidden hussy once again.

'I would like to begin by undressing you, Rebecca; I seem to recall we skipped this part last time,' he commented softly. If any of my previous lovers had tried to give a running commentary on their moves during sex, I would have laughed and asked them to stop, but with Nicholas I rather liked it, his words were compelling and his tone somehow putt me at ease. Maybe this wouldn't be so different to my previous sexual encounters after all.

'Such beautiful eyes. Let me look at you.' His blazing blue stare didn't leave mine as he reached down and began to undo my jeans without so much as a glance. He'd clearly done that before. Unfastened, my jeans slid down the overheated skin of my legs and crumpled around my ankles. 'Step out of them and kick them to the side,' Nicholas instructed me in a husky voice and I did as I was told, luckily not getting tangled up and also not saying anything because, to be honest, I wasn't sure if I was allowed to talk, or even capable of speech in my highly aroused state.

Ever so slowly, Nicholas reached out and began to unbutton my shirt. I was hugely overexcited by this point, my body thrumming with desire, my breath coming in jagged pulls, and my head spinning. Closing my eyes for a second I drew in a long breath to try and recover myself so I didn't look like a blathering idiot.

Before I knew it, Nicholas had me turned around and I felt a hard, stinging slap to my right buttock. *Ow*! Pulling me sharply against him so my back was pressed to his front, he leant around and nipped my neck with his teeth, before soothing the skin with a lash of his tongue, then in my ear, 'Eyes open, Rebecca, you know my rule on that. I won't tell you again.'

Jeez, eyes open. OK, I must remember that.

'Sorry,' I muttered, because it seemed the right thing to do and, in response, he placed several light kisses on my neck that made me moan with longing and lean into his touch. All the while his hand gently massaged my smarting behind, mixing pleasure in with the heat on my bottom, before reaching around me where he continued to undo the last of my shirt buttons.

Still standing behind me, he pressed his stomach against me and a thrill ran through my body as I felt the hard length of his erection digging into my lower back. I hadn't really got a proper look at his tackle last time, and hoped that perhaps I would tonight.

I was totally under his spell, standing there enthralled while he did his thing and wound my arousal higher and higher. I could barely even muster the ability to raise my arms and join in, but when I finally did, Nicholas tutted softly by my ear and gently guided my hands back to my sides again, apparently intent on running the show. Placing his hands on my waist, Nicholas then proceeded to run a teasing trail up my sides, causing me to flinch and giggle as he passed over my ticklish spots, before he took hold of my shirt collar and slowly started to pull it off me, peeling it lazily down my shoulders and arms until just the cuffs remained.

Taking me completely by surprise, he suddenly did something to the shirt that had my hands trapped behind my back ... I supposed he must have twisted the material while my wrists were still in the sleeve cuffs. Whatever he did, it well and truly trapped my hands, and I stood helpless with my breasts jutting forward as Nicholas stalked back around to stand in front of me.

Cocking his head to the side, Nicholas' eyes twinkled wickedly. 'That should stop you fidgeting while I examine your rather lovely underwear,' he commented lightly, a smile tugging at the corners of his lips.

Trailing his gaze across my already heated skin, I watched his eyes settle on my bra and saw Nicholas' pupils dilate further as a sigh escaped him. His obvious appreciation of me merely added to my arousal, and I squeezed my thighs together as I felt a throb settle between my legs as my groin became slick. I glanced quickly down and was so pleased I had made the effort to pick out nice lacy underwear tonight before leaving the house.

'You have a fabulous body, Rebecca,' Nicholas murmured thickly, his eyes roving over me while his hands stayed firmly at his sides as if he were allowing himself to look but not touch.

I began to squirm on the spot from his scrutiny. How was it possible to get this turned on from just a look?

Finally, Nicholas put me out of my misery by stepping closer and placing his hands on my waist, his warm palms rubbing soothing circles on my exposed flesh and sending electric tingles cascading across my skin. One hand began the ascent to my bra and I couldn't help but moan softly as his fingers finally made contact with my breast. Slowly, his other hand joined in as he massaged and kneaded at my sensitive flesh, his thumb grazing across my nipple through the lace of my bra, making me shudder with desire.

Suddenly, Nicholas reached around behind my back and tugged me against him, finding my mouth with his and invading it with his probing tongue. His kiss was fierce but passionate and I found myself longing to touch him, run my hands through his hair, pull him closer, but I couldn't because my hands were still caught in my damn shirt.

Nicholas undid my bra with one hand while still demanding access to my mouth with his relentless tongue as mine duelled with his fiercely, unwilling to be dominated just yet. Then he tugged the right cup of my bra down over my breast and rubbed the heel of his hand up against my nipple, skin on skin, causing it to pucker and harden under his touch as I gasped against his lips and arched into the contact.

My body's keen response seemed to spur Nicholas on because I felt his thumbs tuck into the waistband of my knickers, then suddenly his lips weren't on mine any more because he'd bent down and slipped off my underwear in one fluid movement.

Rising, he placed a brief, chaste kiss on the small strip of hair at the apex of my thighs, making me gasp again, before standing fully and immediately reclaiming my mouth with his.

His right hand continued rubbing circles across my belly, travelling ever lower until his palm finally rubbed across my pubic hair. My stomach clenched and my hips thrust forwards, desperately seeking contact where I needed it the most. I could barely focus; his lips were ravaging mine but his fingers were teasing me, so close to my clit, but yet so far, until finally they began to work their way ever lower until ...

'Oh God, Nicholas ...' I cried out softly as his fingers lazily circled my already pulsing clitoris.

'Shh,' he admonished me quietly, his fingers slipping first down one side of my wet lips and then the other, and I felt a hint of embarrassment at just how soaked I must be now. But when he dipped one finger inside me, those thoughts vanished and it took all my remaining self-control not to scream out with pleasure. Briefly, he pulled back, and I saw him release a hissed breath through his teeth before he sank a second finger inside me.

I sagged forwards against his chest from the pleasure, but thankfully Nicholas immediately circled my waist with his free hand and supported my weight as his other hand continued it magic. It felt so good that I couldn't believe I would ever get enough of this man.

'So ready, Rebecca. You certainly are keen,' he observed with a dark smile as his fingers began to move expertly in and out of me, rubbing exactly the right spots and making my legs rubbery beneath me within seconds.

After hardly any time at all, my body was building toward a release, but as if sensing my imminent climax, Nicholas pulled his fingers out of me and smothered my attempt at a protest with a firm kiss to my lips. Drawing back, he examined me intently before lifting his hand and placing one of his fingers in his mouth, sucking it with obvious pleasure.

Holy shit, that finger had just been inside me ... That was really *pervy,* but somehow really hot too, and I watched in fascination as his eyes dilated with pleasure.

'Mmm, you taste as good as I thought you would, Rebecca,' Nicholas murmured before offering me his other damp finger. 'Suck,' he ordered softly and I felt my eyes widen as I realised what he wanted me to do. Glancing at his hand, I swallowed. I could see my own excitement glistening on his skin and couldn't decide if I found the idea gross or unbelievably hot.

'Taste yourself, Rebecca,' he instructed in a firmer tone, and so I did. Well, it was only a bit of my bodily fluid after all.

Running my tongue around Nicholas' finger was so ridiculously arousing my groin started to twitch and throb almost painfully. I could taste myself on his skin, salty and warm, and as I sucked harder on his finger, I saw a dark grin spreading on his face. 'Tastes good, yes?' he murmured, before somehow reaching round, freeing my wrists, and removing my bra, all in a matter of seconds.

'Lie on the bed, facing up,' Nicholas commanded huskily. Crawling onto the cool sheets, I was grateful to be off of my wobbly legs into a more comfortable position. As I turned my gaze back to him, I saw to my surprise that Nicholas had already removed his shirt and was now gracefully stepping out of his jeans too.

Sucking in a breath, I swallowed appreciatively and allowed my eyes to explore his revealed flesh. My goodness, did this man have a great body; toned and defined muscles and a soft covering of hair in all the right places. My eyes bulged as he removed his boxers and I got my first proper look at his straining erection, but I reminded myself that regardless of how big it seemed it had managed to fit last time without pain, so we obviously were compatible in that department.

'I enjoy being touched, but for tonight I want to explore your body, Rebecca. You'll get your chance to reciprocate, but not now, so no touching me, OK?' I nodded mutely, my body way too far gone to argue anyway. 'If you break that rule I will punish you, do you understand?' Nicholas warned.

Wow ... OK, there's the dreaded P-word again – not something I was particularly happy about hearing, but I nodded. At least he'd warned me, I supposed; explaining the rules so to speak. All I had to do was not touch him and I'd be fine. Although seeing how he held some kind of magnetic appeal to me, not touching him might be harder than it first sounded.

Nicholas then set off on a journey of pure and utter torturous delight. His lips and fingers skimmed, kissed, plucked, and rubbed all over my trembling body, and I only managed to keep my twitching fingers at bay by clutching great handfuls of the sheet on either side of me and gripping it for dear life.

If being a submissive meant lying back and being pleasured to this extreme then sign me up, because the things Nicholas was doing to me were heavenly.

Unfortunately, from my research I knew there was a good deal more to the whole submissive/dominant thing, potentially including pain, but thanks to his skilled touch I didn't let that thought linger in my mind for too long.

When Nicholas' head finally dropped between my legs and his tongue made contact with my most private of areas I completely forgot myself and grasped a handful of his hair as I let out a keen cry.

Almost instantly, his head was up and I found myself being flipped onto my stomach before a sharp slap landed on my buttock, followed almost instantly by another, and then a third.

My cry of shock was muffled by the mattress; boy, those were certainly harder than last time. I tensed my burning buttocks, expecting more, but it was just the three strikes before he flipped me back over and straddled me across my hips, his cock resting heavily and temptingly on my stomach.

'I said no touching, Rebecca,' Nicholas murmured softly before reaching under the pillow to my left and producing a silk scarf in the most beautiful aquamarine colour. 'You broke my rule; I'm going to tie your hands now. It won't hurt as long as you don't tug. Lift your arms above your head,' he demanded, his dark, sexy eyes burning into mine as if daring me to object. I didn't; in fact, I obeyed immediately, keen to continue the fun and avoid more smacks, and raised them above my head where he proceeded to tie my wrists not only together, but to the metal frame of the bed too. A smile flicked on my lips – I just knew the bedframe would be involved somehow.

An experimental tug showed me I had no room for manoeuvre, but before this thought could bother me, Nicholas had bent over and begun sucking at one of my nipples so softly and deliciously that I forgot all about my hands. Instead, my body thrummed under him and I mewled against his shoulder as his tongue worked its magic on my nipple.

He really was superbly skilled at the whole sex thing.

My heart accelerated in my chest as Nicholas reached around me and produced something else from underneath his pillow causing my eyes to widen. What the heck? I'd seen these before. Well, I'd seen things similar to these before, and I was pretty certain what he was holding was a vibrator. But the reason for my slight uncertainty was because it wasn't like the more lifelike ones I'd seen in an Ann Summers catalogue; instead, it was clinical looking, shaped sort of like a long, smooth, white bullet.

'Open your mouth,' he instructed me quietly and I was struck with confusion. My mouth? I had expected him to put it down below, where his fingers were earlier. 'I won't ask again, Rebecca,' Nicholas warned me softly and I was broken from my trance as I opened my mouth obediently.

'I'm going to put this inside you and make you come,' he murmured with a devious twinkle in his eyes. Oh my goodness, whoever thought that just mere words could get me so frigging excited?

'It needs to be moistened first, Rebecca, lick it,' he instructed, so I did, very tentatively, and I saw Nicholas narrow his eyes with what looked like displeasure at my embarrassed actions.

'Imagine it's my cock. Suck it and lick it as if you want to pleasure me.' God, he was so open with his word choices, did he have no shame? Apparently not. To someone as relatively inexperienced as me he seemed to be the living epitome of sexual liberation in all its glory.

This was so embarrassing. Nicholas was watching me intently but I didn't want to let him down or get another spank so I began to oblige, trying to pretend he wasn't watching me. First, I ran my lips slowly from the tip to the base and back again, then I took it in my mouth and sucked briefly before twirling my tongue around the rounded tip several times. I was just about to take it all in my mouth again when I felt him shudder next to me, apparently suitably affected by my ministrations.

'Christ, Rebecca, we're going to have to do that for real at some point,' Nicholas muttered thickly and I smiled up at him as sweetly as possible before, suddenly, I was lost as he lowered his hand to my groin and eased the vibrator inside me where it begin to hum softly against my oversensitive flesh.

'*Ahhh*, Nicholas …' I immediately began to plead and I saw him raise his head and smile darkly at me as I tried desperately to move my tethered arms.

'Shh,' he whispered, pinching my nipple hard between his forefinger and thumb to the point of pain, but somehow it was a delicious sensation and made me buck underneath him, forcing the vibrator deeper inside me and almost causing me to orgasm on the spot. *Shit*, this was like sensory overload.

Increasing the tempo, Nicholas continued to lavish attention on my breasts with his mouth and fingers while still driving me on with the vibrator, sinking it deeper and harder into me and rubbing my clitoris with his thumb until I could take no more and I exploded around it, crying out his name hoarsely and tugging at my wrist restraints like a woman possessed. At last it began to ebb, and I collapsed back on the bed, breathing hard and completely wrung out.

Holy fuck! That had to be the most powerful orgasm I'd had yet. The things this man could do to me! He was totally focused on pleasuring me; there seemed to be no selfish intent like with some men, and I moaned contentedly, my insides still convulsing spasmodically from the aftermath of my delicious orgasm.

The rush of adrenaline from my earlier anxiousness had passed, and with the amazing orgasm I'd just experienced, exhaustion washed over me and my eyes began to close sleepily, but as they did I felt Nicholas loosening the scarf at my wrists and rubbing them gently in turn. 'Eyes open, Rebecca,' he instructed next to my ear. 'I'm not done with you yet.'

There was more? Although deep down I knew we hadn't finished yet because obviously he hadn't climaxed, but I seriously doubted that my body could take any more orgasms like that last one. However, before the thought could properly plant in my brain I heard the rip of a condom packet and felt Nicholas pushing my legs apart with his knee and settling himself over me. Surprisingly, the weight of his body relaxing above me seemed to awaken me somehow.

'I can see you are tired, Rebecca, so we'll stay in this position. I doubt I'll last long anyway. Watching you come like that was an incredible turn-on,' he muttered and I smiled despite my tiredness. He was aroused and apparently pleased because of me, and this thought made me happy in return. Knowing Nicholas liked eye contact, I made a real effort to keep my eyes open as he used his hand to manoeuvre himself into position. His gaze was wide and clear as he slid inside me in one smooth motion with a low groan, before setting off at a fast pace from the outset.

With my hands now free I clutched at his broad back, loving the feel of his strong muscles rippling and twisting under the skin as he ploughed himself into me over and over again. He certainly liked it rough; that was for sure.

My body obviously did too, because even after the amazing orgasm I had just experienced, I felt the pressure building in my abdomen again, and after two more strokes I climaxed violently around Nicholas, my muscles clamping on to his length and causing him to come almost immediately, groaning my name before collapsing on top of me, panting.

Several minutes later, he eased himself out of me, dispensed with the condom, and rolled to the side. Propping his head up on his hand he looked down at me closely.

'That was a bit of an introduction into some of the things I like to do, Rebecca ... what did you think?' There was an edge of concern to his voice, possibly because of the spanking. I hadn't thought I would like that element of it, but actually, it had been quick and relatively painless and had just seemed like part of the whole act, although I suspected it was mild compared to what he was capable of.

The realisation that I had almost enjoyed being spanked surprised me and I stored it away to consider in greater detail later, when I was alone. What *did* I think about what had just occurred between us? Overall, it had just been great sex with a few toys thrown in, plus Nicholas' obvious like of leading the way, of course. My body felt like lead; I was utterly exhausted and completely replete, but instead of saying that I tried for something that might please him a little more. 'Quite frankly, that was amazing, Nicholas.'

A low chuckle escaped Nicholas' throat, but as he continued to examine me, I saw a small frown tweak his brows before he chewed briefly on his lower lip. 'You should probably leave now,' he muttered and I sat up hastily, my cheeks flaming at his words.

Right. Of course. This was sex, nothing more, although I had to admit that I'd almost forgotten about that proviso. After several seconds where I tried to work out the least embarrassing way of gathering my scattered clothing, I glanced back at him and saw he was still staring at me. Finally, just as I was about to slide from the bed, he spoke again. 'I never knew it could be like that,' he murmured in a tone that confused the hell out of me. Never knew it could be like that? But surely that was what he did all the time?

'What do you mean?' I asked, sidetracked from the idea of getting dressed, and definitely more awake now. 'Wasn't that what you usually do?' I cringed at my words. Could I sound any more clueless?

Raising an ironic eyebrow, Nicholas looked across at me. 'For some reason, the two times I've been with you I've been ... different, Becky ... Controlling, yes, but what you've seen isn't the real dominant me. It's just how I seem to be with you.' He shrugged nonchalantly but sounded just as confused as I was.

Wrapping my arms around my bent knees, I bit my lip before asking the question I had to know the answer to. 'The orders and toys aren't the dominant you?' I squeaked. What else could there be?

Still scowling, Nicholas looked at me intently. 'I'm always domineering, in all walks of life, I know that and I can't avoid it. Yes, the accessories play a part, but I was referring to how I feel and act around you.' He looked torn, like there was some conflict raging in his mind that I couldn't see. 'For example, we're in my bedroom for a start.'

'Where else would you go?' I whispered, praying he didn't say something like "my torture chamber". I'd read all about that on the internet too; some dominants had an exclusive room set up with all the paraphernalia they needed for their habit. Some people have a sewing room, or an art studio, others a home cinema, and apparently dominants sometimes have a sex room. *Lovely*.

'The spare room. I never bring women in here,' Nicholas stated matter-of-factly.

'But the scarf and –' I paused, embarrassed all of a sudden, '– *vibrator* … were under your pillow, so surely you had planned this?'

I saw Nicholas' frown deepen at my words. 'I had considered sex as a possible outcome tonight when you decided to continue your lessons and started to relax around me, and yes, earlier I got these things ready … It hadn't occurred to me that I'd put them in here, though …' The troubled expression remained on his face, like he had no idea why he'd acted the way he had.

Wanting to get to the bottom of this while he was in the mood to talk, I persevered. 'So dominant Nicholas is different?' I wrapped the sheet around me tighter to hide the quivering of my limbs.

'Yes. You wouldn't like him,' Nicholas replied tightly, running a hand roughly through his hair he fidgeted in the bed, apparently tiring of this conversation. 'I'm not sure I like him any more,' he added quietly.

'Different how?' I asked, cursing my own grim curiosity.

'You're starting to push your luck with all these questions, Rebecca. If you don't stop talking and get dressed I may just have to show you what it is I normally do,' Nicholas snapped, causing me to flinch at his sudden change in mood. Then he rose from the bed lithely and pulled on his shirt with his back to me.

Chewing on my lip nervously, I watched his back muscles flowing and rippling as he dressed, but after his dismissal of me I was distracted and couldn't fully appreciate the sight. Clearly, our discussion was over and I was now required to leave. I suppose I shouldn't have expected anything different, really, not after his blunt description of how he liked to "fuck women for an hour or two", which he had certainly done to me. Once dressed, Nicholas left the room without another word or glance in my direction, effectively putting an end to our evening and leaving me to get dressed in privacy.

Wow, what a night! I wanted to roll over and allow the exhaustion to sweep over me after the amazing sex I'd just experienced, but somehow I managed to dress myself and head toward the lounge with a straight, confident back, trying to look like I hadn't just been used for sex and asked to leave. How shameful.

Although I could hardly claim to have been "used for sex", could I? I had been just as up for it as he had. God, I'd practically initiated it by bringing up my research into his lifestyle. No, what had just occurred between us had been just as much my doing as his. As the saying goes, "it takes two to tango" ... or shag rampantly, as we had done.

I was beyond mortified as I made my way down the stairs and bumped into Mr Burrett in the hallway. God, how embarrassing. He was so inconspicuous that I had totally forgotten he was here. My already pink cheeks reddened further as I wondered if he'd heard us and I dipped my head as I hurried past him.

When I appeared in the lounge, Nicholas was waiting for me and insisted on driving me home, which was unexpected. After his abrupt mood swing in the bedroom I wasn't going to attempt to start up another conversation, so the short drive was mostly in silence. Needless to say, the quiet tension simmering between us did nothing to ease my discomfort about what I had just done.

As he pulled up alongside my block of flats, I couldn't help but feel a pang of shame. The exterior of my building was pretty shabby now, waiting for a paint job from the lousy landlord, and was a far, far cry from the beauty of Nicholas' home.

'Same time next week?' Nicholas asked, appearing not to

notice the state of my house. His comment caused me to look at him, startled, and raise my eyebrows at his presumption. I saw him flush and narrow his eyes at me. 'For your piano lesson,' he added softly, and I thought I saw a trace of something else in his eyes; humour perhaps, but the moonlight made it impossible to read.

Nodding jerkily, I agreed before getting out of the car and marching to my door without so much as a backwards glance, even though I was secretly dying to see if Nicholas was watching me leave.

FIVE

Flicking through the diary that I kept in my desk drawer I found the first Friday that I had marked with the word "piano". It was in red ink and underlined once. That was when my lessons with Nicholas had started. As I turned the pages, I saw each consecutive week was marked in a similar way, but on the fifth Friday where I'd written "piano", a smiley face had been added next to it and this was underlined three times, serving as a reminder to myself about when I had started sleeping with him. What can I say? I'm a very visual person.

The Friday diary pages from then on each had smiley faces on them, and so it had continued; our weird piano-sex-relationship that really wasn't a relationship at all.

Nicholas had been insistent that we continue my piano tutorials, but each week, once the lesson was finished, he would introduce me to some new sexual joy or act. It was a rather nice way to end the week, really. After overcoming my initial concerns about "being used" for sex, I had realised that this was exactly what I'd asked him for in the first place. Nicholas had told me from the start he didn't do relationships, and what was it I'd said in reply? Oh yes, I remember. "Can't we just have sex?"

Classy girl. I still couldn't believe I'd suggested it, but now, looking back, it was clear to me that my experience with Nicholas had taught me one thing – stable, normal relationships were the way to go. Even if the physical side might be a bit watered down compared to what I'd had with him, at least my body and heart would be safe.

Every Friday night we'd met, and it had been blissful and nowhere near as scary as I had initially thought – just a bit more imaginative, if you like. As well as normal – admittedly fairly vigorous – sex, we had used scarves, vibrators, and some soft handcuffs but that was it, really. None of the chains or dungeons or dressing up in leather that I'd seen on the internet.

My vague attempt at learning the piano continued for several weeks, but Nicholas had started to get more and more impatient until we barely made it thirty minutes through my hour-long piano lessons before he ordered me into the bedroom and began the sexual assault on my senses. In fact, I had begun to wonder why we didn't just skip the pretence of piano lessons and head straight to the bedroom.

In hindsight, I know I should have headed straight for the door.

Another warning sign I should have heeded was the fact that Nicholas never asked me to stay over. Not once. I was a sex toy to him, nothing more. Although he would sometimes hold me afterwards for what seemed like an eternity, eventually he would always peel himself from my side and begin dressing, which I had quickly learnt was his discreet way of asking me to leave. Then he'd drive me home without another word, and we'd repeat it all the following week, like Groundhog Day.

One night stuck in my mind as being slightly different, though. It was the night that had given me a tiny glimmer of hope that maybe he was starting to see me as more than just a bed buddy – but in the stark light of retrospection was probably nothing more than his ego needing a boost.

I'd had a tough week at work, and to top it off, my sister, Joanne, had called twice already. Odd, really, seeing as routine was vital to her and she usually only called on a Wednesday night.

As I saw her name again on my phone's display on Friday afternoon, I frowned. 'Hi, Jo-Jo, how's it going?' I asked in the soft, considerate tone reserved just for my sister.

'Good. Great.' There was a pause where I could hear her chewing on a fingernail, her teeth clicking together noisily and making me wince. 'Actually no, not good. Not good at all. I think the pills the nurses are giving me are the wrong ones. I know it. I do. I know it. Wrong pills.'

I grimaced at her obvious agitation and turned away from the shop floor to walk down the corridor for more privacy.

'It's OK, sweetie, would you like me to come down and see you? I could check with the nurses if it'll make you feel better?' I said soothingly.

'Yes please! Oh yes!' Her relief over the phone line was practically palpable. 'But no … you're so busy. Always busy. Busy, busy, busy. Don't want to disturb you, Becs … Mustn't disturb you …' God, she was rambling; it must be a really bad anxiety attack this time.

'It's not a problem, sweetheart, I'm not busy. I'll be with you straight after work.' As I hung up I knew Nicholas wouldn't be happy with me cancelling my lesson, but my sister came first so I called him, briefly explained that I wouldn't be going over that night, and then hurried through the remainder of my work so I could get to Joanne as quickly as possible.

It had turned into a long, sleepless night with Joanne, but the following morning when she had settled again, I made my way home, and made an on-the-spot decision to turn up at Nicholas' house to apologise for cancelling. It was breaking from our usual Friday-night routine, which he might not like, but having spent the entire night with my sister, talking to her and her lovely nurses, I needed a bit of "me time", and at this moment in my life that involved Nicholas as well.

When he answered the door, he certainly looked shocked to see me then stood back without a word and ushered me toward the kitchen before disappearing in the direction of his study. What a welcome that was! Perhaps it was a bad time, I thought nervously, but surely he'd have asked me to leave if that was the case, so I decided to stick around for a few minutes and see if he reappeared.

Placing my handbag on the kitchen counter I glanced around, as the delicious scent of freshly brewed coffee hit me, and my mouth started to water instantly. My eyes landed on a full coffee pot sat under the gleaming machine on the surface and I grinned happily – perfect. It was just what I needed after my exhausting night. Pouring myself the largest mug I could find, I took a sip of the rich, dark beverage and sighed happily as I turned to find Nicholas leaning on the counter behind me. His arms were crossed over his chest, shoulders tense, and the foreboding look on his face told me everything I needed to know – he was majorly pissed off that I had cancelled on him last night. And possibly annoyed that I was making myself so at home and stealing his coffee, I thought with a flush.

Just as I was considering telling him about Joanne he took me completely by surprise; stalking forward, pouring himself an equally large mug of coffee, and then casually asking, 'How's your sister?'

'She's ... Hang on, how did you know about Joanne?' I asked in a shocked whisper.

Relief flooded his usually controlled features as he pushed one hand into the pocket of his trousers and let out a long low breath. 'So it's true, then? You do have a sister at the Oaks Residential Centre?'

My frown deepened at his mention of her care home. 'Yes, but how did you know?' I repeated slowly, trying to remember if I had ever mentioned her in passing and almost certain that I hadn't. Not that I was ashamed of her or anything, that wasn't the case at all. In truth, I tended to avoid talking about Jo because of the guilt it evoked in me. Even talking about her now made my stomach churn.

Sipping his coffee, I then turned as Nicholas lowered his cup and pursed his lips. 'You sounded distracted when you cancelled on me yesterday, and I thought perhaps you were seeing another man,' he explained simply, without actually answering my question at all.

'So ... what? You followed me?' I guessed, my tone rising with disapproval.

'No, of course not!' Nicholas flushed. 'I got Mr Burrett to follow you.' My eyebrows flew up at his words, but from his expression Nicholas clearly didn't think he'd done anything wrong by getting his hired help to stalk me. 'He called me when you got to the centre and told me where you were going.'

Mutinous thoughts were circling my mind, firstly toward Nicholas for his ridiculously controlling and possessive behaviour, and secondly about the staff at the Oaks. There was no way they should be breaching patient confidentiality by giving out Joanne's details over the phone, which was presumably how Nicholas had found out who I was visiting.

As if reading my mind once again, he shook his head. 'The centre didn't give anything away; I just got lucky. Mr Burrett saw you through a window meeting with a young woman around your age. He said you ha similar features, so I guessed at sister. Apparently I was right.'

Shit, I had fallen straight into his trap.

'Why's she in there?' he asked softly, his tone gentler and more considerate than I had ever heard it.

Clutching my coffee like a life jacket, I made my way to the sofa by the window and dropped onto it, keeping my eyes averted from his in case the guilt I felt about my sister's condition showed in my features. It wasn't my fault, I reminded myself sharply. *It wasn't my fault.*

'Jo is two years older than me. Seven years ago, she ...' I paused, floundering for what to say about that horrible day and the month that had followed. 'There was an ... *accident.*' A chill ran through me, making me shudder, and I gulped at my coffee in an attempt to warm up, even though I knew my shivers really had nothing to do with temperature. 'She suffered a lack of oxygen to the brain that has left her with some issues,' I finished.

Taking a seat beside me Nicholas then raised a hand to rest upon the nape of my neck where he began to rub gently. His touch was infinitely reassuring and began to warm me again as I took several deep breaths. 'Brain damage?' Nicholas asked quietly, and despite the topic, I found myself surprised by just how lovely he was being, completely at odds to his usual domineering persona.

'Yes.' My eyes were still trained on the sofa and actually starting to ache from staring so hard. 'It's affected the part of her brain that deals with rational thoughts and sensibilities. She has to stick to a routine or she panics, and she gets easily obsessed by things. She freaks out around strangers, and security is a big thing to her, so we decided she'd be better off living in the Oaks.'

'Wow, I'm sorry, Rebecca. What happened, the accident?'

At his question, I felt my entire body tense. I couldn't tell him that, *wouldn't*. He'd think I was despicable; I certainly did when I allowed myself to think back to that night, that entire horrible month.

'I … that's not something I want to talk about, Nicholas. You have your secrets, and I have mine,' I added, knowing I sounded bitter but not caring in my exhausted state.

Although he hadn't seemed happy with my refusal to share my story with him, Nicholas was surprisingly gentle and considerate with me for the following few hours, insisting that I have a snooze on his sofa and stay for the rest of the day.

His gentleness even lasted through an exhausting sex session that he had claimed would make me feel better, and after he'd brought me to my second blissful climax of the afternoon I had to say Nicholas had been right, I felt a whole lot better now.

Afterwards though, instead of dressing and leaving as he usually did, Nicholas sat up on the bed, crossed his legs, and gazed down at me with a peculiar expression on his handsome face.

'Why are you here, Rebecca?' he asked suddenly, causing me to worry that I'd outstayed my welcome. After all, I'd been here the entire day and it was getting late now. Once again, it crossed my mind that I really should consider getting myself a normal relationship where I didn't constantly need to be on tenterhooks, but somehow I just couldn't bring myself to walk away from Nicholas just yet.

'I don't mean now specifically,' he said quickly, seeing the slight panic on my face as I frantically tried to sit up. 'I mean each week, why do you come here? You don't strike me as a fuck-buddy kind of girl.'

Oh God, was I that obvious? I winced at his unerring ability to read me, because Nicholas was right, of course, I had always been the relationship type and since starting this … *thing* … with him, I intrinsically knew that deep down I wanted more. Why else would I have run here today after my heart-wrenching night with Joanne? I was clearly starting to see Nicholas as a support mechanism of some sort. Not that I was going to admit that to him; it would well and truly scare him off and I was enjoying myself too much for it to end just yet. Maybe I could get away with some light remarks and half-truths to placate him.

'I come for an amazing piano lesson,' I said with a shrug and a small smile that I hoped appeared light and humorous.

One of his eyebrows arched high as he continued to study me in silence. Apparently, he wanted more detail and was simply going to wait until I provided it.

Touching his leg to placate him, I rolled my eyes. 'OK, OK, an amazing piano lesson followed by some average sex,' I remarked casually, but my heartbeat was racing in my chest. You had to be brave to toy with Nicholas Jackson; it was an adrenaline-raising experience.

Watching him carefully, I saw his eyes darken and narrow as something very like annoyance crossed his features. God, he could be so touchy, but perhaps I shouldn't push him too far. He was an incredibly proud man and joking about his sexual prowess appeared to be pushing him toward the edge. Time for a bit of truth.

Raising my hands in a gesture of surrender, I grinned. 'Calm down, Nicholas, I was only joking!' *Jeez*, he needed to find his sense of humour.

'You're right, I wouldn't have thought myself a "fuck-buddy" type of girl either,' I acknowledged, dropping my gaze at my crude phrasing, Nicholas might curse easily, but I very rarely swore out loud, only in my head. Remembering his virtual obsession with eye contact, I raised my eyes again as I continued. 'But I'll be honest with you, Nicholas. I'm twenty-five years old and until now the only sex I've experienced has been fumbled and pretty lame.'

Pulling the sheet tighter around my waist to give me something to distract myself with, I finally spoke again. 'Until I met you, I never realised sex could be this good,' I admitted, watching as his eyes widened marginally at my undisguised compliment, He was obviously surprised by my words, his face somehow looking open and younger and showing a brief lapse in his usually controlled façade. I shrugged and bit my lip. 'You don't do relationships and I want to experience some great sex while I can, so that's why I come here each week,' I finished in a whisper, pushing aside the tingling sensation of shame that came with my sordid admission, I'd basically just admitted that I was a slut; how shameful. Except for some reason, I didn't feel shamed. In fact, I sort of felt liberated, especially as I saw Nicholas relax after my statement.

In response, he nodded and a marginally arrogant expression settled on his brows as he climbed from the bed. That was much more normal behaviour for Nicholas. Phew, it appeared I had convinced him of my reasons, for now anyway.

SIX

The calendar on the wall of my office told me today was Monday. Now I was single again I was obsessed with Mondays; I couldn't wait for the painfully empty weekends to be over so I could leave my flat and get back to the bookshop. When I'd been dating Nicholas I had become obsessed with Fridays. Perhaps I should rephrase that, because what we had been doing really couldn't be called dating, could it? OK, when I'd been sleeping with Nicholas – although technically I never slept over ... Let's just use Nicholas' terminology, shall we? When I was fucking Nicholas, I'd been obsessed with Fridays.

As I've said, Friday night had been piano lesson night and so, in turn, sex night. I looked forward to my meetings with Nicholas so much that it became all I could do to function properly and get through the day. Most weeks my mind had been far away from work, focused instead on what Nicholas might do with me, or to me, later that night.

One particular Friday, an hour before closing time, a customer walked in who made my heart sink and dragged my mind away from thoughts of Nicholas. This guy, Mr Peterson – although I'd nicknamed him "Mr Moany Pants" – had been a regular in the shop for the past three weeks. He'd ordered a book, a particularly rare first edition, which I had told him would take at least two months for me to source and obtain, and yet he'd still turned up every frigging Friday and asked about it.

Today appeared to be no different, except he looked even more pissed off than usual when I told him it still hadn't arrived and then proceeded to give me a right earful about my customer service skills. The cheek of it! Unable to contain my annoyance,

I gave as good as I got, and in the end Louise had to intervene and push me in the direction of the staff room, telling me to head home half an hour early while she placated him.

Arriving home, I took out some of my aggression by kicking the couch and shoving at my ironing pile with a frustrated grunt. Feeling marginally better I took a long, hot shower and changed into some comfy clothes, deciding to stay at home tonight and relax. Although it was Friday and I was supposed to be heading to Nicholas', I couldn't face it after my run-in with Mr Peterson.

What I really wanted was to skip the piano and just see Nicholas to take my mind off my shitty day. But seeing as he'd made it perfectly clear that I was simply his fuck buddy and not his girlfriend, I didn't feel able to tell him that all I wanted was to go to bed with him then snuggle until I fell asleep, especially not after the other week when I'd turned up at his house unexpectedly after my night with Joanne. If I wasn't careful, he was going to think I was getting too attached to him and end our tryst, which I didn't want. No, far better to just have a night off to cool down.

Sighing miserably, I picked up the phone to call Nicholas. In reality, I needed to sit down and consider what to do about the situation between Nicholas and me. It really wasn't healthy to sleep with someone you actually wanted more from, was it? Especially seeing as I didn't even sleep with him – we fucked and then I left, I concluded dismally with a grimace, but that was a whole can of worms that my frazzled brain couldn't begin to tackle today.

Fidgeting with the TV remote in one hand, I held the phone to my ear with the other as I nervously waited for him to answer. I didn't have to wait long, because he picked up on the second ring. 'Hi, Nicholas.' My voice was a bit pathetic. God, I was definitely feeling sorry for myself.

'Rebecca?' I heard what sounded like concern in his voice and arched an eyebrow in surprise.

'Yeah, hi, I've had a bad day at work today so I'm going to give my lesson a miss tonight. I'm in a really lousy mood, Nicholas. It wouldn't be fair to impose it on you,' I explained lamely, fiddling with a loose lock of my hair.

'Oh.' There was a long, drawn out pause on the other end. 'Fine.' He sounded distinctly pissed off. Great, now as well as a customer and my employee being annoyed with me, Nicholas was also in a mood with me.

I sighed again, dropping the remote and instead lowered my forehead into my palm while wishing my life were easier and that Nicholas was just my boyfriend. If he were, then I could vent my anger on him while he listened patiently and then fall into bed with him to work out my stress. I rolled my eyes. He's not, so deal with it, I ordered myself as he politely but speedily ended our call.

Feeling utterly miserable, I settled onto the sofa with my favourite cookery programme, hoping to distract myself from thoughts of Mr Peterson and my "going nowhere" relationship with Nicholas. It wasn't an entirely successful distraction, because the guest chef had dark runaway hair and bright blue eyes which immediately reminded me of Nicholas, but on the plus side, at least the food looked good and drew my attention for a while.

Half an hour or so later, I was vaguely considering going for a relaxing bath when the doorbell rang. Not expecting anyone, I guessed it would be Louise coming to check up on me after this afternoon's little exchange at work. Hopefully she'd have Chinese takeaway with her too as she often did when she visited. God, I hoped she'd brought sticky spare ribs; I could really do with some comfort food right now.

It would be fair to say I was beyond astounded as I pulled open the door to find Nicholas standing in the hallway of my flat with a very peculiar look on his face. Dressed in black trousers, a pale grey shirt, and a dark leather jacket he looked beyond sexy and I heard my breath wheeze a little as I tried not to moan. Leather? Good God, he looked incredible. Was he trying to give me a heart attack?. He was leant against the wall next to my door, with his head turned down, but he was looking up at me from under his brows in a way that could only be described as dark, brooding, and downright desirable. Wow, I totally had not expected this tonight.

Cringing, I glanced down at my "around the house" clothing; a tatty Nirvana T-shirt and baggy tracksuit bottoms that had definitely seen better days. I literally couldn't look scruffier if I had tried.

'Rebecca,' he murmured in greeting, sending an instant shiver down my spine. Mmm, the way he did that low, raspy thing was just so sexy.

'Nicholas, what are you doing here?' My tone was probably a little sharper than I'd intended, but to be honest, he looked just as confused by his presence on my doorstep as I sounded.

'You seemed tense on the phone so I thought I'd drop by and see if you were OK.' Again, an oddly bemused expression flickered on his face but it was gone before I could read too much into it. 'The trouble at work, is it anything I can help with? Or is it more issues with your sister?'

OK, time out, I thought. Let me just take a moment to process this. Nicholas is here to see if I'm OK and he wants to help ... That sounded very much like the type of stuff a boyfriend would do, so why the hell was Nicholas-fuck-buddy-Jackson here doing it?

Standing back in silence, I indicated for him to enter my flat, which he did with a small nod of his head. As his gorgeous spicy pine scent caught in my nostrils, mixed with a hint of leather from his jacket, I found that I was ridiculously pleased he was here.

Remembering his question, I belatedly answered, 'No, no, Joanne's fine.' I'd visited her more than usual this week and was pleased that she seemed back on track. 'It's a guy at work, just some stupid customer giving me a hard time. He keeps coming in and getting aggravated with me when I've told him repeatedly that the book he wants will take me time to get.' My tone had risen from reliving my anger but I shrugged and headed for the couch, flopping down limply, before watching as Nicholas surveyed first the room, and then me with narrowed eyes.

Thankfully, Nicholas made no comment about my scruffy clothing or the slightly messy state of my flat – the pile of washing that had borne the brunt of my anger when I'd first got home from work was still spread in an unappealing fashion across the other sofa where it had tumbled.

'He's hassling you?' he enquired sharply, and I may have been mistaken but I could have sworn there was a protective note to his voice, a suspicion further fuelled as I watched as his hands tense at his sides. How interesting.

Struggling to make sense of Nicholas' reaction to my bad day, not to mention his appearance in my flat, I tried to adjust to his presence. Having him here, four feet away from me in my little front room felt strange, and not just because he'd never been here before. It was more the way his tall stature and tense, dominant posture suddenly made the place feel incredibly claustrophobic, but not in an entirely bad way.

'Yeah, but it's OK. I gave as good as I got,' I said with a weak smile, which was more than true. In fact, I wouldn't be surprised if Mr Peterson didn't cancel his order and go elsewhere after the barrage of rude remarks I'd thrown at him. I believe the words "obnoxious, ill-bred, impatient pig" may have figured somewhere in my tirade.

'I'm sorry I cancelled my lesson, Nicholas, but I knew I wouldn't be able to concentrate and I didn't want to be miserable around you.' He nodded sharply, passing another gaze around my flat, which made me squirm with discomfort and immediately regret not tidying up earlier when I'd had the chance.

'Why do you live here, Rebecca? It's not exactly the best part of town, is it?' he questioned, with a disapproving frown marring his brows. It was true; although trendy and a cool place to live, the areas of central London with cheaper rent were never going to be the safest of neighbourhoods.

'I've lived here for years,' I replied with a shrug.

'But your grandfather left you quite a sum of money. It was easily enough to buy the bookshop and upgrade your housing arrangement,' Nicholas said as he fingered a dusty bookshelf cautiously.

'Yeah, but I got the flat way before Granddad left me the inheritance money ...' Halfway through my explanation, I froze. How the hell did Nicholas know how much money

Granddad had left me?

At my pause, Nicholas' eyes flashed to mine and a flush of guilt coloured his cheeks.

'I …' He winced with discomfort. 'Once things started to get more … intimate between us I may have done a spot of background research on you,' he confessed finally.

My eyes flew wide open as I jumped to my feet incredulously, my brain in overdrive at the implications of his words. 'What the hell, Nicholas? Did you hack into my bank accounts?' I yelled, my arms flailing in all directions. How dare he?

'No, I didn't hack your accounts. I'm a pianist, not an international criminal mastermind,' he replied dryly, seemingly oblivious of my distress. 'But thanks to your review I'm quite famous now, and as such have friends in high places who do have the skills to obtain information for me.' Which I took to mean "hack my account".

'I merely asked a good acquaintance of mine to do me a favour,' he said, as though it were an everyday occurrence, which for someone like Nicholas it more than likely was.

'Jesus, Nicholas, this is crazy!' My voice was high and disbelieving, however I couldn't help but find his digging slightly flattering. After all, if he was doing background checks into me then he must be seeing me as more than just a casual fuck, mustn't he?

'I was merely curious about you, Rebecca,' he said by way of apology, without actually uttering the word "sorry".

'I'm not after you for your money, if that's what you think,' I muttered quietly, hurt by the sudden thought that that might be how he saw me. Because being viewed as a gold-digger was so much worse than being thought of as a woman who sleeps with a guy casually once a week, I thought shamefully.

'Clearly not; you have more than enough money of your own,' Nicholas stated with a satisfied smirk as he took a step closer, but I countered by stepping back and dropping stubbornly onto the couch again.

Sighing, he ran a hand through his hair, leaving it messy and dishevelled. 'Look, I'm sorry if my actions have upset you.'

Wow, he actually said the S-word! 'But you have no idea how many women have tried to get close to me because of my money. It's so refreshing to know you're different.' Seeing my continued glower, Nicholas let out another deep breath and shook his head as if at a loss for words.

We simply stared at each other for several seconds, his gaze hammering into my eyes, and mine refusing to budge either. After staying silent for a long period, Nicholas apparently decided he'd had enough of that topic and, as he often did, he simply moved on to what was on his mind. 'So, this business with this guy at your work, you're sure you don't need me to do anything?'

After glaring at him for several moments, it was clear that our previous discussion was over and that I wasn't going to win this battle. Or any battle where Nicholas Jackson was concerned, I thought, almost laughing out loud at how stubborn and single-minded he was. 'I'm fine, honestly,' I conceded in a lighter tone. 'Decided to distract myself from it all.' I jerked a thumb at the television.

'With cookery shows?' he asked, eyeing my choice of *MasterChef* rather dubiously, an eyebrow rising in apparent amusement. It caused me to blush and nod simultaneously as a goofy smile returned to my lips. I knew I could use my free time more productively by reading, or extending my skills with a useful hobby or two, but when I needed to kick back and relax after a stressful day like today, then a shot of easy watching TV was just my thing.

'You didn't think I would be a suitable enough distraction for you?' he asked suddenly, his voice dropping low and dark and full of the tantalizing promise of distractions far more exciting than television .

Shocked, and almost instantly aroused, I looked up at him, my eyes widening marginally as I took in his heated stare. 'I know you would be, but I thought you might get annoyed if I couldn't concentrate on the piano,' I conceded weakly. God, his penetrating gaze was getting me overexcited already and he wasn't even near me.

Oh so slowly, Nicholas nodded. 'I see. I can leave if you

want to be alone.' He paused, cocking his head to one side. 'Or I would be more than happy to act as a distraction from your bad day, if you like? I can think of several things that would take your mind off work, Rebecca,' he promised in a low tone that made my stomach quiver with excitement.

Several things? That just sounded too tempting to pass up ...

'Take my mind off work?' I tilted my head at him and absently fiddled with a loose tendril of hair. 'I'd like that, Nicholas,' I whispered decidedly with a nod of my head.

Blimey, sex with Nicholas Jackson at *my* house, who'd have thought it?

With a slightly arrogant but hugely sexy smile, Nicholas stalked toward me with heavy lidded, desire-laden eyes. His gaze never left mine as he held out a hand for me. Wrapping his strong fingers around mine, he proceeded to pull me up but kept tugging so I fell against his chest and had to strain my head back to see him.

'Lead me to your bedroom, *now*,' he instructed quietly, but for such a soft tone it was amazing how much authority he managed to lace into his words and a shiver of anticipation ran through me.

I walked toward my bedroom on decidedly wobbly legs, his hand clutched in mine the entire time. As soon as we were over the threshold, Nicholas kicked off his shoes and pulled a box of condoms from his pocked that he then tossed on the bed, but as he did so he caught sight of the frown that creased my brows.

'What it is?' he asked, stepping toward me again.

'Nothing, I just hate those things.' I indicated the condom packet. 'I know we have to use them but I think I'm slightly allergic to them.' I had always had issues with them; in fact, the first time I'd had sex I'd thought for days that I'd caught something because I'd been so itchy, but after a very embarrassing trip to the doctors it turned out to be just a reaction to the latex.

I could see approval in Nicholas' eyes as he narrowed his gaze and nodded. 'Agreed, I dislike them too. I have tests done regularly. My last one was only three weeks ago and was all clear, I think I still have the results in my wallet,' he said, fumbling in his trouser pocket before handing me a folded copy of his results that I ran my eyes over vaguely before returning. I shifted on the spot with frustration – this interlude was getting a little more business-like than I had first anticipated.

Gripping my chin between his forefinger and thumb Nicholas stared at me with such heated longing that I nearly moaned out loud. 'It's not something I would usually do, but God I would love to fuck you without a barrier between us,' he muttered hotly, and at his dirty words my legs very nearly gave way. 'If you get yourself tested too we can dispose of them, as long as you're on some other form of contraception?' he enquired.

'I have the contraceptive injection every three months,' I told him before blushing. 'And the clinic where I get my smear tests always runs a full sexual health check as standard; mine was all clear when I had it done seven months ago.'

'Seven months?' He scowled as his hand dropped away from my face. 'Maybe you should get tested again. That's quite a while, Rebecca,' he added, which was surprisingly tactful considering he normally just said whatever was on his mind.

Maybe seven months was a while for him, but personally, I knew I had nothing to worry about. 'Um, actually, its fine, I haven't –' Blushing furiously I shook my head before finally meeting his eyes. 'You know … I haven't slept with anyone since that test … only you.'

Open amazement filled his face at my statement and I briefly wondered just how many women he had been through in that time-frame. A shudder ran through me at the thought. On second thoughts, that was something I definitely *didn't* want to know about Nicholas Jackson.

'You haven't slept with anyone for seven months?' he exclaimed gruffly, but I just blushed an even deeper shade of red and started to fidget and shift my feet on the spot.

'More like just over a year,' I mumbled, now embarrassed beyond belief and desperately wishing I could dive past him and switch the lights off to hide my burning features, because, believe me, right then I felt like a frigging glow worm.

'Christ, Rebecca, you're sex on legs – why the hell not?' He looked completely stunned by my claim, but I was distracted by his description of me as "sex on legs" and giggled nervously.

I just shrugged as I often do when embarrassed. 'I finished with my last boyfriend about thirteen months ago and was just too busy to look for anyone, I suppose.' That, plus sex with my ex had been far from thrilling and I wasn't in a rush to go out and experience any more drab fumbling. I saw Nicholas' disbelieving look so I explained further. 'It was about the same time that I got my inheritance from my grandfather and bought my business, so life was pretty hectic for a while. I didn't have time for dating.'

Raising a hand, Nicholas scratched at the back of his neck in apparent agitation. 'How many people have you slept with before me?' he asked suddenly, his eyes boring into mine. This wasn't exactly a topic I wanted to discuss, but his tone didn't really leave me any room for refusal.

Goodness, this was like a game of truth or dare. Squirming on the spot, I held up two fingers.

'Just two?' he whispered, his face both solemn and shocked.

'Yep. You're number three,' I added weakly. I *was not* going to ask for his number. I truly didn't want to know. His answer would no doubt give me far too much fodder for unnecessary jealousy. Clearly, with his level of skill, Nicholas had had a fair amount of practice in the bedroom and I briefly wondered if he even kept up with his number any more or had simply lost count.

Before I knew what was happening, I found myself spun into Nicholas' arms and being kissed so deeply I thought my legs would give way. Actually, my legs did give way, but luckily he was gripping me to him so firmly that he easily supported my lolling body. One of Nicholas' hands thrust into my hair, trapping my head as his tongue invaded my mouth, staking a claim over mine and ripping the breath from my body with its intensity. From the strength of his response, I could only assume he was quite pleased with my relative inexperience in the bedroom.

After several moments of phenomenal kissing, he raised his head and I saw his handsome face was flushed and his eyes blazing as he stared down at me intently. 'Would you like to take your frustration from work out on me, Rebecca?' he asked, his lips hovering just millimetres from mine as our breaths mixed.

'Yes,' I muttered thickly. More precisely, I wanted him to take me rough and hard enough to make thinking about anything other than him completely impossible, but there was no way I was going to say something as rude as that out loud.

Stepping back, he removed his gorgeous leather jacket, folded it, and placed it on a chair. 'Would you like to use one of my toys on me?' he asked as he produced a leather thing which looked a lot like a longer, thinner version of a table tennis bat, and caused me to frown. 'This is a paddle, for spanking. I brought it along in case you needed to let off some steam,' he explained softly.

My body tensed. *Me hit him?* I thought he was the one who did the punishing. 'Do you normally let people hit you?' I asked in a confused whisper. A scarily dark look that spoke of something frightening and horrible flashed in his blue eyes before it was gone, replaced by a neutral expression again that almost verged on blank.

'No. But I will make an exception for you if it will make you feel better,' he said, his tone unreadable and hinting at an underlying something that I was obviously missing.

I didn't even have to consider it. Hitting him was not something I wanted to do, ever, so I shook my head firmly. 'No. I just want you.'

Tossing the paddle aside, Nicholas stepped toward me again. 'As you wish, Rebecca,' he said, with that familiar side tilt of his head again. 'Undress me,' he instructed.

Undress him? Gosh, this was all very different; normally it was him doing everything to me while I just stood there and absorbed the Nicholas Jackson skills. Pausing for a second, I realised that was probably Nicholas' intention – to mix things up a bit so I was too busy thinking about what I was doing to worry about work. If that was his plan, it was certainly working. He had my full attention.

Nicholas stood perfectly still for me, patiently waiting for me to control my composure before I forced my trembling fingers to undo his pale grey shirt button by button and peel it from his body. I was shaking from excitement so badly that I fumbled the first few buttons and had to lower my gaze to know what I was doing, but I was fairly certain that his burning eyes never left me as I did it.

'Now remove your T-shirt.' He might not be doing anything to me, but I noticed Nicholas was still keen to give instructions. But actually, I liked being told what to do by him; it was kind of sexy when he was in charge.

Just as well, really, considering his preference for control, I thought with a small roll of my eyes. As I shook away the thought, I whipped my shirt over my head before it promptly joined his on the chair.

'My trousers next.' I smiled as I saw Nicholas' hands forming fists at his sides; apparently it was quite an effort for him not to join in.

Feeling braver now I could see his excitement tenting the front of his trousers, I briefly cupped his visible erection through the cloth and looked him directly in the eyes as I gave it a gentle squeeze, running my fingers up and down his length teasingly and then giving a harder rub. A breath hissed from between his lips and his blazing eyes narrowed as he reached down and gripped my wrist.

'Trousers off, Rebecca,' he reminded me firmly. 'Otherwise I'll come in my underwear and I don't think either of us wants that.'

The realisation that I had so much power over him made me giddy, and with a cheeky grin, I gave him one last teasing squeeze before lowering his zip and beginning to slip off not only his trousers, but his boxers too. Given how excited he was this was no mean feat; I had to pull the waistband right out before he finally sprang free, allowing me to lower his clothes.

I drew in a deep breath as I admired his naked form again, and then let the air out as a breathy sigh of contentment. Nicholas really was a fantastic specimen of a man and I couldn't help but take a second to run my eyes appreciatively over him while pulling down my tracksuit bottoms and chucking them aside.

'What would you like to do now, Rebecca?' he asked seductively as he stood there completely relaxed and naked, and totally at ease. Not that he had anything to be embarrassed about, all anatomy was present and correct and more than adequate from where I was standing.

My choice? Actually, I'd had such an exasperating day that I just wanted him to sex my brains out, but once again I found I was way too shy to say that, so I shrugged instead, dropping my eyes as a blush heated my cheeks.

Rapidly, Nicholas spun me around and bent me over the bed, landing a stinging slap on my behind that made me shriek in shock. God, surprisingly it had actually felt really good to shout out loud and vent my frustration.

Leaning over my so his lips brushed my ear, Nicholas spoke firmly, 'Don't drop your eyes from me.'

Before I even knew it, or had properly considered the implication of my words, I was speaking. 'Do that again … please,' I whispered, immediately shocked by my own words. But instead of giving me the slap that I had requested, Nicholas gripped my shoulders, pulled me upright, and turned me to face him.

'What?' he demanded, his grip tight on my shoulders and clearly confused by my request for a spanking, which, to be fair, even I was questioning.

'I … it – it felt good to scream, let off a bit of steam, you know. I just wanted you to spank me one more time,' I explained sheepishly, staring down at my entwined fingers and feeling like an idiot.

'You're very confusing, Rebecca, but as you are staring at your hands and therefore breaking my rule yet again, I shall oblige you this time.'

Suddenly, I found myself bent over my bed again and yelling loudly as another, harder slap landed on my arse. Nicholas didn't stop at one; in fact, he landed a further six slaps to my now stinging behind, each one slightly harder than the last and sending spasms of pleasure to my groin.It was crazy but I found it incredibly therapeutic.

After finishing with the slaps, Nicholas held me still with one hand at the nape of my neck and slowly pushed first one, then two moistened fingers inside my already slick channel while I was bent forward. God, it felt so good. My heart was pounding from the slaps and now my body seemed alight for him. I wanted him inside of me right now, and I realised I'd never felt so wanton. It was like a drug.

Nicholas had other ideas, and dragged out this sweet torture for several more minutes. Eventually my frustration got the better of me, and I began to push backwards onto his fingers to increase the pressure, causing him to chuckle softly behind me. Taking my keenness as a prompt to move things on, he slipped his fingers out of my moistness and climbed onto the bed next to me, propping himself up on some pillows and dragging me toward him so I was kneeling next to him and in the perfect position to kiss him, which I promptly did, enjoying the chance to have a little bit of control for a change.

'Straddle me,' he ordered darkly. Me on top … this was new too, but I did as instructed before he took hold of my hips, guided my entrance to the tip of his erection, and then pulled me down hard and fast onto his solid length.

'*Ahhh*!' I cried out from the pleasure and the deepness of this position, grasping at his chest with my hands. I was literally impaled on him, skin to skin, feeling every inch of his shaft inside me, and it felt divine, especially as we were no longer using the condoms.

'You control the tempo, Rebecca; use me as you wish,' he instructed next in a gruff, breathless tone, and so slightly hesitantly, I began to move on top of him, a combination of pushing myself forward and back at the same time as lifting myself off him and dropping back down. Being in control was exciting, and I enjoyed bringing us both close to orgasm, but what I really wanted was for Nicholas to be slamming into me and relieving the last of my tension.

'You finish it, Nicholas, I want you to take me … *hard*,' I whispered, finally plucking up the courage to voice my inner desires. I saw his eyebrow arch and his nostrils flare at my request, but without a word he shifted me off him and lay me on my back. Then he lifted both of my legs up and knelt facing me so that my legs rested against his chest and my ankles were over his shoulders.

'As requested this will be hard then, Becky,' he murmured, *'and deep.'* Holding on to my knees to stop me moving and leaning over me so my legs bent back toward my torso, Nicholas then pushed into me so hard that I yelled out loud. Really frigging loud. Fuck, it was even deeper than before, and just what I had needed.

In this intense position, it only took about a minute of Nicholas' pounding onslaught to bring us both speeding towards a fiery climax, and then with one final hard thrust that contacted perfectly with my G-spot we both exploded into a loud and brutal climax, our limbs thrashing and breaths colliding as we attempted to control ourselves.

As soon as Nicholas had regained his steady breathing, he eased himself from me and pulled me into his arms.

'Frustration relieved?' he asked softly against my damp temple several seconds later, but all I could do was nod against his chest, sigh quietly, and blush beetroot red. Crikey, that had been phenomenal

'It felt so good to fuck you without a condom,' he muttered hotly into my hair, causing me to agree with an appreciative moan before flushing with embarrassment as I realised I could feel his sticky, warm evidence between my legs. How he managed to sound so freaking sexy when he was being that crude I had no idea, but he did, and I loved it.

After a while, Nicholas gently removed me from his arms and headed into the bathroom, leaving me feeling decidedly unsure what to do now. I wanted him to stay the night but even though we'd had sex so many times now, he'd never given any indication that he wanted to spend an entire night with me, so, knowing he would no doubt be wanting to leave, I reluctantly slipped from the bed, cleaned myself with a tissue, and began to pull my T-shirt on.

Emerging from the bathroom, Nicholas paused when he saw me dressing and an unreadable expression crossed his face. Was it regret? A rush of frustration crept up on me. I wished I were better at reading him, or just brave enough to ask him how he really felt.

'That's a pretty impressive bathroom,' Nicholas commented, before tilting his head and observing me for several seconds. 'Shower with me before I leave?' he asked suddenly, sounding vaguely uncertain about whether I'd accept or just chuck him out.

First, his protective little show of turning up to see me because I was upset; now, showering together ... Nicholas was confusing me – nothing new there – but he was acting almost like a boyfriend again and I had to forcibly remind myself that he really only wanted me for the sex.

Realising I'd been silent for several seconds, I answered him by removing my T-shirt again and smiling shyly up at him. We'd done so many things together in bed that showering with him shouldn't be embarrassing for me, but for some reason it felt much more intimate as I took his hand and followed him into my walk-in shower.

Nicholas flicked on the taps, yelping like a child as cold water cascaded over him and soaked his hair, plastering it across his forehead. He grabbed me, practically rugby tackling me backwards as he tried to escape the chilled spray until we were both crumpled against the far wall of the cubicle.

I couldn't help it; I began to laugh, attempting to smother my mirth with my hand as I saw Nicholas scowling at me. Then he relented and grinned along with me, looking a little sheepish.

'I should have warned you, it does that. Here ...' I reached past his goose pimpled skin and adjusted the tap toward the blue arrow – my taps did the opposite of what they were supposed to – causing warm water to splutter from the shower head and then gush over Nicholas' chilled skin.

Sighing contentedly, he slid a wet hand around my shoulders and tugged me under the water for a soft kiss, after which he covered my jaw and neck with feather-light touches of his lips before placing a kiss on the corner of my mouth, which had suddenly deepened into something far more passionate when his tongue pushed inside my lips.

When he broke the kiss several minutes later, I saw Nicholas had somehow picked up my sponge and shower gel from the glass shelf and was smiling broadly at me. If I hadn't been wet in the shower, I might well have grabbed my camera at this point to record his playful mood for posterity, because *boy*, did he look good when he was grinning like this.

'I would like to wash you,' he told me, before squirting a big blob of orange blossom shower gel on to the sponge and squeezing it, causing bubbles to dribble from his hand. 'Turn around,' he instructed, and once again under his spell, I did so immediately. 'I'll do your back first.' He paused. 'Your breasts would be far too distracting,' he murmured, dropping a kiss on my shoulder and making me giggle.

I sighed contentedly. 'This is my favourite shower gel. I love the scent of orange blossom,' I murmured as he began to lather my shoulders with rhythmic swirls of the sponge.

The sensation of Nicholas carefully washing my back was somehow relaxing while also thrilling at the same time. As I stood there allowing him to wash my body, it occurred to me this was probably the most gentle he'd ever been with me, caring almost, but I tried to focus on enjoying it and not allowing myself to read too much into it.

Once Nicholas had thoroughly worked my back, neck, and legs over with the sponge, he wrapped a soapy hand around my waist and bent his lips close to my ear.

'Turn.' His one-word command was so soft I almost didn't hear it, but the gentle coaxing of his hand on my hip alerted me to what he wanted me to do and I slowly spun around to face him again, my thigh brushing against his jutting erection as I did so.

The dark expression on his face was matched with an equally intense fire in his eyes, and as he began to slowly, sensually wash my shoulders, his eyes never once left mine. I felt almost as if he was worshipping me with his actions and it was a completely euphoric feeling, even though deep down I knew it was really just a run-up to something sexual.

Dropping the sponge, Nicholas began to massage his soapy hands over my clenched stomach, slowly making his way up to my eager breasts and sensitive, slippery nipples. Oh, this was so heavenly I couldn't help but moan out loud. My sound apparently drove Nicholas' careful control over the edge because suddenly he ceased his washing and pressed me back against the tiled wall, which was warm from the cascading water.

At the same time as kissing me soundly on the lips, Nicholas gripped my hips, lifted me, and proceeded to thrust into me so gently and beautifully that for the first time it was almost like he was making love to me and not just fucking me.

It was like being with a completely different man. Trying desperately not to let myself get carried away with the marked contrast in Nicholas' behaviour since we'd entered the bathroom, I concentrated instead on enjoying the seemingly endless surprises of the man now buried inside me and clutching me against him.

SEVEN

Even if the shower experience goes down in history as one of my best-ever sexual encounters to date, I should have twigged then how weird Nicholas was because after it, he had returned to the bedroom with a peculiar expression on his face, closed himself off again, dressed rapidly, and left with barely another word to me.

Just like that.

If I hadn't already been totally confused about what was occurring between us, I certainly was after that night.

It was just as well my office was poorly lit because a tear escaped from my eye and dribbled pathetically down my pale cheek, not that anyone was here to see it. Rubbing at my face with the back of my hand I huffed out a sigh. I'd shed so many tears in the last three weeks that I was actually quite surprised I wasn't dehydrated by now.

Wiping another tear from my face, I recalled crying after he'd left that night too. It probably resulted from the stress of the day, Mr Peterson the jerk at work, and then my muddled emotions over Nicholas, but whatever the reason I'd certainly had a little sob before climbing into bed. He'd seemed so loving in the shower and then so distant five minutes later that I had been left reeling. In truth, I still was; Nicholas Jackson was just so bloody changeable it was impossible to keep up with.

At my piano lesson the following week, Nicholas had seemed relatively normal. Although "normal" for Nicholas meant dominant, brisk, and intense, with glimpses of a protective, softer, almost caring side popping up every now and then. He'd certainly made no mention of his random appearance at my flat the previous weekend, nor had we talked about the oddly tender lovemaking we'd shared in the shower. Deep down there had still been a part of me wondering just how much he was holding back from me and his words, "you wouldn't like dominant Nicholas, I don't think I do," had kept nagging at me when I'd allowed them to.

One thing I've learnt from this whole mess with Nicholas is that in future I need to trust my gut instincts and act on them. In fact, I'd printed out that very motto and stuck it on the wall of my office to remind me never to make the same stupid mistake again, and my stinging eyes glanced at it now as I chewed on my lip.

As well as Nicholas' authoritative personality and assertiveness in the bedroom, I had on occasion seen traces of his temper and dominant side spreading beyond our sex sessions. It only added to my concern of what he might be like if he really flipped, although intrinsically the bond between us made me trust him. I had been so torn, often thinking things along the lines of whether I should stick with him and hope to break his hard shell, or get out while I could and lick my wounds.

Given the outcome of our messy little affair, I now know the answer, but unfortunately, my obsession with Nicholas Jackson hadn't allowed me to walk away as my gut had told me to.

I cringed, remembering back to a prime example of his easily erupting jealous anger. Then I shifted uncomfortably in my chair, as I grudgingly had to accept the slight feeling of arousal that this particular memory also brought with it.

I'd been having lessons with Nicholas for over three months, and we'd been having sex afterwards for the past eight weeks, but still neither of us had brought up the discussion of exactly where we stood. As far as I was concerned, from all he'd said we were merely "fuck buddies" – not a particularly nice term, but appropriate for what Nicholas and I did together. After all, seeing someone once a week for sex could hardly be called a steady relationship, could it?

We never did things couples might do, like go to the cinema or for meals together, and rarely spoke in between our Friday-night meetings. Even then, we simply pretended to learn a bit of piano then shagged each other silly for an hour or two before I left.

Yep, this type of situation was definitely wholly new and unknown for me. I'd never done anything as reckless as sleep with a random man, especially one I wasn't even in a relationship with! Goodness, what would my mother say! But with Nicholas, I didn't seem to be able to help myself; it was as though I was growing addicted to him.

Against my better judgement, my heart was becoming more attached by the day too, and even though I knew it could never happen, I was starting to want more. Nicholas was like a drug, I didn't seem to be able to get enough, and even though my brain was repeatedly warning me to get away from him and his dominant side, I couldn't seem to stop our arrangement or finish my lessons and end my weekly visits to him.

That night, as I lay flaked out from a particularly lively sex session, I did something that happens often to me; I let my mouth say what I was thinking before I had considered it properly.

'So, do you have a submissive at the moment, then?' I asked, trying to keep the jealousy from my tone and the horrible images of him with other women from my mind. I'd wondered this on several occasions recently. Seeing as I certainly wasn't fulfilling that need in Nicholas's life, I'd thought maybe he had someone else who did? As soon as I spoke, though, my brain caught up with my mouth I realised that seeing as he'd said he was all clear to have sex with me without condoms he probably wasn't seeing anyone else. But it was too late; I'd already said it.

Unless he just had a submissive to order around and punish in his house … Ugh, what a thought.

Although an even worse thought was Nicholas in bed with another woman – any woman, submissive or not. That just made my guts clench with horribly acidic jealousy, but I had to admit I was still curious as to what the whole "submissive" thing might entail that was different from what he and I did together. Strengthening my failing composure I ground my teeth together and shook my head, he's not your boyfriend; you have no right to be jealous of him, I reminded myself bitterly.

'No, of course not.' Nicholas' tone seemed strained somehow and I tipped my head up from the pillow to look at him to see why. He was standing by the side of the bed half dressed in his shirt and boxer shorts, looking ridiculously sexy ... but as my eyes made it to his face I saw he also appeared to be ridiculously mad as he glared at me and tightened his fists into clenched balls by his side.

Holy shit. What had I done or said to make him look so furious?

Nicholas closed his eyes for a second, his chest heaving as he drew in several jagged breaths before opening his lids and pinning me with a heated stare. 'Are *you* seeing other men as well as me?' he suddenly demanded, stalking around the bed toward me, his intense gaze never leaving mine. 'You said I was your first in over a year,' he stated, in a deadly tone.

'I wasn't aware we were seeing each other – I thought we just fucked once a week,' I remarked with a sweet smile, attempting to lighten his mood, but boy, what a big, *huge*, *enormous,* mistake that had been. Within seconds of my flippant remark, Nicholas had leapt onto the bed and was straddling me. His position completely pinned me down, my arms were trapped against my sides by his legs and my head was held immobile by a firm thumb on my chin as he leant over me.

'Answer me,' he growled, 'are you fucking other people?' His eyes were boring into me; fury, pure and undiluted, was radiating from his every pore. He was, in short, absolutely livid and I thought that perhaps I was getting a little taster of dominant Nicholas in all his glory.

'No,' I whispered, attempting to shake my head, but unable to move it under his firm grasp. Shit, I was completely helpless and actually quite overwhelmed by his incredible strength.

'Not that guy at the book shop?' he demanded, confusing me utterly. Guy? What guy? A customer I'd mentioned, perhaps, or Robin who worked the Saturday shift?

'Which guy?' I asked, briefly forgetting about my pinned

position.

'The arsehole who answered the phone when I called the other day,' he snarled. 'He asked who I was, sounded pissed off. He clearly wants to sleep with you, Rebecca.' He could tell all this from one brief phone conversation? And when had he called me? I'd never spoken to Nicholas at work, never. Had he been phoning to check up on me? Seeing his glare, I decided now wasn't the best time to broach that particular subject, but it was certainly something I'd jot down to look into later.

'Robin?' I mused out loud; no other men ever answered the phone at the shop so it had to be him. 'No,' I answered, wanting to shake my head but still unable to.

'Don't lie to me,' he warned quietly but in a tone that made my blood feel icy in my veins. 'I will punish you if you are lying, Rebecca.'

'I'm not lying, Nicholas,' I said in a squeaky tone. 'We went out for a drink about three years ago but when he asked me out again I told him I wasn't interested.' Rather than getting defensive about him prying so forcefully into my private life I found the truth just rolled from my tongue.

'Did you fuck him?' he asked, his voice deathly quiet, the grip on my chin increasing to the point where I thought I might bruise tomorrow.

'No, of course not! I didn't even kiss him!' I shot back. I might have opened up sexually with Nicholas in recent months but I was a long way from being a slut of any kind, and I certainly hadn't lied when I'd told him I'd only slept with two other guys in the past. 'If he still likes me now, then it's not because I've been encouraging him,' I added defiantly.

Nicholas sat glaring at me for several seconds as if trying to gauge if I were telling the truth or not. His chest was rising and falling rapidly as he dragged air into his lungs but all I could do was look back at him with wide, honest eyes, trying to implore him to believe me.

'I'm not seeing anyone else, Nicholas, only you,' I assured him again in a more persuasive voice. In hindsight, it was probably the answer I should have given earlier instead of the smartarse remark I'd made to him. *Idiot*.

I literally saw the tension leave his shoulders as his body loosened again. Nicholas leant over me and, using his grip on my chin, dragged my head up for a blistering kiss. In his rush, our teeth clashed briefly, but I kissed him back desperately, trying to show him he was the only one for me. How ironic this all was because if Nicholas knew just how attached I had become to him these last months, he would no doubt throw me out of bed quicker than a bedbug.

'You only fuck me,' he ordered against my lips. 'No one else. Understand?'

'Yes ...' I panted, bemused and thrilled by the odd claim he seemed to be making over me when he had been the one to state that he didn't do relationships. I wriggled below him, trying to free my arms so I could touch him and reassure him, but in the blink of an eye Nicholas was off me, pulling my body from under the sheets and turning me over so I was kneeling in front of him, facing the wall.

'Grip the headboard,' he instructed. Sensing his urgency I did so immediately, taking hold of the cold, wrought-iron frame tightly in my trembling fingers.

'Hold on tight, I'm going to remind you why you only want to fuck me,' he whispered hoarsely, and then, with no warning or warm-up, he thrust inside me hard and fast from behind. Holy shit, it was just as well I was still wet from our activities earlier or that could have really hurt, as it was though, it sent a shot of pleasure searing though my system and made me cry out loudly.

One of Nicholas' hands reached round and began to tease my nipple with a series of hard pinches and tweaks causing me to arch into his touch, while his other hand gripped my shoulder to give him something to pull against. There was none of his usual grace or skill; instead this seemed to be more primal, rough round the edges like a lion claiming his mate or something.

Nicholas' rhythm was demanding from the outset and almost seemed to be punishing me for being cheeky to him, but as I held on to the headboard and joined in his pace by thrusting my hips back to meet every one is his strokes, I realised I was loving every single hard, body-bruising second of it. What had this man done to me?

'*Ahh, Nicholas …*' I gasped, as his hand left my breast, travelling down across my stomach where it began to work similar magic on my clitoris, rubbing soft circles across the swollen nub.

'Say my name again – *louder*,' he insisted raggedly against the sensitive skin of my back.

'Nicholas!' I cried, louder and clearer, and in response, his fingers increased their pressure on both my shoulder and clit until I could feel the imminent explosion building inside me.

Suddenly, Nicholas removed his fingers and buried himself deep inside me, before stilling completely as he curled around my back, gripping me protectively against his sweat-slicked body and holding me as close as he could. 'Who fucks you?' he demanded, his voice low and his breath hot against my neck.

Talk about possessive. Dominant Nicholas was well and truly out to play tonight.

'You!' I yelped, between ragged breaths. 'Only you, Nicholas!' As soon as I had spoken, he groaned against my shoulder and after placing a swift kiss on my neck he picked up his hard, plunging rhythm again, driving me wild with both his strokes and his fingers until I climaxed powerfully, screaming his name and clutching at the bedframe while he powered toward a violent climax of his own that had us both collapsing flat onto the bed.

'I love it when you scream my name,' Nicholas murmured into my hair between his gasped breaths several seconds later.

Unable to reply properly, I simply grunted as I lay on my stomach, flattened like a pancake below his weight, while we attempted to recover from his onslaught. God, I would be walking like John Wayne tomorrow, but I had loved every second

'So, I take it possessiveness and jealousy are traits of your dominant personality, then?' I panted. Jeez, what was it with my sarcasm? I just couldn't seem to stop!

Thankfully, this time I heard him laugh deeply against my back, the rumble passing through my skin before he landed a light, playful slap on my left buttock.

'Get used to it, baby,' he murmured against my shoulder, rubbing my bum soothingly and massaging it with his strong fingers until I groaned and wiggled my bottom more firmly into his touch.

Baby? Had he really just called me that? And what did he mean, get used to it? Did that mean he liked having me around, or just wanted more sex? Once again, I was left utterly confused by the bewildering man currently buried inside me.

EIGHT

Baby. Yep, it had become quite a regular nickname that Nicholas used for me, and I rubbed the heels of my hands across my eyes to try and avoid the more pleasant images it conjured up in my mind.

I grimaced. Speaking of images, I really should do the job that I'd been dreading for the past few days – delete the photographs of Nicholas from my mobile phone. We were over, if we ever really started to begin with, and I didn't need them to torment myself with any longer.

I'd already erased his number; I'd had to because the temptation to call him in the days immediately after our break-up had all but consumed me. In the end, Louise had snatched my phone from my hand and done it for me, deleting his number from my phone and even going a step further by erasing his email address and all old emails from my computer.

But Louise didn't know about the pictures, they were my little secret.

Not a particularly healthy secret, though. In fact, I lay awake most nights looking at them. Sometimes I got really angry with the images of him, until I'd take out my rage on a poor, unsuspecting pillow. Yes, it was definitely time to get rid of them.

I dragged my phone from my pocket and turned it over several times in my hand before finally sliding a finger over the screen to activate it. My heart accelerated as I clicked on the "Images" folder and was presented with a series of photographs of Nicholas, or Nicholas and myself, usually looking flushed and rather pleased with ourselves. Biting down painfully on my lower lip, I deleted the first three before I came to an angled arm's length picture of Nicholas and me. A breath leaked weakly from my throat as I paused to look at the photograph. It was one of my favourites; we were sitting on his bed, him with his glorious bare chest fully on display, and my giggling next to him wrapped in a sheet. I'd taken it after possibly one of the best nights of my life.

A shuddering sigh escaped my chest; I was sorely tempted to keep this photo because it was linked to one of my most treasured memories of him – the first night Nicholas had asked me to stay over.

A soft glow was permeating my eyelids and I blinked against the intrusive light wanting to snooze for a little longer if I could. Was it morning already? I must have slept like a log, although that was hardly surprising seeing as last night's efforts with Nicholas had been just sublime. Not to mention his strangely possessive declarations afterwards, that were just downright bizarre. He'd told me point blank that he didn't do relationships and yet now he didn't want me seeing other people. What was that about?

I smiled at the memory of his persuasive sexing. I shouldn't have liked the way he practically laid claim to me, but I had. In fact I'd *really* liked it. Shaking my head a fond smile curled my lips – Nicholas really was something else. Stretching out my limbs I decided I felt marginally refreshed but still tired. Opening my eyes, I blinked several times then looked around for my clock to see how much longer I could sleep.

Groggily, I tried to make sense of what I could see through my blurry, sleep-filled eyes. Hang on, this wasn't my bedroom … I gasped. Nicholas was sitting bare-chested and cross-legged on the bed next to me, watching me intently.

I had fallen asleep at his house. *Shit.*

'Hi,' I murmured, hugely embarrassed that he had been watching me sleep and desperately praying that I hadn't been dribbling or talking in my slumber.

'Hi yourself. Sorry if the light woke you,' he said softly. Looking past him, I saw the bedside clock showing 3.30 a.m. Jeez, it was *so* early.

When I sat up self-consciously, the duvet fell away but I dragged the thin sheet with me for cover. 'Sorry, I didn't mean to fall asleep, I'll leave,' I muttered, embarrassed at my slip, although technically it was his fault for exhausting me with his sexual antics.

His eyes darkened and his brow creased as he seemed to consider something that obviously took great concentration. 'No,' he said finally, with a small shake of his head, 'stay, I was just enjoying watching you sleep.'

Enjoying watching me? That was slightly weird, but he didn't want me to leave, which was a very interesting development.

Again, there was a monumental pause where I considered grabbing my stuff and leaving before Nicholas surprised me by leaning over and taking hold of my hand. OK, hand holding – this was new. My eyebrows had risen with surprise, but instead of saying anything that might break the moment, I opted to stay quiet for the time being and see how this played out.

'What you said earlier about me being possessive and jealous ...' He paused, his frown deepening and shoulders tensing. 'It's a new experience for me, but you were right, it's true, I do feel possessive over you, Rebecca, hugely so. I don't want any other man going near you.' His eyes visibly darkened with jealousy.

Jealousy over me, I registered with surprise.

OK ... my sleepiness was well and truly cleared now; Nicholas had my full attention and as I returned his grasp with one hand, I clutched at the sheet around my chest with the other, waiting in anticipation for him to continue.

Shaking his head as if he couldn't believe what he was about to say, Nicholas then raised his eyes to mine. 'Once a week with you isn't enough, Becky. I want more. Do you have plans this weekend? Can I see you?'

Holy cow, I so had not expected this! Keeping my eyes locked with his, just how he liked it, I smiled to myself. He wants more of me? This just kept getting better! Then, as always, the sensible part of my brain kicked in and I frowned.

'What is it, Becky?' he asked, edging closer to me, looking

almost, well … vulnerable. Now that was a word I never thought I'd use in the same sentence as Nicholas' name, but as I looked at him it was true. His usual arrogance was gone, washed away by a torrent of other emotions that ran across his handsome face, making it impossible to read what he was thinking.

'If I'm to see more of you I want to know all of you … No more hiding, Nicholas, I want to know why it is that you do what you do. Why are you a dominant? You hinted before there's a reason and I want to know it – I want to know the man I'm involved with,' I finished softly. That really translated to "I want to know the man I think I'm falling for", but I certainly wouldn't be saying that out loud any time soon.

I knew immediately that this was a step too far because Nicholas withdrew his hand from mine and I watched his open expression disappear as his face darkened and closed off, eyes shuttering and jaw clenching until the only visible emotion was irritation. 'Isn't it enough that I've told you it's different with you?' he said tightly, clearly annoyed with me.

Pausing, I considered this. Perhaps it should be enough, but for some reason I needed to know how he'd spent his life so far … and *why*. I was so in control of every other element of my life, and even though I was happy for Nicholas to take the lead in the bedroom, I didn't intend to quietly go along with his demands without asking what I needed to know. I'd be stupid to ignore the fact he'd liked to punish the women in his life before me. Why did he do that type of thing? He'd told me before it affected every part of his life so I needed to know more.

Maybe I wanted to know so I could tell myself that it wasn't as bad as I thought, or maybe to test the tiny part of me that was telling me his lifestyle was way more dangerous than I wanted to believe and that I should get the hell away from him.

'I don't wish to share that with you, Rebecca,' he growled. So there *was* a reason behind it all. I'd thought there would be.

It occurred to me then that he only ever used my full name when he was annoyed with me or sexing me, which I now realised meant he was in semi-dominant mode. I thought maybe I'd seen a peek of dominant Nicholas earlier tonight when he'd got all possessive and pinned me to the bed, but according to him I still hadn't seen his real dominant side yet. What else could there be?

Quite possibly, I'd had some sort of sensibility transplant because the next words were out of my mouth before I could stop them.

'OK ... will you take me to the spare room then? Show me what you're like? Just once, so I know the man I'm getting involved with?' Holy crap, what the hell was I doing? Being braver around him was one thing, but asking him to do God only knew what to me in his spare bedroom was totally frigging crazy.

The look on his face was one of complete and utter shock – shock that was quickly replaced with pure, furious anger. Nicholas' eyes widened but the irises were the darkest, most dangerous blue I'd ever seen them. *Uh-oh.*

'I should punish you right now for being stupid enough to request that.' He spat, still glaring at me, but after a second, his eyes left mine and I saw his posture slump slightly, his head lowering until his chin almost rested on his chest.

'I'm trying to put that stuff behind me now ... if I show you that side of me, Rebecca, I have no doubt that you will leave me.' After a second of absently flicking at the knee of his pyjama bottoms, he went on in a tone so quiet I barely heard him. 'I don't want you to leave.'

Wow. A heartfelt statement from Mr Fuck-'em-and-leave. Well I never; this was turning out to be one hell of an eventful night.

'It's not fair for me to expect you to change just for me, Nicholas ...' I explained, as the nagging fear that he'd go elsewhere to fulfil his dominant needs rose in my mind again, 'but also I'd be stupid to ignore that part of you. I want to see what you do. Maybe I could handle it; maybe I'd even like it?' I whispered.

'I very much doubt that.' He ground the words out through clenched teeth, his anger returning to his eyes. Or perhaps it was frustration with my endless questions, I couldn't tell.

'The things we've done together so far ... I've enjoyed

them. Surely it can't be that different?' I persisted, realising how naive I probably sounded.

'It's different, Rebecca, believe me. *I'm* different.' Nicholas' voice was low and quiet and I should have taken it as a warning to back down, but I didn't. Stupidly, I went on regardless. Perhaps I should have a zip installed on my lips to force me to shut the hell up at times like these.

'How can I, when I don't know what it's like? You say you want to spend more time with me, but how can I ever get to know you if you won't share this huge, important part of your life with me?' My voice rose along with my hands, which were now waving in the air, frustration clearly evident in both my tone and actions.

'What is it with you and fucking questions?' he spat, climbing from the bed and pacing across the room like a caged tiger, the muscles in his torso rippling and bulging with tension. 'This is why I've never done relationships,' he muttered darkly under his breath, stalking back and forth and raising a hand to run almost viciously through his hair.

'I'm sorry if I ask too many questions, but I'm a woman who wants to get to know you better, not some submissive you can order around,' I fired back hotly, equally as angry as him now.

'Exactly!' he roared, looking absolutely livid and making my pulse spike with a mix of adrenaline and fear. 'I've told you I don't view you as a sub when we're together but for some reason you want me to treat you like one so you can *learn* about me?' He sneered as he spoke, his handsome face twisting almost unrecognisably. 'What am I? A fucking science experiment or something? When I'm like that, it's as though I'm a totally different person. You would hate it; trust me. You'd be better off leaving me now because you'll sure as hell run away once I'm done with you,' he snarled.

His hot, explosive anger had shocked me, but not enough to stop me continuing. 'I'm stronger than you think and I don't think I would leave,' I challenged, rising from the bed and slipping his discarded shirt on to hide my nakedness. 'But then at least we'd be on an even playing field. You know all about me, so why shouldn't I know all about you?' I demanded, knowing it was the truth. He'd used his influence to find out about my bank account and business and goodness knows what else. The only thing he didn't properly know about was the history with my sister.

As my initial temper died away, I was suddenly brought up short. Why the hell was I pushing for this? Did I really want to see the darkness hidden inside Nicholas Jackson? Why couldn't I just be happy that he wanted to see more of me? Take it one day at a time …

'Fuck it,' he snarled suddenly, interrupting my thoughts, then, before I even realised it, Nicholas had crossed the room to me, grabbed me around my waist, and tossed me roughly over his shoulder. 'You want to see all of me? Fine, have it your way, but don't say I didn't warn you Rebecca,' he growled as he turned for the door and headed into the dimly lit corridor.

Fuck, fuck, fuuuck.

What the hell had I been thinking, getting him so angry? I was over the shoulder of a self-confessed dominant and punisher of women and I had no one to blame but myself. Good job, Rebecca, well done, I chided myself. I could literally feel his fury radiating from his overheated skin under my hands as the tight muscles rippled with each of his long strides. The arm around me was tense and gripping me tightly against the sharp point of his shoulder, and my heartbeat accelerated to a painfully fast level until it was thundering in my ears.

It vaguely occurred to me to shout for help. Mr Burrett – Nicholas' assistant, butler, whatever the hell he was – was no doubt somewhere in the house, but I refrained, my unfounded faith in Nicholas making me stupidly determined to see this through. Whatever "this" turned out to be.

Stopping at a door toward the end of the corridor, Nicholas roughly deposited me back on my feet and I staggered, dizzy from the adrenaline shooting through my system. 'Last chance to change your mind,' he murmured darkly, but I stood my ground, silently blinking up at him as I pulled in long, calming breaths through my nose. I had to know what he did, what he could be like. Besides, I was so frigging nervous that my throat felt as though I was choking and I didn't think I would be able to speak at this particular moment anyway.

'You are so fucking stubborn,' Nicholas declared hotly, his eyes boring into me.

Then, like a switch had been flicked, I saw him changing before my very eyes. His expression altered, becoming blank and emotionless, as if a mask had been lowered over his features. His shoulders hunched menacingly and every muscle in his body seemed to tense and expand, making him seem taller, broader, and a hundred times more intimidating. As he turned back to me he was radiating power and control, authority seeming to flow from every pore, with his eyes blazingly intense but oddly vacant.

Shit, so this was Dominant Nicholas.

'When we go through this door you do not speak unless I ask you to. Do you understand?' He ground out the words in a voice I hardly recognised and I nodded rapidly, my heart hammering in my chest.

'If you are required to speak you will address me as "sir" or "master", because as far as you are concerned, I am in charge. Is that clear?' His blue eyes were glowing now, but in a wholly different way to what I was used to. I nodded again, blood rushing in my ears and almost drowning out his words as I raised a hand to rub at my chest to try and calm my pounding heart. I don't think I had ever been more terrified in my entire life.

'Say it,' he instructed me, his face shuttered and unreadable, a muscle twitching and jerking in his clenched jaw.

'Yes,' I squeaked.

'Yes *what*?' he demanded, his tone low and deadly and completely unfamiliar as he took a threatening step toward me.

Crap. 'Yes, *sir*.'

'I will take responsibility for your safety, you will be safe, but if I set a rule and you break it, you will be punished as I see fit. Do you understand?' He glowered down at me and I was seriously starting to doubt my resolve to see this through. What the hell had I been thinking? Just as Nicholas had warned me earlier, he now seemed like a completely different person and not one I was keen to get particularly well acquainted with either.

'Yes,' I whispered thickly. One of his eyebrows rose and I panicked. '*Sir*,' I added quickly.

'When we go inside, I want you to remove your shirt and sit on the wooden chair.'

With that, he opened the door and stood back, indicating for me to enter in front of him. So, taking a deep breath for courage, I tentatively stepped into the room.

The first thing that registered in my panicked mind was relief, because it looked normal and fairly similar to Nicholas' bedroom. A large four-poster bed sat in the middle of the room, covered with light blue bedding; soft blue curtains hung at the windows and the furniture comprised of several smart oak dressers. Phew. No obvious torture devices in sight. There were no racks on the wall, or scary contraptions to tie me to either, all in all it looked pretty normal. Maybe he was just getting himself worked up over nothing; maybe this was going to be fine. Maybe I was on the verge of a panic attack and just trying to distract myself with rambling thoughts and maybes …

Moving my gaze around the room I saw the wooden chair he had referred to and started to try and unbutton the shirt with trembling fingers. I made my way unsteadily toward the chair as Nicholas disappeared into a walk-in wardrobe at the back of the room. Finally managing to remove the garment, I hung it over the back of the chair and shakily sat down, feeling very nervous and rather silly sitting naked on a chair in the middle of the room.

Nicholas returned then, still in only his pyjama bottoms, and walked over to stand in front of me. As stressful as the situation was I really couldn't help but admire how sexy he looked dressed as he was; the soft cotton trousers hung loosely from his hips, clinging to his legs and groin, and giving a hint of the amazing body that I knew lurked beneath.

Moving my gaze back to his face, I found him examining me intently, his expression still unreadable, and so I simply sat there silently, my back straight, looking up into his eyes. I had asked for this – I *would not* show him my fear. But by God, I *was* scared.

'Avert your eyes,' he stated. *What?* Usually he was all about eye contact.

'*Do it*,' he spat, his face lit with anger. Scowling, I gave him one last look before dropping my eyes to the floor and immediately hating the loss of our usual connection.

'That's better,' he said, reaching across and gently stroking my cheek. Confusingly his voice was now soft again, almost that of the Nicholas I was used to, and I very nearly looked up at him for reassurance. Follow his rules, my poor, terrified brain reminded me hastily.

'If at any point you wish to stop, the safeword in this room is "bubble",' Nicholas explained quietly, but his soft voice only made his words even scarier and I couldn't help but look up at him with wide eyes.

Bubble? 'Why would I need a safeword?' I squeaked without thinking, my heart pounding so desperately it felt like it was trying to break free of my ribs.

'No questions! Eyes down!' he growled, glowering at me. 'It is as I said; if you wish to stop, you say the word. What was the word, Rebecca?' he demanded, his voice radiating authority and making me quiver slightly on my seat. Thank goodness I was sat down, my legs were so shaky that I might well have fallen on my arse by now otherwise.

Holy cow, this was actually really frigging scary now. I was a bookshop owner for crying out loud, a boring, *boorrring* bookshop owner; what on earth was I doing putting myself into a position that required the use of safewords? That just took this to a whole new and terrifying level and made me seriously question my sanity.

'Bubble,' I muttered thickly, staring at the ground again and gripping the sides on the chair seat hoping for some stability. Spots of light began to dance in front of my eyes as I tried to control my breathing and take in the oxygen I needed. That definitely wasn't a good sign. This was terror and arousal at their most heightened and as they mixed in my belly, I started seriously to think I might faint.

'Excuse me?' Nicholas snapped, clearly annoyed, and I

jumped in my seat, realising my error.

'The safeword is bubble, *sir*,' I repeated, a dollop of sarcasm evident in my tone from my nerves. Jeez, I really needed to remember the "sir" thing and stop pissing him off.

'Are you mocking me?' Nicholas demanded, his tone incredulous and utterly terrifying, before he stalked off to the cupboard again and reappeared a few seconds later. I was about to apologise when I saw the thing in his hands. Forget the possibility of fainting; I think I very nearly died on the spot.

Moving to stand behind me, Nicholas leant down and spoke next to my ear. 'I will not tolerate sarcasm from my sub, Rebecca. Open your mouth.' His voice was silky smooth but I'd seen the thing in his hands and I panicked, clamping my lips firmly shut and wondering if maybe I should just walk out now.

As ridiculous as it was, though, I wanted to prove to Nicholas that I was strong enough for this. I'd asked him to show me his darker side so if I walked away now I'd always feel weak and be left wondering what would have happened. No, damn it, I must try and stay, I decided firmly. Ninety-nine per cent of me trusted that Nicholas wouldn't push things too far with me … and if I'm being truthful, deep down I was curious to see what else he had in store for me.

I should also admit that for whatever perverted reasons, I was also hugely aroused by all of this. I could feel the moisture between my legs and even as my brain was telling me it was wrong, I knew my body was disagreeing.

'You wanted me to treat you as my submissive, Rebecca. Well, this is what would happen if someone defied me. Either use the safeword to stop this, or open your mouth, it's your choice. I won't ask again,' Nicholas' tone was so icy that my arms erupted in a sprinkling of goose pimples and I quickly wrapped my arms protectively around my chest to try and hide the quaking of my limbs.

Holy shit. Breathing was suddenly getting much more difficult. I was having a hard time registering what I should do; run, or stay? Discover his dark side? Or walk away from the first man I had ever truly felt a connection with? My brain was spinning.

This was wrong on so many levels but regardless of that fact I was still unbelievably turned on – my nipples were so hard they hurt, and I was now throbbing between my legs, desperate for some contact. For whatever reasons, there was no getting away from the fact I didn't want him to stop. What the heck was wrong with me? Surely it was sinful to want this? Swallowing hard I steeled my emotions and stowed my confused feelings away to consider in more detail later when I was alone. Maybe I'd need to read a few home psychiatry books tomorrow to work through my issues.

Taking a deep breath for courage, I unclenched my teeth and, in a moment of immense bravery, I opened my mouth as he had asked. I was fairly sure I heard Nicholas gasp in surprise behind me – apparently he had been expecting me to use the safeword and chicken out, and even through my fear a tiny part of me felt pleased that I'd shocked him.

Recovering his composure, Nicholas reached around and placed a small white ball in my mouth, just a little smaller than a golf ball. Attached to the ball on both sides was a leather lead, or collar I suppose, and I felt him lift my hair and fasten it at the back of my head, effectively gagging me. Actually, the ball was small enough that I could still breathe through my mouth but it pushed my tongue down and made talking impossible.

It briefly flitted through my brain that I wouldn't be able to use a safeword now, but before this thought even had time to settle I felt Nicholas's breath flutter across my neck as he leant down to speak to me. "You might find it tricky to safeword now Rebecca, so if you wish me to stop at any time just raise your hand and the scene will immediately cease." His lips brushed my skin as he spoke and goose-pimples raced across my heated flesh, making me shiver with desire. Nicholas' sudden gentleness, combined with the fact that he was still giving me a way to stop things helped me relax, and I felt my muscles slacken as I rested back on the chair again. It was strange, given the situation I felt oddly calm and peaceful, it seemed that I must trust Nicholas a whole lot more than I had realised before.

'Finally, you are subdued,' he murmured, perhaps more to himself than me, frustration evident in his tone.

Giving my shoulders a gentle massage for a few seconds he then came to stand before me, producing something from behind his back and holding it out for me to see, causing my already heightened breathing to speed up to the point where I was practically panting.

Holy fuck! It was a ... a *thing* I had never seen before. He must have had it tucked in the elastic waistband of his pyjama trousers because I was sure he hadn't been holding it a second ago. I definitely would have noticed *that* in his hand.

For a second, I thought the object was the "paddle" he'd offered me use of in my flat a few weeks ago because the handle was similar, but as he let it drop down I saw it was completely different. In his hand, Nicholas held a stout handle, but hanging from the handle were lots of thin strips of material. Looking closer, I could see leather, suede, and a few strands that looked rougher but were an unfamiliar material to me, a knotted fabric, perhaps? The way he was holding it made it look a lot like a cheerleader's pom-pom, with all the thin strands hanging down limply, but I was guessing that wasn't what this was.

Looming over me still dressed only in his thin navy pyjama bottoms and somehow looking both scary and sexy as hell, Nicholas gently swung the object back and forth. I drew in a shaky breath, his scent catching in my nose as I stared at it.

'This is a flogger,' he stated calmly, causing my eyebrows to leap to my scalp. Well, that had eased my curiosity. It was *a flogger;* the name didn't leave much to the imagination, did it?

'Regardless of what you may initially think, this can be used for both pleasure and pain, Rebecca. If you do as I ask without hesitating, it shall be used for pleasure; if you disobey me or break any of my rules, I will use it to punish you. Do you understand?'

Again, his voice was low, steely and laced with an authority that for some reason thrilled me to the point where I was almost quivering and shifting in my seat to try and ease my raging arousal.

I nodded numbly, but my eyes were still focused on the flogger. It looked harmless hanging there, but I was fairly sure those little, thin strands would sting like a whip if he wanted them to. The thought made me shudder but I wasn't sure if it was through fear or excitement.

Good God, what dark path had this man led me down that I was now starting to see these things as acceptable, potentially pleasurable even? I blinked several times to clear my mind, unable to focus on the internal conflict in my brain and knowing that I needed to keep my wits about me right now.

'You asked me to show you this side of me – remember that, Rebecca,' Nicholas reminded me as he stalked around me again with the flogger hanging at his side.

'Stand up, walk to the dresser next to the bed, and hold on to the edge,' he instructed shortly, so I did, just like a good little sub. Once the anticipation had built to the point where I could hardly bare it any longer I tried to speak to ask him to ask him to start, but the ball in my mouth made my words nothing more than a lusty moaning sound.

Finally I heard him move behind me. One of his hands snaked around me from behind, splaying across my stomach and pulling me against him so I could feel his erection digging into my lower back. He was hot, hard, and ready and I found myself shuffling my hips backwards into his body. Apparently from that display, Nicholas was rather enjoying himself. Lowering his lips to my shoulder Nicholas gave a small nip at the skin, 'Keep still,' he warned me, then used a knee to push my legs further apart into a more braced position.

'Keep holding on to the dresser,' he instructed briskly, as his hands pulled my hips backwards even further, so I was bent right over, facing the drawers. As I leant over, I noticed that the gag in my mouth was starting to make me salivate rather excessively and I had to concentrate on swallowing regularly so it wouldn't dribble from my mouth. What an unpleasant device it was.

'So far you are doing well for your first time, Rebecca,' he conceded hotly at my ear, 'but you have defied me once by speaking without permission. You need to learn not to question everything. I am going to punish you briefly for disobeying me, then pleasure you immensely,' he told me in a calm but utterly suggestive tone.

Oh boy, punish then pleasure me? What a heady combination. I tensed all over from a cocktail of lust and fear and against all sensible reactions felt myself moisten further between my legs. Jeez, I was such a freak.

'Relax your muscles,' Nicholas instructed me in a whisper as he gently rubbed his warm palm over my bare backside. 'If you relax this will be pleasurable, as opposed to painful.'

I tried to relax my muscles, I really did, but when you know someone is about to spank you – no, not spank, *flog you* – it becomes rather difficult to get your muscles to comply with your brain. Maybe he sensed that because I became aware of something soft trailing over my back in a swirling sensuous pattern. It was almost hypnotic and made my muscles soften instinctively. It didn't feel like his fingers any more, but I couldn't work out what else it would be. A feather, perhaps? Suddenly, a stinging blow bit into my buttock as the first strike of the flogger made my body jerk forward. I realised the soft sensations on my back a few moments ago had been the ends of the flogger being trailed over my skin. *Holy shit.* He was right, this thing could be used for pleasure and pain. I bit down on the ball in my mouth and moaned at the unexpected stinging pain that was warming my skin.

'Shhh. Relax, baby,' Nicholas said softly, his voice suddenly seeming calmer now. And there was that word again, "baby"; it seemed so reassuring from his lips, even in this bizarre situation. As I felt his body shift away, I knew what was coming next and tensed in anticipation for the next blow. It rained down again but this time on my other buttock. Nicholas then leant down and placed a hot, open mouthed kiss on my back before moving away and hitting me with the flogger once more. Kissing me and hitting me, how messed up was this? He continued with his blows for about a minute until both my buttocks were burning and starting to sting more than a little.

Expecting another hit on my backside, I was completely taken by surprise when Nicholas flicked the flogger up between my parted legs and caught me directly on my sex. Fuck, that stroke had been much gentleer and unbelievably erotic. I moaned against the ball in my mouth, then, drowsy with the remnants of my fear and growing pleasure, I hung my head and clutched at the top of the dresser for support.

'Was that a moan of pleasure or pain, Rebecca?' Nicholas asked softly. 'Shake your head if you wish me to stop, nod it if you would like me to hit you between your legs again.'

I considered it for the barest of seconds and then, feeling almost ridiculously pervy, I raised my head and nodded it.

A rumbled noise escaped from his chest, possibly one of approval, and the flogger flicked up against my sensitive flesh again. Jeez, if he did it much more I would probably come standing up, and I wasn't sure my body could take that after all our exertions this evening, morning ... whenever.

'Remove your hands,' he instructed, and then, gripping my hips, Nicholas shifted me to the right so I was now leaning over the bed, my breasts hanging down heavily and my hands sinking into the soft mattress. Behind me, I heard the soft noise of his pyjama bottoms falling to the floor and I felt a thrill of expectation running through me and to my groin.

'You have behaved yourself very well, Rebecca. I'm going to remove your gag. No speaking, though,' he reminded me firmly.

I felt his hand tangling under my hair, gently smoothing away some wayward strands before unfastening the collar, but once again, Nicholas took me completely by surprise, because as one hand was busy at the back of my neck I felt something begin to prod gently at the entrance to my vagina. *What the heck?* It wasn't his fingers; it was wider than that, and made of a strange material, cool and slick against my damp, throbbing flesh.

The ball-gag, complete with copious amounts of saliva – *ugh* – fell free from my mouth onto the bed and I licked at my lips and swallowed several times, glad when Nicholas removed it from my view. Next, Nicholas' hand splayed on the nape of my neck, warm and soothing, as he rubbed circles on the top of my spine. After thoroughly relaxing me his hand moved to my shoulder, gently tugging me back onto the object between my legs so it buried itself inside me in one smooth movement.

'*Ahh,*' I moaned softly at the pleasurable intrusion, then, as I felt a tickling on my upper legs, I realised it must be the handle of the flogger that he was pushing inside me. It was surprisingly thick, but I could not concentrate on its dimensions as Nicholas began to move it in a circular motion inside me, causing pleasure to radiate from my core, and occasionally brushing my clitoris with the pad of his thumb.

Feeling drowsy with need I closed my eyes, but luckily my bent position meant that Nicholas couldn't see my lapse. '*Fuck ...*' I murmured, overcome with arousal. I didn't mean to speak out loud but as the adrenaline rush from earlier began to pass, the sensations in my body were almost too much to take.

Even though I had broken his "no talking" rule, I heard a low chuckle from Nicholas, and felt the hand on my shoulder give an appreciative squeeze. Apparently, his earlier anger had subsided and he seemed more like the Nicholas I knew again, which helped me to relax into the moment.

'Oh, I intend for us to, Rebecca. In fact, I'm going to fuck you so fast and hard you won't know if you're coming or going. But you will be coming, I promise you that,' he muttered darkly. 'That's why I'm getting you nice and wet with this, although I have to say you already seem rather lubricated. You appear to have enjoyed your flogging; perhaps you and I are more alike than I first thought.'

Oh boy. My insides clenched at the thought of him taking me fast and hard, and I very nearly came around the damn flogger handle, wishing Nicholas would replace it with himself instead.

Easing the flogger out of me, Nicholas then spent several minutes rubbing his hands across my back and my behind, almost as if massaging me, then helped me to stand uprght and gentle turned me to face him. 'Lie down on the bed. Bend your knees up and place your feet on the edge of the mattress,' he instructed me. I knew I wasn't supposed to, but I risked a glance at him and saw his strong features were glowing. A grimace crossed his face as he caught my gaze though, so I quickly lowered it again and positioned myself on the bed as he had asked.

Unravelling the chains that were wound around each bedpost – how had I not seen those earlier? – he silently attached a soft leather cuff around each of my ankles. I followed the path of the chains with my gaze and saw they ran from my ankles up over a bar across the top of the four-poster bed before falling to the other side where Nicholas stood, holding the loose ends.

A dark smile played on his face as he slowly and deliberately lowered his right arm, pulling the chain, which shocked me by raising my left leg off the bed so it was at a right angle to the rest of my body. I gasped in surprise as he quickly followed suit with the other chain so I was lying flat on my back with my legs straight up in the air.

Apparently, I was the puppet and he was my master. How very apt.

I could hear rattling as he fastened the chains off. He then placed his hands between my knees and opened my legs just as if he were opening a pair of curtains. The chain slid across the bar at the top and I was now lying with my legs splayed and my lower back slightly raised off the mattress. I had never felt more exposed or vulnerable, but somehow cherished too.

'What a beautiful view I have from here,' Nicholas murmured, his eyes taking in the skin of my legs and my sex, no doubt parted, wet and in full view for him.

How embarrassing. I flushed and closed my eyes.

'*Agh*!' A sharp blow from the flogger across the back of my thigh had me opening my eyes wide and looking up in surprise; that one had really hurt.

'Don't close your eyes, Rebecca, and don't look embarrassed,' he admonished me firmly. 'You are beautiful. Be proud.' Easy for him to say; he's not the one giving a grand display on the bed, I thought sourly as I tried to relax again.

He then proceeded to flick the flogger lightly across my belly in sweeping motions, causing my muscles to clench and relax on each pass of the stands. From the look of amusement on his face, it must have done funny things to my down below area too. These strokes were soft and teasing, nothing like the ones to my backside earlier, and I found myself writing below him and almost desperately craving the next sweep.

Having teased the flesh of my midsection Nicholas suddenly delivered a flick of the flogger to my right breast and I felt the nipple tighten harder under the delicious contact causing my hands to claw at the bed sheets as pleasure seared through me.

'Ahhhh ....'

'Do you like that?' he murmured and I blushed. Why did it feel so wrong to admit it?

'Yes, sir,' I replied softly, not embarrassed by having to use the stupid title for him any more.

'Hmm ... I thought so.' Lazily, he brought the flogger down on my left breast with similar results. 'You are full of surprises, Rebecca,' he observed, managing to strike both breasts simultaneously with another gentle blow.

Back at ya, I thought wryly, but then all thoughts were lost as he flicked my nipples again and I arched my back off the bed, feeling the delicious onset of an approaching orgasm.

I was left feeling utterly bereft when Nicholas stopped with his attentions but I quickly realised his intentions as he took hold of my hips and remained standing between my legs, his naked, fully erect body just centimetres from the top of my thighs.

'You may look at me now,' he instructed softly, and I raised my eyes to his for the first permitted time. He looked incredible; his eyes were blazing with need, his hair a complete sexy mess on his head, and his frame tall and muscular between my legs emanating such total control that I let out a small moan of longing. I watched as he gripped my hips and pulled me onto his straining erection in one slow, gentle slide. With my legs hanging from the bedposts, there was nothing I could do – Nicholas had full control of our movements. After gazing at me for several seconds with a face full of deep emotion, he suddenly blinked several times and then set about a pounding rhythm of strokes that had me gripping the sheets as I tried desperately not to close my eyes.

Our flesh slapped together loudly as Nicholas drove himself into me relentlessly but after all his teasing, it didn't take long before I exploded around him, my body pulsing exhaustedly as

I threw my head back and cried out in pleasure. He didn't break eye contact once through the entire time, although I did notice his jaw was tense from his attempt at self-control.

Burying himself inside of me several more times, Nicholas then thrust himself deep as I felt him silently empty inside me in a series of pulsing, hot bursts before collapsing forward between my legs and falling onto my chest.

Holy shit, so now I had met Dominant Nicholas. He certainly wasn't a man I'd forget easily, that was for sure, especially at the beginning when he had been so angry and, if I'm honest, quite terrifying. I was either crazier than I'd ever believed possible or braver than I gave myself credit for, I decided with a deep breath. Or perhaps a little bit of both.

Somehow, I had managed to turn his anger around because by the end, he was much more like the Nicholas I knew. Well, it was official, I had survived my encounter with his dominant side; and apart from a slightly sore rear end and a very well exercised heart, I wasn't any the worse for wear. Although I might walk a bit funny tomorrow after the three hard sessions he'd given me today, I thought with a smile. I'd never had so much sex in my life.

After several minutes, Nicholas wordlessly eased himself from inside me, uncuffed my ankles, rubbed some life back into the joints, and then scooped me into his arms before carrying me back to his bedroom. The first rays of the sun were seeping through the curtains as he gently laid me on the bed before crawling up beside me, dragging the covers over us and pulling me against him.

'Are you OK?' he asked against my ear, concern filling his voice as he practically burrowed his face into my neck and seemed to tense in anticipation of my response.

Was I? I mulled it over; it had certainly been quite an experience … but yes, on the whole, I think I was OK. Apart from my behind, which still felt quite delicate, and was no doubt very pink at the moment.

Rolling onto my back, I looked up and saw his wide, wary gaze, mixed with that weird, vulnerable look again. Dominant

Nicholas Jackson looking vulnerable was not something I could ever imagine getting used to. 'Yes,' I said finally, which was probably a bit less wordy than he'd been hoping for, but I was still unsure how to vocalise the thoughts running through my head about what had just occurred between us.

'You're very quiet, Rebecca ... you're not going to leave, are you?' he whispered and I almost laughed out loud because the difference between dominant, "stick this in your mouth and like it" Nicholas, and terrified, "please don't leave me" Nicholas was unbelievable. What a frigging contrast!

'No, I'm not leaving.' I raised a hand to stroke along the stubble now darkening his cheek. 'There's no denying I was scared for a little bit,' I admitted softly. 'You were ... so forceful, almost aggressive at times ...' I said weakly, shuddering as I remembered how he had reacted when I'd been sarcastic to him. Ugh, the gag.

Before I could continue, Nicholas sat himself up against the headboard, and then I found myself being dragged into his arms and cradled against his chest as if merely holding me in bed hadn't been enough for him. He proceeded to bury his face in my hair and kiss my scalp over and over again, and for a second I thought he might actually cry.

'I'm so sorry, Becky ... I told you you wouldn't like me like that ... I tried to warn you ...'

'Is that as bad as it gets?' I asked softly, and under my touch, I felt his entire body tighten.

He gave a harsh, dry laugh. 'No.' His voice was no more than a whisper, but spoke volumes. 'That barely touches the surface of how I used to be ...' He grimaced. 'I would be far stricter and the punishments were much more severe. But I didn't want to do that to you ...' Well, that was good to hear at least. 'If you'd been my submissive you would have worn the ball-gag for the whole session after being sarcastic to me, but I could see your fear of it so I removed it. You might not make a champion submissive, but you were so close, baby,' he joked softly as he pulled me even closer against his chest, allowing me the space to wrap my arms around him.

'Yeah, I don't think I'm really cut out to be a full sub, and wearing the gag isn't something I'm keen to repeat ...' I observed, trying to sound light and unruffled. 'Did you use them often?'

'I really don't want to talk about it, Becky – I'm trying so hard to put that behind me ... Things with you are so different. I used to enjoy all that stuff ... but tonight it was harder, so much more difficult ...' He swallowed loudly and I heard it rumble through his chest.

'That's why I said no eye contact,' he admitted softly. 'If you didn't look at me I could pretend it wasn't you I was doing those things to.'

'That makes sense. I had wondered why you'd said that.' Lifting my head, I looked into his eyes now, feeling guilty for making him do something that he had clearly been so uncomfortable doing. 'I'm sorry if I forced you into that ... I didn't realise it would be so hard for you.'

'Becky, these past few weeks ... what we've had together –' He shook his head, clearly bewildered by his feelings. 'I wouldn't be lying if I said I've never felt a connection like this with anyone before. The idea of yelling at you, punishing you ... it just feels wrong,' he murmured, stroking my cheek gently with the pad of his thumb.

As he ran his hand across my face, I noticed the rough scar on his left wrist again and forgot about our discussion for a moment. 'How did you get this?' I asked, smoothing my fingers lightly across the bumpy skin.

A deep frown marred his forehead. 'Childhood accident,' he said, clearly not wanting to discuss it further. 'I don't want to take you in the spare room again,' he stated suddenly, returning to our previous conversation.

'OK. Did you enjoy any of it?' I asked tentatively, guilt eating at my insides until I finally felt him relax beneath me.

'Well, making you come is always a delight, Becky, regardless of the situation,' he murmured, and I could hear the smile in his tone. 'Plus I enjoy using toys for added interest sometimes.'

'Yes, the flogger was quite fun,' I said shyly, surprised by my own admission. 'When you used it for pleasure,' I added.

My arse wasn't looking for a repeat performance any time soon; that was for sure. In fact, it still felt like it was glowing from his earlier treatment even after all the time that had now passed.

Lifting me from his lap Nicholas slid from the bed in all his magnificent nakedness and then bent to place a chaste kiss on the top of my head. 'You must be a little sore, let me sort that out,' he murmured, before disappearing into the en-suite bathroom and then reappearing again almost immediately with a tub in his hand. 'Roll over, Becky,' he said, approaching the bed, but I frowned, wondering what he was planning to do to me now.

'Why?'

'I'm going to make you feel better,' he said with a definite smirk as I noticed that the tub was actually cocoa butter. 'Don't look so worried, I'm just going to use some cream to soothe the skin where I used the flogger.'

Hmm … well, that actually sounded rather nice, so with a shy smile up at him I rolled obediently onto my tummy, exposing my no doubt red arse to him. I heard a rumbled, appreciative noise from his throat. 'I have to say the colour suits you.' he murmured, before I felt his hand press some cool soft lotion onto my heated bottom and begin to rub it in. Once my bum was very thoroughly seen to, and feeling much better, Nicholas climbed back into the bed, scooped my pliant body into his arms and resumed our earlier cuddled position.

'So are you satisfied now you've seen my darker side?' he asked, a strange tone to his voice as he settled me in his lap.

Not entirely, I wanted to tell him. I still wanted to know the story behind his dominant side; I was sure there was some deep-rooted reason that made him act that way, but now I had experienced it, I at least felt I could wait until he was comfortable enough to tell me the rest himself. 'Yes. Thank you for sharing with me. I feel I know you better now, Nicholas.'

Snuggling closer to his warmth, a thought occurred to me. 'I'm curious. Why did you bring me back in here when there is a bed in the other room?'

I saw his eyes darken again. 'Because I associate that room with submissives, and you, Rebecca, are not my submissive,' he said with a wry tweak of his eyebrows.

'What am I, then?' I asked automatically, the words out of my mouth before I could stop them, and I felt his body tense below me.

Damn my stupid runaway mouth, I thought, aware of how rigid he'd gone beneath me. 'Sorry, I didn't mean to ask that … It's OK, I like what we have going … no pressure,' I babbled, rubbing Nicholas' chest and trying to soothe him again.

'I told you earlier I want to see you more often, Rebecca. Now I've shared myself with you, will you stop questioning me and let me try this relationship thing properly?' he asked in exasperation, his tone serious and quiet against my ear.

Surprised, I sat up and looked him in the eyes. 'Is that what you want, a relationship?' I said tentatively, excitement immediately building in my stomach. When Nicholas had suggested seeing more of me, I had assumed he just wanted more sex … but an actual relationship, that was exactly what I craved, but more than I ever thought him capable of.

'It is, yes. If you still do after what you've just been through?' He sounded so unsure that, in response, I leant up, took his face between my palms, and kissed him lingeringly on the lips.

Even after the highly unusual introduction to Nicholas' lifestyle, there wasn't any reason for me to hesitate. 'Very much so,' I murmured against his mouth.

Like a button had been pressed, I felt the tension leave Nicholas' frame on a breath that rushed over my lips. 'I'm warning you now, you will need to be patient; I've not done this type of thing before. I'm pretty sure I'm going to screw up and need you to set me back on track,' he said as he skilfully returned my kiss for several more seconds until I felt his groin stirring below my thigh. God, he was insatiable.

Groaning, Nicholas pulled away with a shy smile that I hadn't seen before but liked immensely. 'It's nearly sunrise and after recent events I think I need to detach you from my lips and let you sleep, otherwise we will both be exhausted later.'

Gently helping me shift off his lap and onto my side, Nicholas snuggled up behind me – distracting erection and all.

As I began to drift off to sleep I decided I felt ridiculously contented for a girl who had just been subjected to her first BDSM sex session. Within a few minutes, I was fast asleep in his arms for the first time.

NINE

Pushing my office chair back so hard that it spun into the wall on its rickety castors, I let out a small yelp of frustration and balled my fists tightly on my thighs. This break-up with Nicholas was getting ridiculous, life consuming almost. I might own the bookshop I sat in, but for me to hide away moping in my office while I thought of nothing but him was just so unprofessional. Not to mention pathetic.

Deciding to be more productive, I vented some anger by ripping open a box containing a new order of books. Usually, this was a task that would keep me thoroughly focused as I scanned each title excitedly and spent a good few hours reading the blurbs, but today I merely unpacked and piled the books to my left, my thoughts still lingering on what could have caused Nicholas to flip so monumentally that fateful, final day.

The act of tearing apart the box was cathartic, cleansing almost, and seeing as there were several more still to open, I set about the mindless task. Soon, my office was full of chunks of cardboard and polystyrene pieces and I found I'd worked up a slight sweat from the exertion.

There had to have been some reason Nicholas had acted like that with the cane that night – something that could explain his completely irrational behaviour? Even with all the kinky stuff we'd done together he'd never hurt me before and I'd been convinced he cared for me ... There simply had to be an explanation, but as hard as I tried, I couldn't think of one, and Nicholas certainly hadn't attempted to contact me to provide one.

Dumping a pile of books onto my desk, I chewed on my lip guiltily. Thinking back, I probably needed to shoulder some of the blame for his outburst that day; I'd deliberately provoked his anger in a way I knew would wind him up. But he'd left me no choice. What else was I supposed to do when he had called me up out of the blue and finished with me for no reason, and all after we'd spent amazing morning in bed together?

God, what a ridiculous mess it all was. I kicked my office door fully closed and allowed my eyes to flutter shut. I recalled the awful day that had seen not only him finishing with me, but also, in a bizarre twist of fate, me walking out on him. I sighed heavily. It had started as such a great day too.

Grinning broadly, I sat up and allowed Nicholas to put the breakfast tray on my lap. Fresh orange juice, toast, jam, and coffee with just the right amount of milk. *Perfect*.

Well, well, would wonders never cease? First of all, his declaration last week that he wanted to try a relationship with me; then I'd experienced seven days of Nicholas on his very best behaviour. I'd seen him almost every night and stayed over at his home, all at his insistence. He'd driven me to and from work and he'd even bought me a beautiful bunch of flowers, which still looked glorious on the kitchen windowsill.

What on earth had happened to "I don't know how to do relationships" Nicholas, because as far as I was concerned he was doing a pretty great job so far.

Plus the sex was still utterly mind-blowing, which helped.

Grabbing a slice of toast, I chomped greedily on it as Nicholas slid back into bed, helping himself to some too and grinning at my impatience. 'Hungry this morning?' he inquired with a sly, knowing smile.

'Yes,' I mumbled around another crumbly bite. 'Dating you is certainly good for my waistline. I think I burn more calories in bed with you in half an hour than I would on a treadmill in a week.' I laughed, spraying crumbs on my lap in a very unattractive manner.

'We are getting rather good at it, aren't we?' He smiled, looking contented and quite pleased with himself. 'Although we have been practising a lot,' he added smugly. Wasn't that the truth! I was actually quite sore by now, but every time Nicholas initiated something, I couldn't seem to say no.

As if reading the naughty direction of my thoughts, he turned to me with a gleam in his eye. 'I bet you the last slice of toast that I now know your body better than you do,' he challenged me with a sly grin.

Copying his smile, I raised my eyebrows. 'And how would we test that theory, Mr Jackson?' I asked tentatively, wondering where on earth he was going with this.

'We see who can make you come the quickest, you or me.'

Wow, I had not expected that. 'Really? You're rather confident, seeing as I've had twenty-five years with this body and quite a bit of practice doing what you're suggesting.'

I blushed at the mention of masturbation; well, it wasn't something you discussed often, was it? However, given my unlucky choices in men up until Nicholas, it was something I'd done a fair amount of since becoming sexually active, because it seemed I could get myself off far better than either of my previous boyfriends ever could. If I hadn't met Nicholas, I'd have gone through life thinking sex was all about clammy hands and unsatisfying, fumbled rubbings.

'I still bet I'll win,' he boasted with a shrug and an arrogant smile that made me want to take him up on his bet and prove him wrong.

As I narrowed my eyes at him, considering his proposal, an idea popped into my head and a broad smile burst onto my lips. 'OK, deal, but only if we try the same thing on you too.'

Now Nicholas was grinning like a kid at Christmas. 'You he you can make me come quicker than my own right hand?' Nicholas chuckled, wiggling the fingers comically. 'You know I'm a kinky bugger with plenty of practice in this area, right?'

'Yep.' I shrugged. 'But I still think I can do it,' I replied with a sweet smile up at him.

'OK, deal.' Nicholas moved the tray off the bed and picked his watch up from the nightstand. 'You go first,' he instructed, with a dark smile.

I scowled, mock disapproval on my face, and made a little tutting sound with my tongue. 'No, that wouldn't be fair. If you watch me, it might get you excited and give you an unfair

133

advantage when it's your turn. I think we should go at the same time.' Not only was this a more logical solution, it would be less embarrassing if Nicholas was doing it at the same time as me.

Laughing, he nodded. 'Fair enough.' He swapped his watch for his phone and set it up on the bed with the stopwatch timer ready, then settled himself back on the pillows next to me.

'Why, Rebecca, I do believe you're blushing,' he teased, looking young and excitable. God, he was sexy when he was like this. Actually, he was sexy all the time. I was such a lost cause I almost rolled my eyes at myself.

'Yes, well, this isn't something I would normally do in public,' I muttered, starting to regret accepting his challenge as the reality of what I had to do in front of him sank in.

'I would hope not.' Nicholas admonished me with a small frown, causing me to raise my eyebrows at him.

'Calm down, Nicholas – believe me, you will be the first person to ever watch me doing this,' I mumbled, suddenly feeling decidedly flustered.

'And the last,' he warned darkly. Gosh, he really was so possessive. This time I really did roll my eyes and he finally smiled. Mind you, from his words it sounded a lot like he was planning for a future together, which was amazing.

'Are you ready?' Lifting his hips, he pulled down his pyjama bottoms, letting his already erect manhood spring free.

'Clearly *you* are,' I murmured dryly, eyeing his sizeable tackle with wide eyes.

'As always, baby.' He grinned. 'OK, ready? Go!' He took hold of himself with his right hand and slowly moved his fist up and down his length. Nervously, I slipped my hand under the sheet and ran it across my already damp sex.

Jeez, just talking sex with Nicholas got me wet. Although I have to say, the sight of him running his fist up and down the silky skin of his erection was a mighty big turn-on for me too.

'That's cheating, Rebecca. Move the sheet; I want to watch,' he instructed huskily. So, blushing further, I pushed the sheet down and exposed my nakedness. Lifting my right hand to my mouth, I moistened two fingers by sucking on them and then dipped them back between my legs. Well, if I was going to do this I might as well do it properly. The effect of my actions wasn't lost on Nicholas, who let out a hissed breath between his teeth as he increased the speed of his hand.

'Christ, you have no idea how jealous I am of your fingers right now,' he groaned, but I giggled, both hugely embarrassed and massively aroused.

Starting to relax into it, I moved my hand rhythmically across my throbbing flesh until I finally dipped two fingers right inside me and increased my pace. Moving my left hand down, I used it to help put pressure against my clitoris and, after a few minutes, I began to feel an orgasm building.

'I'm close,' Nicholas murmured. Gosh, that was quick, I thought, noticing how his eyes were firmly glued to the movements of my hands. Just as I increased my speed in an effort to beat him though, I saw his torso tense, his legs straighten out, and with a low groan, Nicholas came onto his stomach in soft, creamy spurts; a sight that turned me on more than I could ever believe.

Holy shit, that was hot. Spurred on by the vision of Nicholas touching himself to a climax I followed suit seconds later, my muscles clenching around my own fingers as I brought myself to a quiet orgasm., my head pushing back into the pillow as I finished with a soft groan.

'What was the time?' I asked between breaths, as I watched Nicholas cleaning his stomach with several tissues and then fiddling with his phone.

'That would be telling. I've saved the times in my phone so we can check for a winner at the end.' Resetting his phone, he turned to me with a dark smile and a devilish twinkle in his eyes. 'Now for the really fun part. Do you need a break before I prove you wrong and make you climax in record time, Rebecca?'

I definitely needed to recoup before experiencing Nicholas' skilful sexing so I nodded. 'Just let me go and grab a drink of water,' I said, sliding off the bed and swaying my hips provocatively as I walked across the room naked, causing Nicholas to growl behind me.

'If you wiggle that arse at me much more I'll be following you into the kitchen, bending you over the nearest counter, and taking you,' he warned huskily.

'Mr Burrett might see; you wouldn't dare,' I said, glancing back at him as I reached the door.

'Wouldn't I?' Nicholas said in a threatening tone as he slid nimbly from the bed and began stalking toward me, making me giggle and dash away before he could grab me.

Donning a robe in case I met Mr Burrett around the house, I dashed downstairs for my drink, but found the bedroom empty on my return. Losing the robe, I slipped back into bed and waited expectantly. I had a cunning plan up my sleeve that I was fairly sure would win me this bet and I was keen to test it out.

Several seconds later, Nicholas strode into the room with his hands behind his back and a knowing smile on his face.

'Ready for round two, Rebecca?' he asked, a mischievous glint flickering in his eyes.

'Yep. Bring it on.' I grinned nervously.

'Close your eyes,' he instructed as he climbed onto the bed with his hands behind his back, and so with a confused expression I did. 'No peeking, Rebecca, I just have a little surprise for you that might help me win our competition. This will be fun … intense, but fun,' he added cryptically.

I felt a nervous frisson run up my spine. Intense? What was he going to use on me? A vibrator again? I'd enjoyed it last time he'd used one of them on me but surely that would count as cheating in our current competition.

Wasting no time, Nicholas moistened two fingers and moved them straight between my legs where he began expertly rubbing small circles around my already swollen clitoris. Well, this was a competition after all; no point taking it slow, I supposed. Trying to keep my eyes shut, I felt his breath on my chest; the first indication that he was about to suckle at one of my nipples, which he promptly did. After several seconds of his wet tongue working on my hardened tip, I felt a sharp tweak as he nipped at it with his teeth. Ahh, that was good …

The tugging sensation carried on for longer than I had

expected and then, confusingly, he was kissing and suckling my other nipple while I could still feel him biting the first. What the heck?

Deciding that cheating was my only option, I broke his rule and opened my eyes to see him sucking and licking one nipple while a small silver clip had been attached to the other one. Grinning up at me, Nicholas leant back and fastened an identical clip to my other nipple. The ends around my sensitive skin were budded in soft, thin foam and they were attached together with a chain. The pressure from them was similar to a hard suck or gentle bite and, as Nicholas had warned, was incredibly intense, but surprisingly pleasurable.

'Nipple clamps,' he said, a wicked expression on his face, and as he gave the chain a gentle tug, I couldn't help myself arching off the bed and gasping as the pain in my nipples sent pleasure shooting directly to my groin.

Nipple clamps? Wow, that was a first for me, but I have to say they felt a damn sight better than the name suggested. Somehow, by dating Nicholas I'd discovered that pain was indeed close to pleasure if administered in the right ways, which unsurprisingly he always seemed to know how to do.

Giving me no time to adjust to the clamps, he slid first one and then two fingers inside my wet channel and began to circle them seductively in a way that he had learnt excited me very quickly.

'Ahh.' As I moaned my approval, Nicholas tugged gently on the chain, causing wave after wave of pleasure to spike in my nipples and travel directly to my groin like a spear.

'Oh!' I gasped out loud, surprised by the intense pleasure, before surrendering myself to the moment and letting Nicholas' expert hands tease me as he tugged on the chain in time with his fingers at my groin. He brought me to possibly the purest, most intense orgasm of my life, and I cried out his name and clutched at the sheets as pulse after pulse spiralled through me, clamping around his fingers as if I would never let him go.

Unfortunately, given our current bet, it was also probably one of the quickest orgasms of my life too – damn him and his sexual trickery.

'That wasn't fair, you cheated!' I panted, my insides continuing to convulse spasmodically around his fingers, which were still lazily moving inside me.

'I did,' he agreed with a nod, 'but so did you. I saw you looking when I said no peeking. You're lucky I'm not punishing you for breaking my rule,' he said generously, but the wicked glint in his eye told me that he was only joking this time.

After a few moments of recovery I sat up, excited that I would be able to try my trick next and see if I could win the bet. Not that I particularly wanted the slice of toast, you understand, more because I really wanted to beat Nicholas at this. After all, this was his area of expertise and to do better than him would be a monumental victory for me.

'Right then, Rebecca, you think your hand can beat mine, go for it,' Nicholas challenged, propping himself into a half sitting position and grinning from ear to ear. Predictably, after having his fun with me, he was already aroused so I knelt between his legs and tentatively wrapped my hand around his solid length. I loved the feel of him in my hands. It still amazed me how he could be so hard and hot and yet so silky to touch.

'Ahhh,' he groaned, his eyes blazing and focused intently on my face. 'God, I love it when you touch me, Rebecca.' Hopefully he'd love what I was going to do next even more, then.

Instinctively, I moistened my lips with my tongue and then, before he could realise what I was doing, I bent over him and twirled my tongue around the tip of his penis, tasting his salty, manly essence, and loving it.

'Fuck!' he cried between clenched teeth as his hips bucked under me. 'What are you doing?'

I looked up at him with an innocent smile, my tongue still on the tip of his cock. 'I would have thought that was obvious, Nicholas,' I said sweetly before dipping my head and taking him in my mouth, sucking gently as I pulled him as far toward the back of my throat as I could manage.

This was something we hadn't done together yet; in fact, I'd never given a blowjob before in my life, just hand jobs, and

138

even then quite a long time ago and not particularly enthusiastically. But for some reason, with Nicholas I wanted to do this. I wanted him in my mouth.

Maybe it was the feeling of power that having him in my hand and mouth gave me, or maybe it was a bit of his kinky side rubbing off on me, but I found myself looking up and pausing briefly to speak. 'I'm going to suck on you until you come in my mouth, Nicholas,' I promised in a tone similar to the dark, sensual one he used on me so frequently.

'Holy hell, Rebecca,' Nicholas groaned, gripping the sheets in white-knuckled fists, seemingly unable to take his wide eyes off me but clearly starting to lose control. Ha, my plan was working! Rhythmically bobbing my head up and down his shaft at the same time as my fist, I took him as deep into my mouth as I could, occasionally swirling my tongue around his tip and increasing the rhythm until I felt his stomach and balls tighten below me. He was close, very close; time to make good on my promise, then. I'd never let a man come in my mouth before, but with Nicholas there seemed to be lot of firsts happening recently.

His fingers left the sheet and splayed through my hair as I sucked harder and brought him to a violent climax, sending salty fluid spurting into my mouth and causing his body to convulse below me. The taste wasn't wholly unpleasant, but I swallowed to clear my mouth, then gazed up at him with innocent eyes as I provocatively licked the tip of him clean, causing him to throw his head back into the pillows and moan loudly.

'Fuck, Rebecca, that was incredible,' he gasped. 'I *do not* want to know where you learnt how to do that,' he stated, a low, protective tone entering his voice as a predatory look settled on his face.

Almost laughing at how jealous he could be, I crawled up his body and laid myself on his heaving body, my hand trailing though the soft covering of hair on his chest. 'Actually, that's the first time I've ever done that,' I whispered, embarrassed by my probable lack of skill.

Lifting his head off the bed, Nicholas grasped my shoulder

to tilt me back so he could look down at me with a disbelieving expression on his face. 'You've never done that before? Seriously?'

Shaking my head, I blushed. 'Nope. Never wanted to … but things are different with you … I like pleasing you.' God I sounded like such a sap, but crazily it was true. Beside me, Nicholas groaned and buried his head in my hair, kissing me hard on the temple.

'You seemed to like the way I licked the vibrator that time, so I just tried the same stuff on you,' I explained shyly, giving a small shrug. He pulled me protectively against him, apparently rather pleased to be the recipient of my first blowjob.

'Apart from the fact that I really enjoyed that, I think it probably counts as cheating with regards to our bet, Rebecca.' He chuckled, tucking his head against my hair. 'If I wasn't completely exhausted after two orgasms in ten minutes I'd definitely have to punish you. First opening your eyes when I told you not to and now this …' he mused, still gasping for air. Oh God, there was the P-word again. I tensed within his embrace. 'But as you did such a good job, I'll let you off.'

Relaxing back into him, I kissed his chest. 'I think it was a draw,' I murmured.

'Yeah … so in conclusion we're both damn good at pleasing each other,' he murmured contentedly, shortly before I heard a low snore escape from his throat.

TEN

Things went from amazingly, stunningly great to downright awful after that.

First, there were my disturbing discoveries as I'd helped Mr Burrett with some tasks around the house. Nicholas had been busy preparing for a concert that night, so I'd been at a bit of a loose end reading a book when Mr Burrett had wandered past the lounge with a Hoover. He'd been rather embarrassed by my offer to take over the vacuuming from him, but the poor man seemed to multi-task so often that I felt it was the least I could do while I was staying here so frequently.

Starting upstairs with the hall and main bedroom, I then worked my way along the corridor and into the music room before finishing with the spare room. Once I was finished, I had plopped onto the bed and wiped the sheen of sweat from my brow while looking around the space again. It looked like a completely normal bedroom in the light of day, except for the chains discretely attached to the bed post. As promised, Nicholas hadn't brought me in here again, but stupidly, as I thought back to our night in here with the flogger I let my eyes wander to the large cupboard in the corner. Seeing the door open, my ever curious mind began to wonder what else Nicholas had in there alongside the vibrators and things we'd used together.

I should never have bothered looking because after discovering an entire rack of bizarre that looked more like torture devices than anything pleasurable, I actually felt quite sick. Quite evidently, Nicholas hadn't been kidding when he said he was different with me because there was so much stuff in there that we'd never used together. Most of it pretty horrific looking, and it made me feel ill to imagine him in his full-on dominant mode using it with other women.

As well as the unrecognisable stuff, there were things I did know – floggers of different materials and sizes, paddles, handcuffs, the ball-gag he'd used on me, plus a much larger one that looked like it would stop you breathing through your mouth. Not to mention a wall with makeshift pegs containing more "toys", although these hadn't looked fun at all – a crop that up until now I had only associated with horse riding and a whip like that belonging to Indiana Jones – I kid you not – had hung there innocently.

Alongside them was a cane like the ones that used to be used in schools. At the time, I'd grimaced at the sight, but thinking back now I realise it must have been the very cane Nicholas would use on me later that day.

My curiosity had certainly been satisfied by my exploration, but part of me had wished I hadn't seen the other stuff in Nicholas' cupboard; it merely left a particularly bad taste in my mouth as I wondered what types of things he had done to other women in the past, and whether I was truly satisfying all the urges he clearly had.

Attempting to be mature, I had tried to forget what I'd seen – he'd told me he'd moved on from that life, and besides, it was none of my business what he'd done with other women. Then, after stowing the Hoover away, I had wandered to Nicholas' piano room for a bit of solitude. Sitting for a while at his piano, gazing out at the garden below, I had eventually calmed myself. I remember how I had told myself that the stuff in that room didn't matter. Nicholas had told me he was changed, was different with me, so that was all in his past.

Little did I know that it obviously wasn't *all* in his past and that I'd be on the receiving end of the cane before the night was out.

Unfortunately, the day had continued on its downward path, because shortly after leaving the piano room I had decided to head upstairs to Nicholas' study to see his handsome face and cheer myself up. Halfway up the stairs, however, I could hear him speaking, and paused. After listening for a second it became apparent that he was on the phone, so I had tiptoed up the final few stairs not wanting to disturb him.

'She's not your submissive? Are you mad?'

I heard a voice, not Nicholas', and his words made my blood freeze. Had I been mistaken about him being on the phone? Was someone in there with him? And was it *me* they were discussing?

'This is none of your business, Nathan. Rebecca's different, she accepts me. I'm trying to be normal for a change.' Nicholas sounded very pissed off and his mention of my name brought me to a standstill as I froze outside the door, knowing I shouldn't listen in, but finding myself unable to move away.

Nathan. I ran the name through my mind before remembering that he was Nicholas' older brother. He'd mentioned Nathan before now, but so far, I'd never met him. Hearing how disdainful he sounded I was actually rather glad that was the case.

'We're not capable of that type of relationship, Nicholas; it will never work. It's not how we were brought up.' From the light crackle around Nathan's words I realised he was on speakerphone with his brother, and from his use of the word "submissive" he was familiar with Nicholas' lifestyle, possibly even having the same inclination himself.

'Well, maybe we were brought up wrong.' I could just tell from Nicholas' snarling tone that he would be frowning his deepest, scariest grimace, the one that used to make me feel a little frightened of him when we first met. 'Our family life wasn't exactly normal, was it, Nathan? I know you can't see it but Dad was seriously fucked up.' Nicholas sounded mad; I could sense his tension and his words gave me a hint at a history that might explain why he was the way he was. Clearly, it had something to do with his father.

'I don't want to talk about Dad, Nicholas, but he was our father, our role model. Part of him is inside us both, brother. Deep down you know it.' What the heck did that mean? Frowning I leant back on the bannister and began to fiddle with my hair nervously.

There was a tense silence where neither brother spoke and

then, with a sigh, Nicholas bade his brother good afternoon and hung up.

Confused and shocked by what I'd overheard, I quietly made my way back down the stairs and sat in the lounge while I tried to digest it all. I didn't want Nicholas to know I'd been eavesdropping; I shouldn't have listened in and he'd have every right to get angry with me if he knew, but it was so confusing. Their father had clearly done something to make them both dislike him. Was he a criminal, perhaps? It occurred to me that Nicholas had never mentioned his parents before; maybe I'd bring them up in conversation and watch his reaction.

Nathan's tone and words had left no doubt about his feelings toward me dating his brother, though, but I was fairly pleased about Nicholas' reaction. He'd defended me to Nathan, so maybe he really was making progress. One thing was sure: I wasn't keen to meet his brother any time soon.

ELEVEN

The books were ready to distribute around the shop but I was trying to delay the moment when I'd have to go out onto the shop floor for just a little bit longer. The bright lights were not going to be very sympathetic to my tear-stained, heavily bagged eyes, that was for sure. Louise had been lovely since my split from Nicholas, but her never-ending sympathy was wearing me down and couldn't help making me want to cry even more. Thinking of crying made me remember the evening when everything had ended. God, I'd cried enough tears that night to fill an Olympic-sized swimming pool.

Nicholas was getting seriously stressed as he tried to prepare for that night's concert and as a result I'd barely seen him all day, which was probably just as well really, because after my discovery of his bizarre sex toys and then overhearing the unpleasant phone call with Nathan I was liable to say something I might have regretted later.

Another thing that was irking me was that he hadn't asked me to attend the concert with him, which I had found a little hurtful at first. We'd been together 'properly' for a while now, so I'd naturally thought that we might progress to public outings soon. But seeing as the media seemed to surround him like flies because of his introvert behaviour and lack of a girlfriend, I suppose deep down I understood that things between us were too new to flaunt in public just yet.

The morning had left me with an uneasy feeling in my stomach that suddenly made me crave my own space for a while, so I decided to head back to my flat for the first night in ages. I wished Nicholas good luck for the evening, although he seemed too distracted to notice, and then gratefully accepted Mr Burrett's offer of a lift home.

Walking through the door to my flat was like entering an uninhabited apartment. It smelt a bit stale and felt too cold and empty so I cranked up the heating and lit a few nicely scented candles to try and re-adjust the place again. It was strange how quickly I'd adjusted to living with Nicholas nearby; I'd always been so independent that I'd never envisioned myself being so comfortable sharing someone else's personal space.

I made the best of my quiet time by treating myself to a glass of wine and working my way through a pile of post – which predictably was mostly bills and junk mail – before settling down in front of the television to catch up on a few of my favourite shows.

After watching several excellent episodes of *CSI: Miami*, I headed to bed at around 11.30, wondering how Nicholas had got on in his concert tonight. He'd seemed so out of sorts beforehand, nervy and twitchy, which had been very disconcerting for me, as he was always so calm and in control of everything. It had been strange to see him so jittery, and I'd been surprised by just how nervous he had appeared.

Lying in the soothing darkness of my bedroom with thoughts of Nicholas still in my mind, I couldn't help grinning to myself when my phone rang and I saw his name flash up on the screen. Rolling over in my warm duvet I pushed my hair out of my face as I reached for the phone. Perhaps he's missing me just as much as I'm missing him and is calling to say goodnight, I thought with a satisfied smile as I popped the phone open.

'Hi, how did it go tonight?' I asked, flopping back down and stretching, then sinking, into my pillows, wishing he was here with me now.

'Fine. Good. Full house, actually,' he replied stiffly, definitely sounding odd. His tone caused a cool chill to run across my skin as a strange sensation had started to stir in my belly. Sitting up, I frowned. Something was wrong.

'Nicholas, what's the matter?' I asked in a hushed tone, biting my lip as I waited for his response while desperately wishing I could see his face to judge his reaction.

I heard a long, heavy sigh from the other end of the line, and my stomach clenched further. 'Rebecca, I don't think we should see each other any more,' he stated calmly, but my blood froze in my veins as I processed the unthinkable meaning of his words.

The darkness that just minutes ago had been calming suddenly turned oppressive, making me feel like I was suffocating. Scrabbling from my bed, I managed to flick on my bedside lamp and suck in a breath, but still my throat closed up as if I was being strangled by some invisible force.

This didn't make any sense to me. *He* was the one wanting to try a relationship just last week, *he* was the one making great statements about how different he was with me around, and *he* was the one initiating fun little sex games just this morning … Everything had been going so well, and now this? Dumped out of nowhere. I truly was at a loss for what to say.

'*What*?' I finally managed to whisper.

Nicholas didn't pause like I had though, in fact his reply was crisp, clear and almost immediate. 'I don't want to see you again. I'll send you the number for another piano tutor if you need one. Goodbye, Rebecca.' The line went dead and then, to my utter astonishment, he was gone. Just like that.

As fast as he'd entered my life, Nicholas Jackson had left it.

TWELVE

The tea Louise had brought me earlier was stone cold now but I downed it anyway as a distraction to the horrible images now churning in my mind. What happened that night after Nicholas had finished with me was the one part of the whole horrible mess that I kept reliving not only in my waking hours, but in my dreams too. And it wasn't a pleasant thing to dwell on, let me tell you.

It was only after I banged on the door that I realised I was still in the tracksuit bottoms and scruffy pyjama shirt I'd gone to bed in. *Bugger*. Oh well, I was practically in meltdown mode so I decided I could wear what I liked – besides, there was no time to go home and change now. Impatiently, I began to ring the doorbell too before I stood back and stiffened my shoulders in preparation for a confrontation. Nicholas was going to be freaking furious with me; I just knew it.

But I didn't care. In fact, if he looked furious then I'd know that my instincts were right – he did care for me, and his break-up phone call had been a load of rubbish brought about by goodness knows what.

Initially, after Nicholas' call, I had sat in shock hugging my pillow, then I had cried briefly, then I tried to make sense of his sudden actions and kept coming back to one thing – his tense phone call with his brother earlier that day, where Nathan had basically told Nicholas he shouldn't date me. After how well things had been going between us it was the only logical explanation I could think of, and right now, I was clinging to it and hoping I could change his mind about us.

The noise of a bolt being unfastened behind the front door

alerted me to someone's presence and I felt my body tense, then seconds later it was swung open by Mr Burrett. He looked immaculate, as always, but an uncharacteristic frown marred his brow and his usually jovial lips were pulled into a tight line. Behind him, pushing past the older man, was Nicholas, still dressed in his concert shirt and trousers and looking at me with wild, dark eyes.

'Rebecca?' He looked shocked momentarily and then scowled. 'How did you get here at this time of night?'

'I got a cab,' I replied blandly, noticing how Mr Burrett tactfully disappeared when he heard the tension in our voices.

Rather satisfyingly, Nicholas' eyes almost popped from his skull. '*What*?' he screeched. 'You got in a car with a complete stranger at –' he looked furiously at his watch '– 12.40 in the morning? What the fuck were you thinking?' he demanded, glowering at me.

Ah good. Knowing Nicholas rather well, I had been practising an answer to this exact question in the taxi on the way over here.

'I was thinking, *Nicholas*,' I replied dryly, tipping my chin up to point at him, 'that being dumped didn't make sense seeing as we had an amazing morning in bed together when everything seemed fine.' I rested my hand jauntily on my hip before continuing. 'And I was *thinking* that it was strange how my boyfriend dumped me just hours after a phone call from his brother telling him not to date me.' I was yelling now, probably loud enough to wake his neighbours, but I didn't care. I needed to get this out of my system even if he still wanted me to leave afterwards.

'You heard my call with Nathan?' Nicholas asked suddenly, seeming confused.

'Yes, Nicholas, I did.' I sighed. 'Look, if you want to end things because you don't want to be with me any more then I'll deal with it, but if you finished with me because your brother told you to then I think it's only fair that I get to say my piece too.'

A brief flash of sadness crossed his eyes before he rolled his head back to stare at the night sky. When he lowered his gaze a second or two later, the sadness was gone, replaced instead with, flourishing anger. 'You deserve better than me. I'm broken; a relationship with me would never work in the long run. Like I said on the phone, I don't want to see you any more.' His eyes were wide and blazing, his body full of tension and fidgety as he repeatedly moved on the spot.

Trying to swallow the hard lump in my throat that had risen from his last seven words, I continued. 'So you're sticking with your decision?' I asked in a ghost of a whisper.

'Yes,' Nicholas replied bluntly, lowering his eyes from mine in uncharacteristic fashion.

Shit. I'd thought that seeing me might change his mind, but it hadn't. I'd officially been dumped and now snubbed. How humiliating.

But something in his twitchy demeanour nagged at me and I didn't think he was quite as set on his decision as he was making out. There was only one way to find out for sure and that was to target his one weak area – his jealousy.

'Fine. So you're OK with me dating other people, then?' I asked innocently, which immediately caused Nicholas' gaze to flash back to mine.

There was a pause in which we both glared at each other, his blue gaze hammering into mine as I stubbornly refused to look away, even when my eyes began to glass over with approaching tears. 'Yes,' he said, but his thick tone said the exact opposite to his words. Building on his reaction, I then realised how I could really rile him.

'Although I might not date anyone, maybe I'll just fuck some different guys for a while, get some more experience,' I said as casually as possible, rather proud that I hadn't flinched when I'd sworn. It was a pretty low move on my part, but what else could I do?

That was it; they were the words I'd needed to say. Jealousy, pure and furious, rose in Nicholas' face as his eyes widened and his nostrils flared. 'No!' he growled, stepping toward me menacingly. '*Only me*,' he muttered, but the tone of his voice changed as he reached out, dropping his hand back to his side without touching me.

It seemed that Nicholas was struggling with an internal battle, the need to possess me, and his belief that I deserved better than him.

'You should not be with me,' he rumbled angrily, hesitating just a foot in front of me. 'I'm no good.'

'Nicholas, you are!' I assured him firmly. 'You showed me your so-called dark side and I survived, didn't I? I don't care about it, I want to be with you,' I finished weakly, realising just how desperate I sounded and hating it.

God, was this what I'd put my last two boyfriends through when I'd finished with them, I wondered, thinking back to how I had thought they were being quite pathetic and needy at the time and feeling guilty for the cool brush-offs I'd given them.

'You don't know what's really inside me, *you should not be with me*,' Nicholas snarled, spinning away from me and stalking into his hallway, pushing the door closed behind him in an attempt at ending our conversation.

Unperturbed, I dived forward and caught the front door before it could shut. I followed him in, closing it behind me, and stood with my hands on my hips. 'Nicholas, we can do this, you can do *us*, you were doing so well,' I pleaded with him.

'You want to be with me?' he demanded, spinning on the spot, his eyes glaring at me fiercely as he ran a hand through his already dishevelled hair.

'Yes! Unless you want me to go off fucking other guys?' I taunted in desperation.

Knowing how exceedingly jealous he could get, I really shouldn't have made that final comment because the next second, Nicholas was facing me full on, the muscles in his neck bulging, his eyes dark and incensed as he looked like he might literally explode on the spot. I could feel the stress and tension crackling in the air around us and it made the hairs on my arms stand up.

Suddenly a noise similar to a growl resonated from Nicholas' chest before he dived forwards and roughly scooped me off my feet, tossed me over his shoulder, charged up the stairs, and turned toward the spare bedroom.

Shit. I'd made him ridiculously mad and now he was taking

me back to the room where he used to punish his submissives – the room he'd said he never wanted to take me to again. That really couldn't be a good sign.

Kicking the door open he strode into the space and threw me roughly onto the bed. I had barely landed on my stomach before Nicholas' fingers gripped the back of my shirt and ripped it clean off, sending buttons flying everywhere as the fabric was dragged up my arms and thrown to the ground. Before I could recover or get my bearings properly he had grabbed my hands and was tying them with a scarf attached to the bedposts, before disappearing into the walk-in cupboard.

'Nicholas ...' I started breathlessly. 'We need to talk ...' As much as I usually enjoyed having sex with him, this wasn't the answer at the moment. He'd dumped me, for God's sake. I needed to understand why, not get fucked into silence.

'Shhh,' he murmured surprisingly softly, returning to the room as I squirmed on the bed trying to free myself. Nicholas disappeared behind me out of my line of sight, and the next second I felt his hands on my waist. My tracksuit bottoms didn't fare much better than my shirt, because with a rough tug that had me collapsing forward onto my elbows he had pulled them off and thrown them on the floor. The next second, Nicholas had dispensed with my knickers by digging his fingers through the lace and ripping them clean from my body, causing me to yelp with fast-rising fear.

Shit, he might be talking softly now, but his barely controlled actions showed that he was really fucking mad.

'You want to see what's inside me, Rebecca? You want to know the real me?' he demanded, his voice low and menacing beside me.

'Yes!' Knowing how much Nicholas needed my confirmation I yelled my declaration, but no sooner was the word out of my mouth than something slapped across my exposed behind with so much force that I couldn't help but shout from the shock. My eyes nearly popped from my head when I looked to Nicholas and saw the long, thin cane held in his white-knuckled fist.

Holy fuck, he was beating me with a frigging cane. Before I

could consider this prospect in too much detail, I watched him raise it again and closed my eyes as it slapped down on me for the second time.

Fuck, that really hurt. There was no way that could be deemed as pleasurable by anyone, or *ever* be seen as acceptable in a consensual relationship.

Bizarrely, in the stew of emotions flowing around my brain, the thing that made me realise Nicholas had completely lost it was his groin, as odd as that sounds. For some reason as my face was craned to the side, squashed into the mattress, I registered the fact that Nicholas didn't have an erection – and this flooded me with panic. As kinky as it was, I had adjusted to the fact that a little bit of control or light punishment turned Nicholas on – it was just one of his things, I supposed – but right now he wasn't aroused and the blows were getting harder which meant he had lost control and was simply fucking furious.

'You want to be with me?' he roared, his voice strangled and unrecognisable; but I didn't attempt to answer this time. This wasn't my Nicholas, clearly he was not with it any more. 'You want to be with *this*?' he screeched. Any control he'd had was now gone and the cane snapped down on my behind over and over again with each thrash seeming harder than the one before.

There was no way I could stand much more of this. I was fairly sure I was bleeding now; the pain was excruciating, and as hard as I tried to get my wrists out of the scarf restraints, I was pushed too far down the bed to manage it. I had thought that Nicholas had just needed to vent his frustration, but the cane was so much worse than the flogger had been and before I knew it, tears were flowing down my cheeks into the mattress as I sobbed silently.

'Stop!' I wailed, but panic rose in my throat as Nicholas continued with his barrage. 'Nicholas, stop! Please!' I choked out, but suddenly something clicked in my brain and I remembered his rule about stopping in this room.

'Bubble,' I wept. '*Bubble! Stop ... stop*,' Nicholas flinched, but my words had been muffled by the mattress; perhaps they were too soft for him to hear the safeword? Then he moved to raise the cane again and terror began to overwhelm me.

Desperately, I pushed forward, leaning all my weight onto my elbows and twisted myself enough to raise my left leg. With all the volume I could muster I screamed the safeword again, making sure he heard it this time while also planting my foot into his stomach as hard as I could to stop his next approach.

Thank God, it worked this time. It was like I had flicked a switch inside Nicholas, and through my tear-blurred eyes I saw him stagger backwards, a look of absolute horror on his face as he frowned at the cane in his hand and then took in my position on the bed like he was waking up from some kind of trance.

I immediately shuffled myself up the bed, ripping at the scarf and managing to free one of my wrists. Nicholas leapt forward, swearing profusely as he tried to help me with the other wrist, but I completely lost it, adrenaline and anger coursed through me, replacing my fear and filling me with pulsating rage. Freeing my other arm, I pushed myself upright and slapped him across the face as hard as I could, which even in my current state I noticed made a satisfyingly loud crack against the soft skin of his cheek.

'Don't touch me!' I half yelled and half sobbed as Nicholas knelt wide-eyed on the bed in front of me. 'You are seriously fucked up! I actually thought you felt something for me, how fucking stupid am I?' I screeched manically, then in my anger, I shoved him in the chest so violently he fell backwards, slipping off the bed and landing in a heap on the floor with a resounding crash. 'You need to get professional help for this crap, Nicholas,' I snarled, tossing the cane at him with a grimace.

Leaping up, I dragged my tracksuit bottoms on over my smarting behind, not even bothering to try and find my ripped underwear. Then, forcing my arms into my button-less shirt, I ran a shaking hand over my face to try and clear my tears before heading for the door.

Glancing back, I saw Nicholas was still sprawled on the floor, frozen in place, one hand raised to his reddened cheek as he looked at me with disorientated panic rising in his eyes. He seemed to have no clue as to what had just happened.

'You wanted to break up with me, Nicholas? *Fine*, I'm gone, and don't worry, I won't be back. Don't try and contact me,' I snarled through my tears before walking out and slamming the door behind me so hard I was surprised it didn't fall off its hinges.

THIRTEEN

That had been that, really. Single again. No more Nicholas.

Once again, I amazed myself how I could cram the entire events of a three-month relationship into a few hours of daydreaming, but I had and here I was three weeks later, still dazed, still miserable, and still left wondering what the hell had happened that night.

I'd taken two days off work immediately after the cane incident, mostly because my face was too puffy from near-constant crying to dare show in public, but also because I couldn't walk comfortably with my bruised and welted behind and didn't want Louise asking questions and forcing me to lie to her.

Now, life had resumed, on some levels at least, and I was back at work. I might have been active again, but the pain of being without Nicholas seemed worse somehow and the bruises on my behind had paled into insignificance compared to my breaking heart. I hated feeling this pathetic over a man, but in short, I felt wretched. I'd finished with people and been dumped in the past, but always at a time when I was convinced the relationship was going nowhere. With Nicholas, even though our relationship was far from easy, I had felt a genuine attachment to him. He might have had a seriously messed-up view of things, but even with his issues, I had actually thought that for the first time in my life I might be falling for a man properly.

Letting out an aggravated grunt, I leapt to my feet decisively. This really had to stop; the shop was doing fine under Louise's leadership, but I needed to get a grip and move on with my life. Sighing heavily, I decided I couldn't hide in the back office for any longer. Piling the last book onto the stack in front of me, I pulled them to my chest to distribute around the shelves.

Heading down the narrow corridor back to the shop floor, I shook my head. How could I have been so stupid? In hindsight, Nicholas had probably always been out of my reach – too successful and handsome for a start, and then far too damaged for me to ever claim his heart. What a pathetic case I was, moping over a man who had treated my arse so badly that I'd had trouble sitting down for days.

Well, *no more*. As of today I would move on, I decided firmly.

'No, I'm afraid you can't see her. Rebecca might be my manager but I'm her friend too. She's been an absolute mess since you dumped her. She's barely stopped crying for three whole weeks; I'm not going to let you upset her again.' Louise said, stepping out from behind the book display she was setting up and folding her arms boldly across her chest.

'I don't know what she's told you, but it was Rebecca who finished with me in the end,' Nicholas explained quietly, a frown creasing the soft skin between his eyebrows and causing Louise to look up in surprise.

'Really? Well, why's she been so upset then?' Louise muttered, more to herself than Nicholas.

At that moment, the focus of their conversation – me – walked out into the store. Talk about dreadful timing. I'd been hidden away in my back office for the best part of three weeks, but the exact moment I decided to make a reappearance, so did frigging Nicholas Jackson. Fate really sucked sometimes.

As my eyes fell on Nicholas standing in the middle of my shop, I promptly dropped the stack of books I was holding, sending them cascading around my feet like a cardboard and paper puddle.

The breath stilled in my lungs, my body somehow feeling both flushed and shivery at the same time as I simply stared at him, totally unable to move. How could I still be so affected by him after three weeks apart?

It was a slight reassurance to me that he looked as awful as I felt, with his skin pale and grey, eyes dull, and posture deflated. God, even looking as terrible as he did, Nicholas was still so handsome. How unfair was that? I looked like crap warmed up and he still looked great. Bloody bastard.

Seeing him again brought it home to me that even with all his monumental fucked-up-ness I loved him, loved him so much, *so deeply*, and it took all my willpower to remember why I'd left him and not run straight into his arms for the comfort I so desperately craved.

This blinding realisation of love very nearly brought me to my knees in the middle of the shop floor as my world seemed to tilt and rock around me.

Fuck. I was in love with Nicholas Jackson.

Blinking rapidly, I tried to compose myself, but to no avail. I ran the thought through my mind again. I was in love with Nicholas Jackson … and he was standing ten feet away from me, staring at me like I was the last woman left on earth.

How had I not realised this sooner, I wondered. More importantly, how could I have allowed myself to love him? After everything I knew, everything he'd done. Oh God, I'd never been in love before but as I felt my throat closing up and heart aching painfully in my chest I knew once and for all that I was now. My breath was coming in short, hyperventilated drags by this point but still I couldn't seem to move my frozen body.

Nicholas straightened his posture and I saw some of his characteristic confidence return as he skilfully sidestepped Louise, who was attempting to block his path and looking rather unsure about what to do. Then he strode to my side and ducked down to gather the books from around my feet while I tried to steady my spinning head.

Shit, shit, shit. I was so not ready for this.

Placing the recovered books on a table, Nicholas stood up just two feet away from me. If I raised a hand I'd be able to touch him, but I didn't. Instead I clenched my fists, closed my eyes, and drew in a long, steady breath. I could smell his scent, spicy and fresh, and my eyes snapped open again, noticing now that his hair looked a little damp. He must have showered recently.

Closing my eyes again, I clenched my jaw so hard that my teeth hurt. Thinking about Nicholas naked in the shower was *not* going to help me get through this encounter. Forcing myself to shut off my nose, I tried to breathe through my mouth instead so I could avoid his alluring smell and visions of his glorious body all soapy, wet, and naked.

'Rebecca,' Nicholas murmured almost reverently, causing a shiver to run down my spine and my arms to wrap around myself defensively. Three weeks without that voice and yet still I found that I had goose pimples across both my arms.

Breathe. Breathe, I reminded myself as the urge to vomit registered in my brain. Oh God, I wasn't sure I could do this. I wanted so much to fall into his arms, or run away shrieking, but I couldn't for the life of me decide which.

This must be what going into shock feels like, I thought. Serious post-traumatic shock. A brief dizzy spell overwhelmed me for a second or two and then, snapping back to focus, I realised that I was still stood in the bookshop with Louise and Nicholas staring at me expectantly, waiting for me to say or do something. Assuming I couldn't get away with screaming and running for the hills, I instead managed to coax my forehead into a scowl. Not intentionally, really, it was just the easiest facial expression to muster up at the current time, but upon seeing my firm look, Louise scuttled off to busy herself and give me some privacy. Unfortunately, my expression didn't have the same impact on Nicholas and he held his ground in front of me, causing me to sigh heavily.

'Nicholas … what are you doing here?' I managed to whisper, rather proud that I hadn't thrown up on him, or burst into tears and fled to the sanctuary of the staff room the second I'd seen him. Especially seeing as I had spent the last several hours recalling every detail of our time together.

How had it all come down to this? Awkward, stiff exchanges out on the shop floor. Less than a month ago, we'd been sharing dinners and exploring each other's body, and now we were like feuding parties in a conflict.

Oh yes, that's right, I remember now, I thought sourly; he'd beaten the hell out of my arse with a cane. I still had some lingering bruises to remind me every time I sat down.

'Let me talk with you, Rebecca,' Nicholas insisted in his familiar soft but demanding way. Seeing the raise of my eyebrow, he frowned. '*Please,*' he added, his tone gentler, desperate even. 'I won't touch you, I promise. We can go somewhere public if you'd feel more comfortable; get a coffee, maybe? Or a drink? There's a bar across the road.'

Chewing on my lip, I considered his offer. We did need to talk, even if just to finalise things between us. Besides, I still had belongings left at his house that I needed to collect. Sighing heavily I made my decision. Seeing as it was a quiet afternoon, I would get this over with now; I'd already coped with seeing him again, so rather than drag it any longer I might as well get it all finalised. After speaking briefly with Louise and then, handing her the shop keys, I silently exited the shop and walked stiffly across the road to an Irish pub with Nicholas by my side, but just out of reach as he had promised.

'Would you like a drink? Medium white wine?' he murmured, remembering my drink of choice, a simple gesture that made me grit my teeth with longing for him.

Words didn't seem to be forming in my mouth properly so I answered silently with a tight nod. I was going to need a drink to get me through this. Possibly several, I thought with a grimace, only just resisting the temptation to ask him to get me an entire bottle.

Once we were seated in a quiet booth, me with my wine and him with a Coke, he looked at me for a long while as if reacquainting himself with my face. He looked ... well, *sad.* As poor as that description was, it was true; soul-deep sadness seemed to radiate from him. That and the look of virtual devotion that I saw in his eyes very nearly broke me straight away.

'How are you, Rebecca?' he asked huskily.

Did he seriously just ask me that? Sighing heavily, I sat back in my seat and crossed my arms. 'Are you really going to start with that, Nicholas?' I asked, wearily rubbing a hand across my tight face. 'Seeing as we both look like shit I don't think it's really worth discussing, is it?' I lowered my tired eyes and almost dared him to chastise me for it.

After a long pause, I took a shaky sip of my drink and then finally raised my face again, only to find his gaze was wide and intense and focused solely on me. 'You were right ... that day when you overheard me on the phone, Nathan told me I wasn't capable of a relationship so I finished with you,' Nicholas admitted quietly.

'Why did you listen to him? You're a grown man, Nicholas,' I said, amazed he appeared to be about to open up to me. Why couldn't he just have done this three weeks ago instead of grabbing a frigging cane?

Shrugging at me, he then looked at his Coke – a gesture I knew meant he felt uncomfortable because he had always been the one to push for eye contact. 'He saved me,' he said simply, whatever the hell that meant. 'He always saves me.'

In our weeks apart, I might have stewed in a good deal of self-pity, but I had at least decided that I was too strong a person to stay with a man who beat me; that much I knew.

But why couldn't I just hate him? To be able to sit here and physically hate this man with every fibre of my being would have made this so much easier and surely should be the logical emotion in a situation like this? The fact that I now knew I loved Nicholas, *was in love with him,* was overwhelming to me and, quite frankly, I was really struggling to not break down and completely freak out in the middle of the pub.

The fact remained that the cane had been a one off incident. Even when showing me his dominant side Nicholas had never hurt me before that night, which might go some way to explaining why I was having such trouble hating him. He wasn't serially violent; if that were the case I could easily walk away, but if anything, he'd been the complete opposite in our time together. Perhaps if he'd explain to me why he'd done it, *the cane*; what things in his past had created those dark feelings and urges and his sudden uncharacteristic outburst ... then maybe I'd be able to understand and, *maybe*, consider a future with him. But as it was, I couldn't. No, *I wouldn't.*

'I'm not going to ask you to choose between your brother

and me, Nicholas. It wouldn't be fair; clearly he's very important to you,' I stated bitterly. 'I need to leave.' I stood to go, leaving my wine hardly touched. The chemistry between us was still so strong I was struggling to concentrate. The tingling static that hung between us and seemed to pull me toward him was just too much for my sanity to take. My mental breakdown was just around the corner, I could feel it, and I needed to get out now before it engulfed me.

'Wait! Rebecca, stay ... I'll tell you ...'

Swallowing hard I paused in my departure. Tell me? Tell me what, I wondered. Why Nathan is so important to him? Why he's fucked up like he is? Why he's a dominant?

Nicholas' voice had faded off but he stood with me and I could see a trembling in his hands as his fixed, blue gaze practically pleaded with me to stay. Seeing him so shaken was a new experience for me. Perhaps if I'd been hell bent on revenge I'd have taken pleasure in his obvious anguish ... but I didn't. In fact, it was heart-breaking to see him looking so broken.

'*Please. Don't leave*,' Nicholas implored me, I was still fully intent on leaving but it was the haunted look in his eyes that finally broke me, and without saying another word I sat down again.

'Thank you.' He ran a hand through his hair, looking distinctly uncomfortable, before finally returning his cloudy eyes to mine. 'When I was a kid, my father was very strict. He used to beat Nathan and me with a belt or cane if we broke his house rules. At the time, the cane was an occasional punishment in our school too, so we grew up assuming it was normal to be punished like that at home.'

As opening lines go, that's a pretty shocking one, I thought, my attention now fully on Nicholas and his tale.

He seemed to be on autopilot now; his eyes were fixed on the table and his shoulders stiff as he continued to speak. 'He was the same with our mother. In fact, I can remember several times when he literally put her over his knee and spanked her in front of us when she upset him.' Briefly closing his eyes, he paused for a moment, apparently trying to calm himself, or perhaps reliving the memories in his head, and I found myself clenching my teeth at the images flooding my brain.

'My father was ex-military. As such, our household was one of discipline and rules. From as early as I can remember, we weren't even allowed to look him in the eye unless he told us to, which I hated because I could never judge his mood or see when his temper was going to erupt.'

Shifting in his seat, Nicholas leant forward on the table. His hands began to snake across the polished wood toward mine as if he required comfort, but I wasn't ready for contact with him yet so I tucked mine in my lap. With a heavy sigh, he halted and pulled his arms back. 'That's why eye contact is so important to me now, Rebecca. I was never allowed it before. You have no idea how much I love seeing your feelings and emotions in your eyes; they're so expressive I feel like I could have an entire conversation with you without words.'

Hearing the emotion and deep, heartfelt statements from Nicholas was tearing me apart and making it harder and harder to stay away from him. My chest felt like it was being ripped open and I was wringing my fingers together painfully with the effort not to touch him. At least I understood his obsession with eye contact now, and could see why it was so important to him. I nodded slowly to encourage him to continue, choosing to remain quiet for the time being.

Raising his glass, Nicholas took a shaky sip of his Coke. It really was very alarming to see his cool façade gone, replaced with a rattled half-version of the man I knew. *The man I loved.* Yep, that juicy little thought still kept popping up in my mind like a nagging ache.

'My father was a classic dominant, probably a sadist too; I just didn't realise it at the time,' he summarised.

OK, so Nicholas had grown up to be like his father because he knew no different. This was starting to make sense but wasn't easing my discomfort. If he was a classic dominant like his father, or God forbid, a true sadist, then he could snap at any time like he had three weeks ago, and if that was the case there was no way I could go back to him. No way I *would* go back to him, which officially made me sitting here pointless. Before I could state this fact, however, he continued.

'It went on like this for years. As I got older, the punishments grew more severe. I was beaten daily, even if I'd been on my best behaviour and hadn't done anything wrong. He just got his kicks from it, I think,' Nicholas murmured, a look of disgust crossing his face. 'On my 16th birthday it got even worse ...' He shook his head slowly, his eyes now glassy and staring at the table. 'Too much for me to take, really. He'd tied my wrists to a radiator and he beat me so badly with the cane that I passed out from the pain. When I woke up I was still on the floor tied up.'

Holy shit! I stopped breathing as I tried to digest his words, this went way beyond the realms of strict parenting. Gazing at him, sat there ashen and hunched, I saw that Nicholas looked nothing like the man I knew, and my heart constricted painfully in my chest. He seemed incredibly distressed now, understandably so, fidgeting in his seat and showing none of the proud self-confidence that I was used to. I found it very unnerving, especially as I was having to fight the urge of every cell in my body, which wanted to slide around the booth and comfort him.

Pausing, Nicholas looked at me with eyes wide and glassy from the terror of his relived memories. 'Excuse me a moment,' he murmured, then, standing up, he headed to the bar and returned moments later with two large glasses of an amber liquid that I assumed was whisky.

Pushing one toward me, he cradled the other one in his hands and I noticed the uncharacteristic tremble in his fingers had got even worse. Surely there couldn't be more to his story? Biting down on my lip and gripping the edge of the leather seat was the only way I managed to stop myself moving closer to him.

'I tried to pull the rope from my wrists but I couldn't. I managed to reach my school bag with my feet and pull it over to get my pencil case. I got out my scissors to cut myself free.' Slinging his head back, Nicholas downed his whiskey in one go and pushed the empty glass away from himself before rubbing agitatedly at his left wrist.

'I was going to cut myself free ... but I didn't.' His voice was low and rough and I had to strain to hear him, leaning forward in my seat as I did so. 'I'd had enough of his abuse, I didn't want to take the beating any more so –' He ran a hand through his hair again, leaving it spiky and messy and wild like his eyes, '– so I slashed my wrist instead, cut myself with the scissors until there was blood everywhere. I only stopped because it got in my eyes and I was too weak to wipe it out.' His words were spoken in a low, monotone rush but I heard each and every one of them and they chilled me to the bone.

As he finished, a great, whooshing breath escaped my lungs and I felt an icy chill run under the entire surface of my skin. Holy fuck! He'd tried to kill himself. I stopped breathing for several seconds as I tried to absorb the enormity of what Nicholas had just told me; and the stunning similarity that his story held to that of my sister, Joanne. I couldn't believe it; in fact, I was struggling to breathe, almost panting now as I stared at him. Nicholas was so strong, so confident, just like Joanne had been before that night ... He just didn't seem the type, if there was indeed a type, but then neither had my sister.

Gripping the edge of the table I realised my head was spinning almost painfully. I swallowed hard, closing my eyes for several seconds to try and get a grip on my thoughts. Now was not the time to bring up Joanne; this was about Nicholas and his horrifying past that he'd just shared with me, so I focused back on him and continued to try and take in steadying breaths to calm myself.

Nicholas looked so distraught by this point that I just had to comfort him somehow, but I still couldn't bring myself to move to his side just yet, so instead I pushed my untouched whiskey toward him. As he reached out for it, his fingers brushed mine, sending electricity shooting up my arm and causing me to gasp. Even now, in these traumatic circumstances and after three weeks apart, the chemistry between us was just phenomenal. Withdrawing my hand as if burned, I watched Nicholas slide the glass toward himself, a sad smile curling his lips downwards at my hasty movement.

It has to be said that maintaining a distance from him when he clearly needed comfort made me feel like a complete and utter bitch, and I chewed on my lip guiltily as my fingers dug into my thighs to stop me taking his hand.

I realised his story explained the scar on his wrist, his one imperfection, and I now understood why he'd been rubbing at it so impatiently before. From the size of it, I had assumed it was a burn or the result of some accident. But no, teenage Nicholas had hacked at his arm to try to escape from his father's abuse. I felt sick at the pain he must have endured. Again, images of Joanne flashed in my brain and I felt physically drained, needing to rest my head in my hands for a moment until my nausea subsided.

'I thought about doing it again when you left,' he murmured softly, causing my head to shoot up, my eyes wide, only to see Nicholas shaking his head. 'I'm not saying that to get your sympathy, Rebecca. I don't want pity, I'm telling you because after you left I realised I was better than that. Stronger than that. Regardless of whether you'll take me back or not, I know now I am not a coward like my father ... I am not my father at all, I'm better than that. *You made me better*,' he finished in a determined whisper.

Once again, I found myself stunned into silence. He's not like his father and he wants me back? My overwhelming urge was to pull Nicholas into my arms and kiss the scar on his wrist until his hurt went away, but I somehow refrained. This was all so monumentally screwed up; I needed to think before I gave him false hope and ended up hurting him, and me, even more.

'Anyway, the reason Nathan is so important to me is because he's the one who found me that day. I was unconscious in a pool of my own blood. He cut me free from the radiator and took me to the hospital. He literally saved my life that day.'

Shaking his head, Nicholas continued, 'I've never understood it but even in spite of the abuse, Nathan worshipped dad. It was so hard for him to do it but we told the police everything and eventually my parents were put in prison for child abuse.'

His brother worshipped their abusive father? *Jeez*, my instincts about Nathan had been right then. I definitely wanted to avoid him now. I tried to get my head around how someone could have any kind of respect for their abuser, but Nicholas continued talking so I switched my focus back to him.

'I was sixteen. Nathan was eighteen, but he had no income so they were going to separate us and put me up for fostering. That's when Nathan saved me again. He got himself on to a paid apprenticeship scheme with an architecture firm and begged them to give him custody of me. Eventually, the council agreed so we stayed together.' There was warmth in his voice now; real affection for his brother. 'He's always looked out for me, Rebecca,' Nicholas concluded, as if willing me to respond somehow.

Finally, I felt the need to speak. 'This is starting to make sense, Nicholas. I'm so sorry for what happened to you.' Which was such an immense understatement that I grimaced at my lack of eloquence. 'So I guess the –' I blushed and leant in closer so I could whisper '– control over sex, the cuffs and punishments, just developed in response to your father's treatment? Your need to take back control?'

A small frown tweaked Nicholas' forehead and he actually averted his eyes, something so rare for him until today. 'Partly, but that came from Nathan too.'

What? Nathan had introduced him to kinky sex? I grimaced at the visions in my head. God, did I even want to hear this? Seeing my horrified expression, Nicholas looked deflated again but began to explain.

'It's not like that, Rebecca,' he replied quickly, looking almost as disgusted as I felt. 'He's older than me, and he'd put up with Dad's treatment for longer. He'd watched him in action, I suppose; learnt from him. Anyway, once we were free of my parents he started to date a girl. He'd never had a girlfriend before, neither of us had; we'd never been allowed to socialise.'

Nicholas sighed and ran a hand through his hair. In other circumstances, I might have laughed. He'd said in the past that touching my hair was my sign when I was nervous, but it was certainly becoming clear that it was Nicholas' tell that he was anxious. 'Apparently, she accused him of being too overbearing, yelled at him that he should get himself a submissive before she stormed out.'

He finished the second whisky and put his glass down, shifting it on the table and then linking his hands. 'Nathan had no idea what she was talking about, but looked it up when he got home. He found a surprisingly large number of websites on dominant and submissive relationships – an entire community of likeminded people used to discipline, who either enjoyed giving or receiving it.'

Cringing slightly, I recalled some of the websites I'd discovered when researching what a dominant was. They were eye-opening to say the least. As for the photographs and images the sites had shown … Jaw-dropping was more like it.

'After years of living in Dad's shadow, Nathan craved the control that being a dominant gave him. It suited him perfectly; he was able to get the power in life that he'd never had, but I actually think he likes the fact it allows him to be like dad in a small way,' Nicholas explained with a shrug. 'He got himself a submissive then and he's never looked back.'

So Nicholas' brother was a dominant too. What a family.

When he raised his eyes to mine, Nicholas looked thoroughly ashamed. 'When I was eighteen, I was finally starting to come out of my shell. I'd been incredibly insular; Nathan had done the parent thing and tried his best to inform me about girls and relationships. He explained to me what he did and suggested it might suit me too so I tried it.' Nicholas took a deep breath and once again ran a hand through his hair. 'In a totally fucked-up way, it was his way of trying to show he loved me, I think.

'This will all sound crazy to you, Rebecca, but you must remember I had no idea what was normal. I'd grown up seeing my parents' screwed-up relationship and I thought that was what submission meant. It was all I knew; I had no idea what was usual, no clue what I wanted.' Another helpless shrug. 'It went from there but I never felt quite right with being a full dominant; having someone there 24/7 didn't suit me. I knew I had a lot of suppressed anger and I lost my temper quickly, and I knew I liked to control things because I'd never been able to before, but for me I only liked the girls with me for short periods of time.'

I grimly translated this to "I only wanted the girls there for sex", but kept quiet.

'Nathan has always had a submissive who lives with him; they change occasionally. In truth, he's probably more like Dad than he likes to believe. I could never do that, I never wanted someone living with me, not until ...' His sentence faded but the look in Nicholas' eyes as he gazed across the table at me told me the final word. 'You.'

Not that he'd ever officially asked me to move in with him, but after his declaration that he wanted to try a relationship I'd barely left his house, mostly at his insistence. It had felt so natural, so right, that I'd been more than happy with the arrangement.

Rubbing both hands vigorously over his face as if he could wash away the memories, Nicholas then sat back violently against the cushions, causing a whoosh of air to escape the aged leather seat. 'So that's it. My fucked-up life in a nutshell,' he concluded with a grim twist of his mouth. 'And now you know.' He wriggled his intertwined fingers in front of him on the table.

Wow. Just wow. My head was spinning as I sat in stunned silence, unable to think of one thing that was remotely comforting or reassuring enough for the enormity of what Nicholas had just told me. It wasn't often that I was lost for words – usually the opposite, in fact, with my mouth in overdrive – but right now I had nothing. Nada. Zilch. The similarities to Joanne's history made Nicholas' story all the more painful for me to listen to, and my head was now too full of information to try and begin to sort through it all with him watching me like a hawk.

'I'm seeing someone now,' Nicholas said several seconds later, breaking the tense silence that hung between us.

What? Nicholas was seeing someone else? A new submissive? If that was the case, why the hell had he just poured his heart out to me? I gripped the table edge and struggled to breathe, feeling distinctly like the world had just been ripped out from under me.

Obviously seeing my reaction, which was close to hyperventilating terror, Nicholas almost smiled at me. 'A *counsellor*, Rebecca, just like you suggested. I'm seeing a counsellor for my condition and my anger. I went to him the day you left me and paid for a three-hour session. Now I'm going weekly. I've told him everything,' he explained with a simple shrug.

'Everything?' I asked, amazed that he was taking such a huge step toward his recovery but at the same time mortified that I would have been discussed with a complete stranger, let alone all the things we'd done together. A shudder of embarrassment ran through me.

'Yes.' Nicholas was solemn. 'I hate myself for what I did to you. I can't begin to tell you how much I regret my actions that day. After talking with Dr Philips, I at least think I understand why I did it now.'

I swallowed, forcing myself to ask the question I needed the answer to. 'Why?' I whispered, almost too scared to hear his response. Please don't let him say, "because I wanted to hurt you", I thought. If he said that, I just wouldn't ever be able to go back to him; my self-preservation just wouldn't allow it.

'I was scared of the feelings I had for you and believed you deserved better than me, so to prove to myself that I was no good for you I regressed back to my childhood and beat you with a cane like my father used to beat me. Dr Phillips thinks I was trying to make you leave because I didn't feel worthy of you.' Nicholas leant forward, looking like he wanted to reach out for me, and I desperately wanted to let him. But again, I made myself refrain by keeping my arms firmly crossed over my chest and digging my nails painfully into my palms.

'Dr Philips said if I was a true dominant I would have enjoyed it when I beat you,' he murmured in a low, disgusted tone as a huge sigh escaped his chest. 'But I didn't feel good about it. In fact, I can barely remember what happened. I suppose on some fucked-up level my subconscious plan worked though, because you left. Truthfully, I didn't even realise I'd done it until you said the safeword. It was like I was in a fucking trance.' He sounded scornful, apparently disgusted with himself, but as he said this part I remembered back to that horrible night and how I'd thought the same thing at the time. I'd been upset, yes, but I'd still noticed when he'd snapped out of it and seemed completely horrified at what he'd done.

Looking utterly traumatised, Nicholas leant forward and stared at me intently. 'I swear on my life it will never happen again. Please, *please* give me another chance,' he pleaded in a rush as if he couldn't hold back the words any longer.

After his huge confession, I was completely shell-shocked. My emotions were in free fall. No wonder Nicholas was so monumentally fucked up. My overwhelming feeling was to comfort him, help him somehow, but this was all just so much to take in.

'I don't know,' I whispered almost apologetically. 'I have to go home; I need time to think.' With thoughts of Joanne and Nicholas filling my head, it was getting too much for me to deal with. I needed to compartmentalise my mind and deal with one thing at a time. Preferably with a huge tub of chocolate ice cream to aid my thinking skills. His shoulders sagged at my words but, reluctantly, Nicholas nodded.

'You'll call me?' he asked, all the wind seemingly knocked from his once arrogant sails.

'I will,' I promised as I stood up to leave. I took a step away, then realised I no longer had his number after Louise erased it from my phone. Talk about awkward. I turned back to him. 'Uh, do you have a business card on you, Nicholas?' I asked uncomfortably.

Fumbling for his wallet, Nicholas stared up at me with horror-filled eyes. 'You deleted my number?' he whispered, apparently both stunned and hurt by my admission.

I took the card from him and clenched my teeth. 'I did. You beat me with a cane,' I reminded him sourly before scooping up my coat and heading out into the cool of the evening with my head spinning like a top.

FOURTEEN

I must have looked like a complete weirdo as I stood at the bus stop chewing my lip frantically and scowling deeply, but looking like a freak was the last thing on my mind right now. People could think what they liked; I truly didn't care. I almost felt like I had motion sickness as I tried to keep up with my mind, which had sped into overdrive trying to replay every detail of my meeting with Nicholas.

My plan today had been to walk home from work – avoiding the piano restorers, of course – but Nicholas' arrival in the shop had changed all that and thrown me completely off balance. My brain was now so full and confused that I seriously doubted my ability to walk in a straight line, let alone navigate the route to my flat successfully, so I decided on the safer option of the bus.

Trying to slow my mind from its current dizzying speed, I rewound the conversation with Nicholas and ran through all he had told me again. What a shitty life he'd had. Although that didn't really do it justice, did it? Abused by his parents to the point of trying suicide to escape them, then brought into a world of kinky sex by his equally damaged brother.

It was a wonder he was as "normal" as he was, I thought with an ironic shake of my head.

As I thought back over all he'd told me, I realised guiltily that I'd completely taken everything in my childhood for granted; loving, supportive parents, a safe home, encouragement, advice, and near-constant laughter. Things every child *should* have, but things that Nicholas had never experienced. I made a mental note to call my mum tomorrow and thank her.

How on earth could I expect him to understand love, trust,

and relationships if he'd never witnessed these things? It would be like asking me to fly an aeroplane without any lessons – impossible. All he'd known was violence, domination, silence, and fear. No wonder he was screwed up. Without realising it, a huge breath escaped my chest and I puffed out my cheeks at the enormity of the decisions I now had to try and make.

Telling me the secrets of his past had clearly been a torturous experience for Nicholas. He'd looked so lost, so vulnerable, nothing like the confident man I was used to. I sighed heavily as I leant back on the glass wall of the bus stop, realising this was probably when he needed me the most and I'd just walked away from him. A fresh wave of guilt washed over me and I began chewing on my nails to give my sore lip a rest.

An uneasy sensation settled in my stomach as I realised that this was the second time in my life when I'd deserted someone I loved at a time when they needed me the most. My sister, Joanne, had been the first, and I still regretted my actions regarding that situation every single day. Until now, I'd thought of myself as a fairly well rounded individual; was it possible I was actually just a selfish cow in disguise?

As I mounted the bus steps and paid the fare to take me just one stop up the road the driver gave me an odd look, as if wondering why I was being so bloody lazy, but I just ignored him, barely seeing him as thoughts of Nicholas still filled my brain. Grunting my thanks as my ticket spewed from the machine I took a seat in the second row and resumed my nail chewing. Really, what my decision rested on was one simple question – could I really walk away from Nicholas, the man I loved, when he was at his lowest point and in need of my support?

By the time the bus reached my stop I hadn't really come to any solid conclusions; I was still so confused. I loved him; that much was clear. Loved him so much more than I'd ever thought possible … but could I forgive his monumental fuck-up with the cane and go back to someone with such severe anger management issues? Although he was getting help for that from his counsellor. Plus, technically, the cane had been the only time I'd ever seen that side of him. I considered the alternative with a grimace – living without Nicholas, knowing how much I loved him, but not having him.

Once again, nerves made me want to throw up, which seemed to be happening a lot lately, along with biting of my lip and my almost obsessive fidgeting with my hair. I was a veritable catalogue of nervous tendencies these days; a shrink would no doubt have a field day with me. But I pushed aside my nausea with a sardonic smile. I was supposed to be a boring bookshop owner. How on earth had my life become this complicated?

Twenty minutes later, I pushed the key into the front door before pausing. Then, withdrawing the key, I chose to ring the bell instead. After the almost concussing volume of thoughts running through my mind on the bus, I now stood outside Nicholas' shiny front door, not my tatty flat entrance, and decided that barging in unannounced might not be the ideal arrival.

Mr Burrett answered almost immediately, looking immaculate as always and with an expression of pleasant surprise crossing his face as he saw me on the step. Even after four months, I still found it amusing that Nicholas had house staff, and even more amusing that I'd actually dated someone who had a butler. How grand was that!

'Miss Langley.' He greeted me with a warm smile and a nod; if I wasn't mistaken, he looked distinctly relieved that I was there.

'Hi, Mr Burrett, is Nicholas in?' I asked tentatively as I slipped the spare key that Nicholas had given me back in my bag. If things didn't go well in the next half an hour, I'd have to give the key back and try my hardest to forget all about Nicholas Jackson and the huge part he had so briefly played in my life. That would be practically impossible, seeing as he was the most charismatic, domineering, and sexy man I'd ever met, but I decided not to dwell on that.

'Mr Jackson arrived home about ten minutes ago,' he confirmed, with a small, tense glance over his shoulder. 'He was rather agitated and went straight to his music room.' Oh dear. An agitated Nicholas. Looked like I might have my work cut out for me then.

Straining my ears, I could just about hear soft piano notes floating down from the room above. It sounded a melancholy tune and I almost rolled my eyes; he was obviously feeling sorry for himself.

'Would you like to go up? I'm sure he wouldn't mind the interruption from you,' Mr Burrett offered, his bushy, grey eyebrows rising hopefully.

Images of the music room with its piano and memories of the naughty things we'd done together flashed through my mind, making me swallow rather loudly. It wasn't exactly an ideal place for a heart-to-heart; far too distracting for my already baffled brain. 'Actually, would you mind telling him I'm here? I'll wait in the lounge,' I suggested with a tight smile.

'Of course,' Mr Burrett replied genially, a look of understanding crossing his face. Even if Nicholas hadn't confided in him about our split, my absence over the last three weeks would have made it obvious to the older man that something had happened between us. Mr Burrett started to walk away, then hesitantly turned back. 'It's nice to see you here again, Miss Langley … we've all missed you.' Seeing as no one else lived there, I took this as a discreet reference to the fact that Nicholas had missed me, and had probably been an absolute nightmare to deal with. For a brief second, as his mouth hung open, I thought Mr Burrett was going to say more, but then he snapped his lips shut and gracefully turned for the stairs as I let myself into the lounge and nervously lowered myself onto the sofa.

A few moments later, the house went suddenly silent as the piano stopped and then I heard Nicholas' disbelieving voice from upstairs. 'Rebecca's here? *Where*?'

'In the lounge, sir.' But before Mr Burrett had even finished uttering the sentence, I heard clattering footsteps descending the stairs at a great rate of knots, each bang reverberating through the brick of the house. Clearly, Nicholas was coming down them two at a time. He appeared in the doorway, wide-eyed and flushed, with his hair tousled across his forehead.

For some time we simply stared at each other, the atmosphere thickening as if by some strange chemical reaction that always seemed to occur between us. Looking at his guarded but expectant face, I knew I'd made the right choice to come here. I loved him, and although I didn't ever think I would be able to fully accept the way Nicholas had treated me with the cane, I was at least some way toward understanding why he had done it.

'I thought you said you were going home,' he murmured uncertainly from the doorway.

'I did,' I said simply, my cryptic answer causing him to frown. So, with a sigh, I explained myself. 'My flat is just that, Nicholas. It's a place to eat and sleep. But home is where the people you care about are ... so I got off the bus and came here instead.'

As he processed my words, I saw a glimmer of hope flicker in Nicholas' eyes, but, obviously still wary, he stayed standing, holding the doorframe for support, knuckles white from the tension he was holding in his body. It seemed I would need to make the first move so I patted the sofa next to me, causing him to raise his eyebrows in surprise. After assessing me intently for several long moments, I saw him nervously lick his lips and then begin to walk toward me cautiously before folding his tall frame into the seat space next to me.

The tension was palpable between us; from the stiffness of his body Nicholas was clearly trying his hardest not to touch me, but even with the gap between us the old familiar magnetism sparked up again. Steeling my nerves and taking a deep breath, I decided to be brave and get the difficult part out of the way first. Nicholas had been open enough to tell me his painful past, so I needed to do the same, even though I'd done everything in my power to avoid discussing this topic out loud ever again. Sucking in a huge breath I let it out through my nose and nodded once; I needed to tell him about Joanne and the horrible guilt I lived with daily, make him understand that to a certain extent I could relate to how he felt.

'Firstly, I want to apologise for leaving the pub so abruptly ...' I started, but Nicholas interrupted me with a dismissive wave of his hand.

'Rebecca, the blame for all of this lies solely on me, you have nothing to apologise for,' he muttered with a shake of his head.

'Yes I do, Nicholas,' I said with determination. 'I walked away from you when you needed me the most.' Pursing my lips, I wondered how to tell him the next part, deciding that keeping it quick and to the point was probably best. Short and sweet, wasn't that the phrase? Except there would be nothing sweet about my story.

'I left partly to give me time to think about us, but also because your story reminded me of a painful time in my own past – well, my sister's past,' I clarified. 'I need to tell you this before we talk about us because it has certain similarities to your story and, in a way, it helped me to understand how you must have felt as a teenager.'

Looking confused, overwhelmed, and thoroughly un-Nicholas-like, he had turned himself on the sofa so he could pay me full attention, but was still careful to maintain a distance between us as he nodded for me to continue.

Keep it short and sweet, I reminded myself as I prepared to get my horrible secret off my chest.

'When we were younger, my sister and I didn't get on. Actually, we pretty much hated each other,' I clarified with a grimace. 'Jo wanted to be best at everything and after a while I started to resent her for it, I suppose.' My fingers were desperately twining in my lap; better add that to my list of nervous habits. 'Anyway, when we were teenagers, we partied a lot. My parents insisted that we always arrived together and left together for safety, but apart from that we barely used to speak two words to each other while we were out.'

My stomach was churning now, so I sucked in a breath to try and settle it; this story was harder to tell than I had anticipated.

'One night, we got invited to a college party. As soon as we walked in the door, Joanne hooked up with some random guy and was all over him. She was doing her usual and smirking at me, showing off the fact that she was prettier than me and always got more boys to look at her.' I let out a long sigh – this had all seemed like such a long time ago, but now that I was talking about it, the details seemed so painfully fresh in my mind.

'I had a headache that night and about an hour after we arrived I told her I wanted to go home, but she thought I was sulking and told me to stop being miserable and have a drink. But I wasn't sulking, I genuinely did have a headache,' I added, trying to convince myself that I'd been right to go home. 'I broke my parents' rule that night by getting a cab home on my own and leaving Joanne at the party.' I got this far and then felt my throat tighten up, making words almost impossible.

Noticing my growing distress, Nicholas shifted beside me and placed a hand on my shoulder for support. 'You don't have to share this with me if you don't want to, Rebecca,' he said softly.

'No, I need to,' I replied resolutely, twisting my hands in my lap. 'After I left her there, she went off with the guy into the garden to talk and kiss but ... but he forced himself on her.' I heard Nicholas draw in a sharp breath next to me and I grimaced because that was nowhere near the most horrendous part.

'Unfortunately, it gets worse,' I murmured. 'She didn't tell anyone what had happened to her that night but a couple of months later, my mum found her in the bathroom, unconscious, with empty pill bottles by her side.' Next to me, I felt Nicholas tense, obviously realising why I'd said their stories were similar. 'It turned out the rape had got Jo pregnant.' I licked my dry lips and shook my head sadly before continuing, 'She didn't feel she could tell anyone and was so ashamed and distressed by it that she wanted to end it all. She found some online concoction of pills that was supposed to be a home suicide kit.'

I couldn't even draw up the courage to look Nicholas in the eye as I concluded my story in a rush. 'The baby died. Jo survived, but she ended up brain-damaged, partly from the drugs and partly from the lack of oxygen to her brain. If I hadn't left her at that party ...' I shook my head desolately, but surprisingly my eyes stayed relatively dry. 'None of it would ever have happened and Jo would be normal now,' I said quietly, hating myself all over again.

There was a moment of pause before I felt Nicholas shift beside me. 'Jesus, Rebecca, that's truly terrible. But you can't blame yourself for what happened that night, it's the arsehole who took advantage of her who's to blame, not you,' Nicholas stated, squeezing my shoulder, but I merely shrugged.

'Maybe, but I still feel guilty for it. She's quite unstable now, very dependent on medication and not good around strangers. She doesn't blame me but I just can't forgive myself. Maybe if I'd been a better sibling, like Nathan was to you, Joanne wouldn't have ended up in trouble in the first place.'

Turning to him, I took a deep breath and returned my focus back to the small matter of our broken relationship. 'I wanted you to hear the story so you know I understand what it's like to live with someone who has gone through something that traumatic. I can't begin to imagine what you went through with your father, Nicholas, but it obviously affected the way you've grown up.' Understatement of the year.

Now my story of Joanne was out in the open, I decided to act on instinct, so I turned to Nicholas and pushed him back into the sofa while swinging my leg across his lap so I was straddling him. Now I could sit looking straight into his eyes, just how he liked it. My move obviously took him completely by surprise because he sucked in a shocked breath and blinked in disbelief at my sudden close proximity.

'I love you, Nicholas,' I admitted, causing his eyes to widen like saucers. 'You don't have to say it back,' I added hastily, shaking my head and fairly certain that declarations like that would never come from his lips, 'but deep down I know you care about me.' That much had been blatantly clear from his expressions in the pub earlier.

I sighed softly but maintained eye contact. 'I can't walk away from you like I did Joanne. I love you too much for that,' I said with a deep breath. 'An awful lot has happened between us in a short space of time. I can accept your controlling ways and the kinky bedroom stuff – I actually quite like most of it – but if we are to try again you need to know two things,' I told him firmly.

'Anything,' he urged, tentatively placing his hands on my hips, his gorgeous blue eyes blazing with hope.

'First, you need to sort things out with Nathan. I get that he's always looked out for you but I'm not having you freak out about us every time you see him. I won't ask you choose between us, I wouldn't do that, but it's up to you to decide what to do.' Silently, I prayed that it wouldn't come down to an ugly face-off between myself and Nicholas' tough-sounding brother.

A trace of a smile graced Nicholas' lips and his eyes burned into mine as his hands ran restlessly up and down my thighs, heating my skin though the denim of my jeans. 'It's already done, Rebecca. I had a big talk with him the day after you left and got everything off my chest. Actually, he was the one who finally persuaded me to come and see you today. I'd wanted to since the day you left, but you had asked me not to contact you so I tried to stay away for your sake,' he explained softly. 'Nathan has seen the difference in me, especially after you left. I think it's confused him, but he could see I was better because of you. He actually told me to go to you.'

That was surprising news, but I nodded, pleased by his words. I had thought Nathan might be a bigger obstacle than that and felt quite relived he wouldn't be more of an issue.

'Secondly?' Nicholas asked, wary again.

'Secondly, and this is not up for discussion, if you *ever* hurt me the way you did three weeks ago I will leave, and I will not come back,' I stated bluntly, my jaw clenching just at the thought of that awful night.

I felt his hands tighten around my waist. With a pained expression, he closed his eyes and lowered his face into the crook of my neck, where he rested silently for several seconds breathing deep, ragged breaths. 'Never, Rebecca, I promise ...' he murmured, his breath hot against my skin. 'That wasn't me. I was so confused, I'd never experienced feelings like this before and I was so scared about how I felt about you ...' He tugged me closer and wrapped his arms tightly around my waist, his breathing rapid and jerky next to my ear.

'Things were getting serious between us and yet you hadn't left me. I couldn't understand it; all I could think about was my father and how I must be like him, and then Nathan was saying I would never be capable of loving someone ... I was so confused,' he confessed in a soft voice.

'And now?' I asked softly, rubbing my hand in soothing circles on his back, like I'd wanted to earlier in the pub when he'd been so distressed.

'Now I know I'm not like my father.' He raised his head and I was shocked to see tears staining his cheeks. 'I'd refused to acknowledge it before, but now I know ... I ... I love you, Rebecca,' Nicholas whispered hoarsely, his eyes wide and sincere as if doubting I would believe him, let alone want him.

Now it was my time to sit wide-eyed and silent. *He loved me?* I knew Nicholas cared for me, I knew he'd given up things for me, changed the way he lived, even, but I never expected him to admit he loved me. I'd assumed that was beyond him, especially after hearing about his loveless upbringing.

'I can never apologise enough for what I did to you, Rebecca. I hate myself for it every day. Please, *please* try to forgive me. You are so important to me. You're *everything*,' he amended with a shake of his head. 'I'm trying hard to work on my anger and possessiveness, Dr Phillips is fantastic ... I can't promise not to get upset sometimes, but I swear I will never hit you like that again. *Never*. Please, Rebecca, please come back to me,' he implored me, his fingers nervously rubbing up and down the sides of my ribs, making my skin tingle and jump with awareness.

Using the pads of my thumbs, I brushed away Nicholas' tears and lowered my lips to his face, softly kissing both his cheeks before gently pressing my mouth to his. It wasn't passionate, like most of our previous kisses had been, instead, it was a deep, slow kiss that spoke volumes about how I felt for this man.

'OK. You have me back, Nicholas,' I agreed, a smile playing on my lips as he pulled me to him and squeezed the breath out of me. 'You need to bin the cane, though,' I added tersely; I didn't even want to think about that being in his house.

'I've already done it. It's all gone,' he replied as his lips lazily ran across my jawline, scattering a trail of feather light kisses.

'All gone?' I asked, sitting back in confusion.

'Come,' he instructed, then, shifting me off his lap, Nicholas stood and held a hand out to me. Keen to get as much contact with him as possible after our three weeks apart, I grabbed his hand far too eagerly and gave his fingers a squeeze. Gosh, I really was so pathetic when it came to this man.

Leading me up the stairs, Nicholas must have felt me tense as he approached the door to the spare room because he paused with his fingers on the handle and looked back at me cautiously. Thinking of the last time we'd been in here made me shudder. I wasn't sure I'd ever be able to walk back in there again without feeling sick to the stomach.

'Trust me?' Nicholas whispered, his eyes urging me to have confidence in him again. I wanted to trust him again, really wanted to, so slightly nervously I nodded. He opened the door, keeping his eyes fixed on me as I hesitantly peeked around the doorframe and looked inside.

From his statement – "it's all gone" – I'd assumed he meant the canes, cuffs, and other toys, but as I took in the sight before me, I gasped and looked up at him questioningly.

'I couldn't stand myself after you left. Even if you wouldn't take me back, I knew I'd changed too much to want to come in here ever again. I scrapped the bed, burned the sheets, and cleared the cupboard,' he explained with a shrug. 'I wasn't sure what to do with the room at first, but I know how much you love books, as do I, so a library seemed like a good use.' His voice faded at the end of his sentence as he gazed around the transformed room.

Blinking several times, I stepped into the spare room that was now fully fitted out as a library. Wide wooden bookcases filled the walls, soft rugs covered the floors, and two leather armchairs sat by the large window. Wow. It was beautiful. Shaking my head in shock, I noticed he'd even got rid of the old curtains, allowing the early-evening moonlight to flood into the room with a pale glow.

I ran my fingertips across the spines of the books filling one bookcase as I wandered towards the cupboard. Glancing inside, I saw it was now completely empty. The shelves had gone, along with the toys and accessories, most of which we'd never even used together. As I turned back toward the main room, my gaze caught on a small box on the floor and I looked at it curiously.

'Oh … I kept a few things that reminded me of you. Stuff you seemed to like,' he mumbled, looking embarrassed as an uncharacteristic blush reddened his cheeks.

Pulling back the lid of the box, I couldn't help but smile. Inside were the soft handcuffs, nipple clamps, flogger, and some scarves and vibrators.

'I do like,' I agreed, smiling up at him shyly as my cheeks quickly heated to match his own.

Suddenly, Nicholas approached me and pulled me into his arms, clutching me to his chest so desperately he knocked some of the wind from my lungs. 'Oh God, Rebecca, you have no idea how scared I was that you wouldn't come back to me …' Tugging roughly on my hair, he tilted my head back and kissed me deeply and thoroughly, as if reassuring himself that I was really there. His tongue was hot and fierce as it explored my mouth and reacquainted himself with me, and I joined in just as eagerly, lifting onto my tiptoes so I could really give the moment everything I had. Now *this* was a real kiss; not like the chaste one I had given him downstairs.

Oh, how I had missed his kisses, I thought hazily as his lips moved skilfully over mine. His passion was so intense it was all I could do to cling on to Nicholas' shoulder and stay upright. As his soft lips moved to trail along my jaw so insistently, a fire erupted in my heart that had me melting against him and tugging his mouth back to mine so I could meet his kiss with an equally demanding one of my own.

Breaking our lip-lock and panting, Nicholas held me securely but closed his eyes for several seconds, apparently seeking to calm himself.

'Thanks for sharing your history with me today, Nicholas,' I murmured, pulling him even closer to me and rubbing my hand soothingly over his hip, causing a low rumble to escape from his throat.

'I've never told anyone all that before. Apart from the police the day my parents were arrested,' he admitted, his lips thinning at the unpleasant memory. 'But I'm glad I did. I feel better now you know.'

'Me too. I'm glad I told you about Jo. Maybe you can meet her one day,' I suggested, thinking it was highly unlikely that my sister would want to meet any strange male I brought along. 'But I'll have to see how she settles on her new medications first.' Deciding I didn't want to focus on those unpleasant memories at the moment, I brought the conversation back to Nicholas. 'Are your parents still in prison now?' I whispered, unsure of whether he would want to open up about them any further.

'No. My mother served three years for assisting in child abuse, and was released halfway through her sentence for good behaviour. My father got six years but got out after five, I think. Social Services told me they split up. My mum lives in America, apparently, but I've had no contact with them. I don't know where my dad is, and quite frankly, I don't care,' he muttered, his tone suddenly devoid of any emotion.

Such short prison sentences for inflicting years of pain and a lifetime of emotional scarring. It seemed completely unbelievable to me.

'Have you eaten?' Nicholas murmured against my forehead, apparently also wishing to change the subject, which was fine by me. Today had been pretty tough as it was and must have been equally traumatic for him with all our deep confessions.

'No,' I said, 'but I'm not really hungry. Actually, after three weeks of sleepless nights I'd really just like to go to bed. Can I stay?' After all our ups and downs, my tone was tentative, but I was fairly sure that Nicholas would agree, and knew that I stood a good chance of sleeping well tonight with him back at my side.

'There's not a chance in hell that I'm letting you leave,' he confirmed, his old possessiveness seeming to flow easily back to the surface. 'But you need to eat something first. How about a quick sandwich and then bed, Rebecca?' he asked, dropping a persuasive kiss on my lips.

Feeling the warmth of his body against mine, I gave in without a fight. 'OK.'

Leading me in the direction of the kitchen, he gripped my hand tightly the entire time. 'And I know what you mean about the lack of sleep. It's just as well my neighbours are heavy sleepers because I've played piano into the early hours most nights.'

After I'd devoured delicious bacon sandwiches, which I hadn't thought I'd wanted, Nicholas once again refused to let me go and led me by the hand up to his bedroom. Except he referred to it as *our bedroom,* which was a term I rather liked. It was only nine o'clock, but after sleep had evaded me for the best part of three weeks, I was more than ready to retire for an early night.

Once I had persuaded him to let go of my hand for a brief period, I entered the en-suite bathroom and immediately came to an abrupt halt when I found all my things still present. Toothbrush, hairbrush, make-up; everything sat exactly where I had left it three weeks ago. For several seconds I just stared at it, wondering why Nicholas hadn't moved it. Gosh, it must have been really weird for him to have my stuff here on display after we'd broken up.

Shuddering, I pushed those thoughts aside and rushed through my wash to get ready for bed.

After I had brushed my teeth and run a brush though my hair, I emerged into the bedroom to find Nicholas sitting on the edge of the bed in nothing but a pair of black boxer shorts, awaiting my return. I'd almost forgotten how great his body was, so I indulged myself for a moment by staring openly, my eyes skimming over him appreciatively. Standing up he smiled at me like I was the most precious thing left on earth, then he shook his head as if bemused by something and went into the bathroom without a word, dropping a brief, chaste kiss on the top of my head as he passed me.

One simple kiss and I felt like a rubbery lump of nerve endings. I was a totally lost cause, I thought with a smile as I pulled off my work jumper.

Not having a nightshirt or pyjamas at his house, I simply undressed and climbed into bed naked; it wasn't like this was unusual, Nicholas hated wearing clothes in bed, so we'd always slept this way when I stayed over. It wasn't long before I was joined by Nicholas who snuggled up behind me, making a contented growling noise when he discovered my lack of clothing, and allowing his hands to briefly skim over my body before pulling me firmly against him.

Even though I was tired, more tired than I could ever remember being, the feel of Nicholas' warm, naked body pressed up against me again was just too much of a temptation for me to pass up. Especially after three weeks of abstinence. Engaging my full tease mode, I pressed my bottom against his groin and wiggled it briefly, a grin splitting my lips when I felt him start to stir to life, and then rolled over to face him, smiling impishly in the low light of the bedroom.

'I thought you were tired,' he reprimanded me, but there was an excited twinkle in his eyes that betrayed his attempt at chastisement.

'I am, but it's been over three weeks since I've had you inside me and I don't think I can wait a minute longer,' I whispered, a flush reddening my cheeks at my blunt honesty and causing a hissed breath to escape from his parted lips.

'Let's see what we can do about that then, shall we?' he murmured salaciously. The darkness of Nicholas' eyes mirrored my desires, and my hands immediately moved to his chest and began to greedily explore. Smiling seductively, he leant forward and kissed me. His lips moved across mine slowly and tenderly at first, nipping and teasing my mouth until I was moaning against his lips for more but then, as the familiar electricity shot between our bodies it was all we could do not to rush our reconciliation and claw at each other's skin.

Pushing me on to my back, Nicholas set about worshipping my body in every way he knew how. He spent an eternity kissing every inch of me until I was a quivering mess below his teasing lips. 'Nicholas, please ...' I begged as he once again returned to one of my breasts to suckle on it and run lazy streaks across it with the flat of his tongue.

'Please what, Becky?' Nicholas asked while gazing intently into my eyes, his mouth still busy with its relentless teasing.

'Please ...' I paused, not really liking to beg, until a sudden thought hit me and I smiled. 'Please make love to me,' I whispered, loving the fact that I could utter the words for the first time and know they were true. Nicholas loved me, as I did him. Tonight we would make love, not fuck.

Nicholas growled possessively at my request his mouth leaving my breast as he lunged up the bed towards my face again. His lips crashed down upon mine, kissing me deeply, his tongue plunging past my lips and stroking across mine fiercely. 'With pleasure,' he murmured a second later. As he positioned himself between my legs, he gazed deep into my eyes with a look of absolute adoration on his face, before pushing himself inside my heat slowly and tenderly. We both groaned loudly as we were reconnected, and Nicholas had to stop and rest his forehead against mine for several seconds while he regained his composure before starting up a leisurely, loving pace.

Nicholas showed me in both his actions and words that he truly did love me as he rained kisses down upon me and made slow, delicious love to me that night. It was possibly the knowledge that he loved me, or perhaps just the three weeks apart, but he brought me to one of the most blissful orgasms of my life. I had never felt happier as my body clenched around his and he found his release while buried deep inside me, calling out my name into the darkness.

FIFTEEN

The following morning, I woke feeling well rested for the first time since I'd walked out on Nicholas just over three weeks ago. The reason I'd slept so well was still wrapped around me like a blanket, his head resting on my chest with his right arm and leg thrown over me protectively, and I couldn't help but let out a contented sigh. I'd slept through the entire night – well, what was left of it after Nicholas and I had finished reacquainting ourselves with each other's body.

A childish grin spread over my face as I thought about last night's naughtiness. It has been sublime. Three weeks apart had done nothing to dull his insatiable sexual appetite; that was for sure.

I shook my head in disbelief at everything that had occurred yesterday and I shifted myself out from under him so I could lie there watching him relaxed in sleep. Despite all of Nicholas' many, many, *many*, issues, I had no regrets about my decision to take him back. He'd opened up to me so much yesterday that I was sure we could work through any difficulties that arose between us.

With his head now turned on the pillow, his hair had fallen back from his face, revealing the strong cut of his features, and I actually found myself feeling breathless, although this was nothing new. Nicholas' handsomeness had always affected my ability to breathe and after three weeks without the glorious sight of him, I took a moment to soak it up greedily once again.

As I gently trailed a finger down the soft stubble on his jaw, I nodded to myself. Yes, I was convinced I'd done the right thing, especially when I thought about that horrible night when I'd deserted Joanne. Not that that was why I was with him – this wasn't a guilt thing – but my experience with Joanne had taught me that I was strong enough to support him in any remaining conflicts he had and to help him through them. And although it would kill me to do it, I knew I would be brave enough to walk away from him if he ever flipped out on me again.

Sliding away as gently as I could, I did my best not to disturb Nicholas' sleeping form and reached for my phone to check the time. Managing to grab my mobile, I was amazed to see it was gone ten o'clock already. Mind you, after those delicious hours spent sweatily entwined with him last night it was no wonder I had been tired, I thought with another self-indulgent grin. Just as well it was Saturday and I didn't need to be in work because Louise and Robin ran the show on a weekend.

I felt Nicholas stir beside me, obviously having sensed my movement. Before I knew it, he was deftly rolling me back over, straddling me, and leaning down to plant a soft, lingering kiss on my lips.

'I hope you weren't planning on getting up without waking me, Miss Langley,' he murmured against my cheek, making me smile happily as I ran my free hand through his sleep-tousled hair. Mmm, he smelt so good; faintly of aftershave but more predominantly of warm skin, fresh sheets, and me. What a combination.

'Morning, sleepyhead.' I grinned, trying to ignore the heat of his groin, which was laying on my tummy. 'You looked so peaceful I didn't want to wake you,' I murmured at exactly the same time as my phone began to ring in my hand, making me jump. Sliding it out from between our bodies, I glanced at the screen and saw my mother's number flashing up.

'It's my mum, let me get up,' I said, pushing at his chest above me and expecting him to move so I could take the call.

'*You* giving *me* instructions, Rebecca? *Really*?' he said with a saucy raise of his eyebrow. 'Answer it,' he instructed, with a sly smile breaking on his lips. Uh-oh, he had a devious twinkle in his eyes, and when Nicholas got that look, it always led to mischief of the sexual kind.

'Nicholas, I'm not answering the phone to my mum with

your gloriously naked body straddling me.' I laughed, pushing uselessly against him again.

'Glorious, eh? I like that,' he said with a smirk. Then, to my complete surprise – and horror – he grabbed the phone from my hand, pressed the green speak button, and held it out to me, grinning. My eyes widened in shock and I barely had time to realise what he had done before I heard my mum's voice echoing from the speaker, saying my name.

Throwing a look of annoyance at him, I took the phone and tried to calm my heart rate, which was harder than it sounded given that I was pinned below a naked Nicholas whose morning excitement was becoming more evident against my stomach by the second. Goodness, he was keen, I thought with a blush as I glanced down.

'Hi, Mum!' I exclaimed, probably in a slightly too enthusiastic tone due to my current state of panic. I raised my eyes from Nicholas' groin, locked with his gaze, and glared at him, but in return he merely grinned wickedly down at me and wiggled his eyebrows. My glare faded. He was hard to stay mad at when he looked so playful.

Trying to focus on Mum's voice and not Nicholas' aroused nakedness, I listened to her for a moment before I slapped a hand to my forehead. 'No, no, of course I haven't forgotten, Mum.' Which of course meant that I had.

Nicholas then began to very slowly grind himself, and his almost fully developed erection, against my pelvis causing me to completely lose my train of thought once more. Gosh, that was so distracting … Who was I talking to again?

Desperately trying to focus on my phone call, I managed an answer to the question Mum had just asked. 'Today, yep …' I muttered breathlessly as I desperately fought against Nicholas' hands as he tried to reach up and fondle my breasts. Of course it was a losing battle, because one of my hands was busy holding the phone and I couldn't defend both my bare breasts against his fast-moving fingers. I struggled for several seconds, which only caused me to get more breathless, but in the end gave up and flopped back on the bed, giving him full access. He celebrated with a triumphant smile and a gentle tweak of a nipple.

'*Ahh ...*' I groaned as Nicholas ran his fingertips around both my hardened nipple tips. 'Sorry, Mum, I was just, um, *stretching*,' I lied with a grimace. 'Yep, 12 o'clock at my flat.'

To my horror, Nicholas grinned at me, made a show of seductively licking one of his fingers before his hand dipped lower – far lower – and within seconds, he'd slipped it straight inside me. *Holy shit!* Somehow, I managed to muffle the gasp that escaped me at his intrusion, but as he started to lazily slide it in and out of me, I was blushing bright red and squirming below his skilled touch in no time.

'Looking forward to seeing you, Mum. I've gotta go. Bye!' I ended the call as quickly as I could, then threw my phone onto the duvet and began to thrash at Nicholas' chest with balled fists.

'That was my mum, Nicholas!' I screeched, trying to make him realise how inappropriate it was to insert a finger into someone while they were conversing with a parent. Unfortunately, with him grinning down at me like an excited puppy, my anger lasted all of about six seconds, before I greedily grabbed his biceps and pulled him down on top on me for a heated kiss.

Ten minutes later, feeling sated after a very speedy lovemaking session, I finally managed to disengage Nicholas from my limbs and sat up feeling decidedly dishevelled in a wholly pleasant way. 'I've really got to go – I completely forgot that my mum's coming down from Penrith to spend the weekend with me. She's already on the train now. It's her birthday tomorrow and we always have a girly weekend together to celebrate,' I explained as I tried to detangle my leg from the twisted sheets.

Clambering from the bed and reaching for my pants and jeans, I stopped, frozen to the spot, as a thought occurred to me. 'Shit! I haven't even got her a bloody present!' I looked at Nicholas with horror spreading over my face. 'I've been so preoccupied with what was going on between us that I completely forgot about it,' I mumbled guiltily.

Preoccupied was an understatement – I'd been an absolute

zombie these past few weeks.

I grabbed my phone to check the time again and my heart sank. It was nearly half past ten now. There was no way I could get back to my flat, tidy it up, make up the spare bedroom, and go out to buy a present before Mum's train arrived. *Bugger*.

'I haven't got time now. I'll have to see if I can nip out tonight once she's gone to bed and get some flowers or something.' Pulling on my bra and shirt in record time, I dashed around the bed to where Nicholas was lounging back in the pillows, watching my flustered state with apparent amusement.

'I'm sorry to run off like this,' I said, leaning down and cupping his chin. The night's worth of stubble felt rough beneath my thumb and I briefly rubbed it in fascination, loving how he leant into my touch. 'Especially seeing as we just made up. But I really need to go and get my flat ready. Shall I come round Sunday night after Mum's left?' I asked hopefully, turning to find my handbag.

'Sounds good. I'm assuming it's a bit soon for me to meet your mother?' he enquired lightly, completely confusing me. I stopped sorting through my bag to look at him. Did he want to meet my mum so early on in our relationship? It was a pretty big step, after all, besides, we'd only just made up.

'Umm, you can meet her if you like?' I offered, unsure what response he was looking for. From my experience, which admittedly was limited, men didn't usually want to meet parents until wedding bells were in the air. 'But I should warn you it will mostly be us catching up and gossiping.'

Nicholas grinned then made a funny face where he wrinkled up his nose. 'Sounds a bit girly for me; maybe next time,' he said and I took this as his polite way of getting out of it. Fair enough.

He climbed from the bed in all his naked glory, totally distracting me from my packing, and I stood gaping at his masculine beauty as he walked toward me and enfolded me gently in his arms. 'Thank you,' he whispered next to my ear, dropping several light kisses on the corner of my jaw.

'For what?' I asked, trying not to get distracted by the warm nakedness of his body wrapped around me. He now smelled faintly of sleep but more obvious was the scent our recent sex that lingered on his skin and made me feel horny all over again. I buried my head in his chest and inhaled deeply, trying to commit the scent to memory.

'For giving me a second chance. You won't regret it, Rebecca,' he assured me, his voice sincere as he leant back to look in my eyes. 'I love you. I wish you didn't have to go, but I understand.' He sounded regretful as he pushed me in the direction of the door. 'Mr Burrett will drive you.' He turned for the bed, giving me a superb view of his equally superb behind which had me grinning broadly. 'Go now, before I drag you back to bed,' he growled, and I left the room giggling like a teenager.

SIXTEEN

The spare bed was made, the flat was tidy, and I had showered and changed, all just in time for Mum's prompt arrival at midday. Luckily, the place had been almost immaculate anyway because I'd cleaned like an obsessive-compulsive loon over the last three weeks while trying to take my mind off of Nicholas.

Mum and I were sat having coffee and planning what to do with our afternoon and I had to say I was feeling pretty content – first the reunion with Nicholas, and now great catch-up time with my mum. It was a pretty perfect day, really. I hadn't let on that I had no present or plans for her birthday tomorrow, though. I was hoping I might be able to magic up something tonight when she had gone to bed, but to be honest I wasn't expecting anything too amazing.

Late-night Tesco, here I come, I thought.

Just as I had topped up our mugs, the doorbell rang. Wandering to the door, I pulled it open expecting a salesman of some kind, and was startled to find Nicholas leaning on the wall outside my flat. Crikey, he looked stunningly handsome. How was it possible to make dark navy jeans and a simple grey polo shirt look that good? By his feet was a large cardboard box but he stepped over it, entered my flat, and, after a brief glance in my mother's direction, pulled me firmly against him and kissed me hard on the lips.

Wow, what an entrance! Part of me should have been mad that Nicholas was staking such an obvious claim to me in front of my mother, but deep down I couldn't help but feel pleased that he was this possessive.

I've never really been one for public displays of affection, but even though I was well aware that Mum sat on the sofa not ten feet away – with a full view of this passionate exchange, might I add – I couldn't pull away. Didn't want to. With the usual electricity pinging between us, I simply couldn't do anything except place my hands on Nicholas' shoulders, drag him closer, and return his heated kiss.

Leaning back slightly, Nicholas ended the kiss and smiled down at me, his eyes bright and burning with something so naughty that I couldn't even consider it with my mum in such close proximity. 'Hi,' he murmured.

'Hey,' I replied shyly, still half wondering what he was doing here. Had he forgotten my mum's visit, because I had been fairly sure from his reaction this morning that he hadn't been hugely keen on meeting her just yet.

We were seemingly stuck in a little bubble of our own, but I suddenly caught a glimpse of my mum out of the corner of my eye; she was looking at us with obvious interest and a fairly healthy blush reddening her cheeks too. Oops, that was probably from witnessing our heated exchange of lips.

Slipping an arm around Nicholas' waist, I turned toward her to make the introductions. 'Mum, this is Nicholas …' I glanced at him. 'My boyfriend,' I explained awkwardly, hoping he wouldn't mind the title. 'Nicholas, this is my mum, Leanne.'

As Mum began to stand, Nicholas leant down toward me. 'Boyfriend?' he asked in a peculiar tone that made my stomach clench with worry. Had I gone too far by assuming the title for him? But what else could I call him in front of my mother? My lover? Hardly. '*Boyfriend …*' he said again, pronouncing the word slowly as if processing it. 'No one's ever called me that before … I like it,' he concluded with a grin.

Phew.

Mum barrelled across the room to be introduced properly and I watched in amusement as her jaw dropped slightly when she took in Nicholas in all his glory. Yep, he could probably stop traffic with his handsomeness, I thought proudly.

'Mrs Langley, it's a pleasure to meet you,' he gushed in a honeyed tone, extending his hand to hers before bending to place a gentle kiss on her cheek. I smirked inwardly at his "Mr Smooth" impression – gone was Dominant Nicholas, here was

Nicholas at his most charming, and I shook my head in wonder at his ever-changing personality.

Mum was clearly susceptible to his charms and I watched as she blushed furiously –that was obviously where I got that particular trait from – before briefly embracing Nicholas and standing back with a broad grin on her face.

'Call me Leanne. It's lovely to meet you, Nicholas. Rebecca was just telling me about you.' She beamed.

Giving my hip a discreet squeeze, Nicholas smiled at Mum with a look of pride on his face before looking at me with a hint of a raised eyebrow, which I took to mean "I hope you haven't told her everything about me". I smiled up at him cheekily but no, there were certain areas of my life that I wouldn't discuss even with Mum – Nicholas' preference for a little light bondage being one of those things. I hadn't told her about the recent split either, deciding there was no need to worry her now that things were back on track. Blushing, I looked back at my mum and saw her in her element. Clearly she was loving seeing me with a boyfriend for a change.

'Anyway, Rebecca, I didn't want to disturb your girly weekend together, but you left the box with your mum's birthday stuff at my house,' Nicholas said indicating the box outside my flat and flashing me the briefest of winks.

Box with my mum's birthday stuff in it? *What*? I hadn't got round to getting her anything yet. Had Nicholas been out and got a present for my mother? Blimey, that was thoughtful, not to mention totally unexpected.

'I know your birthday is tomorrow, Leanne, but seeing as I won't be here then would you like to open it now? I helped Rebecca pick it out, I'd love to see your reaction,' Nicholas said.

My stomach dropped. I had absolutely no idea what was in the box. God, what if it was awful …? After all, men sometimes had very odd taste when it came to presents, didn't they? What if he'd got her an ironing board cover or something equally hideous?

'Ohh yes! I'd love to!' Mum exclaimed, smiling broadly at Nicholas. He bent to retrieve the enormous box and, after kicking the door shut behind him, placed it on the dining table.

Either his possessive streak was running riot today or he simply couldn't keep his hands off me, because once again he stepped to my side and draped an arm casually over my shoulders. I have to say, after the previous night's reconciliation I didn't mind in the slightest, and returned the action by slipping my hand back around his waist, dipping it into the back pocket of his jeans, and giving his bum a quick squeeze.

The movement of my hand caused a faint rumble to escape from Nicholas' throat, but luckily, it was hidden by the sounds of Mum pulling open the cardboard box. Tentatively, I looked inside, but couldn't see a great deal past the flaps of the box. As she pulled out a huge bunch of flowers, I relaxed. Phew, they were beautiful; Nicholas had done well.

'Oh, these are just lovely. Thank you both!' Mum exclaimed, sniffing the colourful bouquet with a grin and then gently placing the flowers on the table.

Nicholas reached into the box and pulled out a card and smaller, gift-wrapped box. Handing me the card, he gave the box to my mum. 'Maybe you should give your mum the card tomorrow morning so she has something to open,' he suggested, and after a quick glance, I realised the card was blank and ready for me to write in. Gosh, he'd thought of everything.

Meanwhile, Mum was busy unwrapping the small box. I couldn't see what it contained but Nicholas gave my waist a squeeze as she let out a small sob of pleasure. 'Oh! Darling, it's beautiful!' she cried, clearly overjoyed with her present, before she welled up with tears on the spot.

Craning my head, I saw a stunning silver bracelet with tiny blue jewels in it that looked suspiciously like sapphires. Blimey, it was gorgeous, and looked very expensive. No wonder Mum was crying.

Glancing up at Nicholas wide-eyed, I found his gaze firmly on mine. I mouthed the words "thank you", and he smiled at me shyly. Wow, real, genuine shyness; that was a side of him I hadn't really seen before.

'Oh, don't forget this,' Nicholas added, reaching into the seemingly empty box and removing one last envelope.

'Actually, this one is a surprise for Becky too, my treat.'

Mum opened the envelope and I watched as she skimmed the card inside, before her eyes boggled and she looked up at Nicholas with stunned shock on her face. She silently passed the card to me and I turned it over to read the few sentences before gasping. It was a luxury spa day for three at one of London's top hotels and it was booked for tomorrow.

Holy cow, this lot must have cost him an absolute fortune.

'I thought maybe you could take Joanne too?' Nicholas said, sounding uncertain. 'They have private spa rooms so it would just be the three of you, no strangers around.' Could this man – *my man* – get any better? How incredibly thoughtful; Joanne would love to spend the day with mum and me.

Oof. Mum was suddenly embracing me so hard she knocked the wind out of my lungs. 'Oh Becky, this is the best birthday ever, and to see you so happy ...' I hugged her back before she hugged Nicholas and then excused herself to the toilet. Probably to allow herself a private little cry and to fix her make-up.

'Nicholas, this is –' words failed me and I shook my head '– so thoughtful, thank you. I'll pay you back,' I added, wondering how many books I'd have to sell to afford the price of the bracelet alone.

'No need, Becky, I wanted to do it,' he reassured me, pulling me into his arms so I rested on his firm chest, probably one of my favourite places to be. Perhaps this generosity was just another of his ways to make things up with me. 'You liked the bracelet?' he asked uncertainly, stroking a hand over my hair.

'Absolutely. It will suit Mum perfectly; we both prefer silver over gold so it was a great choice,' I murmured as I buried my head in his shirt and inhaled his glorious scent. He'd showered so, disappointingly, the smell of this morning's bedroom activity had gone, but it had been replaced by the lovely, piny, fresh fragrance that I loved so much.

'That's good to hear because I got you something too,' he whispered, producing another box from his trouser pocket and holding it out to me.

Clicking open the square velvet box, I found a solid silver

bangle glinting up at me. It had a line of gems running through the silver which looked rather like diamonds and was exactly the type of thing I would have bought myself if money were no object. Gasping, I looked up at him. 'Nicholas, it's beautiful,' I whispered, 'but this is all too much … This lot must have cost you a fortune,' I babbled in my surprise.

'You forget that because of your review I'm now a rather famous and well-paid pianist. I can afford it – and believe me, Rebecca, you are worth it.' Bending his head, Nicholas proceeded to kiss me deeply and thoroughly until we heard the bathroom door open and had to break apart quickly, both of us panting and flushed and thoroughly aroused. As much as I loved my mum, right now I'd have killed for ten minutes alone with my amazing boyfriend, but as it was, he stayed for a coffee with us and then departed to leave us to our girly weekend.

SEVENTEEN

Two weeks had passed since our reconciliation and I had to say Nicholas was like a completely new man. The protective, slightly dominant side was still there, and although he was working on softening it in his weekly sessions with Dr Philips, I suspected it would always be a part of his personality. Mind you, it was elements of these traits that had attracted me to him in the first place, so as long as he could work on his temper, I was more than happy for the rest to stay.

After the drab relationships I'd experienced in the past, it was overwhelming just how much Nicholas seemed to love me, but incredible too because for a change I actually felt the same way. I'd never been romanced quite like this in my life and was loving every minute.

Things between us had basically returned to how they'd been before I left. Our connection was still just as intense; it was like we were linked on some primal level, sex was frequent, intimate, loving and always mind blowing, and once again I found that I was practically living at his house.

Popping my head round his music room door, I found Nicholas absorbed in playing a beautiful piece and couldn't help but marvel again at his skill. God, he was sexy when he played the piano. Actually, he was sexy most of the time, I thought with a roll of my eyes. I was such a lost cause.

Not wanting to disturb him, I loitered just inside the doorway watching him play. When he finished, I wandered toward him smiling and, to my surprise, he promptly pulled me onto his lap with a look I now knew well – "I am going to kiss you".

Unfortunately, before he'd even managed to lower his lips to mine there was a knock on the door and Mr Burrett appeared. 'Nathan to see you, sir.'

'Show him in,' Nicholas said, casting an odd look at me when he felt me tense in his arms as my hand clutched a handful of his shirt.

Oh God, the infamous older brother. I'd still not met Nathan in person but I now knew so much about him and his problems, not to mention his sexual tastes – which by all accounts were even more twisted than Nicholas' – that I didn't know what to expect from him.

What I didn't expect was the absolute hunk of a man who entered the room about two seconds later. Wow, he was good looking, almost an exact replica of Nicholas. Tall, broad, and facially very similar, nearly as handsome but with more tension lines in his forehead and blond, slicked-back hair instead of his brother's dark, unruly locks.

Jeepers, he didn't look like the kind of guy who kept women chained up at his beck and call … More like the kind of man you might find auditioning for a part in a Hollywood blockbuster. Then again, I hadn't thought Nicholas looked like the kind of man to wield a cane. And how very wrong I had been about that, I thought, the memory bringing with it a pang of pain that I quickly buried. Leave the past where it is, I reminded myself firmly.

Embarrassed to be caught in our intimate position, I struggled to stand from Nicholas' lap. However, instead of helping me up he tightened his arms around me as if sensing my discomfort and choosing to keep me close.

'Nicholas, I'm not interrupting, am I? I can come back later,' Nathan said coolly as his ice-blue eyes bore into me unnervingly, clearly assessing the woman currently residing in his brother's lap.

Finally, Nicholas stood, placing me at his side and wrapping an arm protectively around my waist, which was actually quite nice given how nervous I was suddenly feeling. 'Not at all. It's good to see you, Nathan.' He glanced between the two of us and smiled. 'Nathan, this is Rebecca,' he said, trailing his hand down my arm and sending a tingle shooting across my skin.

'Rebecca, this is my brother, Nathan.'

'Hi. Nice to meet you, Nathan,' I said in a bright tone with as much of a smile as I could manage, although I wasn't entirely convinced my tone backed up my words and was fairly sure my smile looked stretched and false.

'Likewise,' was all Nathan said in response.

Gosh, this was awkward. This man knew that his brother had beaten me with a cane till I bled just over a month ago, and I felt myself blush as I wondered what else these two had shared in their discussions. Shuddering at the idea of him knowing my intimate secrets, I felt the sudden desire to escape. 'I think I'll get a cup of tea. Would either of you like a drink?' I asked in a surprisingly calm tone.

'Coffee, please – you know how I like it,' Nicholas said with a secret smile, seeming somehow to make those simple words mean so much more. Reluctantly, he let me go – but not before placing a soft kiss in my hair.

'Coffee for me too – black, no sugar,' Nathan said briskly, a strange edge to his voice. Although I'd only just met him, so I really shouldn't judge him. Perhaps that was how he always sounded.

After a few minutes alone in the kitchen, I started to relax again. It was probably just as well I'd finally met Nathan. After all, he was Nicholas' brother so I'd probably be seeing a fair amount of him in the future. But because Nicholas had finished with me after a discussion with his brother, I couldn't help but worry what they might be talking about upstairs at this very moment.

I pulled the box of teabags from the cupboard, and promptly dropped them when I was disturbed by a soft cough behind me. Spinning around, I found Nathan eyeing me with apparent amusement. God, he had almost the exact same look of arrogant smugness as his bloody brother.

'Hi, Rebecca,' he said. His voice was calm, but I found myself trembling with embarrassment as I looked at the scattered teabags around my feet. What an idiot I was.

I bent to scoop the box up, and nodded. 'Hi,' I managed, gripping and crumpling the teabags in my hand as I rounded them up shakily.

'You have no reason to be nervous,' he offered, apparently thinking he was being generous, but his comment only prompted my stubborn side to emerge.

'I'm not nervous,' I replied smoothly, wondering why I felt the need to lie because clearly I *was* anxious around him. Who wouldn't be? He was huge and his eyes had to be among the most intense I'd ever seen, and considering I was dating Nicholas don't-defy-me Jackson, that was quite a claim.

'That's good,' he murmured softly, humouring me. 'I merely wanted to apologise for the bad advice I gave Nicholas when I told him to leave you,' he said, tucking his hands into the pockets of his chinos.

Oh. An apology. Wow. I had not expected that and it left me slightly lost for words. Seeing as I wasn't exactly sure what to say in response, I just shrugged as casually as I could. 'OK. Accepted.'

'Clearly you are good for him,' Nathan observed, narrowing his eyes and watching me as I desperately tried not to squirm under his heavy appraisal.

Just then, I caught sight of Nicholas leaning on the kitchen doorframe with a smile playing on his lips and his eyes focused solely on me. Just catching his gaze made my skin heat and I felt my cheeks redden. I would never get sick of the way he gazed at me like that.

'Just checking you two are playing nicely,' he observed dryly before stepping into the kitchen and slipping a protective arm around my waist. I sensed he was claiming me in front of his brother, which I found a little odd. In fact, he couldn't have been much more obvious unless he'd territorially pissed on my leg, but given the way Nathan unnerved me I found his touch reassuring so I simply leant against him and absorbed his calming strength.

'We are, don't worry,' I assured him with a smile.

'Perhaps you two would like to come for dinner at my place tomorrow for a proper catch-up?' Nathan suggested, to my horror. 'How about supper time, say about seven?'

'Sounds good,' Nicholas agreed with a nod, but my stomach

dropped. I hadn't even managed to get through a coffee with Nathan without making an idiot of myself. God knows what ridiculous things I'd do or say during the course of an entire evening around him. Clenching my teeth, I forced a smile too. Nicholas owed me one for this, big time.

EIGHTEEN

The following day, I was standing at the island in Nicholas' glorious kitchen preparing a quick salad to tide us over until dinner at Nathan's that night. We were discussing locations for a weekend away, something Nicholas had suggested after reading about Lake Como in a magazine this morning. Typically, he wanted to go somewhere extravagant, but I'd tried to limit the cost by volunteering the Lake District as a possible destination. With us both being so stubborn, it was currently still up for negotiation but I had the distinct feeling I wouldn't win.

'It feels so normal having you here, Becky, so good,' Nicholas mused quietly, 'Is it usual to feel this comfortable so early on in a relationship?' he asked suddenly as he flipped idly through another travel brochure at the counter behind me.

I didn't know how to answer his question. My two previous relationships had never developed to this level of intimacy. Yes, I had slept with both men, eventually, but I'd never lived with either of them and certainly never felt as closely linked with them as I did with Nicholas.

'I'm not sure,' I replied honestly, picking up a cucumber. 'My previous relationships never really progressed this fast so I've never been in a situation quite like this.'

Next to me, I was vaguely aware that Nicholas had placed the brochure down and taken a step back. Continuing to slice the cucumber for a few seconds, I finally glanced across at him to see why he had moved away from me and felt my muscles freeze on the spot.

He was leaning on the opposite counter; his knuckles were white from the pressure of his grip and his face held an expression I hadn't seen for quite a while. Dominance.

He was glowering at me, apparently fighting to control his growing temper, and my stomach dropped to my boots as I wondered frantically just what I had done to bring on this sudden mood swing.

'I want to punish you, Rebecca,' he murmured, his dark eyes probing and examining me intently, his use of my full name indicating his seriousness and making my stomach clench further.

Oh shit. When had I forgotten how intimidating he could be? He hadn't got this annoyed for ages. My blood was thundering through my veins as if I'd just completed a marathon and I tried to suppress the urge to run the hell away from him, knowing that would only make it worse for me if I did.

Clearly, Nicholas was having a little relapse. I wasn't naïve, I knew the fact that he was seeing a counsellor wasn't a magic wand that had removed all his issues. In fact, I was resigned to the knowledge that the ingrained scars of his childhood would take years to heal fully, if ever, and that he was likely to maintain some of his character traits for the rest of his life, but it was still a shock to see him so enraged again.

Remembering Nicholas had told me his counsellor advised us to discuss his emotions if he ever got angry, I tried to calm myself and think what to say. Placing my knife down, I slowly turned to face him fully. I kept my back straight and forced my posture to appear confident and unthreatened, even if below the surface I was a quivering mess.

'Why, Nicholas?' I asked, keeping my voice soft and using his name to keep him focused on the fact that it was me here with him.

'For having sex with other men before me,' he answered thickly, his nostrils flaring with his obvious displeasure at the idea.

Of course ... his insane jealousy – I should have realised that. It was understandable, I supposed; I got jealous too sometimes, but it wasn't a reason to beat the living crap out of me. After all, I hadn't met him until four months ago. Trying desperately to stay calm, I considered the best way to reduce his anger. I knew one thing that would work – *sex*. That always seemed to relax him, but he looked so furious I was actually worried he might even hurt me while doing that.

'Nicholas … I'm twenty-five; it's hardly likely that I would still be a virgin. Besides, I hadn't met you then,' I stated calmly and rationally. Really, if one of us was going to get upset about ex-partners it should be me, not him, because Nicholas must have had an absolute stack of women in his bed over the years, which hardly compared to my lousy figure of two, did it?

'What was his name? The one to whom you gave your virginity?' Nicholas' tone was deathly quiet – too quiet – and I felt my heart accelerate further in my chest to the point where it was thumping painfully against my ribs.

Truth at all times – the other thing Dr Phillips had advised.

'James,' I whispered, causing his eyes to narrow further. Shit. 'If it makes you feel better, I didn't love him and it wasn't very good. Nothing compared to you, Nicholas,' I explained awkwardly, but truthfully, hoping he would see how much he meant to me. 'I love *you,* Nicholas. You are the only man I've ever loved.'

I was doing well; Dr Phillips would be proud of me, I was sure. I sounded much more confident than my rampaging heart implied. And so far, Nicholas seemed to be maintaining his control too, which was definitely a good sign.

'How old were you?' Nicholas asked through clenched teeth, ignoring my last declaration.

'Nineteen.' Yeah, I'd been a bit of a late starter to the whole sex thing, and after the disappointing experiences with my two exes, I kind of wished I *had* stayed a virgin until I'd met Nicholas. At least then it would have been good and with a man I loved.

Studying Nicholas' posture, it was clear to see the tension radiating from his body. Boy, he was really worked up. Jeez, if he put me over his knee now he might just lose control, like the time with the cane. What would I do if he did? Would I leave again as I had promised? Could I?

I bit my lip, strengthening myself internally. Yes, I could, and if he hurt me again I would, no matter how hard it would be for me. Regardless of how much I loved him, if I couldn't trust Nicholas, my love was worthless. What a truly depressing thought, but it brought me back to my senses. I could trust him; I just needed to remind him what we had together.

'Nicholas, I don't want you to spank me, or beat me,' I said, quietly but firmly. 'I don't want you to punish me and I know you don't want that either.' I desperately hoped my words would sink in. I knew that harming me and hurting me was a huge issue for him; he still hadn't forgiven himself for the incident with the cane that had caused us to separate so I hoped this was the right way to go.

Something flashed across his face, regret possibly, before he slowly pushed off the counter and lithely began to stalk toward me like a graceful panther, his eyes never leaving mine.

Oh God, here we go, I thought. This really could go either way. Panic registered in my brain; it was Mr Burrett's day off so I was well and truly on my own if Nicholas freaked out on me now.

Forcing myself to stand my ground, I straightened my back again and tried to keep my courage, which was hard given that my fear had caused my muscles to rubberise and my blood to pound in my ears, almost deafening me. Nicholas stopped in front of me, his eyes dilated and blazing with a dark desire – but a desire for what? My pain, my submission, or my pleasure? I couldn't tell, and that knowledge scared the living daylights out of me.

'You are mine now,' he declared quietly.

Despite his intimidating stance, the softer edge to his voice showed his vulnerability and I found that slightly reassuring.

'Yes,' I agreed softly, because regardless of his many issues, I really was well and truly his now, just as he was mine. As long as he didn't freak out and beat my arse with a cane again, of course.

Without any warning, I suddenly found myself being pinned up against a cupboard as Nicholas advanced on me, gripped my shoulders, and forced me backwards. As my back hit the wood I registered the sound of a jar smashing inside as the cupboard's contents wobbled from the impact of our bodies, before his lips desperately sought mine and pushed all other thoughts from my mind.

Somehow, he smoothly managed to pin both my wrists above my head in one of his strong hands while his other sought my hip and held me still to face his passionate onslaught.

Well, this was a turn-up for the books. I had quite honestly expected to be thrown over the kitchen counter and spanked to within an inch of my life, but this was much, *much* more preferable.

Dominant, non-spanking Nicholas I really liked – his masculine assertiveness made the muscles in my groin tighten and his desperation to claim me was a heady feeling, making me instantly wet with desire.

'Mine,' he grumbled against my lips. His free hand roughly pulled my left leg up and dropped it to rest on the counter behind him so it was almost wrapped around him. He tugged at one breast through my T-shirt, causing my nipple to extend below the thin material and a cry of pleasurable pain to escape from my throat.

Within seconds, he was dragging my skirt up and then, before I had time to catch my breath, Nicholas had pulled his tracksuit bottoms and boxers over his straining erection, tugged my thong aside, and pushed himself inside me with an almost guttural roar. Jeez, talk about no warm-up time; and he hadn't even bothered to remove any of our clothing!

'Fuck!' I cried out in surprise, but thankfully not pain, as I dug the heel of my left foot into the edge of the kitchen counter to stabilise myself. Nicholas pounded into me relentlessly and I found the stretched material of my thong rubbing perfectly against my clitoris, an added bonus of not removing my knickers, I thought with a throaty groan of approval.

God this was good; unexpected, but amazing. My body was fast responding to his demanding rhythm, muscles clenching deep in my core, desire spiralling in my stomach as his strokes brought me closer, closer …

Suddenly, Nicholas buried himself deep inside me and stopped dead, panting heavily in my ear, his hot breaths sending a flush across my skin.

'*No!*' I cried out. I was so close! What the hell was he doing?

'Tell me,' he demanded softly, his breathing hot and ragged against my sensitive lobe as his free hand caressed my cheek with surprising compassion.

Oh, so that was what this was – punishment sex. Nicholas wouldn't spank me so he was going to fuck me into submission instead and not let me come unless I told him what he wanted to hear. Well, this was certainly an improvement on a caning session.

'*Tell me!*' he demanded again, his voice harsh now, desperate even, and he tugged hard on my earlobe with his teeth making me wince.

'I'm yours, Nicholas. *Yours.*' I spoke truthfully into the damp skin of his neck, my own breathing just as hitched as his.

This declaration from me was apparently all he needed to hear because as soon as I spoke, Nicholas groaned with pleasure and began moving inside me again, slower now, with more deliberate thrusts that had me arching my back up from the cupboard to meet him stroke for stroke until finally my body tensed around his, blinding me with a body-quaking orgasm and making me cry out his name into his shoulder.

Seconds later, Nicholas emptied himself inside me with a noise somewhere near a growl and finally freed my hands, allowing them to drop limply back to my sides. It was just as well he was pushed against me otherwise I may well have slumped to the ground from the post-orgasmic muscle trembles that were shooting through my legs.

We stood joined together as we recovered our breath, my face buried in his neck, his damp forehead resting on my hair. Leaving his softening erection inside me, he leant back to look into my face.

'Tell me again, Rebecca ... *please*,' Nicholas said quietly, an almost bewildered look on his face, as if he didn't believe my words. How could he be so domineering one second and so vulnerable the next? My heart constricted for the damaged man in front of me, so starved of love as a child that he literally had no idea how important he was to me.

Raising my hands to his face, I cupped his jaw, rubbing soothing circles across his cheeks, and then smiled up at him. 'I am all yours, Nicholas, and you are mine,' I murmured.

Apparently convinced for now at least, he closed his eyes, rested his forehead on mine, and sighed. 'Yes. You own me body and soul, Rebecca. I love you.' A warm, buzzing sensation shot through my chest at his words. I would never tire of hearing Nicholas say those three words. He dropped a kiss on the end of my nose before suddenly frowning and jerking his head back.

'Did I hurt you?' he asked, concern evident in his tone. 'I'm sorry if I was too rough …'

Shaking my head, I stroked his cheek reassuringly again. 'No … I like it a bit rough sometimes,' I admitted with a shy smile. I was about to say, 'When I'm with you,' to show how much I trusted him, but then remembered that talk of my other lovers had started all this in the first place and I hastily stopped myself. Good catch, I thought with relief.

'Do you now?' he replied with a raised eyebrow and a cocky grin. 'That's just as well, because you seem to be the perfect anger management strategy for me, Becky.' I noticed he was using my shortened name again. Phew, the tantrum was over.

'Better than using the cane?' I asked tentatively, and in response, he glowered at me. Damn it, why couldn't I just keep my big mouth shut?

'Different,' he muttered finally. 'I don't ever want to hurt you, Becky. The canes … They were for a different purpose, a link to my past, I suppose. But that's all it is now, my past; I don't need to retain it any more. I still get angry with you sometimes but I see that punishing you in that way would be wrong. I told you I don't want to do it any more.' He shook his head. 'Making love to you, albeit roughly, seemed to be a way for me to vent my frustration but not hurt you.' His eyes had widened as if he had surprised himself with this realisation.

I blushed at his admission. Wow, my body was officially an anger management strategy. Not many people could make that claim, could they?

'Why, Rebecca, I do believe you're blushing,' he murmured,

dropping a chaste kiss on to each of my burning cheeks before taking hold of my chin and tilting it up so I was looking into his eyes. 'The cane was way too extreme.' He frowned. 'But the other stuff can be a good distraction sometimes too,' he added cryptically.

'Other stuff?' I asked, wondering what he was referring to. But as his self-confident smile returned to his beautiful lips, I was fairly sure Nicholas was referring to the toys he sometimes liked to use in the bedroom and was just teasing me now. Oh goody, Teasing Nicholas was even better fun than Dominant Nicholas.

'The cuffs and toys are fun but we've not used them since getting back together because, to be honest, as long as I'm with you, Becky, I'm happy. I don't need all that other stuff.' Wow, he really had made progress. I could see the truth shining in his eyes. He genuinely meant it.

I chewed on my lip. Something deep inside me was disappointed. There, I'd admitted it, even if not out loud. I had enjoyed using the gentler toys with Nicholas; they'd been new, completely unknown, and downright exciting when combined with his skilled touch in the bedroom.

Suddenly he laughed and, seeing as his cock was still inside me, I felt it right to my core. 'Just when I thought your cheeks were as red as they could get you've managed to blush even more,' he observed with narrowed eyes. 'I think perhaps you liked experimenting with the toys more than you'll ever admit out loud, Becky,' he concluded softly as if he'd just read my mind.

A flicker of his old arrogance returned for a brief second but his tone was peculiar, causing me to meet his gaze. As I did, it was my turn to gasp. Nicholas' eyes were blazing again, his intention obvious, and no sooner had I registered the excitement in his pupils than I felt him stirring to life inside me again.

'Perhaps I could dig out that box of toys again ...' he murmured teasingly. 'Wrap your legs around me, Rebecca,' he ordered, rolling my full name across his tongue while gripping my waist in his strong hands. His tone made me comply immediately, and once I was secure, he proceeded to walk me to the bedroom with us still joined at the waist intimately.

Nicholas kicked the bedroom door shut behind him and lowered us both to the bed with a hissed breath. 'Christ, Becky, you're so fucking wet I almost lost control just walking here,' he whispered, dropping his forehead onto mine and closing his eyes while he drew in several steadying breaths. He wasn't the only one who needed to recover. Being carried in his arms while his erection throbbed inside me and rubbed against me with every step had almost been my undoing. As for going up the stairs, I thought I was going to come on each and every frigging step.

'I'll be back in a second,' he murmured, dropping a kiss on the end of my nose and easing himself out of me with reluctance. As he reached the door, he paused, his body still fully erect and a dark smile forming on his lips as he turned back to me.

Tugging his dressing gown from the hook on the back of the door, Nicholas pulled the long cotton belt free and threw it at me. 'Undress and then blindfold yourself,' he instructed thickly, then, without giving me a chance to object, he left the room.

Blindfold myself? Wow, that was unexpected ... but actually kind of hot, I thought with a wicked grin. Was this insanely gorgeous, kinky, sexy man really mine?

Undressing in record time – if there were Olympic medals for disrobing, believe me, I would have won gold – I tied the strip of fabric around my eyes until everything went dark. Then I lay back on the soft bedding and eagerly awaited his return, my body already thrumming with arousal.

Luckily, in my hugely aroused state I didn't have to wait long before I heard the bedroom door opening. If the door hadn't squeaked, I would still have known that Nicholas was back because there was a growl of approval that made me grin uncontrollably.

'God, you are so beautiful, Rebecca.' His voice was surprisingly close by. He must have crossed the room silently and be standing right next to the bed, leaning over me. I shivered in anticipation, my body moving on top of the bed as I grasped a handful of the sheet in a tight fist.

Next, I felt the soft caress of his fingers on my wrist. Gently he unclenched my fingers and turned my palm upwards, lazily trailing across the sensitive skin over my pulse point in a teasing series of circles. 'Would you like to be tied up or not?' Nicholas asked softly.

Tied up ... I'd experienced both sides of that in the past. The intense pleasure brought about from not being able to move while Nicholas stimulated me had definitely given me one of my most powerful orgasms ever, but then on the other hand I still remembered the gut-wrenching, stifling fear of being restrained and unable to escape while he used the cane on me to beat out his fury.

A shudder escaped me at the memory and my fear must have been evident on my face because I felt the bed dip as he lowered himself down beside me. I felt the softness of his lips descend on mine before he slipped my blindfold up onto my forehead. 'We can leave that part, Rebecca. You are safe with me, baby, I promise. Do you want me to stop?'

The obvious concern and love on Nicholas' face made it clear to me that I had no need to worry; he wouldn't hurt me. So with a shy smile, I kissed him back and then readjusted the blindfold over my eyes again.

'Tie me up,' I instructed, raising my arms above my head and hoping the gesture would establish in his heart that I really did trust him again. A small hiss escaped his lips and heated my cheek before he kissed me once more, then set about tying both my wrists and ankles to the four posts of the bed. Once he was done, I was completely spread-eagled and unable to move.

You'd think I'd be mortified in such an exposing position, wouldn't you? But I wasn't, not in the slightest. Perhaps it was the knowledge that Nicholas loved me that did it, or just because we knew each other's body intimately by now, but surprisingly I no longer found this type of position embarrassing and I relaxed back into the mattress, eagerly awaiting his next trick.

The sound of a match being struck to my right made me turn my head, and the smell of sulphur registered briefly in my nose before a lovely waft of something sweet caught my breath.

Orange blossom. Nicholas must have lit an orange blossom candle somewhere nearby and the fact he remembered my favourite scent made my heart tighten in my chest. It wasn't exactly a common scent for a candle either, so he'd obviously gone out of his way to find it – another point in his favour.

Even through my blindfold, I could tell when he turned off the main light because everything went even blacker than before. The thought that he was going to make love to me in candlelight, something so classically romantic, made my heart constrict and sent a shot of lust coursing through my body to my aching clit. I squirmed around, desperate for some contact between my legs to ease the throbbing there, but my bound legs wouldn't allow me to squeeze my thighs together like I wanted.

I might be horny and desperate for release, but a huge smile broke on my lips as I lay waiting for him to return to the bed; the progress Nicholas had made emotionally in the last few weeks was truly phenomenal, both in the bedroom and out, and I had to keep reminding myself he was new to the whole "romance" thing. Although with the candles, flowers, and general obsession with my happiness it had to be said that he was handling it all like a pro.

Suddenly, Nicholas' mouth was on mine. I hadn't realised he was so close, he must have been leaning over the bed because I hadn't felt him sit down but his lips were so soft and gentle that I found myself craning my neck up for more of his delicious pressure.

Then his lips were gone and I felt momentarily lost until they began licking and nibbling at the skin of my breast before latching on to one of my nipples, which he sucked into his warm mouth and gently nipped with his teeth. Being "blind" and teased this way was quite something, making my insides liquefy with pleasure and my body almost beyond my control. Nicholas' other hand began roaming across my skin, touching with feather-light flicks; stomach, thigh, hip. As his fingers found my swollen clitoris, he sucked my nipple right into his mouth harder than before, almost to the point of pain. But oh, what delicious pain it was, so good that I felt it right deep down in my groin as my hips bucked from the bed to press myself more firmly against his hand.

'Ahhh!' I cried out, arching my back for more and almost feeling ashamed to enjoy this fine balance of pleasure and pain that he was bestowing on me. Then Nicholas released my hardened, sensitive nipple, giving it one final swipe with his tongue before kissing his way across to the other one to repeat the treatment.

The blindfold increased my awareness of his touch tenfold, and that soon became almost too much for me to handle. My nerve endings felt as if they were on fire and my body was so hot I had started to seriously perspire. The sensation of Nicholas' tongue running along the seam of my lips and plundering my mouth while his hands worked simultaneously at my breasts and clitoris was overwhelming, thundering me towards my peak, and I pulled back, gasping for air and writhing below him like a wild animal.

Sensing my imminent release, he slowed things down, briefly leaving my side before returning and laying himself alongside me. The feel of his naked body and erection warm and hard against my thigh made me sigh contentedly and turn my head to where I thought his face might be. My aim was right and I felt his lips seek out mine, kissing me lingeringly on the mouth, before something cool pressed against the apex of my thighs.

'I think you might like this,' he murmured against my mouth, before pushing what felt like a lifelike-shaped vibrator deep into my wet channel in one smooth movement.

'Oh yes,' I gasped, loving the feel of the vibrator filling me, so alien in its plastic material and yet so familiar in its form, far better than the bullet-style one he'd used on me when we'd first met.

Hearing a click as he turned it on, I expected it to buzz inside me and gasped in shock as, instead of vibrating, the whole thing circled rhythmically. *Wow*, this thing was incredible, somehow managing to hit all the right spots with its sweeping motion and causing my hips to thrust upwards in pleasure. A second click followed, and as well as circling, the vibrator began to pulse inside me. When Nicholas joined in the fun by grazing his thumb across my clitoris in a teasing series of sweeps I was almost a goner.

'Oh God!' I couldn't help but call out from the sensory overload. The pleasure from the vibrator combined with Nicholas' thumb, not to mention his mouth on my breast, was too much for me to handle silently, especially as I couldn't move because of my restraints. After only a few moments, I exploded in a body-shaking orgasm, screaming his name and writhing below him as much as my restraints allowed.

Still held within the cocoon of my blindfold I felt the mattress shift as Nicholas moved around me undoing each of the bonds in turn. He gently massaged and kissed each limb before moving to the next. Swallowing, I realised my throat was sore from yelling his name, and as he removed my blindfold I regained my focus and saw him grinning down at me broadly.

'Could you shout my name louder next time? I'm not sure the people in the next street heard you,' he remarked lightly as my cheeks flamed with shame.

'Sorry,' I croaked as his lips lowered toward mine invitingly.

'Don't apologise. I love hearing you scream my name, baby.' He kissed me lingeringly on my already swollen mouth.

'Now it's my turn, Becky, but I don't need any toys. I like to enjoy them sometimes but I like to enjoy you even more,' he whispered against my neck. He positioned himself between my legs and entered me so deliciously slowly that I could feel every single inch sliding inside me until he was buried to the hilt, our hips pressed together firmly.

My body was still quivering from the aftershocks of my previous orgasm, not to mention the one in the kitchen, but this felt sublime. Jeez, I was going to sleep like a log tonight, and be walking a bit funny too, but even through my exhaustion, I felt my body reacting to Nicholas' tender lovemaking. How could it not? Instinct took over, and as I met him thrust for thrust, he brought me to yet another mind-blowing climax, murmuring my name over and over against my neck and making me feel like the most treasured thing on earth.

NINETEEN

That night, we were due at Nathan's for dinner and I was *dreading* it. I'd lost count of the amount of times I'd huffed and puffed out my anxiousness in the last few hours, but Nicholas just seemed completely oblivious of my anxiousness. I'd distracted myself from consciously thinking about it for most of the afternoon, but as I settled myself in Nicholas' plush car and pulled the seatbelt tight across my lap I felt my stomach bunch with nerves at the thought of seeing Nathan again. Nicholas would be there with me, which was some solace, but still, Nathan had seemed to be even more intimidating than Nicholas, if that was possible; something I attributed to his overwhelming self-confidence. Probably after meeting him a few times and getting used to his mannerisms, I'd feel more relaxed in his company. Yeah, right.

The drive to Nathan's apartment in Canary Wharf took about half an hour, and was actually an area of London that I hadn't visited before. Although I knew Docklands was a thriving business area of London, I'd had no idea that there were so many residential areas too. In fact, as we made our way between large, skyscraper offices and converted dock buildings, I was surprised to see a variety of trendy shops, bars, and restaurants lining the streets of the area.

Mr Burrett had driven us so we could have a drink tonight, and he dropped us off at the base of a huge apartment block that had to be at least thirty floors high. Blimey. Standing on the pavement I craned my neck backwards and stared at the building in awe. It was all steel and glass, and just as sterile and imposing as the resident we were on our way to visit.

We entered the lift and I wasn't really surprised when

Nicholas pressed the button for the top and then entered a private code. Well, this was Nathan's home; if he was anything like his brother, he would have the best apartment in the place, wouldn't he? The lift came to a stop on the top floor as we exited into a plush hallway complete with some fancy modern art on the walls, I saw there was only one doorway off the small landing. Ah, the penthouse, of course, that was obviously why the private code had been needed in the lift.

Without us knocking, Nathan opened the door to his apartment almost immediately. He practically filled the doorway, making me realise that while the two brothers were incredibly similar in their looks, Nathan definitely had the larger build of the two. He was dressed in smart navy trousers and a pale blue shirt that was tight enough to accentuate just how broad his shoulders were. The colour of his top was an exact match for the startling ice-blue of his eyes, which I then noticed were fixed on me. Ridiculously, I gripped Nicholas' hand tighter as I felt Nathan appraise me with a sweep of his gaze before he stood back and ushered us inside with a brisk wave of his hand.

Oh wow! Clearly Nathan made as much money as Nicholas, if not more, because his apartment was stunning, and I mean breath-taking. We had entered almost directly into the lounge, and the entire front wall was made of glass, allowing the evening sun to stream in, warming the room and illuminating the elegantly stylish furniture that adorned it. The view over London was beautiful and I dawdled for a second to admire the last rays of sun glinting off the water of the smart dock area outside. As I turned back into the room, my eyes swept over the space again. Leather sofas of black and white surrounded a marble fireplace and rich, colourful rugs were spread across the floor; it was like a show home, but far, far better. It was such a contrast to my poky little flat that I found myself feeling just a tiny bit jealous.

As we moved toward the sofas, Nathan introduced us to a woman who was standing by the door and appeared decidedly on edge.

'Rebecca, this is Stella,' he said, indicating the woman who seemed somehow slim but curvy at the same time, with bright green eyes and flowing blonde hair that fell to just below her shoulders. Nicholas had clearly met her before because he smiled at her and nodded his head in greeting, but he sent an odd look toward his brother that completely confused me.

Placing a warm hand on my lower back Nicholas guided me to a soft black leather two-seater where we sat down as Nathan settled himself opposite us on the white couch. Stellá had moved into the room, but was now hovering by the end of Nathan's seat like a frozen puppet. What a strange girl she seemed; she still hadn't uttered a word. She was beautiful and her straight back indicated confidence but the posture of her neck made her seem uncomfortable because her eyes were downcast and her hands twisted nervously in front of her. As I studied her odd behaviour my mind began to think back over all that Nicholas had told me about his brother. It took a few moments for my brain to get up to speed, but suddenly everything dropped into focus for me with sickening clarity …

Stella was Nathan's submissive.

Oh God. Of course she was. Nicholas had already told me his brother always had a live-in sub and it was the perfect explanation for her odd behaviour.

A small gasp left my lips at the realisation and I felt Nicholas tense next to me. Glancing at him, I found his blue eyes on me, a look of concern fluttering on his eyebrows as though he knew exactly what I was thinking. Oh wait … he did know exactly what I was thinking. He already knew about Stella, and knew exactly what role she played in his brother's life. Great, apparently I was the only one in the dark.

Our eye contact was broken as I heard Nathan shift on the white sofa. 'Sit,' he ordered softly, patting the seat next to him and looking up at Stella expectantly. She immediately sat down, perched on the front of the sofa cushion with her hands linked on her thighs, head slightly bowed and her eyes averted toward the floor.

With sick fascination, I watched Nathan as he watched Stella. There was a flicker of something in his eyes – something that told me he had feelings for her, that he saw her as more than just a plaything, but what did I really know? I hardly knew him at all, and I certainly knew nothing about the intricacies of a relationship between a dominant and his submissive.

Gently, Nathan placed a hand on Stella's shoulder and pulled her back against the sofa so he was sitting with his arm lightly draped around her shoulders. As he did this, a tiny gasp escaped her lips and I felt my stomach twist uncomfortably. From her reaction, it seemed that they had never sat together like this before, although ironically he had probably done all matter of intimate and pervy things to her in the bedroom.

Jeez, this was so fucked up.

'Eye contact is permitted,' I heard him whisper in her ear and immediately she raised her eyes to his reverently, as if she worshipped him, a hint of a smile twitching on her lips.

Drawing in a long, deep breath I blinked several times, trying to clear my head. I felt like I was watching some hugely intimate scene unravel before me. Obviously, the eye contact was a very big thing for Stella and it was actually making me feel quite uncomfortable to bear witness to it. Their gazes locked for a second or two before Nathan winked almost imperceptibly and then turned back to Nicholas.

'So how was the traffic on your drive over today?' he asked with an easy smile.

How was the traffic? Really? Given the bizarre circumstances, I thought he might have wanted to talk about something different, although what exactly I expected I wasn't sure. One thing was apparent, though – Nathan definitely appeared more laidback than when I'd met him last week, eyes wider and muscles more relaxed. Perhaps it was due to being on home territory or perhaps he'd properly accepted that I was dating his brother now.

As I thought this, his glance swept across to me and his eyes visibly narrowed for a split second as he looked at where my hand was clasped in Nicholas'. He seemed to have to force himself to relax, and I swallowed hard, the pressure hurting my throat. Yeah, so perhaps Nathan wasn't my number one fan just yet, then.

A horrible realisation dawned on me, distracting me from

what Nathan may or may not think about me. Was this what Nicholas' previous life had been like? He'd said he was different with me, so had he had submissives just like Stella hanging on his every word, doing his bidding like a good little girl or being punished if they didn't?

Fuck. The thought made me sick to my stomach. My guts were churning, so fearing I might actually throw up, I practically threw Nicholas' hand away from me and lurched to my feet, looking toward Nathan a little desperately, anger starting to build in my vision and making my head spin.

'Can I use your bathroom, please?'

I saw Nicholas frowning at me but I kept my eyes averted from him; I needed a minute to clear my head. And possibly be sick.

'Sure – Stella, show Rebecca the bathroom, please, and bring back some drinks for us all afterwards,' Nathan replied amiably.

Was he telling Stella to get the drinks or me? Because with the way I was feeling right now, Nathan I-own-you Jackson could get his own fucking drinks and drown himself in them.

Stella stood up and after smoothing her beautiful black dress began leading me away from the lounge into an equally opulent hallway. Pushing open a door to the left she waved a hand towards a large, spotless bathroom with white fittings and aquamarine towels. Gratefully, I staggered inside.

'Thanks,' I muttered. I slammed the door shut before Stella had a chance to utter even one word, and lurched toward the sink feeling decidedly unsteady.

Breathe, I ordered myself, trying to gather my wits. Flicking on the tap, I scooped up a handful of water and splashed it on my face. The cool liquid seemed to help a little so I repeated the action and even dabbed some on the back of my neck before grabbing a towel and drying myself off. With the towel still gripped in my hand like a security blanket, I put the toilet seat down and sat with my head resting in my hands, trying to settle my spinning emotions. This was all totally crazy, who the hell lived like this? Me, apparently, I thought with a roll of my eyes, wondering just how my life had gotten so surreal.

No more than ten seconds later, there was a quiet knock on the door.

'Rebecca? Are you OK?'

It was Nicholas. I closed my eyes and bit down on my lower lip but remained quiet. Was I OK? How could I be when I knew that not ten feet away Nathan sat with a woman who was at his beck and call like a frigging slave? This was so alien to me, so wrong ...

'Becky, baby?' The concern in Nicholas' voice was evident now, its pitch audibly higher. So, reluctantly, I stood up and opened the door so he could come in.

Closing the door behind him, he immediately stepped toward me. Unconsciously, I stepped back, knocking into the sink unit in the process. Now that I was trapped, Nicholas persevered forward, cupping my face and forcing me to raise it so he could look in my eyes.

'Becky, I'm sorry, I had no idea Stella would be here.' He paused awkwardly. 'Well, obviously, she pretty much lives here, but she's never usually around when Nathan has guests. I don't know why she is today.' Nicholas dipped his head to place a gentle kiss on my lips, and even in my current foul mood, I felt my body respond to his touch and relax marginally.

'Were you like that?' I asked quietly, looking at his shirt buttons intently, my heart hammering in my chest as I awaited an answer I didn't really want to hear.

'No. I told you before I've never had anyone live with me. The women I was with were just ...' But his voice trailed off as he shifted uncomfortably on his feet.

'Just for sex?' I retorted sarcastically, looking at him with an unimpressed expression on my face. 'So you didn't control their whole lives, just their sex lives?' I finished bluntly, not caring if I sounded like a jealous cow.

Nicholas' face hardened at my crudeness and his eyes narrowed. 'Yes, exactly. But as I've told you, Rebecca, that's in my past; please leave it there.' After we'd glared at each other for several seconds, a huge sigh escaped Nicholas' chest and I watched as his dominant expression faded. 'You, and only you, are my future, Rebecca. Please believe me when I say that.'

He might not be the world's most emotionally open man, but when Nicholas chose to express his feelings, he always did it so succinctly and with such skill that I almost found myself forgiving him and falling into his arms. Almost, but not quite – I wasn't feeling quite that lenient tonight. Not that this was exactly his fault as such, but still, he was here and I needed an outlet for my anxiety.

Steadying myself, I attempted to rationalise the situation. I rubbed the towel over my face and blinked several times. I knew Nicholas was right, about us at least – his past was just that, *past*, and his continued declarations left me with no doubt about his feelings toward me.

But Nathan, *wow*, that was a completely different story and the sight of him and Stella together was still sitting heavy in my stomach.

Finally, I drew in a breath and nodded. I knew Nicholas had made a lot of compromises for me so I should try to make some effort too. 'I'm sorry,' I relented. 'It's just a really peculiar situation for me. I'll be fine,' I assured him, hanging the towel back up and heading for the door.

'Let's go before they think we're up to something in here,' I joked, but my tone lacked its usual humour. Apparently, my bad mood hadn't vanished just yet. Nicholas examined me intently, watching my face as if he could read it somehow and not looking overly thrilled by what he saw. At last, he nodded and followed me back out into the lounge, and I'm pretty sure he noticed that I didn't touch him once as we re-joined the others.

'Are you unwell, Rebecca?' Nathan said directly as we re-emerged into the living area of his stunning apartment. I noticed someone had got me a glass of chilled white wine – no doubt Stella – and I picked up the drink, taking a much-needed sip.

'I was a little dizzy,' I lied, 'but I feel much better now. I'm probably just hungry,' I concluded with a smile that was my best attempt at convincing him.

'Well, it's just as well dinner is served, then,' he replied, indicating the large dining table by the huge windows. Dinner with a view, and what a view, I thought, allowing my mind to slip away from Stella for a moment and absorb the sun setting over the London skyline as I took my seat. It really was quite breath-taking.

My thoughts were brought back to earth with a bump as soon as Nathan spoke again, however. 'Stella's been working very hard to prepare us a nice dinner,' he said as we took our seats around the table.

I raised an eyebrow. From any other person, the comment wouldn't have riled me, but knowing the situation here it annoyed me that Stella had prepared the dinner alone and not as part of a team effort, like most of the couples I knew would do. A small snort rose in my throat. God, she'd probably done it because Nathan had ordered her to, I thought sourly, shooting Nathan a frosty glance.

Under the table, I felt Nicholas place his hand on my leg and give my knee a firm squeeze as if noting the return of my bad mood; not that it had ever really gone away. I made a conscious effort to shake it off, then glanced at him, giving a small nod to show that I would try to behave myself.

As dinners go, I have to say Stella had excelled; beef Wellington, creamy mashed potatoes, broccoli, and deliciously rich gravy. It really smelt superb. As good as the food looked, though, I still couldn't help but watch the interaction between Stella and Nathan with fascination.

Initially, after placing all the food on the table, Stella stood staring at the tablecloth awkwardly, as if unsure how to proceed. Perhaps she was used to serving Nathan first, or maybe they never ate together and this was a first? Gosh, this was very peculiar, but luckily, Nicholas was on the ball and spoke quickly. 'Shall we all just dig in?' he enquired, apparently well aware that Stella was stuck about what to do next.

'Excellent plan, brother,' Nathan agreed, but I still noticed that Stella didn't take any food until we had full plates.

Once we all had a dinner in front of us, I tucked in but saw Stella sitting with her dinner untouched in front of her. Was she not even allowed to eat without permission? A bubble of anger rose in my throat and I realised I was dangerously close to saying something I might regret, but just then Nathan leant in close to her ear to whisper something too quiet for me to hear. I watched as Stella's face lit up with a genuine smile of happiness; her eyes were actually twinkling and for the first time, I could see just how pretty she really was. He leant back a few inches then the two of them shared a lingering and decidedly hot look that to any outsider would have given the impression of a lovestruck couple. Wow, how strange! Intrigued, I found myself wishing I knew what Nathan had said to her.

Nicholas remained tense next to me throughout the meal; picking at his food with far less appetite than usual, although I suspect he was merely reflecting my own tense mood. He did, however, touch my hand or leg whenever he had the opportunity, trying to relax me with his contact, I guessed.

At one point when my hand lay next to my plate, Nicholas took hold of it and rubbed his thumb reassuringly across my skin, but I noticed that Nathan watched the action with a frown creasing his brows. As far as I was concerned, he could bugger off. I didn't care if Nathan disapproved of us, and to prove this point, I gripped Nicholas' hand and raised it to my lips, planting a swift kiss on his knuckles. My actions caused Nathan to narrow his eyes further but had the dual effect of causing Nicholas to grin and then blush, something I'm not sure I'd ever seen him do before.

Unsurprisingly conversation was light. Stella did not really contribute, but I noted that she seemed to enjoy the interactions and her eyes genuinely shone as she watched the three of us chatting around her. It was a shame she didn't open up a bit more, because from the few glimpses I caught of her personality, she looked like she might be quite fun to chat to.

After we finished eating, Nathan nodded at Stella and she began to stack our plates. Inwardly fuming at Nathan for not making any effort to help, I flashed him a furious glare and stood up. 'Let me help you clear the dishes, Stella,' I offered, collecting the potato bowl and gravy boat and following her into the kitchen. Almost bumping into her as we passed at the sink, I gave her a reassuring smile before she caught my arm and stopped me returning to the dining area.

'I can see your shock, Rebecca. I can tell you don't approve of Nathan and me, but it's not like you think. I want to be with him.' She tipped her head to the side and smiled. 'Actually, I chose this lifestyle by myself; you might not believe it but I sought him out and I like living this way,' she explained simply, her green eyes burning into mine before she smiled at me and headed back toward the others.

Wow. She'd actually sounded sincere, and she'd sought him out? I'd love to know more about what lay behind that story – so perhaps I shouldn't be so quick to judge other people's lifestyles, I thought guiltily. Suddenly, a flush of embarrassment rushed across my cheeks; if Stella had noticed my disdain then Nathan probably had too. Oh God, I'd already had enough of problems with Nicholas' brother without adding to them with my insolence.

I rinsed my hands in the sink, then I deliberately softened my shoulders and took several breaths to relax myself. Stella was apparently happy with her unusual set-up so it was really none of my business to interfere. I still had coffee and dessert to make a better impression, so I decided I would try my best to do just that as I wandered back into the dining room, smiling my first genuine smile of the evening.

TWENTY

The following morning, Nicholas and I were enjoying a lazy lie-in – me tucked under his arm and contentedly flopped across his warm chest while he rubbed soothing circles on my back. My bad mood from last night had dissipated; in fact, it had pretty much cleared after my quick chat with Stella when I'd realised I shouldn't judge things on first appearances, but Nicholas had still been insistent that we needed make-up snuggling when we got home. Obviously, I hadn't complained, although I was a bit sore between my legs now after all of yesterday's action. Overuse, no doubt, and this from me, a girl who previously didn't really like sex – who'd have thought it! I grinned to myself, I'd had so much sex I hurt, and I felt ridiculously proud of that fact. Gosh, I really had turned into a slut.

Yawning cavernously, I turned my head as I heard the sound of a car crunching up the gravel driveway to the rear of Nicholas' home. Apparently intrigued, Nicholas gently removed me from the warmth of his arms, hopped from the bed, and pulled back a curtain to see who the visitor was. My eyebrows rose in amusement; he was totally stark naked, and clearly not bothered in the slightest who might see him in all his glory.

'It's Nathan's car,' he commented, indicating a shiny Audi TT parking under a tree as I joined him at the window and slipped my arms around his warm waist.

I had been feeling light-hearted and happy up until now, but swallowed nervously as Nathan's slicked blond hair emerged from the black car. Oh God. I hoped he wasn't here to demand Nicholas dump me for my rude behaviour last night.

Nicholas pulled on some jeans and a T-shirt – going

commando, I noticed with a faint smile – before heading downstairs, but I took a little longer to dress, actually bothering to find some underwear and running a brush through my hair before trotting down to join them, delaying the expected confrontation for as long as possible.

Hearing voices in the kitchen, I walked in to find Nicholas making a pot of coffee with his flashy machine. Perfect. Caffeine would help me deal with Nathan, who I noticed was looking just as well groomed as yesterday in a pair of tight-fitting black jeans and a white polo shirt. I could see just why Stella wanted to be with him; he was definitely an attractive guy. Seriously intimidating, but attractive nonetheless.

Nathan nodded to me in greeting as he saw me enter. Well, at least he hadn't ignored me, so that was a good start; perhaps I hadn't made a complete show of myself last night.

'I need to speak to you,' Nathan said abruptly, causing Nicholas to turn from the coffee maker with a frown.

'Whatever you want to say you can say in front of Rebecca,' Nicholas replied in a cool tone, perhaps thinking along the same lines as me, that Nathan might be here to complain about my attitude to his "relationship" with Stella.

'Not you, Nicholas, I want to speak to Rebecca,' Nathan said calmly. 'In private,' he added, turning his piercing blue eyes on me and causing me to take a step back in surprise.

Me? What did he want to speak to me about? Last night? Oh God …

Nicholas turned and leant on the counter, crossing his arms over his chest and giving his brother a long, hard look as if assessing his reasons. 'It's nothing serious, Nicholas; I just want a quick chat.' Nodding, Nicholas angled his head then loped over to me and kissed me firmly on the lips before releasing me, another example of his territory-claiming behaviour. 'Five minutes,' he said to Nathan firmly, 'then I'm coming in,' he murmured, turning back to the coffee.

Confused, but reassured that Nicholas would be interrupting us in five minutes, I went with Nathan into the downstairs lounge, where he paced in front of the fire impatiently before turning to me and catching my gaze with a ferocious one of his own.

'You can't tell Nicholas about this,' were the first words out of Nathan's mouth and they were said in a low tone that instantly set my defences on high alert. For several awful seconds, as he stepped closer and closer to me, I thought he was going to try and kiss me. Then he took me completely by surprise by stopping, averting his eyes, and speaking softly near my ear.

'Nicholas told you about our past? Our father?' he questioned almost urgently.

'Um, yes,' I responded, wondering where he was going with this.

Nathan nodded tightly. 'Nicholas had it a lot worse than me as a kid. Dad used to hit me too, but I always thought he was trying to make me better, punishing me so I could learn, you know what I mean?' He almost appeared to seek my approval of his words.

His eyes penetrated me, demanding an answer, but if I were being honest, then no, I didn't understand his sentiment at all. If you loved someone, there were definitely better ways to help them improve other than giving them a beating. Not that I was going to express that out loud to a self-confessed dominant like Nathan, a man who by all accounts was tougher and rougher than Nicholas had ever been with me.

I recalled how Nicholas had said he thought Nathan idolised their father and considered saying something, but seeing as it was Nathan who stood glaring at me expectantly, I decided to avoid that topic for now and be casual in my response.

'Oh, I suppose so,' I said vaguely. My fingers had linked together in front of me and I was twining them impatiently to try and calm the nerves that Nathan seemed to spawn inside me. But then I suspected even the coolest person would have wilted under Nathan's scrutiny.

'My parents never expressed their love for one another; all I saw was my father's dominance over the household, his unyielding strength. They were united in some strange way but never affectionate.' Nathan's eyes had clouded as if remembering certain unpleasant scenes from his past. 'Never loving,' he finished with a frown and a shake of his head.

'OK …' I began hesitantly. 'Where do I fit in to this, Nathan, what did you want to talk to me about?' I had to ask, because it looked like he just wanted to unload his emotional baggage on me, and right now I wasn't sure how much more I could take. Not without showing the pity I felt for them both that I knew wouldn't be well received.

'I want what you have,' he said simply, crossing his arms over his broad chest and staring at me.

What? What could I possibly have that someone as rich as Nathan couldn't get? Had he forgotten that I'd seen his luxurious apartment? Clearly, the guy had money by the bucket load, and would be able to buy whatever the hell he wanted.

Seeing my obvious confusion, he elaborated. 'I want to be like you and Nicholas. I can see he's happy, *genuinely happy*, with you, Rebecca, and you with him. When you sat together last night, I could literally see the love passing between you; it was amazing. I've never witnessed that before.' Shaking his head, he looked rather bemused now. 'I'm not sure I'm capable … but I want it.' His eyes were on my face again – not directly on my eyes, but close enough that, for whatever reason, I couldn't look away from his inquisitive blue gaze.

'With Stella?' I wondered out loud, amazed and surprised by the emotional sentiment in Nathan's statement, he sounded like he *really* meant it.

'Yes. I … I … like her a great deal, but I don't know how to proceed,' he admitted with difficulty. His eyes that, seconds ago, had been piercing and cold were now firmly fixed on the floor, cloudy and hesitant, and I realised he felt uncomfortable – he liked to be in control but this was something new to him, something beyond his control. It was quite an interesting experience to watch the mix of emotions playing on his strong features.

The combination of adrenaline and confusion in my system nearly made me laugh out loud; somehow, I seemed to have managed to turn into a relationship trainer for ex-dominants. Although looking at his hooded eyes and intense posture, I wasn't sure Nathan would ever completely stop being a dominant. He was just so frigging intimidating that I struggled to draw an image in my mind of him having a softer side.

'Tell her,' I said simply, with a shrug.

'No.' He shook his head defiantly. 'Words mean very little to me. When we were children, my mother would always say she loved us but then whenever Nicholas was hurt by Father, it was always me tending to his injuries, not her. Deserting your child? How can that be love?'

A pained expression filled his face and I almost hugged him for support, feeling sick at the thought of a young Nicholas, hurt and unloved.

His words made another piece of the jigsaw fit and helped me to understand a little bit more about the Jackson brothers. This distrust of spoken sentiments was no doubt why Nicholas always felt the urge to touch me, and why physical demonstrations of love – *sex* – were more potent to him than verbal statements. Shaking my head, I let out a breath as, once again, I realised just how lucky I had been as a child.

'I need to *show* Stella that I want to be with her. What do I do?' he demanded softly.

Thinking on the spot, an idea popped into my head. 'Well, I'd start by ripping up any "submissive" contract you have with her, if I were you. That would make it less of a formal agreement and more like a relationship.' I remembered Nicholas mentioning that Nathan always drew up some sort of document with his live-in submissives, which sounded positively weird to me. 'Take her out for a meal in public, hold her hand, kiss her, make her feel special, make her feel like an equal,' I replied, vaguely aware that five minutes was nearly up and Nicholas would be charging in here at any moment.

I wanted to add, "Don't beat the living crap out of her", but decided not to push my luck with Nathan until I knew him better. If he really was similar to his father, as Nicholas suspected, then I needed to tread carefully. Besides, he might not punish her; I had no idea what he did to Stella in the privacy of his bedroom, and neither did I want to know, for that matter.

'Touch her like you and Nicholas last night?' he asked, frowning. 'When he held your hand and you kissed him?' Wow, he really had no clue, did he? Then I thought back to his description of their childhood home life and wondered if they'd never experienced or witnessed affection, how could they possibly know how to display it?

'Exactly like that,' I agreed with an encouraging nod. Nathan was going up in my estimation, I decided with a smile.

'Do you think she likes me?' he asked next, self-doubt clear in his tone as the lines at the corners of his eyes deepened.

I had to fight the urge to grimace – the thought that Nathan was living with a woman, sleeping with her, and didn't actually know if she liked him or not was disturbing to say the least. Did that mean originally Nathan hadn't cared what Stella thought and would just do with her as he pleased? Against her will, perhaps? A small shudder almost escaped me but I pushed it down. Nathan was trying to change and I needed to help him, I reminded myself firmly.

'Well, obviously I've only met Stella once, but yes, I think she likes you, Nathan. In fact, she told me she wants to be with you,' I confirmed, remembering my kitchen conversation with her. 'And when she looked at you, her eyes lit up; that's always a good sign,' I added with a small smile, feeling myself start to relax with him.

Standing straighter as he absorbed this news, he stepped even closer to me and I had to tip my head back to see his face. 'Her eyes lit up. Explain what you mean?' he mumbled, sounding confused. His voice was low but there was still an edge of demand to it, and I unconsciously shifted myself back a few steps, rewinding my previous feelings of relaxation.

'People can smile but you know it's genuine if it reaches their eyes, and when Stella smiled at you it reached her eyes,' I explained simply.

Seeing the look of utter confusion on Nathan's face, I sighed. This was like explaining something to a child. 'OK, watch me smile,' I instructed, before turning my mouth up in a small fake smile. 'Now watch again and see if you can see a difference,' I instructed.

I took a second to think about Nicholas in the kitchen, and how good it felt when he wrapped his arms around me, and a genuine smile spread across my face. I felt it crinkle the corners of my eyes and even sensed my heartbeat speed up a little.

Nathan's brows rose. 'Yes, I see it …' Cocking his head, his blond hair fell away from its perfection to flop over his brow as he looked like he wanted to touch my face and explore the emotion I was showing, but thankfully, he refrained. 'Your cheeks have flushed and your eyes are … *twinkling*,' he said, sounding bemused. 'When did Stella look like this?'

'As soon as you told her that eye contact was permitted.' I shrugged. 'And at the dinner table when you whispered something to her, she looked genuinely thrilled.' I thought back to my curiosity from last night. 'Can I ask what you said to her?' I blurted out without thinking.

Frowning, he looked away, running a hand through his hair to restore its usual order. 'She doesn't usually socialise with me if I have company but I was very intrigued by your relationship with Nicholas and wanted her to see it too. That was the first time she's joined me for dinner with guests and she was nervous so I said she was doing very well,' he admitted, but I could see from Nathan's face that there was more. 'And I told her –' he paused awkwardly '– I told her she looked very beautiful.'

A grin broke across my face; maybe there was a romantic hidden inside him after all. 'Do more things like that, she'll love it,' I encouraged him, stepping forward and patting his arm reassuringly. 'Girls like it when men express their emotions, so don't be afraid to tell her what's in your head,' I advised just as Nicholas opened the door and disturbed us. His eyes instantly hardened as they settled on where I was touching his brother's arm.

Nodding to me, Nathan moved toward the door. 'I will, thanks, Rebecca. I gotta go.' Evidently, he was keen to get home and try out his new techniques straight away.

As Nathan was leaving, it suddenly occurred to me what I'd just said, and more importantly, *who* I had been addressing, and after thinking about some of the twisted things that were probably in Nathan's head I quickly clarified my final point.

'The good stuff, Nathan – only tell her the good stuff!' I called, and I think I actually saw him grin as he closed the door behind himself.

Turning back to Nicholas, I realised his expression was about as far from a grin as humanly possible. His eyes were shuttered and his lips drawn together in a thin line as his shoulders hunched defensively. Possessive really should be his middle name.

I shook my head in exasperation and clucked my tongue. 'Chill out, Nicholas, he just wanted some advice from me,' I chided, slipping my hands around his waist and tugging his reluctant frame toward me.

'He's only just met you, Rebecca, what could he need advice about?' Nicholas' tone was still low, concerned and wary and his body was tense beneath my hands.

'Girl stuff,' I replied briskly. 'He doesn't want me to tell you just yet, but you have nothing to worry about, Nicholas, trust me.' Rubbing smoothing circles on his back, I could still feel tension in his muscles; apparently, Nicholas wasn't convinced yet.

I decided to ignore his sulk. 'Is the coffee ready?' He nodded silently in response to my question. A plan of how I could relax him formulated in my mind and I ran one hand gently around to his hipbone and slipped it into the front pocket of his jeans, wiggling my fingers provocatively against the upper area of his pelvis, a spot I knew he found particularly ticklish.

'In that case I think we should take it up to bed and continue with our lie-in,' I suggested, using Nicholas' pocket to pull him in the direction of the kitchen. 'Except I'm not tired any more, so you'll have to think of something else for us to do in bed for a few hours. Any ideas?' I asked in a similarly salacious tone to the one he used on me so often.

Hearing a growl from Nicholas as he followed me, I finally felt him relax as his hands wrapped around my waist and roughly tugged me backwards into his waiting arms, my favourite place to be.

TWENTY-ONE

The following Saturday, Nicholas had another charity concert – this one was to raise money for a children's home in one of the outer London suburbs. I have to say I'm actually rather proud of just how much charity work Nicholas does. Who'd have thought that you could be a kinky pervert in the bedroom and still want to help others elsewhere?

After spending several hours in the new library room – a place I found myself quite often now – I wandered over to Nicholas' music room and saw him sat at his piano, engrossed in his practice. Propping myself on the edge of the white armchair by the huge window, I watched him finish playing; his body moving rhythmically, head swaying, and eyes alternating between open and closed as he lost his self to the music. His skill was simply breath-taking.

Once he had drawn the piece to a close, Nicholas took a few seconds to come back to reality, then turned to smile at me, and I couldn't help but shake my head at how different my life was in comparison to just a few months ago. I'd gone from being single and relatively boring to practically living with an exceptionally talented, handsome, caring man in his beautiful Victorian house. OK, so he was a tad on the pervy side too, but no one was perfect, were they?

'What?' Nicholas asked, obviously noticing my whimsical expression.

Pushing off from the sofa, I grinned and made my way across to him. I dropped a kiss on his shoulder and hummed happily. Nicholas' skin was warm through the cotton of his shirt and I could smell his delicious pine scent mixed with fresh laundry powder, which only made my smile even bigger.

'I was just marvelling at how fortunate I am,' I replied cryptically, not wanting to give him a big head by blabbing about just how marvellous I thought he was. 'That piece was beautiful, Nicholas. I won't disturb you for long as I know you're busy, but I thought I might head back to my flat for the night. You'll be out until late anyway and I really need to get my post and check for any bills.' As I spoke, my cruel mind flicked back to the last time Nicholas had played a concert, and I inadvertently shuddered.

Mid-pout at my mention of leaving, Nicholas saw this reaction and frowned. 'What is it, Becky?' he asked, instantly rising from the piano and taking hold of my shoulders in concern.

'Nothing,' I murmured. Seeing his probing look, I sighed. 'I was just remembering the last time you performed at a concert ... afterwards, you called me up and finished with me,' I mumbled, suddenly feeling rather fragile and leaving the rest of my thoughts unspoken. *Then I came to your house and you beat me with a cane ...*

Pulling me into his arms, Nicholas held me tightly to his chest and planted several kisses in my hair. He obviously knew what I was thinking, but didn't want to mention it again either. 'Come with me tonight,' he requested suddenly, leaning back to look at me. 'There's a dinner afterwards; I never usually stay for them but I could tonight. I'm allowed to take a guest – would you like to come?'

Out in public with Nicholas, that would be ... *interesting*. Not to mention new. We'd not exactly been trying to hide our relationship as such, but he was sure once the press latched on to the fact that he had a girlfriend – a first as far as the journalists were concerned – they might be a bit more persistent in their hounding of him, so we'd kept everything low key and mostly stayed at home when we met up.

'Do you want me to? I know you never go out with women in public ...' I didn't want Nicholas to feel pressured into anything and freak out on me again. Sometimes dating him was like walking over broken glass – you had to tread really, really carefully.

'I've never been out in public with a woman because, to be honest, you're the first proper girlfriend I've ever had,' he admitted with a shrug. Cupping my face and circling my cheek with his thumb, he gazed down at me with an expression of uncharacteristic openness on his handsome face. 'I love you and I want the world to see it. I would be incredibly proud if you would accompany me tonight, Rebecca.'

Wow. I had been about to get nervous about the response of the journalists but his last statement made me feel quite a bit better. What a heartfelt sentence. From *Nicholas,* no less. Plus, he would be the main focus of the press, not me, I thought, to reassure myself as I smiled up at him.

'OK, I'll come,' I agreed, before a small grimace crossed my face. 'God, I have no idea what I'll wear, though. How posh will it be?'

'I tell you what,' Nicholas said, glancing at his watch, 'I'll take an hour out of practice time and run you to the shops to get a new dress, then I'll drop you at your flat and head back here to prepare. I can pick you up at five for the concert – how does that sound?'

Almost glowing at the thought of accompanying Nicholas to the concert and meal – in public – I nodded keenly. 'OK, sounds good.' Then I leant up on tiptoe and kissed his cheek. 'I love you too, Nicholas … so much,' I murmured against his skin, causing him to growl contentedly and hold me firmly against him.

With the limited time we had, Nicholas drove me to a posh out-of-town department store quite close to his house. After consulting the floor plan, we headed straight for the second floor, the dress section. With Nicholas needing to get back to practice there was no time to dawdle like I usually would when shopping.

'How smart do I need to be? Cocktail dress or formal eveningwear?' I asked absently as I fondled the soft material of a red knee-length dress. There was no way I was big enough up top to carry it off, but it was so beautiful I couldn't help but touch it.

Nicholas shrugged, showing a man's typical lack of interest

241

in such things. 'I think the women at these things normally get pretty dressed up. Floor-length dresses, I suppose,' he murmured, heading toward a gorgeous strapless silver dress on a mannequin.

'Try this on; it would look stunning on you,' he said, holding it out to me. I nearly laughed at his command, but the dress was beautiful and exactly my size, so I merely shook my head at how funny he was and held out a hand to accept it.

'OK.' I took it, grabbed another, equally striking navy blue dress, and then headed to the changing room sure that one of these gowns would be the one.

'I'll wait out here; come out and show me when you have them on,' he said, once again in a tone that was more instruction that request. Control freak. Although I genuinely don't think he realises just how bossy he is when he talks like that.

Rolling my eyes, I handed my items to the shop assistant and allowed her to lead me to a changing room. Slipping into the silver dress, I immediately knew it was the one. I might not be what you would call a hugely girly girl but even I could see just how amazing this dress made me look.

I was suddenly all breasts and curves. Blimey, who knew I had that figure lurking in me?

Carefully making my way to the entrance of the changing rooms, I couldn't find the assistant but saw Nicholas casually leaning on a nearby wall, looking amazingly handsome as he fiddled with his phone.

Was he really my boyfriend, I wondered as I took in his brooding good looks once more, but then he glanced in my direction and completely distracted me because the heat that seemed to emanate from his eyes was simply breath-taking. As he pushed from the wall and stalked toward me, I suddenly felt my mouth go dry. His frown disappeared and his eyes softened but they remained loaded with heat as they repeatedly ran up and down my body, well and truly checking me out. Gosh, he was so sexy when he looked like this; intense and focused solely on me. There really was no greater turn-on than feeling so completely desired by this man.

Remaining silent, he circled me, taking in the dress like a hunter surveying his prey. 'So beautiful,' I heard him murmur as he stopped in front of me again.

'You like it?' I asked quietly, flushing at the dark, lusty look in his eyes.

'More than like. The dress is stunning and you make it look even better,' he said in a gravelly voice that made me feel like he was about to undress me on the spot, regardless of spectators.

OK, that was a definite seal of approval. 'Me too. I'll get this one.' Smiling shyly, I nodded and headed back to change.

As I pulled the curtain shut to my changing area, I reached behind my back to undo the zip and suddenly found my hands being grasped firmly at the wrists and my whole body being pushed forward. About to yelp in surprise, my gaze fell on the mirror and I realised it was Nicholas joining me in the cubicle. What the heck?

Gently pushing me face first against the mirror, Nicholas split my hands, holding one in each of his and bringing them up next to my shoulders. He pinned me to the mirror with his body, his hips pressing into my bum and chest laying along my back, before burying his head in my neck and kissing it hotly, his tongue darting out and no doubt making my skin redden with excitement.

'You can't come in here!' I hissed breathlessly, my breath steaming on the mirror and dampening my cheek.

'Baby, I can come wherever I want,' he murmured salaciously. 'Quiet now, let me show you.' I had to stifle a nervous giggle, gosh, he was just *sooo* naughty. 'This will be quick,' he told me, then his head dipped again, and as he kissed behind my earlobe, I forgot about my fears and lolled my head back against him.

'Turn,' he whispered, releasing my hands at last and moving back marginally to allow me some space to manoeuvre in.

As soon as I was facing him, I grabbed at his jacket and pulled him back to me again, kissing him furiously and thrilling in his heated response to my urgency. Lowering his hands, he began pulling up the thin material of my dress gently, his fingers caressing my thighs as he did so, making me want to whimper with desire. With my dress bunched around my waist, Nicholas briefly fondled my breasts but obviously didn't want to pull the light material around too much because he only spent a minute or so there before he dropped to his knees in front of me.

Holding my dress aloft with his hands, Nicholas winked up at me before nudging my legs apart with his shoulder. Looking intent on his task, he slipped the cotton of my knickers to the side and wasted no time in ducking forward and running his tongue down the length of my already slick folds. Holy crap, talk about moving fast! But it felt so unbelievably good that I buried my hands in his hair, encouraging him to continue as my eyes rolled shut with arousal.

When Nicholas sucked on my clitoris and gently nipped at it with his teeth, I couldn't help but let out a small moan and I felt his hot breath fan across me as he laughed softly at my keen response. After briefly dipping his probing tongue right into the very core of me, causing me to practically convulse, he stood up again, looking smug and smiling darkly, a trace of my moisture still glinting on his mouth. Oh so slowly his tongue slid along his lips as if savouring the last taste of my juices as he gazed down at me with hooded eyes, not breaking the eye contact once as he undid his zip and pushed my legs further apart with his knee.

'No noises, Rebecca,' he reminded me softly, and as his head nuzzled my neck, he eased himself into me with a groan, gripping my left buttock and bringing my leg up off the floor to deepen our connection before he began to slowly move against me.

This was so naughty! Sex in a changing room cubicle while other shoppers were innocently trying on clothes, completely unaware of what was going on just feet away from them. I could hear a woman in another cubicle fiddling with a variety of plastic hangers. Thinking about it, what we were doing was probably illegal … which just made it even hotter.

Somehow managing to keep his movements small but teasing, Nicholas repeatedly ground the base of his erection against my clitoris. Within a minute or so, I was just a rub away from a climax. A small hiss began to escape from my lips as I felt my muscles tighten around him, and Nicholas immediately placed a hand over my mouth to silence me.

Biting down on one of his fingers, I came hard around his pulsing erection, squeezing my eyes shut with the effort to be quiet and knowing that even Nicholas wouldn't be brash enough to punish me for breaking eye contact in a changing room. Seconds later, he buried himself inside me to the hilt and stilled as he came, removing his hand from my mouth and placing a gentle kiss there instead.

After recovering for several seconds, he leant back and grinned at me. 'Sorry about the hand over your mouth but I thought you were about to shout out loud,' he whispered against my lips.

'S'kay,' I managed weakly, trying to say "it's OK" but not managing to vocalise it in my current post-orgasmic state. When I could finally speak, I told him I was grateful for the way he'd trusted me enough to let me bite his finger – they were the tools of his trade, after all.

Nicholas eased himself out of me and kissed me tenderly on the lips before fishing a handkerchief out of his pocket for me. Flashing me a wink, he departed the changing room as quickly as he'd arrived, leaving me leaning against the wall, a quivering mess.

Wow, he was just amazing, and so was the sex for that matter. I shook my head in disbelief. After using his handkerchief to clean myself up, I began trying to change, which was actually quite difficult with trembling fingers and rubbery legs. Just when I had thought things were settling to normality, Nicholas kept surprising me with exciting activities and new locations. How he had never managed to have a proper girlfriend before was beyond me.

Changing out of the dress, I hung it up carefully while I put my own clothes back on. After smoothing my hair, I tried to walk casually out of the cubicle as if I hadn't just been shagged silly by the hunk of a man waiting for me just outside. But I had, so obviously my face flamed as soon as I saw the assistant waiting at the entrance to the changing rooms.

After relieving me of the navy dress, which I hadn't bothered to try on, she raised an eyebrow at my flushed cheeks – and no doubt post-sex hair. It sent me beetling across the floor to Nicholas where I burst out laughing childishly.

'I told you I could come anywhere I liked,' he stated softly, pulling me against his side and heading in the direction of the tills with me still giggling from embarrassment. 'And it appears you can too,' he added wickedly.

Holding the dress so it didn't drag on the floor, I glanced at the price tag hanging from the label and gasped. I stopped mid-step, wondering if I had time to find something cheaper, but Nicholas saw my look and shrugged.

'Don't worry about the cost, it's my treat. Plus, technically it's used now, so you have to buy it,' he said, referring to our hasty changing room tryst and making me blush yet again.

I wasn't happy with him paying though, so I shook my head, about to complain. The look spreading across Nicholas' face stopped me. His expression became one of pure dominance; eyes darkening, brows lowering, and jaw becoming solid, as if daring me to object. So, not wanting to spoil our good mood, I gratefully carried the dress to the till and leant up to kiss him on the cheek. 'Thank you,' I murmured against his light stubble, my single kiss sparking a smile on his face and seeming to reverse his mood, and suddenly I was even more excited about attending the concert with him tonight.

TWENTY-TWO

Later that afternoon, back at my flat, I was sorting through my disorganised wardrobe – also known as "the black hole" – trying to find a suspender belt that I'd bought but had never really worn. It had to be here somewhere. I'd remembered it when Nicholas was dropping me home, and decided he might quite like discovering me clad in stockings and suspenders underneath my posh dress tonight. I broke out in a smile as I tried to imagine the look he'd have on his face when he undressed me.

Half an hour of searching later, I still hadn't found the suspender belt, or the stockings for that matter, but I had found something I'd long forgotten about that I thought he might like for altogether different reasons. Reasons that caused me to blush and get rather hot just thinking about them.

At 4.45, I heard a knock at my door. Crap, he was early and I wasn't ready yet; I'd wasted so much time looking for the bloody suspenders that I was now running late. Thankfully, I wasn't too far behind schedule – I was dressed and my hair was nicely washed and straightened but I still needed to finish my make-up. Oh well, I supposed I could always finish it at the theatre while Nicholas prepared for the concert.

Dashing to the front door, I yanked it open and immediately sucked in a huge gulp of air when I saw again just how stunning Nicholas looked in his eveningwear. If I were a religious person, I'd be thanking the Gods right now for the steaming hunk of masculinity that, by some miracle, was currently standing on my doorstep. I couldn't drag my eyes away from him. Tonight he was wearing a black tailcoat and trousers, white shirt, black bow tie, and a deep-navy waistcoat that almost matched his eyes.

God, he looked utterly breath-taking, and I had to suppress the urge to mount him in the hallway and have my wicked way with him.

When I finally managed to reconnect my brain and raise my eyes to his, I saw a similar look of admiration and desire reflected in his own eyes as he appraised my appearance, so I performed a quick twirl for him with a giggle.

'You look beautiful,' he murmured thickly, his tone dark and full of his obvious pleasure, which made me glow internally.

'Thank you, as do you. Wow,' I breathed. 'Very handsome,' I concluded with a nod. And all mine, I thought devilishly. Running a hand down the buttons of his waistcoat, I couldn't help but sigh contentedly. 'Come in, I just need five more minutes.'

Leading him back to my bedroom, I picked up my mascara and quickly continued with my make-up application – but my eye was caught by the item I'd found earlier while searching for my stockings.

'I have a present for you.' I smiled, handing him the small blue box. 'Well, it's not a present as such – I didn't buy it, I was given it – but I thought you might like to use it some time.'

Taking the gift from me, Nicholas tilted his head inquisitively. 'That's a mischievous look, Rebecca, whatever is in here?' he asked before opening the box and raising an eyebrow at me as a grin split his face. Recognition of the object was evident in his features.

'Apparently, it's called a love-egg,' I murmured, far more embarrassed than I should be considering the amount of sex toys Nicholas had owned in his time.

'I thought they were called bullet vibrators, but I like the name love-egg,' he said with a sly smile as he examined the small silver egg that was about two inches long and slightly thicker than his thumb. 'Hmm, I didn't know they made them wireless,' he commented, picking up the tiny remote control and pressing it so the toy started to vibrate in his palm.

He grinned wickedly and then frowned, his voice lowering as he dropped the egg back into the box as if it had burnt him.

'Who gave it to you? A past lover?' he demanded hotly, turning to face me with a twisted, dark expression on his face.

His moods changed so quickly it was unbelievable. 'No!' I exclaimed. Jeez, as if I'd give him something I'd used with a past boyfriend. Did he really think I was that stupid? 'Have you ever heard of Secret Santa?' I said, smiling broadly into the mirror as I swiped the mascara wand across my lashes and watched his reaction in the reflection.

'No,' he said, still with a querying expression. 'You're telling me Santa delivers sex toys to good girls now?' His words caused me to giggle and very nearly coat a line of mascara down my entire cheek.

'Not quite; Secret Santa is a way of giving small Christmas gifts to your friends or work colleagues without having to buy for everyone. You all put your name in a hat, pick one out, and that's who you buy for, but it's secret so the presents are anonymous. We did it every year at university with all the girls I lived with. One year we decided to see who would receive the most embarrassing present and this is what I was given.'

Nicholas was smiling his wicked, sexy smile now, all traces of his anger completely gone. 'Your housemates sound fun,' he commented lightly, causing me to frown with unnecessary jealousy. He immediately picked up on my reaction and grinned even more broadly, pulling me into his arms and dragging us both so we were sitting on the bed. 'But not as fun as you Rebecca,' he assured me firmly. 'Was this the most embarrassing present given?'

'We never really decided on a winner,' I said, remembering back to that drunken night. 'Naomi was given edible underwear but she was quite a prude so the look of shock on her face was really funny. Jen got a large packet of penis-shaped jellies that squirted cream out in your mouth when you bit them. Debs got edible body paint.' I paused, trying to remember the other gifts. 'Oh yeah! Laura was given an inflatable man and Samantha got a Rampant Rabbit vibrator. I think she was secretly quite pleased.' I grinned, knowing the vibrator Nicholas had used on me recently was similar to the Rabbit one Sam had received.

'Have you ever used it?' Nicholas asked, fingering the small vibrating egg again.

Blushing bright red, I looked down at my hands. 'Once,' I mumbled.

Suddenly, I found my chin being gripped tightly between his forefinger and thumb as Nicholas jerked my head up toward his. As his sparkling blue eyes met mine I saw his brow had darkened again. 'Who with?' He demanded. God, he was really demonstrating tonight just how his temper could flare from nothing to volatile in the blink of an eye. It was like he had a switch inside him somewhere that had a faulty wire.

'Just by myself. I was curious about it,' I said shyly, telling the truth.

His eyebrows rose significantly and an excited glint twinkled in his dark eyes, erasing all traces of anger – switch flicked to "off" again. 'Really?' His grip on my chin relaxed and he brushed my cheek gently with the back of his knuckles. 'Tell me what you did.'

'What? No, it's embarrassing!' I blushed again. At this rate I wouldn't need to finish applying my make-up because I'd be pink enough already!

'Don't be shy, the idea of you touching yourself turns me on,' Nicholas confided as he pulled one of my hands to his hardening groin to illustrate his point. 'Tell me,' he urged again as I felt his cock twitching below my fingers.

The thought that my words alone could excite him this much was a real power trip so I tried to push my embarrassment down and explain. 'I just pushed it in and turned it on,' I mumbled awkwardly. I wouldn't win any prizes for erotic description that was for sure. 'Actually, I was a bit worried it might get lost inside me so I mostly rubbed it around the outside.' I wondered if I sounded as stupid as I felt.

'Did you climax?' Nicholas murmured, his groin tightening even more under my hand as he shifted on the bed to make himself more comfortable.

Pursing my lips, I shook my head at how kinky he was and gave his groin a gentle squeeze. 'Yes,' I conceded.

My response made Nicholas moan in appreciation and he lowered his mouth to mine, kissing me fervently. His hands began to roam across my body freely, gliding over the thin material of the dress and searing my skin with his heat.

'God, Rebecca, I'm so aroused right now,' he murmured against my lips, although considering my hand was on his very evident excitement it was kind of an unnecessary statement. I was fully expecting him to initiate some brief sexual release before we had to leave, but instead I was surprised when he sat back and took several deep breaths instead. Perhaps he was like an athlete and didn't allow himself any sex just before a concert in case it affected his performance.

'Maybe we could use this tonight,' he pondered with a suggestive wiggle of his eyebrows. Seeing my startled expression, he smiled. 'Don't worry; it's not possible for them to get lost inside you. I believe it's similar to inserting a contraceptive diaphragm, you just slip a finger in to retrieve it,' he said, looking at the egg again. Of course he would know how to use them, I thought, being the pervert that he is.

'Would you wear it and let me keep the remote?' he asked, assessing my reaction with a curious glance.

'At the concert?' I squeaked, trying to imagine just how much of a pervert I'd feel walking around with the love-egg tucked inside me all night.

'Yes. It's only small,' he cajoled. 'God, I would love knowing you had it inside you when we were out in public together. Knowing I had the control over you.' His eyes were positively blazing now and there was a light flush of excitement on his cheeks.

Ah, yes, Dominant Nicholas and his love of control. 'I'm not sure …' I replied hesitantly. I liked his games in the bedroom, but was I really enough of a kinkster to join in while we were out in public?

'I wouldn't tease you too much, Becky, I promise, just occasionally. And imagine how turned on we'll both be when we get home,' he added persuasively, stroking my cheek and making my skin flutter under his touch.

After chewing my lip for a second, I decided to shelve my bookshop persona for the night and go wild. Why the hell not? Besides, the remote control for the egg would probably only work when it was fairly close, wouldn't it? So he'd only be able to use it when he was near me. 'OK, then,' I agreed with a shy smile and a shrug. Part of me actually quite liked letting my naughty side out, which was just as well seeing as I was dating Nicholas with all of his pervy ways.

Gently pushing me back on the bed so I was lying down, Nicholas pulled up my silky dress with ease and seductively licked his tongue around the egg. Just this sight had moisture pooling between my legs. Yanking my underwear to the side, he pushed a moistened finger inside me and then grinned broadly. 'I was going to warm you up a little first, but you appear to be more than ready, Rebecca.' He wasn't kidding either; all this talk of sexy stuff with Nicholas and I practically felt like I was dripping. With one more lick to the toy, he removed his eyes from mine as he concentrated on the task of inserting the love-egg. I felt the coolness of the metal against my heated skin and then the warmth of his fingers as he followed it to make sure it was in far enough.

'How does that feel?' he asked thickly, apparently rather aroused by his task.

I paused for a beat whilst I shifted my hips a little and then nodded. 'OK. To be honest, I can't really feel it,' I said in surprise, giving my hips another wiggle. 'Argh!' Suddenly a vigorous vibration started inside me, right next to my G-spot, and I looked at Nicholas to see him holding the remote, a huge grin splitting his face.

'Feel it now?' he enquired silkily.

Bastard. 'Yes,' I panted, clutching at the duvet with scrabbling, frantic hands. 'God, Nicholas, I can't do this in public, it's too much!' I was squirming from the trembling sensations in my lower abdomen. It felt so strong; surely other people would be able to hear it, wouldn't they?

Just as I thought I couldn't take any more, the vibration inside me reduced to a gentle hum and was much more bearable. Flopping back in relief I drew in a shaky breath and tried to recover myself. I shifted my pelvis from side to side and decided after several seconds that this new setting was rather nice. Very nice, actually. Mmm, perhaps this would be fun after all ...

'How about now? This is a lower setting,' he said, showing me the remote. I noticed it had five different levels and it was now set to the lowest one.

'Better. Nice,' I said, loving the alien sensation deep inside me. Then he must have switched it off because I was left feeling bereft as it stopped.

'Oh, Rebecca, we will have so much fun with this tonight.' Nicholas dropped another heart-stopping kiss on my lips before standing up, straightening out his tailcoat and adjusting the tie at his neck. 'Right, are you nearly ready? We need to get going, Mr Burrett's outside with the car.' Glancing at his watch, he looked back at me. 'I have to warm up for half an hour before the theatre doors open to the public.'

As I stood up I wondered what Nicholas would do without the multi-skilled Mr Burrett to act as butler, housekeeper, assistant, cleaner, and driver.

'Yep, let me just finish my left eye.' I applied another coat of mascara to my lashes and experimentally wiggled about a bit to see if the egg was uncomfortable. To my surprise, it wasn't; in fact, now I was standing up I could barely feel it at all. In the mirror, I saw the reflection of the cheeky smile on Nicholas' lips and couldn't help grinning myself. Tonight was going to be rather exciting, I decided.

TWENTY-THREE

Front frigging row. How Nicholas had managed to get me a front-row seat to a sold-out concert when we'd only decided I was coming four hours ago was beyond me. But he had, and now I excitedly sat gazing up at the piano on the edge of the stage, wearing my beautiful new dress. I felt like a million dollars on the outside, while secretly glowing from the knowledge that I had my love-egg nestled inside me.

Thinking about it, perhaps that was why I was on the front row ... Maybe Nicholas had arranged it this way on purpose, so he could use the toy on me. The piano was up high but probably only about ten feet away from my seat; would the remote control work from there? I had a sneaking suspicion that Nicholas thought it might, and I was now seriously regretting not reading the packaging to learn about operating distances.

The concert was quite a small affair – small in comparison to the one at the London Palladium that I'd attended, anyway – and was being held in a local theatre that had a large function room for the meal afterwards. Just seating myself on the plush velvet chair in the auditorium took me back to memories of the night when I'd first met Nicholas, and a shiver flowed over my skin at the memory. After that initial slightly scary meeting, I'd never have guessed that we'd end up together.

To my right was the aisle but to my left were an older gentleman and his wife, Patrick and Joanna, I think, but it might have been Jemma. The orchestra had been loudly warming up when they'd introduced themselves, and after asking her name twice, I'd been too embarrassed to ask her to repeat it again.

It turned out Patrick was a major donor to several of Nicholas' charities and had also sponsored his first two solo albums – quite an avid fan, apparently. When I told him I was Nicholas' girlfriend, he looked openly astonished for a second or two, before quickly hiding his surprise with a warm smile. He'd been absolutely charming to me ever since, even getting me a glass of complimentary champagne. It seemed that dropping Nicholas' name into conversation had its benefits.

I didn't have to wait long to find out if the egg would work from ten feet away because Nicholas had zapped me as soon as he first came out onto the stage to a standing ovation. The audience's applause had proved to be well timed because the noise covered my small yelp as the egg inside started to vibrate. He only left it on for a few seconds, and thankfully, I had regained my composure by the time I sat down.

Being Nicholas, however, his second use of the egg was a little more intense. Taking a brief break in between his final two tunes, he had caught my eye, winked, turned the toy on and then proceeded to play an entire five-and-a-half-minute, self-written piece as his finale.

Five-and-a-half frigging minutes. By the time he finished and stood to receive his rapturous applause, I was panting like a dog and must have been the colour of a ripe tomato. Grinning like a loon and flashing me a private wink, Nicholas discreetly put his hand in his pocket and ended my torture, which was just as well because I was practically melting out of my chair by that point.

After reminding the audience that the meal would be served in ten minutes, he then surprised me completely by trotting down the steps at the side of the stage, grabbing my hand, planting a wet kiss on my lips and leading us out of the theatre down the central aisle while the crowd continued to clap and cheer around us.

From the audience response, it would seem that a performer exiting via the auditorium wasn't usual, but with my wobbly legs, it was the least of my concerns at the moment. How I could manage to walk after five-and-a-half minutes of egg torture was beyond me, but with Nicholas half-supporting, half-dragging me, I did it.

There was rapturous applause all around and a fair few wolf

whistles too, and I'm fairly sure I spotted one or two women jealously giving me the evil eye as I left with my hugely talented and exceptionally kinky boyfriend.

The meal was delicious– three courses of unpronounceable, but totally divine French food – followed by a charity auction and a series of speeches thanking various donors and, of course, extending appreciation to Nicholas for his time and money. The auction was fun. I'd never been to one before and I even made the winning bid on one lot – a lunch cruise on the Thames with the star of tonight's show, Nicholas. Well, I wasn't going to let another woman win it even if it would take a hefty chunk of my savings to pay for it.

I have to say Nicholas looked absolutely thrilled by my determination not to be outbid on the cruise, and he grinned like a schoolboy as I went up to the podium to collect my prize. He might express his possessiveness in the bedroom by restraining me and licking me to within inches of my life, but I preferred to show mine in a more standard display of territorial jealousy.

Once that was done, the speeches were just getting a little monotonous for me when Nicholas decided to have a little fun of his own. I'd almost forgotten all about the toy inside me, but he must have clicked on the remote control because suddenly the little egg jumped to life once again, causing me to yelp from the unexpected sensation.

Was it too much to ask for just a little warning? Apparently so.

'Are you OK, my dear?' Patrick asked, turning in his seat at our table and raising his bushy eyebrows at me. God, how embarrassing; he'd probably heard me yelp in the concert too and was no doubt forming some strange conclusions about me in his mind. Forget obsessive-compulsive disorder, I sounded like I had compulsive-yelping disorder.

'Fine, thank you, I ... trapped my finger, that's all,' I mumbled feebly. Patrick glanced at my hands in confusion, apparently wondering what I could have trapped it in, but smiled politely before turning back to listen to the speeches. Beside me, I could sense Nicholas laughing softly to himself, and I only just held back the urge to hit him with something.

Thank goodness our table was right in the corner and Nicholas and I were seated at the back, because he left the little egg thrumming away inside me for several minutes, reducing me to goo while everyone else's attention was still drawn toward the stage.

'Don't make a sound,' he ordered as his right hand slipped under the tablecloth. I could feel the warmth of his fingers as he massaged my leg for a few minutes, then, after carefully raising my long dress around my thighs, Nicholas' fingers slid straight below the hem of it to rub softly at my groin through my already damp knickers.

'Nicholas! No! Not here,' I hissed, squirming in my seat and trying to move away from his exploring hand without disturbing the other people on our table.

'Hush. Grip the table if you need to,' he advised sagely, his fingers refusing to be dislodged from their position and his face impassive as he stared at the stage, apparently enthralled in the current speaker.

Panic briefly set in as I realised I couldn't stop him without making a scene or standing up abruptly, but after another minute, I simply gave in to the inevitable and relaxed my muscles. Nothing would stop him when he was set on something so I simply took his advice and clutched at the table top, clenched my teeth, and tried to look calm and normal as if I were simply watching the speeches and not about to explode into an orgasm at any minute.

God, this really was bad. We were in a room full of people and Nicholas seemed to have no qualms about bringing me to climax in front of all of them. Yet another example of him in his full pervert mode.

'Let it go, baby,' Nicholas murmured against my ear several minutes later. My whole body was tense, like a tightly wound spring, and my eye had started to twitch from the effort of controlling my muscles while also trying not to draw attention to myself.

'No,' I muttered, focusing all my attention on not orgasming in a public place for the second time in one day.

'*Yes*,' he demanded, his eyes turning to mine with a heated "don't you dare defy me" look, which was probably quite terrifying to most people. But I was getting used to these looks now and so merely stuck my tongue out at him defiantly.

In response to my provocation, Nicholas narrowed his eyes and then increased both the intensity and speed of his fingers *and* the little egg inside me. Shit, he must have turned it up at least two settings because suddenly I could feel my insides quivering with a building release. It was no good. Even with my best efforts to defy him, several seconds later I exploded around the egg, my body quaking, thighs tensing and my fingers practically biting through the wood of the table as I tried not to yell out loud.

Panting lightly and feeling rather dazed, I flopped back in my seat. Hopefully, the only indication of my pleasure above the tabletop would be my flushed skin but that would be undetectable in the darkened room. My eyes scanned the people closest to us but all were still concentrated on the stage; somehow, we'd got away with it.

Holy shit, had he really just done that to me in a crowded room? Feeling my groin still pulsing and tingling from my release I blew out a low, amused breath. Yes, yes he most certainly had.

Thankfully, Nicholas must have pressed the off switch on the love-egg because it ceased its torment. But his hand stayed protectively near my groin, brushing against me occasionally, and I finally relented and rested my head against his shoulder as I pretended to watch the rest of the speeches.

'You are so bad, Nicholas,' I murmured quietly, almost wanting to fall asleep on him.

'I am,' he confirmed with a sly grin, dropping a kiss on my damp brow.

After the speeches, I excused myself to the toilet and removed the little love-egg, placing it carefully in my handbag. There was no way I was going to be able to cope with another dose of that if he suddenly got the urge to tease me some more – definitely safest removed. Smiling to myself with a blush, I decided I'd liked it, though. It had been exhilarating to know Nicholas had the remote control and it had certainly spiced up the evening's proceedings. Perhaps we could use it again sometime.

When I got back in the hall, I saw several tables had been shifted out of the way and the dancing had begun. Wow, they really went all out for these occasions, although during the speeches they had said tonight's event was of particular importance for the children's home involved so maybe this was fancier than usual. Seeing Nicholas was absent, probably still in the toilets, I headed back to our table but was halted before I sat down by a hand on my elbow.

'Rebecca! I thought it was you! How are you?' Looking up, I saw a blast from the past. Harry Green, someone I'd known for most of my life since we'd met at primary school. In fact, his parents still lived three doors up from mine in Penrith. We emailed occasionally, but it was strange how one look at Harry's dimpled grin took me straight back to my childhood, and the long days our little gang of friends had spent fishing in the lakes or climbing trees up one of the local hills.

'Harry! I didn't know you lived down here now. How are you?' I asked with a grin.

'Really well, thanks, and you look great, Becs! I can't believe it's you. Would you like to dance?' he asked, his eyes shining with pleasure.

'No, she wouldn't,' a cool voice over my shoulder answered as I felt Nicholas' possessive hand wrap around me from behind and splay protectively on my hip.

Frowning and craning my neck so I could see Nicholas' face, I rolled my eyes at him then looked back at Harry.

'I'd love to,' I confirmed. 'Just give me a minute,' I told Harry and he stepped back, casting a slightly nervy glance at Nicholas who was now glowering at him furiously.

Turning to face Nicholas, I regarded him as sternly as possible, which, seeing as he looked positively murderous, was actually quite difficult. 'Nicholas, that's not just some random man asking me to dance. I went to primary school with Harry; he's married to one of my best friends, Andrea, who is pregnant with his baby, and my parents still have lunch with his parents every month.'

I placed a hand on his chest, trying my best to ignore Nicholas' thunderous expression. 'I am *your* girlfriend, but I am my own woman and I can make my own decisions. I am going to dance with Harry to have a catch-up chat, but that's all it is, *a dance*. Don't be mad with me.' I stepped away and found Harry again.

Dancing with Harry, I caught glimpses of Nicholas sitting watching us, still with an expression on his face that I could only describe as somewhere between homicidal and demented. Oh dear. I was going to be in trouble later. But if Nicholas and I were going to be together, he had to know that while he might be in charge of things in the bedroom, the same didn't apply to the rest of my life.

I consoled myself with the fact that at least it was an upbeat number so Harry and I were dancing near each other, but not actually touching, while we chatted. I suspected if Harry placed so much as one finger on me Nicholas would immediately intervene.

As the song ended, I decided I had better not push my luck any further so I wished Harry well and headed back toward Nicholas. He was still sitting at our table but his eyes were averted as he studied his mobile phone intently. Looping around behind him, I bent over and slipped my arms around his tense shoulders, nuzzling his neck and placing several kisses on his pounding pulse point. Apparently, he wasn't as calm as he appeared outwardly.

'Hi. Are you still angry with me?' I murmured against the warm skin of his neck, although I didn't need a verbal answer. I could feel his annoyance radiating from his muscles under my arms; his entire body was stiff with tension.

'Yes,' he replied tightly, clicking his phone shut and pocketing it.

'Please don't be, Nicholas. You can't expect to control my whole life.' I dropped another kiss on his jaw. 'Dance with me?' I asked, walking round in front of him smiling hopefully and extending a hand to him.

He was still scowling at me and refusing to take my hand.

God, he was so stubborn. But so was I, so I persevered with a sickly sweet smile. 'I would really love to have a dance with my boyfriend before we leave, Nicholas; surely you're not going to disappoint me?' I cajoled him.

Finally, after what felt like an eternity, I saw his shoulders start to relax and he gazed up at me with a look of complete confusion on his face as he stood and took my outstretched hand.

'I didn't like you defying me,' he said sullenly as we made our way to the dance floor.

'And I don't like you trying to oppress me,' I countered lightly, before wrapping an arm around his neck and pulling him against me, even though the music was probably a little too fast for an intimate dance. 'But I'm sure we'll learn to compromise.'

Pressing my body against his, I slid my other arm around his neck and rested my cheek on his chest where we swayed together for several silent minutes. 'This isn't how you danced with Harry,' Nicholas commented in apparent bewilderment, wrapping his arms around my waist and holding me against him. I shook my head; in my annoyance at his attitude, I'd forgotten just how little he knew about relationships.

'No, it isn't. This is how I want to dance with you, *and only you*, Nicholas,' I murmured, resting my face on his shoulder again and sighing contentedly.

Seemingly placated for the moment, he lowered his cheek against my hair and held me tightly against him as we swayed to the music. 'I'm sorry if I was overbearing,' he said at last and I leant back to study his expression.

'*Was*?' I teased with a raised eyebrow, but he just frowned in return before stroking my cheek with the back of his knuckles.

'OK, *am*,' he corrected himself reluctantly. 'I'm working on it, Becky, but I still find it hard to see you with other men. I think I always will,' he admitted.

'I understand. I would be just as jealous if you were dancing with another woman,' I conceded. 'But he was a long-term friend, not some guy hitting on me,' I explained again, hoping the difference would be clearer to Nicholas now he'd seen how I danced differently with him.

Unexpectedly, his hands gripped my shoulders and tilted me away so he could meet my eyes with a probing stare. 'You would be jealous?' He sounded genuinely surprised by my admission.

I nearly laughed but, knowing how sensitive he was about our relationship, I didn't dare. 'Of course. You know when you get all possessive and tell me that I'm yours?' I asked him, stroking a hand across the silk of his waistcoat and loving the feel of the soft fabric below my fingertips.

'Yes,' he murmured, looking wary, apparently unsure where I was going with this.

'Well … likewise,' I said with a shrug. 'As far as I am concerned, you are mine too, Nicholas, I just don't express it out loud quite as much as you do. Surely you realise that's why I bid so hard for the cruise with you? It would have killed me to know you were going for lunch with another woman.' Especially the tarty blonde who had been bidding particularly aggressively; she'd looked like a complete gold-digger and had probably cost me an extra hundred pounds in her desperation to try and win the date with Nicholas. Cow.

After staring at me in astonishment for several seconds, a breath he had obviously been holding left Nicholas' lips, and I felt the last of the tension ebb from his body as he cradled me against him gently while we continued to sway together in contented silence.

As the dancing began to wind down, Nicholas lazily slung his arm around my waist and guided me toward the exit with a promising expression on his face. Gosh, *again*? He'd better let me lie down this time because after the effort of two silent orgasms today my body was already exhausted, my muscles feeling like I'd run ten miles.

The crowds in the foyer meant Nicholas had to let go of me briefly, and as we finally escaped to the theatre's main exit, I was astounded to see a horde of journalists snapping people as they left down the red carpet.

'Nicholas! Just a quick photo, please?' one cried enthusiastically.

'Mr Jackson! This way!' Another called.

God, it was like feeding time at the zoo.

Deliberately hanging back, I waited for them to get their photos but watched as Nicholas' right arm reached out into thin air as if trying to find something. Turning, I could see his brow was puckered as he scanned the crowd. Upon seeing me at the far side of the carpet, he strode over and looped his arm around my waist before guiding me back toward the press.

Oh, he had been trying to find *me*.

A visible tremor of excitement ran through the gathered journalists as we approached them and the flash bulbs went crazy. Holy shit. This was insane and my heart immediately began trying to burst from my chest. Gripping his waist with all my might, I did my best to force a smile onto my face but probably only succeeded in looking completely shell-shocked. This was an entirely new experience for me, and not one I was particularly enjoying.

Glancing up at Nicholas, I found his gaze was on me, not the press, a smile lingering on his lips as his eyes danced proudly. Just the look he gave me was enough to relax me and I smiled back, loosening my grip on his hip, which would probably be bruised tomorrow after my talon-like hold.

Lowering his head to mine, Nicholas nuzzled close to my ear. 'I love you,' he murmured, dropping a kiss on my temple and causing the journalists' flashbulbs to go crazy as they all tried to get a picture of our intimate moment.

Wow, the L-word from Nicholas twice in one day; I *was* a lucky girl.

'Nicholas, who's the lovely lady?' a portly man in a slightly too tight tuxedo shouted out.

'This is my girlfriend, Rebecca Langley,' Nicholas announced, causing a brief silence to fall over the press and making my heart constrict at his public announcement of me as his girlfriend.

'How did you meet?' A blonde woman called out, finally finding her voice.

'Over a piano,' Nicholas replied silkily, but the implication was not lost on me – bent over a piano, with him thrusting into me. Thankfully, the press seemed unaware of his double meaning, and with all the flashbulbs popping didn't seem to notice my heated flush.

'How long have you two been together?' another called.

'Long enough to know she's the one for me,' Nicholas stated with certainty, his eyes never leaving mine and making me grin goofily. Let's hope that expression didn't get caught on camera because I had a suspicion it wouldn't be particularly flattering.

'Goodnight.' Nicholas raised his hand in a brief wave, which I copied, and then swung me in the direction of the waiting limos with a sigh of relief as he clutched me protectively to his side.

What a day. Changing room sex, love-egg action, silent orgasms under a table, first encounter with the paparazzi ... Jeez, it was a relief to see Mr Burrett holding a limo door open for us so we could slide into the cool interior away from the flash bulbs.

After settling in his seat next to me, Nicholas sat back and closed the tinted glass of the privacy separator, effectively shutting us off in our own little world. The silence was a welcome relief after such a busy evening. The next thing I knew, I felt my handbag start to vibrate. Thinking it was my phone, I tugged at the zip, pausing when I saw Nicholas' eyebrows dip in disappointment. The vibrating in my bag stopped as I looked up at him in confusion.

'You took it out,' he muttered, practically pouting at me.

Oh, it hadn't been my phone vibrating – it had been the love-egg. Understanding his frown now, I grinned. 'Yeah, sorry, Nicholas, two silent orgasms in one day were as many as I could handle,' I explained, feeling ridiculously guilty as I saw his disappointed expression.

Glancing at the privacy panel, an idea occurred to me that might cheer him up, so, without waiting for common sense to kick in I unclipped my seat belt, dragged my dress up around my thighs, and dropped to my knees in between his legs. 'I wonder how I could make it up to you ...' I murmured, already tugging at the belt around his waist.

God, I hoped that really was one-way glass and Mr Burrett wasn't getting a full-on view in his mirror of what I was about to do to Nicholas.

Realising my intention, a dark smile spread across Nicholas' lips before he helped me with his belt and zip. When I opened up his fly and parted the opening in his boxer shorts, his already excited manhood sprang free, bobbing up to meet me, and I wasted no time in palming it and beginning a slow rhythm with my hand.

Warm, hard, and silky smooth. God, I loved holding him like this, it was so thrilling, so intimate. Nicholas' head lolled back on the leather seat, but as usual his eyes remained firmly on mine. I noticed his pupils were so dilated from desire that in the dim light, his irises looked almost completely black. Dark eyes to match his dark, complicated soul, I thought as I increased the speed of my hand.

Leaning forward, I continued the motion with my hand as I dropped a short, hard kiss on his mouth, forcing my tongue in between his lips and gasping at the heat in his returned kiss. I might be leading the action for the moment, but the fire in his kiss left me with no doubt of who was really in charge here. Then, just seconds later, I bowed my head and used my mouth on a very different part of his anatomy, much to his apparent enjoyment.

As my tongue languorously explored the soft, silky skin, Nicholas' hips bucked under me, and a throaty groan escaped from his chest. Tilting my head so I could look at him, I teased the head of his penis, running my tongue around and under his foreskin; something that seemed to please him a great deal. With another moan, he tangled his hands in my hair, encouraging me to continue.

Using my hand to hold him steady, I took him in my mouth completely, as far toward the back of my throat as I could manage. With my free hand, I cupped his balls before pressing a finger to the hard skin just behind them, the real base of his erection, and rubbed it in time with the bobbing of my head. The combination of my fist, fingers, and mouth were too much for Nicholas to handle, and after only a few minutes, I felt his balls tense and his cock harden further before he let out a strangled groan and came in my mouth in a series of juddering spurts.

Continuing with my motions until he was spent, I swallowed and finally lifted my head, smiling shyly up at him. I had a momentary glimpse of his blazing eyes before he pulled me off the floor of the car and into his arms, kissing me so softly and lovingly that I barely noticed the remainder of the journey home.

TWENTY-FOUR

The following morning, we were awoken again by the sound of tyres on the gravel driveway round the back of our house. Gosh, I couldn't believe how quickly I'd slipped into using the term "our" when referring to Nicholas' house ... but that could only be a good thing, couldn't it?

Without lingering to answer my own internal question, I jumped up to spot who our visitor was. As suspected, I saw Nathan's Audi TT pulling up the drive. I rolled my eyes; this was getting to be a weekly event now.

'It's your brother again.' I was keen to get an update on how things were going between Nathan and Stella, but still the thought of talking with Nathan in all his dominant glory made me feel edgy. Coping with Nicholas' mood swings was hard enough, so how Stella coped with Nathan on a day-to-day basis I'll never know.

'Don't rush,' Nicholas said lazily as he watched me donning my bracelet and starting to dress. 'He has a spare key. If he's going to insist on disturbing us early on a weekend, he'll have to hang around and wait for us.' Then, grabbing the back of my jumper, he gave a sharp yank and brought me stumbling back onto the bed with a giggled yelp.

Gripping my head in his palms, he leant over me upside down and gave me a very thorough good morning kiss that left me breathless. I wasn't sure I'd ever been kissed upside down before, I mused with a smile, almost laughing at how it made his eyes and mouth look a really peculiar shape.

'He's no doubt here to see you again,' Nicholas murmured disapprovingly before narrowing his eyes at me. 'Will you tell me what he's so desperate to talk to you about?'

Smiling up at him, I shook my head. 'He asked me not to …' But as soon as I spoke I saw uncertainty settle in Nicholas' eyes and could tell he was getting protective, no doubt worried about my new apparent closeness with his brother.

Sighing, I stroked his cheek and relented. 'You can't tell him you know yet, but he's asking for my help to mainstream a bit more. He wants what you and I have together, so he's making a go of a proper relationship with Stella,' I explained, deciding that I'd rather break Nathan's confidence than put Nicholas on edge.

Sitting up, Nicholas pulled me with him so we both sat upright. 'Really?' He looked pleased, which was a relief. 'That's great; maybe he's finally putting the stuff with Dad behind him.' He frowned. 'Why didn't he want me to know?'

I had been wondering the same thing but, not knowing anything for sure, all I could do was share my assumption with him. 'I think he's worried in case it doesn't work out. He's your older brother and he doesn't want you to see him fail.' Nathan hadn't vocalised this, but it was a logical guess.

The look of obvious affection that spread across Nicholas' face was rather touching, and I couldn't help but give him another lingering kiss. It had only meant to be a quick peck on the lips, but it escalated rather suddenly into groping hands and very nearly ended up with us spending far longer in bed than planned.

Once we had finally peeled ourselves apart and dressed, we joined Nathan in the kitchen and accepted a cup of coffee that he had already made for us.

'I saw you two in the papers this morning.' Nathan chucked a copy of the local newspaper down. It slid across the worktop and I saw a half-page picture of Nicholas and me, grinning happily at each other at the concert the previous night. Oh my God, we were actually in the newspapers! Snatching it up from the counter, I gaped at it, wide-eyed.

The headline read, *Pianist Nicholas Jackson Saves Children's Home*. To my shock, I saw it was running with the strapline of *And Lands Himself a Woman in the Process*. Well, that wasn't technically the case … but I'd rather they printed it than the truth, which would be along the line of *Pianist Nicholas Jackson Seduces Student on the Veneer of his Grand Piano*.

At least I looked good in the photo, I thought, analysing it again. That new dress had definitely been a good investment on Nicholas' part.

Nicholas smiled proudly at the picture and gave me a kiss on the shoulder before heading off to top up his coffee mug. Glancing up at Nathan, I saw his expression was impassive. It was quite a lovey-dovey pose we'd been photographed in, so he no doubt found it rather sickening. Unless things with Stella had moved faster than expected, of course. Studying his expression, I decided that Nathan didn't look overly offended by the image, so perhaps he was getting in touch with his emotions at last after all.

'Rebecca, can I grab you for five minutes again?' Nathan asked abruptly when I was partway through my coffee.

From his position across the kitchen, Nicholas suddenly appeared at my side. 'You can't *grab her* at all, brother,' he warned with a predatory growl. He slid an arm around my shoulders and gripped me just a little tighter than was comfortable. Jeez, he was so protective of me even with his own brother that I wondered what he'd do if a stranger ever dared to ask me out. After a second's thought where I remembered his reaction to my bumping into Harry, I grimaced. I suspected it wouldn't end well for the stranger.

'You know what I mean, Nicholas. Five minutes' *chat*,' Nathan explained patiently.

With a shrug, I gave Nicholas a reassuring pat on the arm and followed his brother to the lounge.

As soon as we were over the threshold, Nathan turned to me and began to talk urgently. 'I did what you said. We went for a meal last week; I think Stella enjoyed it. We had sex afterwards, no funny stuff, just sex … It was good … really good, actually.' He sounded surprised, but I was beyond embarrassed, wanting desperately for the ground to open up and swallow me. Advice I could do, but discussions about sex with Nathan Jackson, no way.

'Maybe you should discuss this with Nicholas ...' I started, a flush creeping up my cheeks, threatening to engulf me.

'No, Rebecca, you've changed Nicholas, I can see that. I want to change too. I need your advice.' He stepped closer, his eyes once again boring into me. 'The thing is I'm fairly sure my father used to be in charge in the bedroom too, I ... I saw my parents together by accident and my room was next door so I –' He paused, looking embarrassed, a first for Nathan. 'I didn't stay to watch, of course, please don't think that, but I heard certain, uh ... *things*,' he finished with a narrowed expression, as if reliving the experience.

Oh good God, I was *so* not going down this road with Nathan, discussing his sex life was bad enough but now I had to hear about his parents' fucked-up bedroom activities too? Where would it end?

Completely oblivious to my enormous discomfort, he continued. 'Do you and Nicholas do any kinky stuff now, any bondage? Any punishments at all?' he demanded hotly.

'I'm not comfortable discussing this, Nathan,' I said, squirming on the spot. 'It's up to you and Stella to set the boundaries,' I murmured through my blush.

I saw in his expression that Nathan wasn't pleased by my response. Gosh, he really was quite scary when he looked like that, so I relented and tried to give him a little more to go on. 'Look, Nicholas and I talked about what we both liked and what I disliked and there is certain stuff we don't do any more, but it's a personal thing. You need to sit down with Stella and ask her opinions.'

Nathan nodded, running a hand through his hair the same way Nicholas did when he was agitated. 'Right, ask her opinion, got it,' he said, nodding and then immediately frowning. 'You mean what rules we stick to? Which toys she likes, things like that?'

Ground, please swallow me now, I thought. 'Er, yeah,' I replied, blushing as I sought to clarify my point. 'You might want to loosen up on the rules bit, Nathan; normal relationships don't use them quite the way you do. She needs to feel like an individual as well as your partner.' That was an understatement.

Needing permission to make eye contact? *Really?*

'OK ... reassess the rules and ask her opinion on sexual stuff ... I'll go and do that now,' he said firmly, striding for the door and calling goodbye to Nicholas, who I saw was hovering outside the kitchen door, scowling.

Once the front door had slammed shut, Nicholas stalked toward me and entered the lounge. 'I'm not sure I like you being so pally with my brother, Rebecca. Are you certain he hasn't tried anything on? I know how intimidating he can be when he wants,' he observed in a dark, sulky tone.

'Because you'd know nothing at all about being intimidating, would you, Nicholas?' I asked sweetly as I fluttered my eyelashes at him.

My teasing words worked and I saw him relax slightly, although I noticed he still held some tension in his shoulders.

'So did your mum really like that bracelet I picked out for her birthday?' he asked, taking me by surprise at his sudden shift in conversation.

'Yes. She's mentioned it every time she's called me; she says it's the best present I've ever got her.' I grinned. How ironic that I wasn't even the one who had picked it out.

'I'm glad. I notice you wear the one I gave you all the time too,' he commented lightly, brushing his fingers over the bangle that only left my wrist when I was showering or sleeping.

I rubbed fondly at the bracelet and smiled. 'Yeah, I love it, Nicholas.'

'Good,' he said, nodding but looking as though something was troubling him. 'I got you something else that day, but I decided to hold on to it for a while,' he added cryptically, causing me to look at him with an intrigued quirk of my eyebrows.

Digging in his pocket, Nicholas produced a small box in the same blue velvet that my bracelet had come in. Matching earrings, perhaps? I thought, but as I clicked open the box, my breath caught in my throat and my heart began to flutter unsteadily in my chest. Oh my God. Nestled in the blue silk pillow was a ring, a beautiful platinum ring with three delicate diamonds clustered together at the top. Holy shit! Was this one of *those* rings?

My eyes must have been as wide as saucers but as I turned back to Nicholas, I saw that he had dropped out of my eye line onto one knee in front of me. Oh my God, it *was* one of those rings! Struggling for breath, I had to swallow down a yelp of surprise and force myself not to slip into shocked unconsciousness as I stared down into his gorgeous, expectant face.

'We've been together for six months now ... which might not seem long, but I don't need longer to know you're the one for me.' He swallowed, his eyes intense and blazing. 'Rebecca Langley, you've made me understand that I can be a better man. For you I will do anything. I love you – will you marry me?'

Holy crap! I couldn't believe it. Nicholas I-don't-do-relationships Jackson was down on one knee asking me to marry him! To be his wife!

There was no hesitation. The stuff with the cane was a distant memory to me now. Nicholas was dedicated to me and loved me and I knew without a doubt that I loved him back. I shrieked in excitement, leaping at him and wrapping my arms around his neck so exuberantly that we both collapsed backwards in a heap on the soft, carpeted floor.

I sought out his lips with mine and kissed him frantically. Nicholas took control of the situation, rolling us over so he was leaning down on top of me. His eyes were dancing and his cheeks looked as flushed as mine felt.

'Is that a yes?' A wry smile played on his lips.

'Oh!' In my excitement, I hadn't actually given him an answer. 'Oh yes!' I exclaimed breathlessly, causing Nicholas to utter a possessive growl as his head lowered to my lips again.

Sitting up, he pushed his wayward hair from his brow and slipped the ring from the box before slowly sliding it onto my trembling ring finger. Raising my hand to his lips, he kissed the ring and then my palm before leaning down to kiss me on the mouth. 'Mine,' he rumbled against my lips as he began to speedily remove my clothes in celebration.

TWENTY-FIVE

My phone rang just as I was greedily devouring the last of a mountain of pancakes that Nicholas and I had prepared once we'd managed to get up off the living room floor. A carbohydrate recharge was definitely called for after all the energy I'd exerted on sex in the last few days.

Seeing Joanne's number, my brow lowered in concern. It wasn't unheard of for her to call me on the weekends for a chat, but it was certainly unusual, and I felt my heart accelerate as I wondered what sort of state she'd be in today.

'Hi, Jo-Jo,' I answered, going for as soothing a tone as possible. From across the kitchen Nicholas glanced at me, obviously sharing my concern when he realised who was calling.

'Come and visit me today, Becs!' she gabbled, not even bothering with a "hello". Oh dear, she sounded agitated, overexcited even, and I closed my eyes briefly as I pushed away the horrible guilt that swept over me every time I heard her in distress.

'OK, sweetie, I can do that,' I replied in what I hoped was a calming tone. 'I'll just tidy up my lunch things and head over in about twenty minutes, is that OK?' Even though it was a weekend, I desperately hoped the head nurse, Mrs Samson, would be on duty so we could discuss whatever had got Joanne so wound up this time.

'Brilliant! And bring him, Becs, you have to bring him!' She practically screeched down the phone, completely confusing me. Bring who? Dad wasn't due for a visit just yet, especially seeing as Mum had only just been down for her birthday.

'Er ... who?' I asked, bewildered.

'Nicholas Jackson, of course!' Joanne sputtered, sounding like she was grinning. Wow, *grinning*. I couldn't remember the last time Jo had done that of her own accord.

But how on earth did she know about Nicholas?

She answered my question before I even got the chance to ask. 'I've just been watching the local news in the common room and they showed footage of last night's charity do for that children's home round the corner. It raised a record amount and has saved the home from closure,' she tutted at me impatiently, as if I should already know this. 'Anyway, I saw you and Nicholas Jackson snuggling up together on the red carpet! *Nicholas Jackson*!' she repeated in a shriller tone that made me hold the phone slightly away from my ear. 'I can't believe it, Becs, I *love* his music and I can't believe you never told me! I want to meet him!'

Gosh, she was speaking so quickly it was hard for me to keep up, but I think I got the general gist of my sister's words. *I* was the cause for her agitated state, well, more precisely, me and *Nicholas*. What was astounding was that she was openly asking for me to introduce her to a man. That had never happened before. Since her rape and subsequent issues, she had developed an almost total paranoia about men in general. The only male visitor she would accept was Dad. Whenever male relatives visited other patients at her residential home, Joanne would usually go and hide away in her room.

'Um ... OK, I'll ask him if he's free,' I said, catching Nicholas' gaze and giving him a confused shrug.

We arrived at Oak House within half an hour of Joanne's call. I'd been slightly surprised at Nicholas' immediate willingness to accompany me. Perhaps I needed to stop underestimating just how far he'd progressed emotionally over the months we'd been together and start appreciating what an amazing guy he really was. An amazing fiancé, I corrected myself with a grin, glancing down at my glinting ring again.

We had barely been in Joanne's room for two minutes before Mrs Samson came and asked if she could speak with me privately for a few minutes to update me on my sister's new medications. I'd full briefed Nicholas on Jo's insecurities around men, so he stood to leave the room with me, but to both of our surprise, Joanne jumped off her bed and practically begged him to stay and talk to her. Giving me a shrug, Nicholas sat back down as I turned to follow Mrs Samson.

As utterly awful as it sounds, I felt a twinge of jealousy as I exited the room, leaving Joanne fawning over Nicholas like a puppy. It was almost like when we were back in college and she'd try to show me how much prettier she was by deliberately flirting with a guy she knew I liked. Except this was totally different, of course, I chastised myself. She wasn't flirting now, she was barely capable of it. If anything, she was like an excited child meeting her idol, and as I walked away toward the nursing station, I felt like a complete and utter bitch for my horrible thoughts.

As I re-entered Joanne's room five minutes later, I smiled at how happy she looked sat on the bed holding one of the CDs we'd brought with us for her – one of Nicholas'. After she'd told me on the phone that she was a fan he'd grabbed a few copies from his study for her, which I thought was a lovely gesture.

Closing the door behind me. I gave her a little wave and, within seconds, I was thrown backwards as my overexcited sister leapt from the bed, pounced on me, and began to claw desperately at my hands. Finally grabbing my left hand, she stared wide eyed at the shiny new engagement ring before setting off on a ranting conversation that I had no chance of keeping up with. This was one of the side effects of her brain injury; an inability to control her thoughts enough to level out her conversation speed.

Behind her, Nicholas looked slightly shocked at her speedy tirade but I knew from experience that this would pass in a second or two. As expected, it did and she calmed enough to speak at an understandable speed, although she still fired several questions at me in one go.

'This is so exciting! Engaged? Wow! How long have you been together? Do Mum and Dad know? When are you getting married?'

Before I'd even had time to answer one of her questions, Joanne leant in close to my ear to whisper, 'He's really nice, Becs, I approve.' For a second, it was almost like she was back to normal and was a very bittersweet moment for me that caused tears to well in my eyes. I embraced Jo, pulling her tightly to my chest – probably harder than was necessary – before getting a grip on my emotions and sitting down to share our news with her over a pot of tea.

TWENTY-SIX

Though Nicholas had barely been able to contain his excitement about my acceptance of his proposal, which I found very sweet, he had managed not to give the surprise away last night when he'd phoned Nathan and invited him and Stella round to lunch today to share in the good news.

Slightly to Nicholas' annoyance, Nathan had asked to speak to me on the phone, and after secretly putting it on speaker phone to placate Nicholas, we listened to him proudly telling me that things were going exceedingly well between him and Stella. I gave a thumbs-up to Nicholas and in response he had grinned. It seemed that perhaps both the Jackson boys were getting themselves sorted out at last.

Gently rubbing my shiny new ring, I smiled to myself and glanced at the clock. It was one o'clock now and Nathan and Stella were due at any moment. As if someone had read my thoughts, there was a knock at the door, and after dropping a kiss on my forehead, Nicholas stood from the sofa and wandered into the hall to let them in.

After a few seconds of silence in the hallway, I heard a peculiar noise like a dry, choking sob, then an unfamiliar voice.

'Nick,' I heard the voice in the hallway say.

'Father?' I heard Nicholas' hollow tone and the blood froze in my veins.

Father?

As in the man who had so monumentally fucked Nicholas up as a kid?

Standing up from the couch, I turned on the spot and took in the scene playing out in the hall. Jeez, it was like the shop front of a submissive supermarket. Stella, Nathan, and Nicholas all stood frozen to the spot with their heads slightly bowed and their eyes trained at the feet of the man in the doorway.

'Dad popped round to see us,' Nathan muttered thickly his eyes still downcast. 'He wanted to see how you were getting along, Nicholas.'

Dragging my eyes from the sight of my Nicholas looking so lost, I finally took in the man who had damaged him so badly in his youth. His father. He was tall, athletic looking, and handsome, just like his sons, but his blond hair was flecked with grey and he had a few more wrinkles. As his eyes turned on me, I almost staggered backwards. Blimey, how had I ever thought that Nicholas and Nathan were intimidating? This man's stare was like ice being fired straight into my soul and I shivered uncontrollably under his scrutiny, immediately wrapping my arms around my chest defensively. Instantly, I could tell he was not a man who would like to be disobeyed. Images of him beating Nicholas with a cane flashed through my mind and sent a bitter taste to my mouth.

So this wasn't going to be the usual "this is my dad" kind of meeting, then.

He contemplated me inquisitively for several more seconds before apparently dismissing me and turning his gaze back to Nicholas. 'Nick, you have done very well with your piano playing. I've read about you in several journals.'

In response, Nicholas shrugged slightly, looking very much like a lost child in front of an angry parent, which I suppose was exactly what he was.

'You must have got that skill from me,' his father concluded briskly. Arrogant git.

At least I knew now why Nicholas hated being called Nick. His father used the diminutive and I could completely understand how unpleasant the association must be for him.

This was crazy. No one was saying anything. Not a single word.

Glancing at Nathan and Stella, I saw they looked just as subdued as Nicholas. It was as if the two brothers had regressed back to their childhood right before my eyes. It didn't matter that they were older and stronger now; they weren't saying anything because it wasn't the done thing. They'd never been allowed to in the past because it was against their father's rules, so they wouldn't do it now.

As for poor Stella, she didn't stand a chance against someone as intimidating as Mr Jackson; she was visibly trembling on the spot as it was.

Looking again at the arrogant expression on Mr Jackson's face, I felt something inside me snap and I marched over to them. Someone had to do something and as seeing Nicholas, Nathan, and Stella were all practically in a trance, that someone would have to be me. *Great*. Time to bury my nerves and dig out my courage.

'And who are you?' Mr Jackson asked, stopping me before I had even started to say my piece.

For some reason, his tone demanded a response from me. 'I'm Rebecca, Nicholas' girlfriend. Fiancée, actually,' I corrected starkly, stiffening my back and summing up all available courage from my reserves.

In response, Mr Jackson raised an eyebrow and his lips curled snidely as if not believing his son capable of having a girlfriend, let alone a fiancée, and that was the trigger for me. I lost it. I didn't care how frigging intimidating he might like to be; I wasn't just going to stand here and have him ruin all the progress that Nicholas, and Nathan, had made in the last few months.

'These three might be too polite to say anything, Mr Jackson, but I'm not. You are not welcome here, please leave,' I stated in a surprisingly level tone.

In the blink of an eye, Nicholas' father went from calm and haughty to absolutely freaking furious, and I faltered slightly as waves of anger seemed to radiate from him and wash over me.

Uh-oh. I was beginning to think I might have chosen the wrong Jackson man to wind up.

'*Who the fuck do you think you are?*' he roared incredulously, spittle flying from his lips and landing all over my shirt. *Gross*. As he took a step toward me, I suddenly felt very small, but somehow I stood my ground and tipped my chin back defiantly. Adrenaline flew through my system so fast I could feel my veins pulsing with it like a beating drum.

'I'm the woman who loves your son more than you ever did, I'm the woman who's helped him recover from the fucking mess you left his life in, and I'm the woman who will marry him and make sure you never have the chance to fucking hurt him ever again. Now get the fuck out!' I screeched, perhaps with a few too many expletives, but they had felt necessary to bolster my point.

Clearly, I had gone too far, because within a blink of an eye I found Mr Jackson's fingers biting into my upper arms as he shoved me backwards down into the hallway so fast that I was tripping over my own feet repeatedly. *Shit*! I hadn't even seen him move!

'You need to be taught a serious fucking lesson, young lady,' he growled, but his voice wasn't raised any more. It was quiet, too quiet, a tone I recognised only too well from the past; angry, I-want-to-punish-you Nicholas. Oh fuck, this was not good at all.

Suddenly, his biting grip was gone and I fell onto the floor from quite a height, landing hard on my bottom and only just stopping my head hitting the floor as I crashed backwards. The bruising pain in my lower back was almost instantly forgotten, as all hell broke loose above me. Mr Jackson was no longer holding on to me; in fact, he seemed to be rapidly disappearing. As I sat up and gingerly rubbed my lower back, I saw Nicholas, a terrifying look of fury burning in his eyes as he dragged his struggling father off me and down the corridor.

As he threw the man roughly out of the front door, Nicholas practically fell out along with him from the effort. He loomed over him like a predator ready to make the killer blow. 'If you ever touch Rebecca again, I will kill you, do you understand? *Now fuck off out of our lives*,' he roared in a tone so utterly terrifying that goose pimples rose all over my skin. Within seconds, he had slammed the door shut and was by my side, pulling me into his arms and raining gentle kisses all over my face.

Holy shit, had that really just happened? I settled myself more comfortably in his lap and could feel Nicholas' heart hammering in his chest, matching the racing pulse of my own, but tension still seemed to be radiating from his every muscle like a bomb ready to explode.

'Are you OK, Rebecca? Did he hurt you, baby?' Nicholas whispered, his fingers gently rolling up my T-shirt sleeve to examine one upper arm before he raised it to his lips and planted a ring of kisses around the bruising, reddened flesh.

'I ... I'm fine.' Which was a total lie, of course, but I *would* be fine now his dad had gone, so I reassured him in a trembling voice, knowing it was what he needed to hear. Letting out a breath at my words, he lowered his lips to mine and began to kiss me deeply, as if reassuring himself that I really was OK.

'Shit, Nicholas, I'm so fucking sorry for bringing him here,' Nathan said limply from his position by the front door. 'I don't know what I was thinking ...' He shook his head in confusion. 'I guess I wasn't really thinking at all ...' His voice faded away.

Nicholas broke his lips from mine, and we looked up from our kiss to see Nathan approaching us warily, a haunted expression masking his usually handsome features.

'Brother, it's OK. I know what a hold he had on you. I just hope now you can see what he was really like,' Nicholas responded, pulling me even closer onto his lap and burying his head in my hair as his breaths gradually slowed and his muscles began to unclench.

'I do see now. It's all clear to me just how fucked up he is ... I'm sorry, Nicholas, Rebecca ... we'll leave you alone, I'll make sure he's gone.' Nathan ran a hand through his hair then smiled weakly. 'Engaged, eh? Congratulations. Sorry I fucked everything up. Maybe we can have drinks tomorrow? My treat, by way of apologising for this shit and celebrating your good news?' he suggested hopefully, his voice still weaker than usual.

'Sure,' Nicholas said, but he was too tied up in me to watch his brother and Stella leave.

'Are *you* OK?' I asked him as the front door closed, wondering how the sudden reappearance of his abusive father would have affected Nicholas. Please don't let this make him regress back to how he used to be, I thought desperately; I wasn't sure I was strong enough to pull us both through it all again.

Raising his face at my question, Nicholas looked at me, his eyes burning with love and protectiveness before he smiled at me far more brightly than I would ever have expected under the circumstances.

'I am now I have you,' he murmured, kissing me firmly on the lips to ensure I was still with him. 'God, you were amazing, Rebecca. So strong.'

Kissing me again until my head was spinning, Nicholas left me with absolutely no doubt of his feelings for me, and I had to agree with him. Together we would be just fine.

Thank you for reading! If you enjoyed this book please review on Amazon to help spread the word!

Curious about Nicholas' dark and complex brother, Nathan, and his relationship with Stella? Then read *Out of the Darkness*, Book Two of The Untwisted Series, out soon!

I write for my readers, so I'd love to hear your thoughts, feel free get in touch with me:
E-mail: aliceraineauthor@gmail.com
Twitter: @AliceRaine1
Facebook: www.facebook.com/alice.raineauthor
Website: www.aliceraineauthor.com

When I write about my characters and scenes, I have certain images in my head. I've created a Pinterest page with these images in case you are curious. I hope you enjoy this little glimpse into Nicholas and Nathan's world. You can find it at http://www.pinterest.com/alice3083/

You will also find some teaser pics for upcoming books to whet your appetite!

Alice x

Although this book is a work of fiction, if you or someone close to you needs advice or support on issues relating to suicide or abuse, help can be found at www.thecalmzone.net or at www.samaritans.org.

Out of the Darkness

The Untwisted Series #2

Out of the Darkness is the second novel in the highly addictive *Untwisted* series that begun with *The Darkness Within Him*.

Businesswoman Stella Marsden has put her personal life on hold to further her career. But all work and no play leave Stella realising that she misses sex.

Deciding to seek out a no-strings attached relationship, Stella joins Club Twist with the aim of finding some stress-relieving fun.

What Stella finds is the sexy, cool and domineering Nathaniel Jackson. Nathaniel appears to have it all together, but under the surface, he's struggling to deal with a past he'd rather forget.

Can Stella lead him Out of the Darkness…

Into the Light

The Untwisted Series #3

Into the Light, the third novel in the highly addictive Untwisted series follows on with the complex and intensely erotic relationship between the dark and domineering Nathaniel Jackson and timid Stella Marsden.

Passion runs wild as Nathan and Stella continue their illicit 'no-strings attached' meet-ups, but as Stella begins to fall for Nathan, his jealous side rears its ugly head. After a misunderstanding threatens to end their relationship once and for all, can Nathan move past the engrained behaviours of his past and learn to trust Stella, the only woman to ever tempt him to consider a 'real' relationship?

Enlightened

The Untwisted Series #4

Passionate, intense, and formidable, the Jackson brothers return in the deeply erotic final instalment of The Untwisted series. Nicholas and Rebecca are together and stronger than ever as they prepare for their upcoming wedding, but a series of misunderstandings threatens to ruin their big day – and possibly the foundation of their entire relationship. Meanwhile, Nathan and Stella are drawn into complications as Stella hides a secret from the man she loves that could tear them apart forever.

Can Nicholas and Nathan ever truly escape their dark past and find the happiness they thought would always be out of reach?

Christmas with Nicholas

An Untwisted Short Story

From the best-selling author of the Untwisted series comes a sexy seasonal short story.

Devilishly dark Nicholas Jackson is sexy, intense, and domineering but since meeting timid bookshop owner Rebecca, he discovers his softer side. Determined to give Rebecca the best Christmas of her life, Nicholas sets out to find the perfect gift. Only problem – he has absolutely no idea what to get her!

Can Nicholas give Rebecca a Christmas she'll never forget?

Cariad Titles

CARIAD

For more information about **Alice Raine**

and other **Accent Press** titles

please visit

www.accentpress.co.uk